STRANGER

AT THE

VILLA

Strangers Book 3

A Regency Romance

by Mary Kingswood

Stranger at the Villa: Strangers Book 3

Published by Sutors Publishing

Copyright © 2021 Mary Kingswood

ISBN: 978-1-912167-36-4 (paperback)

V2

Cover design by: Shayne Rutherford of Darkmoon Graphics

Author's note:

this book is written using historic British terminology, so *saloon* instead of *salon*, *chaperon* instead of *chaperone* and so on. I follow Jane Austen's example and refer to a group of sisters as the Miss Wintertons.

Stranger at the Villa: Strangers Book 3

About this book: *A new physician arrives in the village, but is he all he seems?*

Susannah Winslade is twenty-six, and drifting into perpetual spinsterhood as she tries to care for her sick stepmother, look after her young brothers and sisters, and keep her father sober and solvent. Her brother Henry isn't much help, either. She doesn't mind. Once upon a time, she met the perfect man and until someone like him comes into her life again, she's happy at home, with her wildflower painting for solace.

Samuel Broughton has come to Great Maeswood to make a new start as a country physician. It's a small practice, but at least it's steady work and everyone is friendly. Finally he's reached a safe harbour where he can look about him for a wife. At last he has a future! But there's something very strange going on at his surgery, and then, just when his hopes of a family of his own might be fulfilled, the unthinkable happens. Is there no escaping the past?

This is a complete story with a happy ever after. Book 3 of a 6 book series. A traditional Regency romance, drawing room rather than bedroom.

Isn't that what's-his-name? Regular readers will know that characters from previous books occasionally pop up. Lawyer Mr Willerton-Forbes, his flamboyant sidekick Captain Edgerton and the discreet Mr Neate have been helping my characters solve murders and other puzzles ever since *Lord Augustus*. Michael Chandry, first seen helping after the shipwreck in *The Clerk* and more recently in *The Duke*, is now a crime-solving partner to Captain Edgerton and his pals. Mrs Leonard Audley, the former Lucy Winterton, appeared in *The Chaperon*, *The Seamstress* and *Woodside*.

Stranger at the Villa: Strangers Book 3

About the Strangers series: There's a famous saying attributed to John Gardner that authors like to quote: that there are only two plots - a stranger arrives in town, or a person goes on a journey. Most of my books have been based on the latter, in its loosest sense (sometimes a journey of discovery, rather than a literal journey, but a major change, of death or misfortune or even good fortune which propels the main character in a new direction). So I wondered what the other side of the coin would look like - a stranger arriving in town. And there was my series title - *Strangers*.

Book 0: Stranger at the Parsonage: a new parson arrives at the village of Great Maeswood, and tragedy strikes the baron's family. (a novella, free to mailing list subscribers).

Book 1: Stranger at the Dower House: a widow moves into the long disused Dower House and makes a horrible discovery in the wine cellar.

Book 2: Stranger at the Grove: an estranged brother is forced to return to his home and face up to his past.

Book 3: Stranger at the Villa: a new physician arrives in the village, but is he all he seems?

Book 4: Stranger at the Manor: a destitute man comes looking for help from his cousin, and uncovers some mysteries.

Book 5: Stranger at the Cottage: an out-of-work governess tries to start a school in the village.

Book 6: Stranger at the Hall: the newly discovered heir to the barony arrives to claim his inheritance.

Want to be the first to hear about new releases? Sign up for my mailing list at my website http://marykingswood.co.uk/

Table of Contents

The Principal Inhabitants Of Great Maeswood

At Maeswood Hall:

Lady Saxby (47), a baron's widow

Her step-daughter, Miss Cass Saxby (26)

Her daughters, Miss Agnes (20), Miss Flora (18), Miss Honora (16)

Her sons from her first marriage, Mr Jeffrey Rycroft (28), Mr Timothy Rycroft (24)

At the Dower House:

Mr Pettigrew Willerton-Forbes, a lawyer

Captain Michael Edgerton, formerly of the East India Company Army

His wife, the former Miss Lucinda Willerton-Forbes

Mr Michael Chandry

Mr James Neate

At Cloverstone Manor:

Squire John Winslade (52)

His third wife, Lilian (28), who is ill

His daughter, Miss Susannah Winslade (26)

His son, Mr Henry Winslade (24)

Eight younger children

Stranger at the Villa: Strangers Book 3

At Lower Maeswood Grove:

Mr Laurence Gage (40)

His wife, Louisa (30), the former Mrs Middlehope

His children from his first marriage, Henrietta (15), Edward (12)

His sister, Miss Viola Gage (46)

At Green Lawns:

Mr David Exton (28), a reclusive widower

At Whitfield Villa:

Dr Roland Beasley (54), a physician

His sister, Miss Phyllida Beasley (40)

At St Ann's Parsonage:

Mr Theodore Truman (28), a clergyman

At Bramble Cottage:

Mrs Cokely (84), widow of a previous parson to the parish

Her daughter, Miss Lucy Cokely (44), a milliner

Note: hi-res versions of family trees and maps are available from my website at http://marykingswood.co.uk/

The Saxby Family

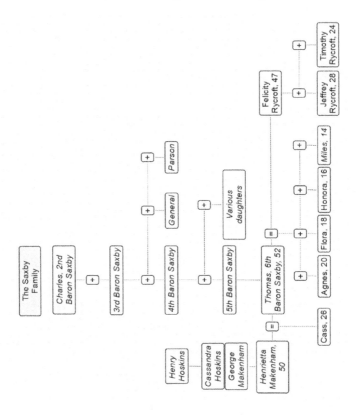

The Winslade Family

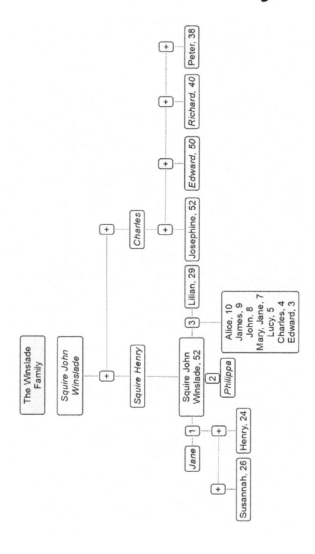

Great Maeswood Map

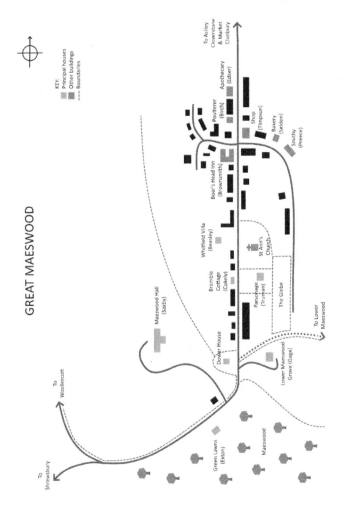

Great Maeswood Environs Map

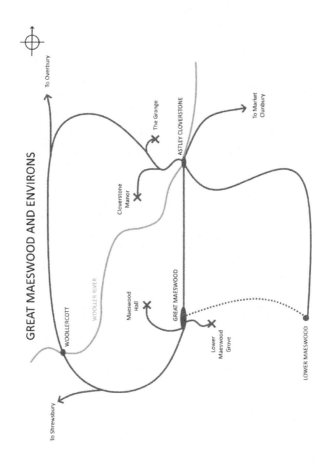

1: A Proposal Of Marriage

JUNE

Miss Susannah Winslade was at her desk on the first floor of Cloverstone Manor. Being a practical soul, she had positioned it to face a wall not a window, so that the summer sunshine and sweet breezes from the river should not distract her from her work. Her mornings followed the same pattern every day. Immediately after rising, she would go to the nursery to check on the children and listen to the long recital of woes from Nurse. Then it was a visit to the kitchens in the basement to discuss the day's menus with Mrs Whiteway, who sampled her own cooking too enthusiastically these days to climb the stairs. After that, Susannah went to her office to begin work on her letters, lists and accounts. Mrs Cobbett, the housekeeper, knew to find her there, so any domestic matters could be attended to.

At ten o'clock precisely it was time for breakfast in Mama's room, which was conveniently next door to Susannah's office, so that she could be summoned immediately if needed. Mama's nurse was very competent, and her companion, Miss Matheson, very willing, but sometimes Mama needed her own family about her.

Mama smiled as she always did when Susannah entered her room. She was still in bed, for she rarely left it these days, but she was propped up against a bank of pillows in a lacy robe and silk shawl, her hair neatly brushed and bound up with a ribbon. Against the pillows she looked tiny, as delicate and fragile as a little doll. The room was overpoweringly hot, for a good blaze burned in the hearth despite the season.

"How are you today, Mama?" Susannah said, bending over to kiss her.

"We are a little better this morning," Nurse Pett said briskly, from her position before the open doors of a large cabinet, as she sorted through bottles of medicine and boxes of lozenges.

The lady herself immediately broke into a cough, and Nurse Pett and Miss Matheson rushed forward, one each side of the bed, reaching for a glass of water and a vinaigrette, respectively.

"Not a good sign," Nurse Pett said to Miss Matheson. "We should ask Dr Beasley to call."

"I agree. Perhaps she is too cold? Build up the fire a little more, will you?"

Nurse Pett was a large woman with a brusque but efficient manner, and Miss Matheson was a wisp of a thing, a fluttering ball of anxiety, but they were united in their care for their charge.

Lilian was Susannah's step-mother, her father's third wife, and the birth of eight children in eleven years had exhausted her utterly. Dr Beasley was of the opinion that careful nursing and regular bleeding would restore her health, but in the three years since little Edward's birth, no improvement had been seen, rather the reverse.

Every physician in the county had been consulted, and every likely remedy tried, to no avail.

The butler and footman came in with the breakfast trays, followed almost at once by Squire Winslade. Susannah's father was more than fifty years of age, but it was not merely a daughter's fondness that thought him a well-looking man, one who was still sufficiently active to display a very manly figure, and cared enough for his appearance to dress in fine London style.

"Well now, how are you, my dear?" he said, bending over to plant a gentle kiss on his wife's forehead. "You look charming, as always."

She smiled and giggled girlishly. She was half her husband's age, and although they had not a great deal in common, there was a fondness between them that warmed Susannah's heart. Money was in short supply at Cloverstone Manor these days, but no expense had ever been spared by the squire for his wife's comfort.

Susannah and her father ate at a small table beside the bed with Miss Matheson, while Susannah's step-mother had a tray resting on her lap, where she crumbled a bun and sipped a little coffee. The squire cheerfully imparted all the news and scandals of the day. Susannah suspected that her father chose to be a magistrate purely to have the earliest intimation of every scurrilous event in Shropshire.

She had more practical matters on her mind. "Papa, James and John both need new breeches, and all the girls need new gowns, and Alice's half-boots are quite worn through. Have the Midsummer rents come through yet? Or can you let me have a few pounds now?"

"I will talk to Jackson, but this is a difficult time of year for our tenants to meet their rent. They have wives and children to feed, and one does not like to be too heavy-handed."

"No, indeed. You are the most generous of landlords, I know, but I must have a little more money soon. We shall need to order coal for the winter before too long and—"

"Caswell will wait. He knows I am plumper in the pocket in the autumn. He will not dun us, you may be sure. We have been good customers for too long."

Susannah frowned. "But he has not yet been paid for last year's supply, and only partially for the year before, and he has a wife and children to feed, just as much as the tenants. They cannot eat coal."

The squire laughed uneasily. "Eat coal? What strange things you do say, my pet, but we must not talk about money, you know, not when your mama is here and looking so fetching. I am sure I have the world's prettiest wife." She blushed and dimpled up at him. "And now I must run off, for Kingly has a little heat in one chambrel and one can never be too careful with a horse of his temperament. Take care and do not overtire yourself, my dear."

And with a quick kiss of his wife's cheek, he was off. She sighed, and her eyes followed his departing back until the door closed with a snap.

"How are we doing with that bun?" Miss Matheson said, in her wispy voice. "We must eat a little, Mrs Winslade. A little more coffee?"

"Is Dr Beasley coming today?" she said, in her tiny voice, barely audible. "Will he bleed me? I do so hate it."

"But it does so much good," Miss Matheson said firmly. "Is it not so, Miss Winslade? The doctor knows best, and no one understands your mama's constitution better than Dr Beasley."

"I so dislike being bled," said the faint voice in the bed. "Leeches are worse."

"Perhaps you would like to see the new doctor, Mama," Susannah said. "He will be here any day now, and he might have new ideas about curing you. He is coming from Edinburgh, you know."

"Oh, perhaps... but I should not like to offend Dr Beasley. If only he would not insist on bleeding me when—" A coughing fit interrupted her, and Susannah had to move aside as Miss Matheson and Nurse Pett swooped in to attend to their patient. The clock struck the hour, and breakfast was over.

Susannah took her coffee back to her office, and began work on her lists. The butcher, the poulterer, the grocer. The chandler, the ironmonger, the vintner — so much wine consumed! It was astonishing in a house with only two gentlemen and very little entertaining how much wine was needed. Instructions for the man who did carpentry work for them. Instructions to the head gardener. The new items to be added to the list for the children — goodness, how fast they did grow!

Silas crept in with his oily smile. He was the first footman, although he liked to call himself the under-butler, and it was true that he did much of Binns' work now, for poor Binns was very elderly and had trouble with the stairs. He insisted on carrying out the principal butler's duties of supervising dinner and announcing callers, but he left much of the lesser business to the younger man.

Silas asked her to order more candles, and that was another item which should not need to be replenished so often at this time of year. But there, Papa liked to play cards of an evening, and grumbled if the light was insufficient. She could cut back on working candles, she supposed, for there was enough light to sew by until quite late on these summer evenings, if she sat on the window seat.

Dr Beasley came to attend to her mama, and looked into Susannah's little office afterwards. He had a brisk manner that Susannah rather liked.

"She is well enough, and I did not bleed her," he said, with a shrug. "It would do her good, but she hates it so much, and it is not yet an urgent matter. I detected no fever or signs of excess in her appearance today, merely the usual lassitude."

"That is good news. Thank you for coming," Susannah said.

"I shall come again tomorrow, but only to introduce my associate, who arrives later today."

"Mama is worried about offending you, if she sees the new man," Susannah said. "She does not quite understand that you have been ill, and must give up your practice."

"Not all of it, I hope," he said, smiling. "I shall still keep on some of my long-established patients, but they will understand that I shall not be riding out to call upon them in the middle of the night any more. I shall leave that to my energetic young colleague. At least, I trust he will be energetic. And my work as coroner — I shall not surrender *that*, you may be sure." He rubbed his hands together with a gleeful smile. Sometimes Susannah suspected he preferred his dead patients to his live ones.

Not long after the physician had left, Binns came in. "Mr Rycroft is here, madam."

"Which Mr Rycroft, Binns?" she said, without looking up from her accounts book, her pen flying across the page.

"Er… the elder… the younger… er…"

She laughed, and raised her head to look at the elderly butler. He had seemed old to her even when she had been a child, and he had not got any younger since then, his accuracy with names receding as fast as his hair, but he was too much a part of the family to be put out to grass. "It is of no consequence, Binns. He will want my father or my brother. Send him to Mearing in the stables. He will know which way they went."

"He asked most particularly for you, madam. A private interview."

"Oh." The elder Mr Rycroft then. "Show him into the Willow Room, and offer him some Madeira. Tell him I shall be there directly."

Carefully, she wiped her pen and laid it down, then sanded the page and closed the book, putting it neatly back on the shelf beside its fellows, adjusting it so that all the spines stood in an exact line. She had no mirror in the room to check her appearance, but she had done nothing which might disturb its symmetry since she had dressed that morning. The Willow Room was seldom used and faced north, so it would be chilled even at this time of year, but it was austere enough to match her mood, and at least it would be private. She picked up a shawl and went to meet her fate.

Jeffrey was gazing out of the window, but when she entered the room he turned and came towards her, hands outstretched, with a warm smile on his face. He was a pleasantly-featured man, not precisely handsome, but personable and good-humoured, when he got his own way. His father had been an improvident man, leaving his family destitute, but his mother had made a fortunate second marriage to Lord Saxby, and so Jeffrey and his brother had been raised as gentlemen, although without the wherewithal to support such a lifestyle. It made him a restless, not to say capricious, man, but in one direction alone had he been steadfast, and that was his devotion to Susannah.

"Susannah! How well you look today."

"Good morning, Jeffrey." She allowed him to take her hands, and for a dreadful moment as he rushed upon her she was afraid he was going to kiss her. He drew back at the last minute, contenting himself with lifting her hands, one after the other, to his lips. Withdrawing her hands carefully, she added, "Has Binns offered you some refreshment?"

"Oh… yes, but I want nothing. Only to talk to you." She sat down on a faded damask-covered sofa and waved him to a chair, but he continued to stand. "I have good news, Susannah. The best in the world, for I have just come from the Grove. The Gages are to build a new house in their grounds, and rework all the pleasure gardens — the whole park, in fact, and they have engaged *me* to oversee the work, contract with builders and suppliers, and so forth. What do you think of *that?*"

His face was so animated, alive with excitement, that she could not but smile at him. "That is wonderful news, Jeffrey. I knew you had hopes of reworking the Dower House gardens, but this is better, far better. It will give you something to occupy you, now that Lord Saxby is no longer with us."

A flicker of annoyance crossed his face. "What has my stepfather to do with anything? I was very sorry about his death, but it hardly affects me, since he would never help me into a career."

"But you used to shoot and ride with him a great deal, and help the gamekeepers and grooms, and all of that will end when the new Lord Saxby is found. It is as well to have some useful pursuit to fill your time."

"Good Lord, Sue, you make me sound like some sort of dilettante, wasting away my days, when you know better than anyone how much I have longed for a profession. Well, now I have the chance to build a career for myself. There is money to be made from it, in time, enough that I shall be able to reclaim Melverley at last, but for now Gage will pay me a salary. It is only a modest amount, but it is a start. Now do you see?" He perched on the edge of the sofa beside her, taking one of her hands in his. "Everything we want is finally within our grasp. Sue, dearest Sue, you know how I feel about you, how I have *always* felt about you, but it was never possible before. I had just about given up hope, I can tell you. But at last we can move forward, and is it not perfect, the way everything has worked out? We can see about the banns any day you like, and be married within the month, but if you want to wait... for your mother's sake... Well, who can say when—?" He broke off sheepishly, and Susannah tried not to be annoyed. Perhaps her mother's days were numbered, but she would never give up hope of an improvement. After the briefest of pauses, he went on, "For myself, I should like us to marry soon, but it shall be as you wish. What do you say?"

To put off the moment when she must answer that question, she said, "You offered for Cass Saxby."

"Oh... well, yes, that is true." He looked uncomfortable, like a boy caught stealing the jam tarts, then abruptly moved closer to her, so close that she had to lean away from him. "I had to make a push for Mother's sake. I mean, Cass has seventy thousand pounds! It would have set us up so splendidly, and I could have cleared the mortgage on Melverley at once and lived like a gentleman, as I should, instead of having to earn my bread like a common tradesman. I had to try, but I knew she would never have me, so I was quite safe. I have never loved anyone but you, Sue. Sweet Susannah!" He ran one finger down her face, smiling at her in a way that ought to have reduced her to water, but somehow did not. "I love you so much, and it would make me so happy to have you as my wife. Please say you will… please?"

His eagerness moved her, but her heart remained untouched. How many times had they enacted this same scene, and yet her part in it never varied? "I am very sorry, Jeffrey, but I cannot marry you. I like you very much, but I do not feel for you that esteem which a wife should feel for her husband. I do not love you, so although I wish you every success with this new venture, I cannot marry you."

"That is no reason!" he cried. "Love… it is not necessary that *you* should love *me*, for that would grow, in time. We get on so well, and the only obstacle has been that neither of us has any money, so—"

"That is *not* the only obstacle," she said crisply. "Really, Jeffrey, I have told you a score of times that I do not love you and can never marry you. Why do you not believe me? I am delighted that you now have a worthwhile occupation, but it does not change my mind in the slightest."

"A worthwhile occupation!" he cried, anger suffusing his face. "You think I have been a wastrel all these years, then. So that is the way of it."

"You are eight and twenty," she said, evenly. "Your stepfather would not *buy* you a career, but there was nothing to stop you making your own way in the world long since. You spent four years at Shrewsbury and three at Oxford, so you are not without friends who could have helped you to a position as a secretary or in government, say. You might even have taken holy orders and found a living by now. Or you could have worked with Barnes to learn to manage the estate properly, got to know the tenants, learnt about farming methods, instead of just dabbling when you had a day with nothing better to do. There are many things you might have done to advance yourself, but you chose not to, Jeffrey."

"I never *needed* to before!" he snapped, but then, with an effort, reined in his temper. "It always seemed easier to drift along, I suppose, in the hope that one day something would happen and money would rain down from the skies." He laughed ruefully. "Foolish, is it not? And one day something *did* happen — my stepfather overturned his curricle and killed himself and his only heir, leaving us nothing, and now we are all to be pushed out of the nest, and must learn to fly whether we will it or no. I am forced to make my way in the world, and I shall! I shall be a success, Susannah. One day I shall be rich and much sought after by those who want a new house or garden, and you will see what sort of man I am. And perhaps, if I do well, you will look more favourably on me?"

His expression was so hopeful that she could have wept, but she had to be honest. "No, Jeffrey. I shall never marry you."

"But why? What is it about me that repulses you?"

"Nothing. In your person, nothing. In your character, I see some weakness, but it would not weigh with me if I had not—"

"Had not what? Are you in love with someone else, Sue? If so, tell me the worst at once, I pray you! Do not spare me."

"No, no! I am not in love with anyone, but I have seen the possibility of love, that is all, and it was nothing like this." She hesitated, for she had never spoken of it before, but perhaps it would convince him that his suit was hopeless. "It happened when I was but fourteen, and had gone to London with Mama — not this mama, it was Philippa, Papa's second wife. She was in great distress about her inability to conceive, so she consulted a very eminent *accoucheur* in town. That was why she went to town so often, to see that physician, and she was always invited to dine. On the last occasion, the very last visit shortly before she died, I was invited to dine there too. The eminent physician had two or three young men staying, young physicians training under his supervision. That night, when the card tables were set up, one of them offered to teach me to play backgammon, for I had not played it before. He spent the whole evening teaching me, talking to me, treating me just as if I were a lady worthy of his time, instead of a girl of fourteen, the daughter of an impoverished squire from a distant county. His whole attention was on me, and I felt... I cannot tell you how I felt. More alive than I had ever been, somehow. My whole life until then had been spent half asleep, but for that one night, for those few hours, I was awake and alert, all my senses tingling. It felt like high summer in the middle of winter, if that does not sound too fanciful. And I want to feel like that again, Jeffrey. Can you understand that?"

"He was just being polite to you, as a guest."

"Oh yes, of course! It meant nothing to him, I know that. And I was not in love with him... how could I be, when I knew nothing of him? But it felt possible... on that night, with him, anything was possible."

"So you are waiting for this man—"

"No!" she cried impatiently. "I shall never see him again, I know that, but there will be someone, somewhere... a man who makes me feel alive, truly alive in that magical way, and with whom there is the possibility of love... and I cannot settle for less. I *cannot.*"

2: The New Physician

Dr Samuel Broughton stepped wearily down from the stage coach to the inn yard, stretching his bruised limbs and aching back. Finally, he had arrived! Tonight he would sleep in a clean bed and, he very much hoped, enjoy a better dinner than any inn could provide. A week of travelling was surely six days more than any mortal body ought to be expected to suffer.

He was the only passenger alighting at Great Maeswood. The guard tossed his portmanteau and small box to a waiting inn servant. A sign above the entrance to the inn proclaimed it the Boar's Head, but oddly the painted sign showed the whole of the beast, not just its head. It was a modestly sized establishment, the yard untidy with heaped-up barrels, oddly shaped sacks and buckets of swill. The usual crowd of idle drinkers sat on benches in the afternoon sun, while the ostlers and kitchen workers stood about watching the stage prepare to depart. Or watching him, if he were being honest. A large woman with a chicken in a cage and a basket of vegetables mounted the steps to the coach, setting it rocking, then the door was closed, the guard hopped up to his perch and the stage rolled ponderously out of the yard again.

"You'll be the new doctor from Edinburgh, I daresay," said a voice from the crowd. A young man stepped forward from a crowd of ostlers, better dressed than his friends. "Welcome to Great Maeswood, Dr Broughton."

Samuel gave a wry smile. "There are no secrets in a village as small as this, I imagine. But you have the advantage of me."

"John Spencer at your service, sir. Groom to Gaius Valerius, the finest horse in the county, and possibly several adjoining counties." He waved to one of the inn servants, and pointed to the box and portmanteau. "William, get these onto your cart and down to the Villa."

"Is it far to Whitfield Villa?" Samuel said. "Do I need to ride with my luggage?"

"No distance. I'm heading that way, so I'll show you if you want."

In Samuel's experience, anything described as *'no distance'* tended to be a wearying long way, almost as bad as *'not far'* or *'only a step'*. Fortunately, the dreaded *'you can't miss it'* was inapplicable, since he had a guide for the journey, and in fact it turned out that the groom to the finest horse in the county had not lied about the distance. They passed no more than a dozen cottages before they came to a house a little set back from the road in its own grounds, and the words *'Whitfield Villa'* neatly inscribed on the gate posts.

"There you go," Spencer said. "I work at Lower Maeswood Grove, just at the far end of the village, but you'll find me at the inn as often as not."

"The ale is that good?" hazarded Samuel.

"The ale is only passable and the food is terrible but the new chambermaid is incomparable," he said with a wink, then, waving cheerily, he was gone.

Samuel walked the short distance up the drive to the house. He was pleased with what he saw. The grounds were not extensive, but he could see chickens and an arch of beans behind a picket fence to one side and a stable building to the other, with what looked like an orchard beyond that. The house was larger than he had imagined for the home of a country physician, neat rather than elegant, but pleasingly proportioned.

But perhaps he should not have been surprised, for he knew nothing at all about his new partner. Dr Beasley was an older man who suffered from a weakness of the heart necessitating a withdrawal from much of his work, but that was as much as Samuel could say of him. The man who had sponsored him in Edinburgh, John McNair, knew no more himself, for although his friendship with Dr Beasley extended over many years, after a chance meeting in London many decades ago they had not met again, and corresponded only on medical matters. He could not even say for certain if the physician were a married man.

Samuel knocked briskly on the door, and almost at once it was opened by a man who could only be Dr Beasley himself, to judge by his dress. He was a spare man of above fifty, greying and slightly stooped, who beamed at Samuel merrily.

"Dr Broughton? Come in, come in." He waved him into a cool, tiled hall, with a large hearth on one side and a painting of a naval battle filling the opposite wall. "Are you exhausted? Ah, there you are, Thomas. Here is Dr Broughton arrived. Do you have luggage, Broughton?"

"A man from the inn is bringing it."

"Excellent. Thomas will show you to your room so that you may wash the dust from your boots, as the saying is. When you are suitably refreshed, you will find me in my book room, just through that door there. You will forgive me if I do not show you myself, but I am avoiding the stairs as much as possible."

Thomas, a ponderous man of some solidity, made a stately progression up the stairs, with Samuel treading slowly in his wake.

"Your room, sir." Thomas threw open a door and Samuel passed inside.

It was larger than he had expected, and well furnished in the style of Queen Anne, solid and practical. A maid rushed in with a ewer of hot water, then rushed away again. A commotion downstairs drew the manservant away, but he returned moments later with Samuel's portmanteau, followed by a puffing William, labouring up the stairs with his box.

"May I unpack for you, sir?" Thomas said, after William had been given a coin and dispatched back to the inn.

"Thank you. You will find a clean shirt and neckcloth in the small bag and my evening things in the box. What time is dinner?"

"Five o'clock, sir. I usually assist the master at four, but I can attend you at half past the hour, if that would suit?"

"That would be helpful, since it will be a few days before my man can get here."

"Oh," Thomas said, his eyebrows rising an inch, as if in surprise that the junior doctor had a man of his own.

Washed, changed and feeling a great deal more presentable, Samuel made his way downstairs again. There was no sign of feminine presence in the house — no girlish chatter or sound of an instrument, nor signs of children at play, so he suspected this might be a bachelor household. That would suit him very well, he decided. He wanted no more doctors with families. Especially daughters.

Dr Beasley was comfortably ensconced in an armchair beside the empty hearth, a book in one hand and a glass of wine in the other, but he willingly laid them down and rose to greet Samuel.

"Well now, have you everything you require? Did Thomas look after you?"

"He did, sir, thank you."

"Madeira? Or port? Your luggage has arrived, I see."

"Madeira, thank you. That is the part that came with me on the stage. There are two more boxes coming more slowly, and my man is bringing my horse and his own by easy stages. I will pay for his keep, of course, as well as my own, and the feed for the horses, and all the taxes."

"You are punctilious — I like that," Beasley said. "McNair pronounces you to be an excellent physician and a good Christian. Would you agree with that?"

"I certainly try to be both," he said. "I cannot comment on my own professional capabilities, naturally."

"McNair's word is good enough for me. That is what I asked him for, and he sent you, so there we are. You are aware, I take it, that this is a country practice, so we undertake whatever is asked of us. Bleeding, purging, bone-setting, cleaning putrid wounds, all of that. I have cut off a limb or two in my time, too. Edser, the apothecary — I will introduce you tomorrow — he is a very good sort of fellow, and keeps the leeches, so between the two of us, we cover all eventualities. But there is no room for a fancy city physician here. Good, steady work and plenty of it, but you will need to get blood on your hands. You are prepared for that, I trust?"

"I would not have it any other way, sir. I have no liking for fancy city physicians."

"Good, good. What do you know of the practice?"

"Nothing at all, sir, or of you, except that you have suffered some illness of the heart necessitating a reduction in your workload."

"Ah. Well, this used to be a much larger practice. I had two consulting rooms, one at Shrewsbury and a smaller one at Market Clunbury. When I inherited this house, I sold the Shrewsbury practice and now I must dispose of the rest. You will take full charge of the Market Clunbury practice. It used to be worth four hundred a year, but it has been somewhat neglected lately, so there is scope for you to improve it. Of my country patients, I will encourage them to turn to you, but some will want to cling to me from long habit, I daresay."

"Of course. Did Dr McNair explain that I am not in a position to buy the practice outright?"

"Oh yes, but no need to worry about that. You may pay me by degrees, as you can afford. We can make some arrangement — let us call it a partnership for now — although there will be a probationary period, just at first. But I am sure there is nothing to worry about there, since McNair recommends you so highly."

"Do you act as apothecary too, or do you keep to the prescribing?" Samuel said.

"A little of both," Beasley said. "I buy my supplies from Edser, and make my own medicines for my Market Clunbury patients. There is not enough profit in mere consultations, but I do not sell potions at the door, like a common apothecary. I recommend you do the same. You will see the prices I charged — all the books are in the consultation room. For my country patients, I deem it courteous to let Edser make up whatever is needed, so I merely advise and prescribe. I get along very well with Edser, and I recommend you follow the same strategy. He is a good fellow, and I should not like to tread on his toes. You are not married?"

"No, sir."

Beasley chuckled. "No need to look conscious, Broughton. You are what, thirty? Thirty-five?"

"Thirty-four."

"There you are, then. You are of an age to be thinking about it, at least. Not that I ever felt the urge to enter the bonds of matrimony, and have never regretted it. My sister keeps house for me, and she is a spinster, so we go on very comfortably together. She is gadding about with Miss Gage today, her particular friend. Thick as thieves, they are. You will see Phyllida at dinner. A little more Madeira? How pleasant this is, to have another doctor to talk to. I have a most interesting case of boils over at Woollercott. What would you use in such a case?"

Samuel quickly realised that he had fallen on his feet. Dr Beasley was a kind man, easy-going and genial, exactly the sort of mentor he wished he had found at an earlier stage in his career. Miss Beasley turned out to be a timid but inoffensive creature, drably dressed although with odd pieces of lace attached here and there, as if she wished to prettify her dress but had no notion how to go about it. She said little, and the household ran on haphazard lines, but dinner, when it arrived, was plentiful and not inedible, which was all he asked of it.

As well as his bedroom, he had a room downstairs set aside for his use, with a desk and chair, bookcases and cabinets, and a chaise longue against one wall. It had a slightly fusty, unused air, all the shelves depressingly empty, with indentations in the rugs marking the position of heavy furniture, now removed.

"It was Aunt Margery's room for her last few years," Miss Beasley said, when he asked. "After she could no longer manage the stairs. She died in this room, but that will not trouble you, I hope?"

"Not in the least. I am very grateful for a room of my own."

"You will be able to see patients in there if you wish, or invite your friends in, you know. This is your home, Dr Broughton, and we want you to be happy here."

He could not have wished for greater kindness, and felt himself very blessed. His prayers that evening were long and heartfelt.

~~~~~

Susannah was returning from her daily walk, her arms full of ox-eye daisies, when she spotted a familiar sight turning into the stable yard — a gig and small pony. A groom rushed to the pony's head, and Cass Saxby carefully descended to the ground. Cass was Susannah's best friend since childhood, and a welcome visitor at any time.

"Cass! How lovely! You have your gig again. I thought it was to be sold. In fact, I thought it *had* been sold."

"So did we all, but Goronwy had other ideas, and kept returning to the Hall." She chuckled, stroking the pony's nose affectionately. "What lovely flowers! Did they come from your garden?"

"No, no! The meadows just beyond the river. Wild flowers are not as showy as garden blooms, perhaps, but I love their delicate colours."

"I wonder..." Cass said, with the faintest blush. "Do you ever see Mr Truman out and about? He is very keen on wild flowers, too, especially orchids."

"Is he? No, I have never seen him in any of the places I go to, and he has never mentioned his interest to me."

"I expect he goes to different places on his walks. Are you rushing off to paint your flowers? We can talk in your studio, if you wish."

"No, these are for the house. I need only hand them to Mrs Haines. Come inside, and we will find a quiet corner for a coze."

The advantage of a house like Cloverstone Manor was that there was always a quiet corner to be found. Built in the reign of King James, it boasted wandering wings and a myriad of interconnecting rooms, most of them shrouded in holland covers, but it was always easy to find a secluded chamber for a private conversation.

"Goodness, I thought I knew this Manor well, but I have never been in this room before," Cass said, gazing around at the heavy oak panelling and ornate plasterwork ceiling.

"This is the Queen's Dressing Room," Susannah said with a laugh. "Not that any queens ever stayed here, but the original owner had great ambitions. Such a pity that he ran out of money almost before the plaster was dry. Oh Cass, it is so good to see you. Are you allowed out and about again? Shall I see you at the Beasleys' card party tomorrow?"

"Correct on both counts. It will soon be six months since poor Papa died, and even Mama agrees that we may step back into the world again. We are to go into half-mourning just as soon as the gowns are made ready. I do not think she would have been quite so willing to brave the hurly-burly of the Beasleys' card party, were it not for the arrival of the new physician. Had you heard? He is expected today, so naturally my sisters are wild with excitement. There is to be a great endeavour with curling papers, and I left them in a positive whirlwind of gowns and fans and ribbons. Such a commotion!"

"Is it known whether he is single or not?" Susannah said. "For such efforts will be entirely wasted if he brings with him a wife and five children."

"Nothing at all is known about him, but naturally one hopes that a man just taking up a medical practice will be young and single, and being now settled in his career, will be desirous of taking a wife."

"Naturally one does, but not you," Susannah said with an arch glance at her friend. "*You* need have no interest in the new physician."

A faint flush coloured Cass's cheeks and she lowered her head bashfully. "That is true. Which reminds me, I am the bearer of an invitation to dinner two weeks from now. Everyone is to be invited and I hope... I have reason to believe..." She stopped, her blushes spreading.

"Cass! Can it be that there is to be an announcement?" Susannah cried, clapping her hands together excitedly. "At last! I never understood the need for secrecy."

"That was all Mr Truman's delicate sense of propriety. He has so much sensibility." She sighed fondly. "I daresay everyone has guessed our secret by now, but if we are to be meeting publicly, Mama feels it is best for the betrothal to be acknowledged."

"So you will be married before the summer is out," Susannah said.

"Oh... as to that, no. Mr Truman is adamant that we must wait the full year, out of respect for Papa and Miles. We will not be married until January." Her face was glum. "He hopes the new Lord Saxby will be here by then to give me away. At least I shall have plenty of time to prepare my wedding clothes, and he says I may have whatever work I wish done to the parsonage."

"The parsonage! You will not live there, surely? With your fortune and his, you could live anywhere, and install a curate. That is often done, is it not?"

"He does not wish to leave the parsonage," Cass said, lifting her chin a little. "He is too conscientious a clergyman to abandon his parish, Susannah."

"Not abandon, perhaps, but he might live somewhere a little more in keeping with his position in society, yet still near enough for him to perform the offices on Sundays. The Grange, say, or even Wellwood Park."

"That would be very grand for a clergyman," Cass said, laughing. "No, it is all agreed with Mama that she will go to the Grange whenever the new Lord Saxby arrives, whoever he is. The money for that must come from my fortune, of course, but Theodore has said — I mean Mr Truman," she corrected herself with another little blush, "has said she must be comfortable and he will not withhold the funds when we are married. But enough of me. Jeffrey is very low, Susannah. Even Tim cannot raise his spirits, and never did a brother try so hard! Is there truly no hope for him, even now that he has steady employment?"

"None at all, as I have told him many times before. I wish, *truly* I wish him to be happily married, just not with me, that is all."

Cass sighed. "I have a natural affection for him, growing up with him almost as brother and sister, so perhaps my preference misleads me, but I believe him capable of making any woman happy, even you, Susannah. You would grow to love him in time, I am sure of it, and he is utterly determined to make the most of this opportunity and build a proper career for himself this time. Will you not give him the chance to prove himself to you? Give him six months, say, so that he can make a beginning with this new venture, and then reconsider."

Susannah could not possibly explain her reasoning, even to so good a friend as Cass. Jeffrey had not understood, and she was tolerably sure that Cass would not, either. In fact, if she were being entirely honest, she was not sure she understood it herself. She was not waiting for the man she had met that night, but she was waiting for *something*, that much was certain, and she could not settle for less.

When she said nothing, Cass went on gently, "Sue, you are six and twenty. Is it not time to be practical?"

That was a question she could answer. "You mean that I have no dowry, no beauty, no great accomplishments beyond the usual? I should settle for what I can get, is that it? But I do not *need* to marry, Cass. I have a home here. Papa will never turn me out, nor will Henry, if he ever marries, and if he does not, then there are still James, John, Charles and Edward in the nursery. I shall *always* have a place here, as a daughter, or sister, or aunt, or even as a great-aunt."

"And you are content with that?"

"I am content. And if I were not, your own situation gives me hope that, even at the age of six and twenty, there might be a happy marriage in my future, based on love rather than practicality."

Cass could not deny the truth of it.

3: The Consultation Room

"When do you wish to ride over to Market Clunbury to look at the house and consultation room?" Dr Beasley said at breakfast.

"Today, if you will instruct me on how to find it," Samuel said.

"Nothing easier. If you can find the Swan Inn, you will see it next door. There is a man in residence to keep everything in good order. Lucas Renshaw, his name is. Been with me for several years. Very reliable. He will let you in, but I shall give you the keys in case he is out. You will want to check the drugs cupboard, anyway. Renshaw has no key for that. You can take my horse. I shall not need him today."

"You are all goodness, sir, but I prefer to keep to a business-like footing. I shall hire a mount from the inn."

"Ah, you young men, you can be too independent sometimes. But have it your own way, Broughton. Have it your own way. In that case, I shall walk into the village with you and introduce you to Edser, the apothecary. Sad story, actually. I had better warn you, in case you inadvertently distress him at any time. Poor fellow had a yearning for Agnes Saxby, one of the girls from Maeswood Hall. Very broken up, he was, but Lord Saxby squashed it, of course. Not at all the thing for the daughter of a baron to wed an apothecary, especially one living in the same village. Lady Saxby could hardly call on Mrs Albert Edser, after all. Everyone should stay in their place or what would the world come to, eh?"

"What were the lady's feelings in the matter?" Samuel said.

"Hardly relevant," Beasley said uncompromisingly.

Mr Edser had a neat shop just beyond the inn on the Market Clunbury road. Samuel's experience with apothecaries was that they were either fussy, elderly men, pedantic and interfering, or else they were jovial middle-aged fellows smelling worryingly of spirits. Albert Edser was neither of these, being only a year or two younger than Samuel, with a cheerful round face and a welcoming demeanour. After Beasley had made the introductions and departed, Edser showed Samuel over every corner of his domain, and answered a couple of carefully chosen questions so comprehensively that Samuel had no doubt at all of his competence. Leaving his servant to mind the shop, Edser sat Samuel down in a comfortably furnished parlour with a glass of Madeira, and plied him with questions about his experiences in Edinburgh.

"Ah, such an interesting place to live — how I envy you, Dr Broughton. How lucky we are to have you here, for you will bring the latest thinking to our quiet corner of England. And is there a Mrs Broughton?"

"I am not married." He hesitated, but after Beasley's warning, he hardly liked to ask Edser the obvious question.

However, he answered it himself. "Nor I," he said with a heavy sigh. "Almost was, once. The lady accepted me and we were betrothed for fully two hours until her father intervened and barred me from any further thoughts in that direction. It would never have done, I suppose. It was presumptuous of me to dare to aspire to the hand of a baron's daughter. Miss Agnes Saxby. Have you met her?"

"Not yet."

"People call her plain, but I've never seen it. She has the sweetest nature imaginable, and such a lovely smile! I should have been the proudest man on earth to call her my wife, but it wasn't to be. That was four years ago, and yet she is still unwed, and she will be of age before the year's end. Perhaps it is wrong of me, but I've not yet surrendered all hope. Another drop of Madeira, Dr Broughton?"

After hiring a workmanlike horse at the inn, Samuel soon left the village behind. Market Clunbury was a distance of some seven miles from Great Maeswood, at first a good, straight road with open fields to either side, and then winding through the dappled shade of oak and beech trees, the hedgerows a mass of slender blooms of white and pink and purple. Musical rivulets burbled beside the road, or beneath it, and once across it, the ford no more than a handspan deep. It was both ordinary, the very essence of England, and yet exquisitely beautiful at the same time. Samuel's spirits lifted a notch.

The town was probably no different from a score of other small towns in Shropshire, with a single main road housing most of the principal shops and other establishments. At the northern end, the road divided around a medieval wool exchange with a clock tower, before turning left for Wales and right for Chester. Samuel passed a bank, an inn, a circulating library and several useful shops before he turned onto Chester Road. Dr Beasley's practice was housed in a narrow building squeezed between the Swan Inn and a linen draper's shop. Samuel left the horse at the inn, and, following Beasley's instructions, walked through the yard to the alley behind and thence to the back gate of the property.

The gate gave access to a small yard, the corners filled with ancient sacks of grain, but the cobbles were clean and weed-free. The back door opened at his touch and he entered a small kitchen, empty of people but everything clean and tidy, a kettle hanging over the fire on one hook and a pot of something simmering on another. The whole room was filled with an appealing aroma that made Samuel's mouth water.

"Hey there? Anyone here?"

Silence.

A narrow stair and heavy curtain screened off another area, perhaps sleeping quarters, but no one emerged at his call. Renshaw must have slipped out for a moment, but he could not have gone far, since the door was left unlocked. Samuel called again, but there was no answer and no sign of life.

On the far side was another door, and this led to what could only be the consultation room, with its polished desk, cabinets filled with patient notes, a shelf of well-thumbed medical books, a worn leather sofa and chairs, a long table for surgical procedures and the locked cupboards containing the instruments and medical supplies. Beyond was only a narrow hall with a bench and a small console with a bell, where presumably patients waited to be seen.

Samuel tried the various keys until he found one that fitted the medicine cupboard. He was in the process of examining the rather dusty assortment of bottles and boxes within when he heard a soft sound behind him.

"Put that back!" said a gruff voice.

Samuel spun round, to find himself looking at a young man, incongruously wearing a bob-wig, holding a business-like pistol in one hand. It was pointing in Samuel's general direction, but the hand holding it wavered so much that it was hard to say precisely which part of his anatomy was the desired target.

"Put it back, you thief!" the young man said. "The constables are on their way, so don't try to run away." The pistol wobbled even more precariously.

"I have no intention of running away," Samuel said warily. He could see that the wielder of the pistol was very young, barely more than a boy, and he doubted that the fellow meant any harm, but a loaded pistol could discharge accidentally and he was still directly in the firing line.

The boy's chin lifted a shade. "Good. Very good." Then he paused, licking his lips, as if unsure what to do next. He was nervous, and certainly more afraid than Samuel was. How odd. "Put the bottle back."

"By all means," Samuel said, replacing it in the cupboard and locking the door once more. "I daresay it has lost its efficacy anyway. It has been here a very long time. I shall have to replace everything, I daresay."

The boy's eyes narrowed. "Who *are* you?"

"Dr Samuel Broughton. I have taken over this practice from Dr Beasley."

"Oh!" The pistol drooped.

"And now you had better put that weapon down and tell me who you are," Samuel said. "What has happened to Renshaw?"

The boy licked his lips again, but then the chin came up again. "*I am Renshaw.*"

"Nonsense. Renshaw has worked here for many years, and you are a mere stripling."

"That was my uncle. I work here now." The pistol drooped even more, and the voice softened.

"Dr Beasley told me nothing of this. I shall have to confirm it with him. Look, for heaven's sake put that pistol down before someone gets hurt."

The pistol lowered to a point such that Samuel's only concern was for his feet. "Are you truly the new physician? We weren't expectin' you yet."

"I arrived yesterday. Do you want to show me around, Renshaw? I have seen the rooms on this floor, but I should like to know what else there is. A bedroom upstairs, I presume. Attics? Cellars?"

The boy cleared his throat. "No attics, just two bedrooms. I… haven't had time to tidy upstairs."

Samuel was amused, but had no wish to intrude on the boy's bedchamber. "Very well. The cellar?"

"There's only the coal store."

"Nowhere to store a few bottles of Madeira or some such?" Samuel said, pointing to a pair of decanters and several glasses laid out on a gleaming silver salver.

"Oh… there's a wine cellar, too."

"Well, bring up a bottle and let us make the place ready for patients, shall we?"

"You want wine in here?" Renshaw waved the pistol around vaguely as he spoke, gesturing around the room. Samuel winced and instinctively shifted to one side, out of range. The boy looked at the pistol with a bewildered expression, as if he had almost forgotten he held it. "Oh... beg pardon. I'll get rid of this." He disappeared into the inner room, and Samuel was left shaking his head. What a strange young man!

While Renshaw was gone, he looked through the medicine cabinet again, noting the principal deficiencies, and then at the instruments, a good array of implements, well cared for.

When the boy returned with a bottle in his hand, Samuel sat in the chair behind the desk, folded his arms, and said, "Just decant it, will you, and then pour me a glass." And waited with interest.

The boy looked at the bottle and then at Samuel. "Decant it?"

"Yes. Is it sealed? You will need a knife, a corkscrew and a strainer, then."

"Knife, corkscrew, strainer. Right." He disappeared again, taking the bottle with him, but returned a few minutes later. "Is this a strainer? It was with the corkscrew. What sort of knife do you want?"

"Never mind. I have a pocket knife. You have never done this before, have you?"

The boy smiled suddenly, abruptly looking about twelve years of age. "No, sir."

Samuel took the bottle from him. "You use the knife to cut off the wax seal, you see? So you need a small, sharp knife. Then the corkscrew goes in like so. Then, hold it firm between your feet, and— There! One heave and it is done. Then carefully pour it through the strainer into the decanter, like this. Oh, this looks like port, so there will be a lot of residue. It is important to keep the wine free of contamination. There, now you may pour two glasses."

"Two, sir?"

"One for me and one for you, Renshaw. Then you can come and sit down."

"Sit down, sir?"

Smiling, he said, "I believe it will become a trifle tedious if you are to repeat everything I say. Pour two glasses and then sit down here." He placed a chair before the desk, then took his seat behind it, watching with amused eyes as Renshaw tried to keep his hands steady enough to pour the wine. Eventually he got it done, then carefully carried first one glass, then the other across to the desk, before sliding into the chair, his expression wary.

Samuel raised his glass. "Let us drink to a long and amicable working relationship, Renshaw." He took a sip and watched as the boy gingerly took a sip too, then choked.

"Ugh! Nasty stuff!"

Samuel chuckled. "Actually, it is very good stuff, but I daresay it is an acquired taste. And now let us talk, and this time you can tell me the truth, Renshaw, if that is indeed your name."

The boy's mouth dropped open, and he wriggled uncomfortably in his chair. "What... what do you mean?"

Setting down his glass and steepling his hands, Samuel said, "Let me tell you what I see here. Firstly, there is a large pot of something cooking in the kitchen, far too much for one person. Secondly, you said *'we'* earlier, so if you tell me you are alone here, I shall not believe you. Thirdly, you wish me not to investigate the upper floor, so I presume you have something, or perhaps some *persons*, hidden away there. Fourthly, you have not explained what happened to your uncle and why Dr Beasley was not notified of it. Fifthly, and finally, you will be relieved to hear, there is the small fact that you are female. So you see, you had much better tell me the truth. What *is* your name, by the way?"

There was a long, agonised pause, then a whispered voice. "Charlie. Charlotte Renshaw." She removed the rather elderly wig with an expression of distaste, revealing a head of shining dark hair, neatly coiled.

Samuel raised an eyebrow. "Oh, you really are a Renshaw, then? That is something, I suppose. Shall we start with your uncle, Lucas Renshaw?"

She nodded. Her face was white with fear, but she answered him readily. "He disappeared... three weeks ago, it was. He took off one night and just... never came back. He used to go away a lot before, but never more than two or three days at a time. But this time he's not come back, and we never heard a whisper about what happened to him or where he'd gone. We didn't know what to do, and that's the truth."

"And who is this *'we'* that you keep mentioning?"

"My brother Matt, and my little brothers and sisters. Lucy, Jack, Rob and Maggie."

"No parents?"

"Both dead, sir."

"And you all just happened to be here?"

She nodded. "We had a little place just off the High Street, and after Ma died three years ago, we just about managed on Matt's pay, and what Mary and Jane could give us. Our sisters. They're both in service — got really good positions, so they helped. We thought we could keep goin', and Lucy will be old enough to go in service herself in a few months, and Jack's tall enough to be a footman, in time. But then Matt lost his place at the brewery and the rent went up and we couldn't afford it, so Uncle Lucas said we could live here, just till Matt got back on his feet, but… but that was two years ago and I don't think he'll *ever* get such a good job again. It's been bits and pieces since then. Day work, that's all. He's helpin' at the Lamb and Pheasant today, since one of the ostlers is sick."

"Why did he lose his place at the brewery?"

"Nothin' to do with his work!" she said, eyes flashing. "He's a good worker, but their rent went up, too, when Lord Saxby bought the land, and they couldn't afford to keep him. He was the youngest, so out he went. He got a good reference, but nobody's hirin' at the moment because of the higher rents. It's been difficult for everyone. When the new Lord Saxby comes, everyone's hopin' he's not such a graspin', thievin'—" She bit her lip. "Not my place to criticise, I suppose. Did you know him?"

"No, I've never been to Shropshire before."

"But you know Dr Beasley and he knew him. He told Uncle Lucas that it was wrong to complain about the nobility because they were put on earth to rule over us and they know best, and we don't want to turn out like the French, gettin' rid of the nobles and endin' up with Bonaparte, and I s'pose he has a point. But a lot of people in Market Clunbury are strugglin' just now because of Lord greedy Saxby."

"Including you," Samuel said gently. "But when your uncle disappeared, you stayed on here and I can see that you have kept everything in good order. The place is immaculate."

"Oh... thank you. We all helped. It was the least we could do, to thank Uncle Lucas for shelterin' us, and when Dr Beasley came to do his surgeries, we all just hid upstairs. He only came once or twice a week, and then he stopped comin' altogether. He wrote and said he was ill and there would be a new physician comin', but he never said when that would be."

"What was the purpose of dressing in boy's clothes?"

"Oh, that was Uncle Lucas's idea. Safer, when he was away so much and Matt was workin'. People could look through the winders and see a man inside, and no one would try anythin', and Matt's always here at night. He left the pistol here for us, too. Are you goin' to throw us out?"

Samuel considered that, seeing the anxiety in the girl's eyes. What would become of them if he made them leave? The workhouse, presumably, and a slide from respectable poverty into destitution and perhaps worse. But he knew nothing about them. They were scavengers at best, and a family of six was not his responsibility.

"As to that, I cannot say. Let me see your quarters and the children, and I must meet your brother also, and then I shall decide."

The anxiety in her face lifted slightly. "Very well."

She led him into the back room, then up the narrow stairs to the floor above. There were two rooms squeezed under the slope of the roof, both set up as bedrooms, with thin pallets and clothes neatly folded on shelves. The larger also did duty as a schoolroom, with slates and chalks and a scant row of books. There were four children here, their clothes patched and worn. Lucy was a shy girl of perhaps eleven. Jack was a well-grown boy of nine or ten. Rob was about eight and Maggie... oh dear Lord, Maggie! A wide-eyed child of four or five, with a halo of blonde curls.

Samuel's heart turned over, but the physician in him took precedence. "What is the matter with your eye, Maggie?"

"It's sore."

"It looks it. Come down to the consultation room. You shall be my very first patient in Market Clunbury." Without ceremony, he picked her up and carried her downstairs, sitting her on his knee in a chair beside the window, so that he could see clearly into her eye.

"How long has it been like this?"

"A couple of days," Charlie said. "She's had it before, and it cleared up all by itself."

"It will probably do so again. Charlie, will you bring me a small bowl of warm water and a clean cloth, if you please."

She was back with commendable promptness, and Samuel cleaned the crusty residue from the eye with gentle movements. "There, does that feel better, Maggie?" Solemnly the child nodded, and Samuel hugged her tight and stroked the soft hair. "It will be better soon, I'm sure. Do you get out regularly? Do you run about in the sunshine?"

All the children nodded. "We go down to the river sometimes, or the woods at the far end of the Welsh road," Jack said.

"Good, good. Try to get outside every day, if you can. I can see that you are well fed," Samuel said with a smile. "Or rather, I can smell it. How often do you have meat? In fact, how have you managed for money?"

"I get somethin' cheap for our Sunday dinner, and it lasts us until Wednesday, as a rule," Charlie said. "I can't afford much. Uncle Lucas kept his money in a jar, but I haven't liked to take anythin' from it, so we've lived on Matt's money. I'll dip into the jar if he doesn't come back soon, 'cos we have to eat, don't we, sir?"

"Indeed you do. But it seems to me that your Uncle Lucas has found himself another means of employment now that you are here to manage matters on his behalf. I think we should regularise the position. Charlie, what age are you?"

"Seventeen, sir, and Matt is nineteen. He can do Uncle Lucas's work here, sir," she said, suddenly eager. "He knows what to do — about sendin' word if someone wants you to call, and keepin' the waitin' room in order, that sort of thing."

"I have a better plan," Samuel said. "I shall employ you as housekeeper and manager here, at the same salary as your uncle. That will leave your brother free to obtain other employment. Two incomes, instead of one, you see? What do you say?"

Her mouth flapped open in astonishment. "Me, sir? Really?"

"Really. And since you have been doing the job for some considerable time already, it would appear that I owe you some arrears." He pulled out his purse and counted out five pounds. "This is the last quarter's wages that have not yet been paid to your uncle. When he returns, I shall discuss with him how much of his work he has left to you and ensure that he pays you accordingly. Is there a school in the town for the children of working families?"

"Mr Drinkwater of St Swithin's has a parlour school for poor children."

"Here is another shilling, and there will be more when you need it. Lucy, Jack and Rob should go whenever they can."

"You're very kind, sir," Charlie whispered. "I thought you'd throw us out, truly I did. I'm very sorry I pointed a gun at you. It wasn't loaded — I don't know how to."

Samuel chuckled, looking at the row of scrubbed faces, and the clean, if well-darned, clothes. "If ever a family deserves a bit of kindness, it is this one, so get yourself back into your skirts, Charlie, and give your pot of stew a stir, and promise me you will not wave guns at any more interlopers. Send for the constable if you have a problem."

He gave Maggie another little cuddle, and planted a quick kiss on those blonde curls, and wondered if he was being kind or merely foolish. He should be more hard-hearted, he knew, but how impossible it was! Surely one day the pain would lessen.

4: A Card Party

Susannah was in her office one morning, industriously working at the household accounts — more tea already? Where did it go to? A faint knock on the door heralded the arrival of Binns, whose discreet cough — *'hem hem'* — was usually a harbinger of trouble. She laid down her pen at once.

"Yes, Binns, what is it?"

"There is a *person* to see you, madam."

"What sort of person?"

"He says he is a business associate of the master's, but he's asking for you, madam, *in private.*"

"He asked for me by name? Not the mistress, or the lady of the household?"

Binns shook his head. "Miss Winslade, he said. A matter of business."

"Does this person have a name?"

"Trent... Bent... No card, madam." His mouth pursed in disapproval of persons wishing to speak to a lady of the house without so much as a calling card.

"Pray show him in, Binns."

Susannah was not some schoolroom miss, terrified to see a man in private for fear of compromising her reputation. She was six and twenty, and had managed the house for several years now, ever since her stepmother's health had begun to fail, and had been deferred to by servants and family alike for several more. Her stepmother was a delightful woman, loved by everyone, but running a household as large as Cloverstone Manor was not within her capabilities, even when she was well. So Susannah returned to her accounts without impatience, as she waited for Binns' faltering legs to convey him down to the hall and back again.

Mr Trent or Bent was not quite what she had expected. It was hard to determine his age, for his unlined face belied the greying hair and slight paunch about the midriff, but his attire proclaimed him a respectable burgess. And yet there was something about him that Binns had noticed, with the infallible instincts of a butler of many years' experience. Something worse than the lack of cards.

"Mr Trent?"

"Kent, madam. Erasmus Kent at your service."

"My apologies, Mr Kent. The butler is a little hard of hearing. I am Miss Winslade. You wished to speak to me privately? On a matter of business, I understand."

"That is so, madam." He smiled, a smile of such charm that her reservations melted away. "I would usually deal with your father, but there are reasons, which I will explain, as to why that would be... inadvisable."

That was concerning, but Susannah was intrigued. "Pray be seated, Mr Kent, and let me hear your explanations."

He sat on the chair she indicated, and crossed one knee over the other, quite at his ease. "You are aware, Miss Winslade, that your father was left a share in a business in Lord Saxby's will?"

"It was a property, I thought, a house in Market Clunbury. Lord Saxby owned a great deal of property in the town."

"He did, and in recent years he expanded his holdings there quite considerably, including the premises where I conduct my business. When it came time to review the rent, he proposed a different arrangement — instead of rent, I would pay him a share of the profits. I did not like it, but Lord Saxby could be very... persuasive."

"He was a man who liked his own way," Susannah said dryly.

"Indeed. When his lordship went to meet his Maker a few months ago, he bequeathed the property to your father. Your father was agreeable to continue in the same way, so when Lady Day came around, I gave your father his share of the quarter's profits. He was very happy to receive it, and told me that he would be able to settle a few small debts, and he talked of you, Miss Winslade. He said you would not be so plagued by the household expenses, and he would buy you some new gowns. And then he sat down at the card table and gambled it all away, every last penny."

Susannah gasped. "No! And here I am struggling to find the money for more candles."

"And that is why I bring this to you, rather than your father," he said, pulling a cloth bag from his pocket and placing it in her lap. It was surprisingly heavy. "The Midsummer profits. I leave it up to you what you do with it. If your father remembers that he is due a payment, I shall tell him that I have given it to you, but not the amount, so you may keep some of it and give him the rest, if you wish. Or you may tell him that you have a better use for it than the gaming tables. The choice is yours, madam. I bid you good day."

And with that, he was gone, and she was left with the heavy bag. She unfastened it and tipped the contents onto the desk in front of her. Coins... so many coins, a mountain of golden guineas and silver crowns and half-crowns. A small roll of linen notes, neatly bound with a ribbon. With trembling hands, she began to count, making a series of piles. Twenty-five, fifty, a hundred. Twenty-five, fifty, a hundred. Two hundred and fifty in ten pound notes, from several banks. Twenty-five, fifty, a hundred...

Seven hundred and eighty four pounds and six shillings. More than she had all year to feed and clothe the household. Three thousand pounds a year, which was more than Papa's income. And Papa had *gambled it away!* How dared he! How could he leave his family struggling to pay for new boots, while he tossed away such amounts of money in a single night, and for what? A few hours of excitement. It was unforgivable!

But he should not do so again. She scooped the coins and notes back into the bag and locked it away in a drawer of the desk, then sat, stunned and still boiling with rage, trying in vain to compose herself.

A faint scratching at the door. "*Hem hem.* Is all well, madam?"

"Oh... yes, thank you, Binns. Mr Kent has left."

"Silas showed him out. He was not... insolent, madam?"

"Not at all. A trifling matter of business. It is all settled now."

"Very good, madam."

When he had left, Susannah had second thoughts. Taking out the bag again, she extracted a hundred pounds in guineas and crowns, tucked them into her purse, and put the rest back in the drawer. If she had to hand the bag over to her father, at least she would have a little extra to spend this quarter. She pulled her list towards her, dipped her pen in the inkstand and doubled the amount of tea in her order.

Then she carefully wiped and laid down her pen, and wondered whatever sort of business brought in profits of three thousand pounds a year.

~~~~~

Susannah always enjoyed the card parties at Great Maeswood. Two families in the village held evening parties each week, open to all their friends, and it was just the sort of intimate occasion that suited her. Her father was more inclined to grand banquets and balls two or three times a year, or a dinner for forty with great pomp, but she liked to sit and talk to her friends, sharing a few rounds of vingt-et-un for fish or whist for penny points. But her father enjoyed his cards too much to forgo even such simple entertainment as Dr and Miss Beasley provided, so to Great Maeswood they were to go.

She had not thought much about the new physician. He would be a charming young man, she supposed, handsome and full of his own importance in the world, who would bow respectfully to her and ask how she did, even as his eyes slid away to look for better prospects — young women of greater beauty and wealth, women he could flirt with. Such treatment never bothered her. She had no great yearning to marry, and she hoped she had better sense than to fall for a smooth talker, another such as Jeffrey. He would be there, she supposed with a sigh, but with luck he would avoid her as much as civility allowed.

Unlike the Saxby ladies, therefore, she had no particular reason to expend greater effort than usual in her *toilette,* having no expectation of wishing to attract the attention of the new physician. She was curious to meet him, naturally, especially as he might very well take over the care of her stepmother from Dr Beasley, so it was important for her to find out what sort of man he was, but beyond that he deserved no special attention from her.

So it was that she walked into the Beasleys' drawing room quite unprepared.

"Ah, there you are, my dear," Dr Beasley said, beaming at her. "Come and meet my colleague and fellow physician, newly arrived from Edinburgh, Dr Broughton. This is Miss Winslade, Broughton, quite the most talented artist in our little community. Painted the prettiest view of the River Wooller you ever did see. John, Henry, come and meet…"

His voice faded. Susannah's breath caught. She could hardly believe her eyes. She dipped into her curtsy, instinct guiding her movements, and when she rose again, there he still was, looking… not unchanged, for that would be impossible after twelve years, but instantly recognisable, despite a few lines about the eyes. There was the light hair, somewhere between brown and blond. There were the steady grey eyes, the strong chin, the well-shaped mouth. His hands… they were just the same, strong but slender. Lord, how she had thought about those hands, hovering over the backgammon board as he explained the game to her, then deftly throwing the dice and moving his pieces without hesitation. Then he would fold his arms, and sit back with a gentle smile on his face.

Dr Broughton. The man who had so enchanted her fourteen-year-old self in London.

Yet how strange that he should be here. She had always supposed that he would set up a practice in London, that he would be rich and much sought-after by now. Yet somehow, he had found his way to Edinburgh and thence to sleepy Great Maeswood. She tried to work out his age, but failed. Her brain seemed not to be working.

After Papa and Henry had been introduced, there were more new arrivals, and Susannah allowed herself to drift further into the room. She found Miss Cokely in a corner, and sat beside her with relief.

"How are you? And how is Mrs Cokely?"

"We are both well, thank heavens. Mama does not grow any less confused, but she is well in herself, which is remarkable for her age. Eighty-four, and still has all her teeth. Quite remarkable."

"Yes, indeed," Susannah said absently, but her eyes strayed towards the door, where the Saxby ladies were arriving. The three youngest, Agnes, Flora and Honora, gathered in a proprietorial huddle around Dr Broughton, eyes shining, laughing and giggling, trying to outdo each other, Susannah guessed. He answered them solemnly, not unwilling to be drawn in by them, she thought, but unsmiling.

That was the most noticeable change in him, when she considered the matter. The young man she remembered had smiled a great deal, a comfortable, lazy smile that had made her want to smile too. He had been so charming, and yet now... he was more serious, as if he carried a great burden that weighed him down. Perhaps that was the inevitable result of greater age, as the light-hearted man with his whole future before him gave way to the responsibilities of maturity. She was not a great smiler herself, nor was Cass Saxby, waving to her as she entered the room, but the younger Saxby ladies, aged from sixteen to twenty, smiled to excess. Yes, perhaps that was all it was that gave Dr Broughton such a sombre air, mere advancing years and not, as she had momentarily feared, some great sadness.

As the manservant moved about with a tray of glasses — ratafia for the ladies, port for the gentlemen — Susannah found herself drawn nearer to the now large group clustered around Dr Broughton.

"He is very handsome, is he not?" Cass murmured, materialising at Susannah's elbow.

"Yes, very." Too handsome for her, but oh, how much she wanted him! Not as a husband or suitor or lover, but as he had been twelve years ago, talking to her, sharing a joke with her, *noticing* her. No man ever noticed her. Well, except Jeffrey, a man she had grown up with and could never see as a lover. He was just arriving now, a little late, his eyes searching the room until they found her. Then a quick nod and that was all. Relief... that was her overwhelming emotion. At least she was spared Jeffrey's reproachful eyes.

Last to arrive, just as the card tables were being set out, was Mr Truman, the very personable and charming new clergyman, and Cass's betrothed. Now there was a man who smiled a great deal. To Susannah's surprise, he made no effort to attach himself to Cass's side, as a lover properly should. Instead, he immediately allowed himself to be drawn into a whist four with Lady Saxby and the Gages.

Susannah shot Cass a quick glance, and the hurt was clear to see on her face. This was the first time she had been properly in company since her father's death five months earlier, yet her betrothed avoided her. Discretion, perhaps, since the betrothal was not yet known? Perhaps, yet what need for it, in such friendly company? It was unfathomable.

Momentarily distracted, Susannah had not realised that the groupings had shifted, and so she found herself, not unwillingly but in some surprise, sitting down with Agnes Saxby, with Henry opposite her and Dr Broughton beside her. He picked up the cards, shuffled and dealt with expert hands. Oh, those hands! Susannah was mesmerised and for some minutes played rather poorly, until she chided herself for her inattention and forced herself to concentrate on the play.

Would he remember her? He gave no sign of it. His attention was mostly on Agnes, for she chattered away to him unstoppably, asking him a myriad of disconnected questions, all of which he patiently answered. But he found time to talk to Susannah, too, asking about her home, her family, her interests. In none of it did he give the least sign that he remembered the girl of fourteen to whom he had devoted an entire evening once, many years ago. And why should he? She could hardly expect it.

After supper, Lady Saxby was tiring and took her daughters away with her, and Miss Cokely left too. As the smaller number of players reformed into different groupings, Susannah found Dr Broughton beside her.

"May I have the pleasure of your company again, Miss Winslade? You ended a little down before supper, and I am sure you wish to have your revenge. Piquet, perhaps? Or cribbage?"

"Backgammon," she said, without thinking. "There is a set in the console over there."

"Backgammon it is," he said.

Now, if ever, was the time when he would remember her, but still he gave no sign. They played, and he won, but whether it was his greater skill or her inability to consider, to think, to *breathe*, she could not say. It was not the same, and it was impossible that it should be, but for that one hour he was hers again, just as he had been all those years ago. He threw the dice, moved his pieces, raced round the board but she cared for none of that. All that mattered was the way he talked to her and those grey eyes gazed at her as if she were somebody of importance. As if he noticed her.

Perhaps she talked, too. It was hard to remember afterwards just what was said, what they talked about that was so absorbing. The others in the room faded away, so that only the two of them remained, and there was nothing in the world but their little table and the board it held and the two of them, lost in some private garden where it was always high summer, where perfumed trees arched over them and butterflies flitted around their heads and birds twittered melodically.

Eventually, her father came to take her away. The carriage was waiting, had she not heard him order it brought round?

"I beg your pardon, Papa. I was so absorbed in the game."

"Must you go so soon?" Dr Broughton said gallantly. "What a pity, when you were doing so well. I was sure you would win this game."

"I must, I regret to say, but thank you for entertaining me so well." And then, because it was true, she added, "It is a long time since I have enjoyed a game of backgammon so much."

"Then I hope we may repeat it very soon."

And he smiled.

Susannah's heart turned upside down. She had arrived at the Beasleys' entirely heart-whole and free, but she left it rather more than half in love.

5: Patients And Remedies

Samuel woke early, filled with enthusiasm for his new home. Last night had been very pleasant, and he had been received, not as an interloper replacing a much-loved local man, as he had feared would be the case, but as a friend. Lady Saxby had been gracious, her daughters spirited, the gentlemen welcoming. The play had been pleasant, but not such as to bankrupt the unwary, and there had been good conversation, too. The Winslade girl, with her undistinguished features and simple dress, had provided him with as entertaining an hour as any he could remember for a long time. He had fallen amongst friends, and it was the greatest relief to him. And today Mac would arrive with his horse, and before long his boxes would make their ponderous way from Edinburgh by a succession of carriers, and he could begin to make his two rooms at Whitfield Villa into more of a home.

He sent for his washing water, and dressed himself with practised efficiency, then made his way to his own study to write some letters. First to McNair in Edinburgh to tell him of his arrival and to thank him for his good offices in recommending him for the position. Then to a couple of friends in London. Finally, to the Clunbury *Clarion* and the Shrewsbury *Chronicle*, a brief notice.

Stranger at the Villa: Strangers Book 3

'Dr Samuel Broughton, son of the late Dr William Broughton of Chester, a fully qualified physician, MD (Oxon), MD (Edin), begs leave to inform the inhabitants of Market Clunbury and all surrounding villages that he will be available for consultations at 12 Chester Road, the establishment formerly held by Dr Roland Beasley, on Mondays, Wednesdays and Fridays from 11 until 3, or by appointment outwith these hours, and would be delighted to call upon the nobility and gentry at their convenience.'

The Beasleys ate breakfast promptly at nine, and even though Samuel was early, he was still the last to arrive. Miss Beasley read the day's collect, and then a short Bible reading, before Dr Beasley said the Grace. It was so restful to be part of a real family again, and one with proper observance of the rituals. The Scots were strong adherents to their religion, but in Edinburgh there had seldom been time for more than a few perfunctory words at mealtimes.

Samuel had barely broached his second cup of coffee when the doorbell clanged.

"Goodness, a visitor at this hour!" Miss Beasley said.

Thomas came in a moment later. "Miss Agnes Saxby is here, madam."

"Oh! My goodness!" Miss Beasley rose from her seat.

However, Thomas said, "To see Dr Broughton, madam. A medical matter, as I understand it. I have shown her into your study, sir."

Miss Beasley turned surprised eyes on the manservant, then on Samuel. "Well! Your first patient, Dr Broughton."

"Indeed. That is... unexpected."

Dr Beasley chuckled. "Not entirely, Broughton. I could see the young ladies all had their eye on you last night. I daresay Miss Agnes wants to steal a march on her sisters, eh?" He chuckled again. "She will have you in parson's mousetrap before you have well unpacked."

Samuel said thoughtfully, "Thomas, does Miss Agnes have her maid with her? Or one of her sisters?"

"No, sir. Quite alone."

"Oh dear," Miss Beasley said, her soft voice fretful. "Dr Broughton, should you like *me*—"

"I should be most grateful, Miss Beasley."

He followed her through to his study, where Agnes Saxby sat composedly on a chair. She jumped to her feet with a wide smile. "Good morning, Miss Beasley. Good morning, Dr Broughton. I hope I am not too early?"

"Not at all," he said politely, holding a chair for Miss Beasley. "Illness and injury do not abide by the hours of the clock, after all. Pray be seated, and tell me how I may help you."

She sat, wriggling herself into a comfortable position. "I have the earache."

"One ear or both?"

"Just this one. It is very painful, and I could barely sleep last night."

"Any pus?"

"Any what?"

"Is anything oozing from it? May I examine the ear?"

"Ooh, yes, please do."

She tilted her head invitingly, but the briefest examination convinced him that there was nothing major amiss with it. "It is not discoloured or inflamed, and you do not look feverish, Miss Saxby. I recommend a warm onion."

"Oh." Her face fell. "That is what Mags said — our old nurse. I thought you would have some clever ointment, or a tonic or lozenge to take the pain away."

"One starts with the simplest remedy first, Miss Saxby. If that brings no relief, then one would proceed to something stronger, perhaps, but I suspect your ear will be better in a day or two, if you apply a warm onion to it."

"Oh. Well, thank you, Dr Broughton."

"Allow me to show you out."

When he returned, Miss Beasley was still sitting in her chair, a little smile on her face. "She is very determined, but you are wise not to see her alone. Not that I think she would attempt to entrap you, but it would not do her reputation any good. Or yours, either."

"Thank you for your assistance."

"Any time, and if ever I am not here, Mrs Haines will act as chaperon. Or Matilda, in a pinch, but she is a very stupid girl, so I would not place any reliance on her discretion."

He raised an eyebrow. "Why employ her, then?"

"Oh, the poor child came from the workhouse. One has to help if one can, in Christian charity, and she is useful enough in the kitchen, if only she would not drop things quite so often. I do not mind a broken bowl here and there, for Roland is quite comfortably placed so the expense is not a burden, but she will drop things *after* they are cooked, and then Mrs Shinn is obliged to begin over. Once she dropped a whole tray of dressed lobster that was for a card party supper, and Roland was so upset. He is very fond of lobster, and we do not often get it. He likes everything of that kind — crabs, prawns, crayfish, oysters, mussels. It is such a pity that we are so far from the sea, but there we are."

"I like a solid piece of mutton, myself, or spring lamb," Samuel said, amused, for he had never heard her talk so much before.

"Well, you have come to the right place, then," she said, smiling. "There must be thousands of sheep in Shropshire. You will never be short of mutton, Dr Broughton."

~~~~~

It had been arranged at the card party that Dr Broughton would call at Cloverstone Manor the next day to see Susannah's stepmother. It was fortunate that Susannah had some warning of the event, so that she could to some degree compose her thoughts. After a sleepless night spent in agitated reflection, a surprise visit would have undone her completely.

He arrived precisely at the appointed time, which pleased her, although she could not say why. Probably his punctuality arose more from the lack of other patients than from any innate virtue, but still, it was a good start.

Susannah's father had stayed at home that day, which was unusual for him. He was a great one for being out of doors, and when Lord Saxby had been alive, the two of them had been out almost every day shooting or fishing or riding about one part or another of their estates. He was never so miserable as when it rained during the game season, and he could not get out at all. Yet today, a fine, sunny day, he chose to stay home and bring Dr Broughton up to Mama's room.

"Here we are, my dear, here is the new physician to see you, Dr Broughton. Beasley's successor, you know. There you are, Broughton, I shall leave you to it. You will not need me, I am sure. Female business, this, and here are Nurse Pett and Miss Matheson, oh, and my daughter, too. No, you will not need me, but I should like a word before you leave."

"Of course, sir. May I thank you for—"

But he had gone.

Dr Broughton looked at the pale figure propped up in the bed, with Nurse Pett and Miss Matheson standing on either side, like guardian angels, or watchdogs, perhaps. "Good morning, Mrs Winslade. How are you today?"

"We're not so good today," Nurse Pett said. "We didn't have a very good night, did we, madam?"

"Not much appetite at breakfast, either," Miss Matheson said.

"Are you going to bleed me?" Mama said, her voice barely there.

"Not if you dislike it," Dr Broughton said.

"Dr Beasley recommended bleeding," Nurse Pett said.

"It did her so much good," Miss Matheson said.

"Do you generally feel better after a bleeding, Mrs Winslade?" Dr Broughton said.

"We're ever so much better, aren't we?" Nurse Pett said.

But Mama shook her head. "No. I feel weak."

Dr Broughton glanced from one to the other of the two watchdogs. "I should like to talk to Mrs Winslade alone," he said quietly.

Nurse Pett bristled with indignation. "I'm her nurse, sir, and I don't leave my patient's side."

"It wouldn't be proper," Miss Matheson said. "Dr Beasley always had us in the room. He said we were very helpful."

"I am sure you are, but I am going to talk to Mrs Winslade about her daily care, and you will not wish to be embarrassed by hearing yourselves praised, I am sure. Nor can Mrs Winslade be open with me if you are by, for she knows you will demur at every compliment. Miss Winslade will stay for propriety, I am sure."

So saying, he held the door open and they had no choice but to leave, although reluctantly, knowing they had been out-manoeuvred. It was cleverly done, and Susannah could only admire his deftness. She sat by the window where she kept a basket of sewing for such times, and settled down with her needle.

Dr Broughton carried a chair nearer to the bed. "Now then, Mrs Winslade, tell me all about yourself — your father, your mother, where you grew up."

"Old history," she said. "Why do you wish to know that?"

"I like to understand my patients, especially the most interesting cases, such as yours. If I know everything about you, I shall have a better idea of how to treat you."

"Oh... the most interesting cases. Well, my father was an apothecary at Market Clunbury. He's dead now, but he was in a very good way of business there. He was well respected. When Mama died, my aunt came to look after me, but then she died too, and so Papa sent me to be a companion — well, a nurse, really — to one of his elderly patients at Astley Cloverstone, and that was how I met John... my husband, for he was her landlord. He was married, then, of course, but he came quite often, and he always stayed for a cup of tea and a little chat, and when the previous Mrs Winslade died, he went straight to Papa and asked permission to pay his addresses. Such a handsome man, and he still is, don't you think? For his age, a very well-looking man. And so we were married, not two months after the funeral."

She chattered on, her eyes shining and a little colour tingeing her cheeks. Susannah could not remember the last time she had seen her stepmother so animated. She paused often to catch her breath, but Dr Broughton said nothing, placidly waiting until she was ready to carry on. Once she was overcome with coughing, and he offered his handkerchief, making no comment.

Susannah soon forgot her sewing, caught up in listening to her stepmother and watching the physician. From where she sat, his face was in profile, not moving, his eyes fixed intently on his patient. Initially his expression was solemn, but gradually, as the tale reached the children and their curious little ways, his face softened and he even smiled. Once he even laughed at some little jest, and Mama giggled too, one hand covering her mouth. He had such an easy way about him, and Mama responded to it, just as Susannah had all those years ago. Who could not respond to such undivided attention? Such pleasing manners and so handsome! She had always thought him handsome, but the years had added something to his appearance so that he looked exceptionally distinguished and gentlemanly.

She was aware of something inside her, an aching hollowness, a yearning such as she had never experienced before. She *wanted* this man, wanted him as she had never wanted Jeffrey. Above all, she longed for him to turn his eyes on her, to smile at her, to notice her again. He was more serious now, so different from the man she remembered. Yet she caught glimpses of him, in the intensity of his focus when his attention was turned in a certain way, but most particularly when he smiled. The man she remembered was still there inside, buried perhaps beneath layers of sobriety, and maybe that man could still be brought into the sunshine again.

Such thoughts astonished her. From the day she had first put up her hair, she had known she was expected to marry — all women were, after all, it was their sacred duty. Yet she had never thought it likely. She lacked looks, accomplishments and dowry, and that had never worried her in the slightest. She had never cared whether she married or not.

Until now.

Yet he was not beyond her reach. He was not nobility or the wealthier reaches of the gentry. His profession made him a gentleman, albeit at the lowest reaches, yet it also meant that he could support a wife without a dowry. All she had to do was to turn his mind to matrimony, yet how that was to be done she had not the least idea.

Now he was asking Mama how long it was since she had left her room. "Oh, months, many months. A year or more, perhaps. I cannot walk far, you know."

"Should you like to go outside? Into the garden?" he said, his voice soft. "You have mentioned the garden and the flowers there so often that you must miss them."

"Oh yes! I have always loved the garden here, for I never had one before, not a proper one, like this. John had new flowerbeds made and filled with all my favourite flowers, but I cannot see them any more. Susannah paints them for me, to remind me." She gestured to the several framed paintings on the walls.

"I do not see any reason why you should not go outside a little in the summer," Dr Broughton said. "I will send the squire a design for a wheeled chair with handles such that it may easily be lifted up and down stairs by a pair of footmen. Then you can sit on the terrace, or be pushed about the garden, if the paths are solid enough."

Her face lit up. "Oh! I should like that of all things! I thank you from the bottom of my heart, sir!"

"You must not overdo it, mind," he said, wagging a finger teasingly at her. "However, the sunshine will do you a great deal of good."

He called Nurse Pett and Miss Matheson back into the room, and a lengthy discussion ensued, after which the two watchdogs were persuaded to throw away the better part of the tonics and chest rubs and lozenges previously prescribed, and somehow he brought them to consider this winnowing as entirely their own idea.

Leaving the patient to their care, he made for the door.

Susannah was there before him. "I shall show you to my father's lair," she said, unwilling to hand him over to Binns or Silas.

"Thank you, but I should like a word with you first," he said quietly.

"My office is next door."

He followed her through, and to her surprise, took the chair she offered and accepted a glass of Madeira. Not a brief courtesy call, then.

"Miss Winslade, how long have Nurse Pett and Miss Matheson been here?"

"Miss Matheson about six years, and Nurse Pett a few months. They are a little over-protective, but the previous nurse was a touch too fond of gin."

"Overprotective? Cerberus would be less fierce, I suspect. But tell me of Mrs Winslade's health. It seems to me that she has been in decline for some years."

"She has, for she is such a delicate little creature, so tiny and fragile, and she has borne eight children in as many years. The first three were not so bad, for although she was exhausted, she recovered after each one, but the twins— That was the start of it, and with each successive child, she became more debilitated. But... I do not think that is all. It is consumption, is it not? The shortness of breath, the coughing—"

"Ah, yes. It is very likely, but it does not follow that her life will be cut short," he said gently. "I have seen many recover from the illness, in time, with good care. But we must ensure that she is not cocooned away from the world so much. Does she ever see her children?"

We must ensure... Susannah trembled at the intimacy. Even though he was talking dispassionately about Mama, yet he regarded her as a part of a united endeavour. *We...* oh, if only there were a *we*. It took her a moment to recover her composure sufficiently to answer his question.

"She used to but... but it distressed her so much that... that Dr Beasley put a stop to it." Be calm, she told herself sternly. Take a deep breath. "Her nerves are easily disordered, and he wished her to have absolute tranquillity."

"I beg your pardon, Miss Winslade. It was not my intention to agitate you. However, if she wishes to see them, it is my belief that it will do her no harm, if care is taken."

"The older children, perhaps..." she said thoughtfully. "They are so well-behaved that—"

"No, the younger children," he said, with sudden fierceness. "The youngest is... three, perhaps? His presence would remind Mrs Winslade how much she has to live for. If she can be recalled from the cycle of decaying health into which she appears to be trapped, then it is the youngest child, her baby, who will do it. No mother can fail to be moved by the living proof of her own life force. Or father, either," he added, half to himself.

"The youngest," Susannah repeated, rather surprised by his vehemence. "Very well."

6: The Frog Orchid

Samuel found himself quite disconcerted by his conversation with Miss Winslade. After all this time, to be overset by the mere talk of children — it was foolish beyond permission. He quickly brought the interview to a close, and she led him by circuitous ways to the small book room where her father waited, and left him there, disappearing back to whatever chores occupied her. A sensible woman, very practical, who would be a far better nurse for her stepmother than those two bird-witted women.

He had expected the squire to be sensibly engaged, reading, perhaps, or writing letters, or working on his accounts, but he found him standing disconsolately before the empty hearth, glass in hand, moodily kicking at the grate.

"Ah, there you are, Broughton. I had begun to wonder if you were ever going to emerge. Whatever kept you?"

"I like to talk to my patients on first meeting," Samuel said. "It gives me a better idea of how to treat them."

"Hardly necessary with Mrs Winslade, I should have thought. Consumption, would you not say? Not much to be done about it, eh? Just have to let it run its course, eh?"

"Well, perhaps but there is much that might be—"

"Never mind that. Come and sit down, Broughton, for I have a matter to discuss with you. A private matter, if you understand me. A glass of port?" He poured a glass for Samuel, then refilled his own and tossed most of it down at a gulp. "Awkward business. Impossible to mention to Beasley. Good chap, and all that, but... he is a friend of so many years that... well, awkward, very awkward."

"I understand, sir. You wish to consult with me on a medical matter."

"Exactly so, but... you will not tell Beasley? He is such a pious man, he would not understand."

Ah, that sort of medical matter. "I am the soul of discretion, Squire. Not a word of what you say will leave this room, you have my word on it."

"Good man, good man. Very reassuring." He hesitated, chewing his lip. "It is damnably awkward, Broughton."

"So let me see if I can guess. You have some manifestation of disorder in a particularly delicate place?"

"Exactly so! You are sharp, I will say that for you. Yes, a particularly delicate place."

Samuel assumed his most solemn expression. "Would you care to describe the precise nature of the problem, Squire? Pain or discomfort? Some kind of discolouration or rash? Or perhaps—"

"A rash! That is it."

"Should you like me to have a look at it?" Samuel said in his most neutral tones.

"Look at it? Good heavens, no! I mean — that is hardly necessary, is it?"

"I am sure I have seen worse," Samuel said mildly. "You would be amazed what physicians encounter. It does make it easier to determine the correct treatment."

There was a long, agonised silence, then with a huff of resignation, the squire unfastened the fall of his breeches and lifted his shirt. "There! You see? It is the pox, is it not? You need not spare me, Broughton, for I am quite prepared for it."

"Actually, I think not. Acquired in the same way, perhaps, but I believe it can be treated."

"Truly? You think so? Then I am not—? Oh, thank God! I know I have sinned, but— Thank God!"

Samuel gazed at him sympathetically. "These things happen, Squire. Your wife has been ill for a long time, after all."

"Precisely so! You understand it exactly," he said, tidying his breeches. "Not that I liked to do it, but... well, you understand how it is. Beasley, now — he would have read me a lecture, and quoted the scriptures at me, and made me feel like a schoolboy again, caught flicking ink pellets at the master."

"Did you do so too?" Samuel said, chuckling. "The most tremendous fun, was it not?"

The squire gave a bark of laughter. "Ah, school! Such happy days. There is something you can prescribe for this? Something to set me right again?"

"I will make up something for you. If I purchase the ingredients from the apothecary in Market Clunbury and mix it up myself, no one will know it is for you. And you should advise the woman you visited of the situation."

The squire patted him amiably on the back. "You are a good fellow, Broughton, a very good fellow not to preach at me."

"You will get no preaching from me, sir, but I would advise you to keep to yourself if you possibly can. You are aware of the risks you run, and although you have been lucky this time, matters could have been a great deal worse."

"I know it, and I am chastened, Broughton, I assure you. Believe me, such habits never crossed my mind until Lilian became so ill, and it became clear that she would not recover. The prospect of a lifetime of restraint is appalling to me, I make no bones about it. I am ashamed to admit that there have been times when I almost wished Lilian dead, instead of lingering in this appalling way. That is dreadful, is it not? But not on my own account — well, not *solely* on my own account, for then she would be free of this dreadful illness that has sucked all the spirit from her. Have you ever been in love, Broughton?"

"Never, sir."

"Then you cannot imagine the pain — ah, my lovely wife! My little sprite, I called her, for she was so full of vitality, and now... I cannot bear to see her so shrunken and faded, like a living ghost. She is trapped by it, and so am I, Broughton, so am I. But there it is, there is nothing to be done about it, except to endure."

~~~~~

Susannah's days were well regulated from the moment of her rising, with household tasks and the many needs of her eight brothers and sisters still in the nursery. Often she was called to her stepmother's room, to resolve disputes between the two attendants. But at four o'clock every day, and at two on Saturdays, she called a halt. The house was left to Binns and Silas and Mrs Cobbett, the children to Miss Norton and the nursery maids, and her stepmother to Nurse Pett and Miss Matheson. In winter, Susannah retreated to her art studio or to her boudoir, but in summer the outdoors called to her.

On this particular Saturday, she knew exactly where she was bound. She had, in fact, already prepared the satchel containing her painting equipment, so it was the work of a moment to change into stouter footwear and don bonnet, spencer and gloves, and set off for the river. There were many beautiful places near Cloverstone Manor, but to her mind the River Wooller bested them all. On one side coppices and fields jostled each other amiably, and on the other a grassy rise provided a meadow of delightful abundance, carpeted from early spring to autumn by a myriad of tiny flowers, alive with butterflies, bees and crickets.

She found the perfect spot, and began to unpack her easel and paints. She had not been painting for long when she saw a man steadily making his way up the hill towards her, his figure familiar enough that her heart jumped in pleasure.

"Good day to you, Miss Winslade!" he called out as he approached. "What a glorious spot! No wonder you wish to capture it for ever."

"Good day, Dr Broughton. This is one of my favourite spots, and I have painted it many times for it is always changing. The seasons, the shifting of the sun, the passing of a cloud — every hour brings some new aspect."

"But are you not facing the wrong way? Is not the river behind you of much greater interest? The varied colours of the trees, the sun catching the water so that it looks like quicksilver, the farms and woods beyond — is that not prettier than the meadow before you, which is so uniform in colour and form?"

She glanced up from her easel with an amused smile. "Uniform? But look at all the flowers, Dr Broughton. The meadow is carpeted with them, and the subtle colours and textures are a great challenge to capture."

"Flowers? I see nothing but grass, of varied hue, perhaps, but still— Oh! Those little spikes? Are those flowers?"

That made her laugh outright. "They are frog orchids, sir, and if you look very closely, you will see some tiny purple flowers here and there. That is wild thyme. And over by that rocky outcrop, do you see a patch of yellow? Kidney vetch. This meadow is alive with flowers from spring to autumn. There is always something new to be seen."

"Fascinating!" he said, casting himself face down on the ground so that he could examine the orchids closely. "So small and yet so perfectly formed, and so beautiful. Subtle colours indeed, Miss Winslade. I never knew such wonders existed."

"Were you never in the country before, sir?"

"No, never. I grew up in Chester, which is quite a substantial place, but we seldom ventured beyond the bounds of the city. My father was a physician there, and felt obliged to be available to his patients at all times."

"And you do not?" she said, intrigued by this glimpse of his past.

He sat up again to face her, crossing his legs neatly. "I believe that sunshine and exercise are beneficial to all, Miss Winslade, even physicians. I watched my father's health decline from the lack, combined with overwork, and when he died, I swore I would live my life differently. In Chester, I began to walk beside the River Dee, and at Oxford it was the Isis. In Edinburgh I climbed Calton Hill every day, and here…" He laughed suddenly, and her breath caught at the difference in him. *There* was the man she remembered! He went on, "Here I can walk in a different direction every day, and find some vista or prospect to delight the eye and lift the spirits. How lucky you are to know it so well, every little corner familiar to you in all its moods."

"But you have the happiness of discovering such corners," she said, with a smile. "I can only imagine your pleasure in seeing such splendours for the first time. We are both lucky, I think."

"That is very true," he said thoughtfully, the serious expression returning momentarily. "Have you always lived here?"

"Yes, I was born in the manor house."

"And have you travelled much?"

"Hardly at all. Papa liked to go to London at one time, but I was too young to accompany him then, and now he prefers to stay at home. Henry visits friends he made at school and at Oxford, but I never went to school, so all my friends are here, in the neighbourhood. I envy you — all of your sex — who are free to come and go as you please."

"Not quite as we please," he said, and there was that smile again, a little rueful this time. "Most men have no independent income to set them free, but must pursue a career as best they can."

"But you have lived in many places!" she cried. "Chester, Oxford, Edinburgh, London… so much you must have seen of life, whereas I have seen nothing but flowers."

"Yet perhaps there is more of truth and beauty and nobility in a single flower than in all of our great cities," he said, his voice abruptly harsh, as he sprang to his feet in one swift movement. "But I disturb your artistic endeavours, and perhaps the light will change and you will lose the image you attempt to capture. I shall leave you to the enjoyment of your flowers. Good day to you, Miss Winslade."

And he was gone before she had a chance to answer him, leaving her bemused and a little hurt.

~~~~~

Sunday saw the whole Winslade family bound for church. This was an unusual enough event to attract comment from several of their friends, but only to Cass Saxby could Susannah admit the truth as the congregation mingled in the churchyard after the service.

"Papa is finally becoming more like his old self again. Ever since Mama took to her bed, he has been... difficult, either too fond of the bottle or else too inclined to gad about on who knows what business. I have been quite concerned about him, if you must know."

"I knew about the drinking," Cass said quietly. "It worried me when you so seldom came to church, for I know you have little leisure for visiting and I missed you. Still, your father's wishes must prevail."

"We had prayers in the chapel, but it is not the same, is it? But for the last week or so, Papa has been much more himself. He had a long chat to Dr Broughton on Friday, and that seems to have had a beneficial effect on him. He has said that from now on we should all attend church every week, even the little ones, so long as the weather is fit for the horses. I cannot tell you how relieved I am. Miss Norton is a very competent governess and between us we make sure the children say their prayers every day, but there is no substitute for the weekly service and a good sermon."

"He does preach a good sermon, I think," Cass said, with that faint blush which warmed her countenance whenever she spoke of her betrothed. "Perhaps I am biased, but his points are always well made, without too much roundaboutation."

"I admit Mr Truman to be an excellent clergyman," Susannah said with a smile. "He is looking our way — will you not call him over? I have a most interesting orchid that he may care to know of."

"Oh... he does not like it if I claim his attention in public. He is so conscious of the awkwardness of our position, and is most careful of my reputation."

"But that problem is easily resolved, is it not?" Susannah said, with a smile. "You need only declare your intentions to the world and—"

"No, no, not yet. Mr Truman is most insistent that there must be no whisper of rumour beforehand. Excuse me, I must have a word with Miss Cokely."

Susannah watched her go with some disquiet. While she understood the difficulties of a betrothal contracted while the lady was still in mourning, after almost six months the time for secrecy was surely past.

"Your friend — she is the eldest Miss Saxby, I think?" said a voice at her side, a voice that was all too heart-flutteringly familiar.

"That is so, the only child of her father's first marriage." Then, turning to face him fully, she said with a little frisson of fear, "Have you a particular interest in Cass, Dr Broughton?"

"A medical one only. That is a worrying limp — is it permanent? Or a recent injury that might need attention?"

Ah, always the man of medicine. "Cass was very ill when she was a child, no more than six years of age. The fever was very great and she could not leave her bed for a long while. When she recovered, one leg was misshapen and nothing could be done about it."

"That would be infantile paralysis. It is not uncommon, and you are correct, there is nothing that can be done for it. Miss Saxby is lucky that she is female, for long skirts cover the visible deformity. Men are less fortunate. She copes well with her affliction, I think, for she shows a cheerful demeanour to the world."

"She does not repine over it, certainly. Ah, good day, Mr Truman, an interesting sermon today — thank you."

"Everyone says that," the clergyman said with his ready smile. "An interesting sermon… or thought-provoking… or well-phrased, or some other compliment, just as if they had listened carefully to every word. I warrant if I were to ask them the precise verse upon which it was based, fully eight or nine parts of them could not answer."

"'My cup runneth over'?" Susannah hazarded.

Mr Truman laughed. "I was not testing you, Miss Winslade. It is enough that my parishioners are here in body, even if their minds are elsewhere, just so long as they do not snore too loudly." He chuckled at his own wit. "How is your mama?"

"Much as usual, but Dr Broughton has given us a new regimen to follow, so we are optimistic of improvement. Mr Truman, I know you have an interest in wild flowers, and particularly orchids. You may care to know that there is a fine display of frog orchids just now on the hill above the river."

"Frog orchids?" He looked perplexed for a moment. "Ah yes, frog orchids. How fascinating. The hill above the river, you say?"

"Yes, I was there yesterday painting them before they fade."

"Before they fade... of course. The colours are so pretty, are they not? I must find time to see them. Excuse me, I must catch Mr Gage before he rushes away."

Susannah frowned.

"Pretty colours?" Dr Broughton said in an undertone. "He has never seen one, has he?"

She gurgled with laughter. "He cannot have done, no."

"I am not the only one who knows nothing about orchids," he said.

"So it would seem, and yet... how odd. He told Cass he had a particular interest in them. How very odd."

"Clergymen are often eccentric, and he *was* testing you, Miss Winslade. *'Thou preparest a table before me in the presence of mine enemies: thou anointest my head with oil; my cup runneth over.'* Psalms chapter twenty-three, verse five."

There was such a teasing expression on his face, that she burst out laughing, and was still chuckling when the carriage drew up outside the lych gate.

7: Consultations

JULY

On Monday Samuel rode over to Market Clunbury. The long spell of fine weather had given way to grey skies and intermittent drizzle, but Samuel's spirits were high. He had his own horse at last, and was accompanied by his groom, Mac, a small, dark Scot who had been in his employ for two years now, and was perhaps his closest friend.

"Are they looking after you below stairs?" Samuel said, as they jogged through Astley Cloverstone.

"Aye, weel enough. Nae complaints. Better than Mrs McFarland's house, that's fae certain."

Samuel chuckled. "True enough. She was a bit of a stickler for the rules, I grant you that. The Beasleys are far more welcoming."

"Proper gentlefolk," Mac said. "Wax candles and cloth on the table in the servants' hall, and everything fine. One thing I dinnae understand, though. Why dae ye live with them and nae at the consulting place?"

"Too small," Samuel said. "It was only ever intended to be a second place for consultations, with just room for a caretaker to live in."

"Nae grand enough for the likes o' ye," Mac said, with a grin.

"I plan to make my permanent home here, so I shall look for somewhere a bit larger when I am settled."

"Ah, ye's plannin' on marryin', I'd say," Mac said knowingly.

"Maybe, who knows?" Samuel said complacently.

"Weel, it's about time. Man o' your age should be wed, right enough."

Samuel said nothing.

The whole Renshaw family awaited him in the kitchen this time, with nary a gun in sight, and Charlie respectably gowned. There was one new face, that of Matt Renshaw, the young man of nineteen. He eyed Samuel warily, but thanked him politely for his generosity in allowing them to stay and employing Charlie.

"I don't know what we'd have done else, sir, and that's a fact," he said, his young face earnest, as Samuel bathed Maggie's eye again.

"We'd have been in the poor house," Charlie said sombrely.

"And that would have been a shame, when you are clearly sober, hard-working people who happen to have fallen on hard times," Samuel said. "There, Maggie, that eye is coming along very well. Lucy, Jack, will you please take Rob and Maggie upstairs? I should like to talk to Matt and Charlie."

"You want to talk about Uncle Lucas," Matt said, when the others had left and they were seated at the kitchen table.

"I do, yes. He has been gone for almost a month now, and that worries me," Samuel said. "Have you any idea at all where he might have gone, or what might be keeping him away?"

The two exchanged glances. "No, but there's somethin' we think you ought to see."

Beneath the stairs was another door, which opened to reveal a steep stone stair leading down. Matt lit a lamp, and led the way. It was quite a small basement, with beer and wine cellars, two bays for coal, shelves of jars and cheeses, and sacks of vegetables. Tucked away behind a partition was another door, with a heavy lock and two solid bolts fitted.

"We found the key in Uncle Lucas's press," Charlie said, as she unlocked it, and slid back the bolts. "We were lookin' for some clue to where he might have gone, and we found it then."

The light from the lamp revealed a much larger cellar, cool and damp, the walls stacked with boxes. Some bore candles or jars of oil, but most were filled with bottles carefully packed in straw. Samuel lifted one up.

"Wine? Your uncle has an excessive quantity of the stuff here. Is it all his?"

"It comes in and out at night," Matt said, his face troubled. "Over here is a hatch to the yard up above, with old sacks hidin' it. Nothing comes through the house. All the boxes go straight down the hatch into the cellar. From time to time they take boxes out."

"That sounds as if your uncle is just renting out cellar space, maybe to the inn next door," Samuel said, puzzled by their concern. "There is nothing untoward in that. People do it all the time."

"But they only ever move them at night!" cried Charlie. "Why would they do that if everything was legal? Is it smugglin'?"

"It seems unlikely, so far from the sea," Samuel said. "Besides, smuggled wine is conveyed in the barrel. In fact, all imported wine is shipped that way. Can you imagine trying to get these fragile bottles onto and off ships?"

"Then why the secrecy?" Matt said stubbornly.

"It may be that the roads are quieter at night, with no coaches to get in the way. It sounds like a sensible arrangement. Your uncle was making a little extra money, and perhaps he helped himself to a bottle here and there as well. But I do not imagine this has anything to do with his disappearance. Have you reported it to the constables?"

"They won't do anythin' unless we lay a complaint," Charlie said. "They told Matt it's not their job to chase round after fully grown men who happen to have gone somewhere else. But he could be *dead.*"

"That is one possibility," Samuel said sombrely. "Dead or injured and unable to return. Equally, he could simply be choosing to stay away. And I think there is a distinct possibility that you may never know what has become of him."

Samuel spent his allotted four hours in the Market Clunbury consultation room. He had no expectation of patients, since the newspaper notices had not yet been posted, but he pinned a sign on the door to show that he was open for business. He spent an hour arranging in the cupboard the supplies he had bought from Mr Edser, the apothecary, and sorting through the patient notes left behind. And then he wondered what on earth he was to do with himself for the rest of his time.

Mac had been left to settle the horses at the inn, and then to look around the town and buy a few basic supplies.

"It's a cosy wee place," he said cheerfully, depositing a collection of parcels on Samuel's desk, and a map of the town. "Three banks, two apothecaries and another inn, a bit better than the Swan." He fished in a pocket. "Brought ye a pie tae keep ye going till that fancy dinner tonight."

"What kind of pie?" Samuel said, eyeing it suspiciously.

"Nae idea. Rat, maybe? Quite tasty, though."

Samuel chuckled, and took a nervous bite. "Oh, not bad at all. Mutton, possibly."

"Aye, it could be, right enough," Mac said, with a grin. "Hello, is that the bell? Ye've a customer, Sam."

And so began Samuel's Market Clunbury medical practice, with a child who had been kicked by a horse. He was followed by a bootmaker's apprentice with a bleeding hand, an elderly man with a boil on his neck, and two young ladies who blushed profusely, talked vaguely about weakness of the limbs and ran away giggling when pressed for details. For those who could pay, he took their directions to send his bill. For those who could not, he treated them anyway, and told them to come to the kitchen door in future.

"And only for emergencies, mind," he said. "I have to earn a living somehow, just like you do."

He was treated to a rather stiff visit from one of the town's apothecaries, a rotund man with iron-grey hair in long Vandyke curls, who hoped Dr Broughton would see his way to the use of his services, when required, rather than his scurrilous and incompetent rival, who was like to overdose and quite likely kill all his patients.

"I am very glad to have met you," Samuel said, "and if my patients wish to obtain their remedies from you I shall not deter them, but if I prescribe a remedy, I like to prepare it myself if I possibly can."

"So you don't trust my work, sir," the apothecary said, lifting his chin pugnaciously.

"It would be presumptuous of me to judge when I know nothing of it," Samuel said mildly. "My considerations are practical only. If a patient is in my consultation room, and I can provide what is needful on the spot, then it saves a great inconvenience to supply it."

An hour later, the other apothecary, a cadaverous man with a tightly-curled tye-wig, came to him with the exact same plea, and Samuel gave him the same answer.

"You'll be taking business away from me and my family," the apothecary said. "I have three babes to feed and another on the way, and a third medical man is more than this town can stand, and that's a fact."

"This practice has been here for some years, although a trifle neglected of late," Samuel said. "But you may be sure that I am no rival to you and your fellow apothecary."

"How's that, then?" the apothecary said suspiciously.

"My fees will be much higher than yours," Samuel said blandly. "I have degrees from Oxford and Edinburgh, have lectured at both of them, and have published a treatise of the circulation of the blood. I am a very exclusive physician, sir, and most people will not be able to afford me."

When he told the tale to Mac on their ride home, the Scotsman said, "Why d'ye say that? No one'll want ye now."

"On the contrary, those two gentlemen will helpfully spread the word of the arrival of the most exclusive and expensive physician in Shropshire. The discerning gentry for miles around will want to know what makes me so special. They will make me fashionable, and then the merchant class will be drawn in."

"What does make ye special?"

Samuel chuckled. "I have no idea. All I do is listen to them. They talk, I listen and they feel better. It is magic, Mac, absolute magic."

"Profitable magic, too," Mac said.

"Let us hope so, or I am sunk," Samuel said.

~~~~~

Tuesday was a Great Maeswood day. Samuel rode over to Cloverstone Manor to see Mrs Winslade, and found her full of excitement after her first visit to the garden. Her two guardians had considered it too damp to venture onto the pathways, but she had sat on the terrace for an hour, while Miss Winslade and a gardener had brought armfuls of flowers from the glass houses and pleasure grounds. Then she had spent the rest of the morning arranging them in bowls and vases. Now they stood on every surface in her room, filling the air with perfume. Miss Winslade was valiantly attempting to paint the best of them before they began to shed petals.

He returned to Great Maeswood to find a note awaiting him — *'Lady Saxby would be grateful if Dr Broughton would call at Maeswood Hall at his earliest convenience.'*

His horse having already gone to the stables to be rubbed down, he set off on foot. This proved to be a mistake, for he had barely left the drive of Whitfield Villa before he bumped into Miss Beasley with a friend, whom she introduced as Miss Gage of Lower Maeswood Grove, a middle-aged spinster with drab clothes covering a spare frame.

"How delightful to meet you at last, Dr Broughton," Miss Gage said. "Of course, I saw you at church but there was no opportunity to talk to you then, so surrounded by the ladies from the Hall as you were." She tittered, one gloved hand covering her mouth. "I should have met you last Thursday at dear Phyllida's card party but we were a trifle unsettled that night. However, you will come to the Grove this evening, I trust. We have cards on Tuesdays and you will be very welcome, you know. We generally sit down at eight."

"Thank you. That is most kind," Samuel said politely. "Where precisely is Lower Maeswood Grove? Is it very far?"

She tittered again. "Oh dear me no, not far at all, Dr Broughton. You can almost see the gateposts from here. Directly opposite the Dower House."

"Oh, so Lower Maeswood Grove is in Great Maeswood?" he said, rather confused.

"What? Oh! Oh yes! Such a joke, but the original house was at Lower Maeswood, you see, which is several miles away."

"Two miles," Miss Beasley said in a whisper.

"Two miles? Is it? It seems further to me. Are you sure, Phyllida? It definitely seems further to me, but it is of no consequence. When the old house burnt down, the new house was built at this end of the estate, not at Lower Maeswood at all. So you will come tonight, Dr Broughton?"

"I should be very happy to do so, if no patients summon me elsewhere. And now, if you will excuse me, I have business that cannot be delayed. Good day to you, Miss Gage. Miss Beasley."

As he strode off, he distinctly heard Miss Gage say, "What business does he have? Do you know, Phyllida?"

He found Lady Saxby reclining on a chaise longue, a handkerchief pressed to her temple. There was a strong aroma of burnt feathers in the room, as all four of her daughters were gathered around her, and a couple of maids hovered nearby with anxious faces.

"Ah, at last!" she cried, as he was announced. "What kept you, sir?"

"I was visiting another patient," he said evenly. "What ails you, Lady Saxby?"

"Why nothing, except my usual palpitations and flutterings of the heart, but they have been my companions these many years, and I no longer regard them. It is Honora who concerns me. She has a fever, and I am sure it is the smallpox. There is smallpox this side of Oswestry... or was it Welshpool? I am not sure, but somewhere in Wales, anyway."

"Oswestry is in Shropshire, Mama," said Miss Agnes.

"Is it? But that is even worse! There is smallpox within the county, and we are all at risk. Tell me the worst, Dr Broughton — is it smallpox? Honora, stand up and let Dr Broughton look at you. Cassandra, bring a chair for the physician."

It was fortunate that she thus identified Miss Honora, for Samuel would not have known one sister from another, apart from Miss Agnes. She was both the plainest of the sisters, and also the one who had had the boldness to call upon him. Miss Honora was as different as it was possible to be, a pretty little creature, blushing furiously.

"Do you have any spots and redness anywhere, Miss Honora?"

"No, sir."

"Is your sleep disturbed?"

"No, sir."

"Have you vomited?"

"No, sir."

"Any change in your appetite?"

"No, sir."

"And you do not appear to be suffering any fever, so I think we may safely discount the possibility of smallpox," Samuel said, rising from his chair.

"Is that all you have to say, sir?" Lady Saxby said sharply. "She is ill, she needs something to restore her bloom."

Samuel did not hesitate. "Of course. I will have Mr Edser prepare something for Miss Honora. I know of a very efficacious tonic much in use in Edinburgh. I am certain it will do her a great deal of good, when combined with exercise in the sunshine, and plenty of sleep."

"Exercise?" Miss Honora said, in outraged tones. "I am not well enough for exercise, Dr Broughton."

"Gentle exercise for a short time each day is very beneficial, Miss Honora," Samuel said, smiling gently. "Every lady needs to maintain her beauty and health with regular exercise. A short walk in the garden, or, if the weather conditions should be adverse, within the house, is greatly to be recommended. Breathe deeply as you walk, and maintain an upright posture, and I am sure you will soon see the benefit."

"But you will send a tonic?" Miss Honora said anxiously. "To perk me up until I am well enough to exercise?"

"I will. Miss Agnes, is your ear better?"

"Her ear?" Lady Saxby said. "Agnes, what is amiss with your ear? Why did you not inform me about it?"

"It was a trivial matter, Mama. Just a little pain, that was all, so I asked Dr Broughton to advise me and now it is quite gone away." She beamed happily at Samuel.

"I see," Lady Saxby said, her eyes flitting from her daughter to Samuel and back again. "Do sit down again, Dr Broughton. Cassandra, pour the gentleman a glass of Madeira. Do tell me of yourself, sir. Your father was a physician also, I understand?"

Stifling a sigh, Samuel sat, dutifully sipped the Madeira and told Lady Saxby in indirect terms everything that she wished to hear, which was that he was not connected to anyone of rank, that he had been educated largely by scholarship at the local school and that he had little money of his own.

"But you have taken over Dr Beasley's medical practice, I understand?" she said, her eyes fixed on him.

"At present, it is more in the nature of a partnership," he said. "Once the business is thriving again, then I shall be in a position to buy Dr Beasley's share."

"Ah," she said, nodding knowingly, and he congratulated himself in successfully diverting any matrimonial ambitions she might have harboured for her daughter.

Miss Agnes herself was less easily deterred. When he deemed he had fulfilled the obligations of civility and made his farewells, she followed him out to the hall.

"Dr Broughton, there is another matter upon which I desire to consult you." Her prominent blue eyes gazed at him without a hint of shame.

"By all means, Miss Saxby. Let us go back to Lady Saxby and—"

"No, no. There is no need to worry Mama over something that I am sure is perfectly trivial. It is a very minor female matter, but it is so reassuring to consult with a qualified medical man such as yourself, and one does prefer such discussions to be completely private. May I call upon you tomorrow, before breakfast?"

"By all means, but you must be chaperoned, Miss Saxby. Miss Beasley would be willing to—"

"Oh no, not Miss Beasley. She would not understand."

"Then your mama, or one of your sisters. Failing that, a maid, perhaps. I cannot see you alone, and I am sure that Lady Saxby would say exactly the same."

"A maid… yes, that could be done," she said thoughtfully. "Mags will come." She smiled up at him. "Until tomorrow, then, Dr Broughton. Oh, but you will be at the Gages' card party, I expect, so I will see you this evening." The smile widened even further. "Goodbye."

Samuel walked home sunk deep in gloom. There was no evading a young lady determined to find an excuse to see him.

8: Another Card Party

Samuel's first impression was that there were far more people at the Gages' card party than there had been at the Beasleys' the previous Thursday. The new faces were the Gages themselves, and three visitors from London who had been engaged to investigate a mysterious body in the Dower House wine cellar, and had somehow managed to dig up more mysteries to occupy themselves since then. They were a strange trio. Mr Willerton-Forbes was a lawyer, although Samuel had never seen one so fashionably dressed before. Captain Edgerton, formerly of the East India Company Army, was a small man who, even in evening dress, had the look of the career soldier about him, as if he were permanently ready to leap aback his horse and charge into battle. The third man, Mr Chandry, was a little younger than Samuel and had the sort of roving eyes and roguish smile that would worry any mother of susceptible young ladies.

Unfortunately, the Saxby ladies were also in attendance and there was no avoiding Miss Agnes. However, Samuel successfully steered her away from the intimacy of whist, and towards a round game of speculation. There was no possibility of rational conversation in such a setting, but Samuel found the sensible Miss Winslade on his other side, who gave him some respite from Miss

Agnes. Miss Winslade, he discovered, enjoyed the rather pretty name of Susannah. She was not especially prettily featured, but her dress and manners were modest, and her conversation pleasant.

"Did you manage to complete your paintings of all those flowers?" he said to her, between rounds of the game.

"I did, and they came out rather well, I feel," she said. "I am quite accustomed to paint swiftly, before the sun or rain or clouds change the view altogether, so vases of flowers which sit quietly before my easel are no great challenge."

"Shall you have them framed?"

"Mama wishes it, and so it will be done. Then she may have a selection on her wall through the winter months to remind her of the summer. Dr Broughton, I cannot thank you enough for suggesting that we take Mama to the garden. It was wonderful to see her enjoyment of such a simple exercise, and tomorrow, if she is well enough, we plan to take little Edward in to see her. I hope that will do her just as much good."

"I hope so too," Samuel said.

After supper, Lady Saxby summoned her carriage and took her daughters home, but the hardened games players continued for slightly higher stakes. Samuel was not so poor that he was obliged to abandon the evening at that point, but neither was he so rich that the loss of five or ten pounds was not a consideration. Luckily, he found himself partnered by Captain Edgerton, who turned out to be a capital player, so they ended the evening twenty pounds apiece better off. The defeated Miss Beasley and Miss Winslade accepted the loss with good grace.

Somehow Samuel found himself one of the last to leave, along with Captain Edgerton, and they set off down the drive together.

"Are you staying at the inn?" Samuel said, knowing that the captain and his friends were visitors, not residents.

"Happily not, for Mrs Brownsmith is the world's worst cook. Mr Gage was so obliging as to accommodate us while we were investigating some matters for his family, but now that we have another affair to interest us, we have rented the Dower House for the rest of our stay, however long that may be."

"Another body in a basement?" Samuel said.

"Sadly not. Two such in one small village would be too much to hope for. However, there is always something arising to catch our interest, and if ever we are at a loss, there is the mysterious case of Dilys Hughes, a housemaid who left the Hall twenty-nine years ago, caught the public stage as far as Shrewsbury and then vanished."

"Surely people vanish all the time," Samuel said. "What is so special about this particular housemaid?"

"Nothing at all," Captain Edgerton said. "It is the usual tragic story — she found herself with child, so she left her position at the Hall, supposedly to return to her family in Wales. Yet she never arrived, and I wonder often what became of her. I daresay we shall never know, after all this time, but such cases intrigue me, Dr Broughton. They intrigue me very much."

"If you would like a more recent case of a person who vanished—"

"Aha!" He stopped dead, and even in the near-total darkness of the night, Samuel could see the excitement on Edgerton's face. "You know of such a case?"

Samuel told him as much as he knew about Lucas Renshaw. "I feel a certain responsibility for the Renshaw children," he said. "If their uncle has gone for good, it would be as well to know that."

"Indeed so. When next you go to Market Clunbury, we shall accompany you, Dr Broughton. If Lucas Renshaw is to be found, then be assured that we shall find him."

~~~~~

Susannah was horribly unsettled. For six years now, ever since her stepmother's health had begun to deteriorate noticeably, she had been mistress of Cloverstone Manor and she liked it very well. Her father made haphazard attempts to keep up with the accounts and deal with estate matters, but everything else was left to Susannah's care. It was not easy to manage such a large household on the meagre funds her father could spare, but somehow she had contrived it.

But now, every time she sat down at her desk, she opened the drawer and looked at the bag that lay within. Even with the amount she had kept to herself, there remained six hundred and eighty four pounds and six shillings. Her father had not asked for it, and so there it remained, untouched and yet calling to her. There was so much that needed to be done! It was not just new boots for the boys and gowns for the girls, there were the worn out kettles in the kitchen and the threadbare sheets that had already been turned sides to middle once. There was so much that could be done with that money, if it were hers to use. It *should* be hers to use, for had her father not said so when the first bag of money had been put into his hand? But then he had gambled it all away, so Mr Kent had done what he could to protect the family from such profligacy.

Yet despite the generosity of the gesture, she was left with a dilemma. Whatever was she supposed to do with that money? If she spent it all, she might find that her father had planned to use it for some scheme on the estate, and a row of tenant cottages would have to suffer leaking roofs for another winter. Yet if she handed it over, he might just throw it all away on the toss of a die. He had not asked for it, but she lived in terror that he would, and then what would she say to him? Mr Kent had suggested that she might simply tell him that she had a better use for it than the gambling tables, but she was not sure she had the stomach to defy her father openly in that way. Could she meekly hand over the bag, and not tell him about the hundred pounds she had taken? And each day that passed where she said nothing at all felt very much like lying, and that made her feel guilty. A part of her wished that Mr Kent had never come. If he had done what was expected of him and given the money to her father, even if he lost it all at the card tables, she would have known nothing about it, and so it could not hurt her. It would not be gnawing away inside her, keeping her awake at night.

Then there was Dr Broughton. She had met him precisely six times since his arrival at Great Maeswood, and each occasion had merely confirmed her first opinion. By this time, she was well aware of her own heart. Despite the shortness of their acquaintance, she knew beyond any question that she loved him. Her first sight of him had awakened all her childish admiration of him twelve years ago, and ignited far more womanly hopes and desires. She would marry him tomorrow if he asked her.

And therein lay the rub. As the carriage made its ponderous way back to the Manor after the card party, gently swaying her about, Susannah contemplated the problem of Dr Broughton, and how to bring him to the point of a proposal. So far, although he was perfectly civil, he had given no sign of especial interest in her. Indeed, she had no idea whether he might be contemplating marriage at all. His age suggested it, and he was now settled in a career which would enable him to support a wife, but he might turn out to be a lifelong bachelor, like Dr Beasley.

Yet if he were not, if there were any possibility that he would take a wife, she desperately wanted it to be her and not Agnes Saxby. Agnes's attempts to find herself a husband had amused the village for years, but it was not at all amusing when the object of her campaign was the man Susannah herself wanted. Perhaps she should simply tell Agnes of her own feelings and hope that Agnes was generous enough to cede the field to her? But then imagine the humiliation if nothing came of it! No, she would have to try to attach Dr Broughton by her own efforts, and the truth was that she had not the least notion how it might be done. She could not throw propriety and dignity out of the window, as Agnes did, and that was certainly a hindrance. Apart from subtly putting herself in his way whenever possible, what else could she do? He would either notice her or he would not, and that was all there was to it. She could do no more.

Had it not been for Agnes, the evening at the Grove would have been a pleasant one, and Susannah had been pleased to see Mr Truman paying some attention to Cass, even though his behaviour was less like a lover than a rather avuncular acquaintance. Anyone not already in the know would never suspect their betrothal. It was enough to please Cass and put a little delicate colour in her cheeks, however. She at least was to have the man of her heart, even if the world knew nothing of it yet.

There was only one uncomfortable moment during the evening. At supper, Susannah had noticed Miss Cokely sitting a little apart and at once invited her to join the table where she sat with Cass, Mr Truman, Dr Broughton and the Beasleys.

"Oh, I would not wish to intrude," she said, a little flustered. "You are such a cosy group... no wish to impose."

"Nonsense, Lucy," said Dr Beasley briskly. "Come and sit with us. We are not talking about you, you know! Truman, make a little space, will you?"

"Thank you. So very kind."

Dr Broughton rose and moved her chair to their table, and she sat rather awkwardly on the very edge of her seat, as if ready to sprint away at the first opportunity. She had always been self-effacing in company since her father had died. He had been the clergyman at St Ann's, but his death had left Miss Cokely and her mother in great poverty. They lived in a tiny cottage where she eked out an existence as a milliner. There were those who looked down on her as no longer being gentry and therefore unworthy of attention, but most of the village treated her kindly, and she always attended the evening card parties, even though she could never repay the hospitality.

"How is your mother, Miss Cokely?" Cass said.

"She keeps quite well, thank you for asking, Miss Saxby. She is wonderful for her age," Miss Cokely said. "Her mind is not what it was, but she is very well in herself."

"May I call on her?" Dr Broughton said.

"Oh, no need, no need," Miss Cokely said in some alarm, no doubt wondering how on earth they would be able to pay a physician's bill. "We go to Mr Edser when... I mean if ever..."

"Naturally I should not offer medical advice unless it is asked for," Dr Broughton said. "No, the boot is quite on the other foot. Whenever I hear of an elderly lady, or an elderly gentleman for that matter, who is wonderful for his or her age, I at once wish to meet that person to ask the secret of such longevity. If only I could discover such a secret, I should at once broadcast it to the world, that all might enjoy the benefits and live long, healthy lives. Would that not be a wonderful thing?"

"Indeed it would," Miss Cokely said, smiling. "I do not imagine there is any secret to Mama's long life, unless a fondness for tea and cake is a contributory factor. She would be delighted to see you, sir, but do not expect to leave quickly. She gets so few gentleman visitors, and none of them newcomers to the village, so you must be prepared for her to tell you her entire history."

"No newcomers? Oh, but surely—" Cass said, with a puzzled glance at Mr Truman.

"I have not yet had the pleasure of meeting Mrs Cokely," Mr Truman said. "She does not attend church, and there are so many calls upon a clergyman's time that it is not always possible for me to visit every one of my parishioners. I hear all about Mrs Cokely from Miss Cokely, however, so I am reassured that she is well and happy and not in need of my professional services. I daresay Mrs Cokely knows all about me, too."

"More than you might think," Cass said with a laugh. "She sits in the window all day watching the comings and goings, and since Bramble Cottage is directly opposite the parsonage, I daresay she sees every time you enter or leave your own house."

"Goodness!" Mr Truman said, eyebrows raised. "I had no idea that I was so observed."

"You will have to be careful, Truman," Dr Beasley said jovially. "No inviting young ladies to visit you, eh? Mrs Cokely will know all about it if you do." He laughed at his own wit.

Mr Truman laughed too, and said, "It is fortunate, then, that I have not been in the habit of doing so. But my curiosity is aroused, Miss Cokely. I feel I should meet your mother for myself. She sounds like a remarkable lady."

"She is, she is," Dr Beasley said. "She and Miss Cokely ran this parish with great efficiency when Dr Cokely was in your place, Truman. Every clergyman should have a wife, in my opinion, to help him with his duties to the poor and so forth, but I am sure you will get around to matrimony in time."

"Would you apply the same rule to physicians, Dr Beasley?" Mr Truman said. "Would you advise Dr Broughton to marry?"

The question was asked flippantly, perhaps, but Dr Beasley frowned and answered sombrely. "The cases are different, I think. A clergyman's living is his for life, and although the tithes may vary from year to year, they cannot be stopped, however great or little effort is expended by the incumbent. We all hear tell of indolent clergy who hold three or four livings with a curate in each, and live high on the proceeds. You are not such a man, and care for your parish. You say yourself that you have not time to visit all your parishioners, and so a wife would be an advantage to you, an extra pair of hands to take on the more time-consuming duties while you yourself concentrate on higher matters of a theological bent. But a physician earns only as much as his own efforts will produce. He must visit his patients to make money, and must visit *more* patients if he is to increase his income, and a wife will not help him advance. So a wife becomes a matter of choice. I was so fortunate as to have a sister to keep house for me, and I have never felt the need for a wife, whether for professional or personal reasons."

Susannah did not dare to comment on a subject so dear to her own heart, but fortunately Cass voiced her thoughts. "Would you agree with that assessment, Dr Broughton?"

"I would," he said quietly. "I would go further, and say that a physician's fortunes are far more precarious than a clergyman's. A physician builds his practice on his reputation as a skilled medical practitioner. If he is perceived to be a successful healer, his star may rise high and he can make his fortune, but if there is any adverse event, any damage to his reputation, then his stock will sink so low that he may be ruined."

"That is true," Dr Beasley said. "I suffered from such a reverse myself, when I was just starting out. The wife of a justice of the peace in Shrewsbury died under my care, and the gentleman considered me to blame. It was a blow at the time, but I weathered it. Happily, such cases are rare, and need not concern you, Broughton."

"Such considerations will not deter me from taking a wife, when the time comes."

Susannah cherished such welcome sentiments. At least he was minded for matrimony. Now her task was to ensure that when he went looking for a wife, he saw her before any other. And that was no easier than it had ever been.

9: Little Mysteries

When Samuel next rode over to Market Clunbury, he had Captain Edgerton and the roguish Mr Chandry with him, as well as Mac. He found Charlie alone in the little house, for Matt had work that day, and all the other children were at school.

"Even Maggie?" Samuel said, when told this.

"She's five now, and Mr Drinkwater will take her, as long as she sits quietly."

"And Matt's work? Something promising?"

"Helpin' the draper next door settle his bills. He doesn't like walkin' round town with a bag of money without a couple of stout young men with sticks, just in case. It's only a day's work, but it's half a crown, and his dinner."

"We must try to get him something more regular. Charlie, this is Captain Edgerton and his colleague Mr Chandry. They are going to attempt to track down your uncle. Can you show them his belongings?"

"We've gone through everythin'," she said. "There's nothin' there to give us a clue where he's gone."

"Then we shall be disappointed," Edgerton said. "Nevertheless, everything is important, or might be. Looking at his clothes, for instance, will give us an idea of the sort of man he was."

"Do you want to see the cellar, too?" she said.

"Certainly. We will scour the whole house from top to bottom, including the cellar. Will you show us around, Charlie?"

Samuel retreated to the consultation room, where he found a neat note — *'Mrs Tilford, West End House, Welsh Road - please call. Mrs Partridge 11am'*. By the time he had visited Mrs Tilford and talked to Mrs Partridge, the surprisingly pretty young wife of a bank manager, the industrious Captain Edgerton had news.

"We have found this little notebook, tucked away inside his mattress, and a bag of money hidden under a loose floorboard."

"Four hundred pounds!" Charlie said indignantly. "We've been livin' on pig's trotters, and he had enough for good beef. And where did it come from, that's what I'd like to know."

"That is an interesting question," Edgerton said. "Tell me more about this wine in the cellar that comes in and goes out at night."

"You think that is suspicious?" Samuel said.

Edgerton raised his eyebrows. "You do not? An honest man does business out in the open, where he can be seen, not sneaking around in the middle of the night. Tell me, Charlie, is it a regular trade — every Saturday night, say?"

"No, there's no knowin' when they'll come. It's not full moons or anythin' like that. They have lamps. The busy times are around Easter and again at Michaelmas, or a bit after that. Three or four days when they come for hours, but in between it's just an hour, maybe less."

"And you have seen them?" Edgerton said.

"Yes. I share a room with Maggie, and she's a really light sleeper, the least thing wakes her, so I'm often up at night, watchin' them creeping into the yard and down to the cellar. Of course, we didn't know until recently what it was they were shiftin' around."

"Interesting," Edgerton said. "March and October are the best times for bottling, so that is when they increase their stocks. The rest of the year, they are distributing their ill-gotten gains."

"You are quite sure they are ill-gotten, then," Samuel said, rather amused.

"Smuggled, what else?"

"We are a long way from the sea."

Edgerton grinned. "Ah, but the River Severn is navigable for most of its length, and certainly as far as Shrewsbury."

"Smugglers are hardly going to haul illicit wine all the way up the Severn," Samuel said.

"Dr Broughton, I regret to say that you will never make a criminal. You do not have a sufficiently devious mind for it, and must resign yourself to living a blameless life. Now I, on the other hand, have a very devious mind. If I were a smuggler, I would, naturally, hide away the French barrels at once. Then, I should transfer the wine to barrels of innocent origin — from Spain or Portugal, say. These may then be transferred openly by whatever means is convenient."

"You are correct," Samuel said. "That is indeed very devious. It is a relief that you are engaged in rooting out crime, Captain, and not perpetrating it, or you would surely be hanged."

"Indeed, and my wife would be quite cross about that," he said with another grin. "So embarrassing to have one's husband hanged. It is not at all the thing. But look at this, Dr Broughton. This is the notebook that was tucked away in Renshaw's mattress. Tell me what you observe."

Samuel turned the pages of the small book. "I see a number of addresses, one per page, each with numbers and letters below. *'Peterson, Low Barn Farm. Willett, Kings Arms, Lowes Heath. Sir Walter Piggott, Littledale House, Whitchurch. Masters, Rose and Crown, Hambridge Cross.'* His friends? People he had worked for or done business with?"

"You notice nothing unusual?"

"No. I have not your acute eye for the suspicious, Captain."

"Ha! True enough. This is the hand of an educated man. See how perfectly the letters are formed? I would hazard a guess that your uncle had not so fine a hand, Charlie."

"He could barely write his own name!" she cried. "He was taught his letters and numbers, but he never had much chance to practise. He used to get me to write things for him. We had a bit more teachin' than he did."

"So now we have two mysteries to resolve," Edgerton said, folding his arms with a smirk of satisfaction. "We have the disappearance of Lucas Renshaw, and the identity of the man who wrote in this notebook."

"It is also interesting that the unknown man left his notebook with Renshaw," Samuel said. "They must have been friends, at least."

"There again, the deviousness of your mind is distressingly lacking," Edgerton said. "Since I am already convinced that something nefarious is being undertaken here, I have no difficulty imagining that Renshaw stole it from the unknown gentleman with the elegant hand. Or that an accomplice of Renshaw's did so, and left it with Renshaw for safe keeping."

"Along with a bag of money," Charlie said. "I don't care about the fancy writin', or the wine that comes and goes, either, but I'd like to know how Uncle Lucas laid his hands on so much money. Not honestly, I'll be bound. He couldn't earn that much by respectable work in a month of Sundays."

"No, indeed," Edgerton said. "On that point we are entirely in agreement. Dr Broughton, I regret to say, is a lone voice speaking out in favour of lawful activity, in the face of strong evidence to the contrary. You like to think the best of people, Broughton, but I have seen too much of treachery and lawlessness to be so sanguine."

~~~~~

Susannah seldom visited Great Maeswood other than for church, but a note from Cass one day caused her to walk in that direction. She found Cass sitting disconsolately beside the lily pool at the Hall.

"Oh, I am so glad you could come!" Cass cried. "It is presumptuous of me to drag you away from your chores, for I know how busy you are, but no one else understands as you do."

"I hope you will always call upon me in need," Susannah said. "Whatever is the matter? It is not Mr Truman? He has not cried off?"

"Oh, no, it is not so bad as all that, but it is not to be made public after all. Not until the autumn, anyway. A relation of his has recently died, a great-uncle, I believe, and he feels he must go into mourning for a while. He does not feel it would be appropriate to be celebrating at such a moment, and he does have such a delicate sense of the proprieties that one must respect his wishes, naturally. Oh, but it is hard, Susannah! I had so looked forward to being a betrothed woman, and being able to order my wedding clothes at last, but I must not."

"Is he to go to the funeral?" Susannah said.

"No, for it is in Newcastle, and he has no one to take the Sunday offices for him while he is away. That is thoughtful of him, is it not? He does not wish to neglect his parish duties for so distant a relation, and one he has not seen for a number of years. Indeed, I never heard him speak of a great-uncle. I thought he had no living family, but then I suppose they were not close, so he would not think to mention it. Susannah, you are very quiet. Tell me what you are thinking."

"Do you want my honest opinion? For I think you will not like it."

Cass lowered her eyes to the hands which twisted restlessly together. "You think he is losing interest, I imagine. That he is not truly in love with me, but he is, he is!"

"A man who is ardently in love generally cannot wait to claim his bride. Such a long delay makes him look... as if his interest is cooling."

"But it is not so." Her voice was quiet, but when she lifted her head, her eyes were flashing fire. "He *is* ardent, truly. He comes to the Hall every Saturday when I am doing the weekly accounts, and we have a glass of sherry together and talk and... and..." She blushed. "You need not worry about his ardour, Susannah. I am in no doubt of it."

"Then neither am I," Susannah said robustly, but inside she worried greatly for her friend.

Cass rose to her feet. "I have some small things to take to the Cokelys. Will you come with me?"

"With the greatest of pleasure. I have not seen Mrs Cokely for an age. How does she do?"

"You may judge for yourself. Her mind is very muddled and she is quite frail, but considering her age she goes on very well. She is never plagued with the grippe every winter, as most of us are."

When they arrived at Bramble Cottage, they found Dr Broughton visiting, which sent Susannah into all sorts of spasms inside. She berated herself mightily for her weakness, but was helpless to subdue it.

He greeted them both with apparent pleasure, rising from his seat beside Mrs Cokely in the window. "I have had the most interesting chat with you, madam," he said. "However, I shall not impose myself upon you any further, since you have fresh visitors to entertain you. And look, here is Mr Truman coming up the path to see you, as well."

"He is a bad man," Mrs Cokely growled, almost under her breath.

"Is he?" Dr Broughton said interestedly. "What makes you say so, madam?"

"He left his horse out in the rain," she answered.

"Oh, Mama, that was Mr Lancaster," Miss Cokely said, with an apologetic glance at Dr Broughton.

"Was it?" the old lady said. "Hmpf. He was a bad man."

Stranger at the Villa: Strangers Book 3

And then Mr Truman was arriving, and Susannah set aside her own turbulent feelings for a moment to watch her friend and the man she was to marry. Was there any sign of particularity in his greeting to her? If there was, she could not detect it. Even though she watched carefully and very much wanted to see some sign of the ardour of which Cass spoke, she could not in all honesty say that she saw it. He was polite, he was solicitous, he was gentlemanly, but he was no more a lover to Cass than Dr Broughton was to Susannah. All she could say was that if he were head over heels in love with Cass, he hid it very successfully.

They stayed for perhaps half an hour, and Susannah made no move to leave for she saw that Cass wanted to stay. That she understood. To be in the same room as one's beloved, even if unacknowledged, was a joy that should not be denied. So she sat quietly, sipping tea and crumbling the small slice of cake she had accepted, for the Cokelys had not an unlimited supply, and listening to Mr Truman's laboured conversation with Mrs Cokely.

Whatever she might have thought of Mr Truman before, Mrs Cokely was not immune to the charm of a personable young man, and she melted under his attentions. He said nothing in particular, merely asking her about her health and how she managed the stairs, whereupon she told him triumphantly that she had no need to, because her bedroom was just across the hall, and so all she had to do was to walk to the sitting room or the kitchen. He was fascinated by the details of what she watched from her window and examined with apparent interest the notebook wherein she recorded the comings and goings of the neighbourhood, but unless he had a great interest in the butcher's boy's deliveries, it was not terribly enlightening. He smiled with unimpaired good humour, however, and Susannah's opinion of him rose somewhat. If he could devote half an hour of his morning to the ramblings of a very elderly and not very lucid woman and yet remain cheerful, there was nothing terribly amiss with him.

When they all took their leave of the Cokelys, Mr Truman chose to accompany them back to the Hall. Susannah walked slowly, so as to give Cass the opportunity to walk on with her betrothed, but she saw nothing in his manner or in the words she overheard, that could be construed as lover-like. Nevertheless, when eventually he left them, almost at the steps of the Hall, Cass had a glow of happiness about her that was very pleasing to behold. Whatever the motive for Mr Truman's restraint in claiming his betrothed, Susannah could only be delighted at the happiness he brought Cass, which would be magnified a hundred-fold when, eventually, they were married.

Susannah would not enter the Hall, for she had stayed away longer than she intended. As she walked home, she pondered the different situations of Cass and herself. Both were in love, but Cass at least had the object of her affections secured. He might be shrinking from the actual ceremony, but he was bound by his word and Cass's eventual happiness was assured.

Whereas her own... Susannah could not be sanguine. Dr Broughton had given every sign of wishing to accept the shackles of matrimony, but none at all of considering Susannah as any part of that scheme. If only one could say to a man — I am willing. If you want a wife, then take me. But it was impossible. She could throw herself at his head, like Agnes, in the most vulgar and obvious manner possible, or she could stay silent, and wait and hope. What other choice did she have? It was disheartening. The one man in the world that she wanted, and yet she could not reach out for him. She must sit demurely and wait for him to notice her, as women had done since time immemorial. It was so frustrating she could scream!

At least she could see him regularly, and Susannah had never been more thankful for her father's fondness for the card table, and the generosity of the Gages and Beasleys, with their regular card parties. When she entered the Beasleys' drawing room that evening, her heart lurched eagerly at the sight of the familiar golden-brown hair and wide shoulders. He had his back to her, but she would know him in any crowd.

But it was Captain Edgerton who bounded across the room to greet her. "Miss Winslade, may I introduce my lovely wife to you? She has come to rescue us poor, lonely menfolk from the hideous prospect of meals at the Boar's Head."

"That is indeed a hideous prospect," Susannah said, laughing. "I wondered greatly why you chose to move away from the comforts of the Grove to the Dower House, with virtually no servants, but I see that you had a cunning plan all along."

"Ah, Willerton-Forbes would have moved in permanently to the Grove, if he could, especially now that Mrs Gage's man cook is installed, but we are working on a new investigation now and could not impose any longer upon the Gages' good nature. Here is Mrs Edgerton, Miss Winslade. Luce, this is the Squire's daughter, Miss Winslade, who painted the watercolour of the Grove that you so admired."

Mrs Edgerton was a lovely, willowy creature, half a head taller than her husband. Unlike his flamboyant style of dress, she wore a gown of stark simplicity, with only a small heart-shaped pendant of pink stone and pearl ear drops for adornment. There could not have been a greater contrast between the two, but he gazed at his wife with such clear adoration that Susannah could not suppress a pang of jealousy.

She was acutely aware of Dr Broughton standing now not three feet away from her, but still with his back to her. With all her being, she willed him to see her, to hear her voice, perhaps, and turn around with pleasure in his face, to greet her as a friend... as something more than a friend.

Miss Beasley was directing people towards the card tables. Now was the moment, surely. Could she inveigle herself into his little group? She had been so successful at the last card evening, please, please let it happen again.

"Will you join us for whist, Miss Winslade?" Captain Edgerton said. "Who shall we find for a fourth?"

She took half a step towards Dr Broughton. He turned, he saw her, he nodded in acknowledgement... and then moved swiftly away to take the last seat at a table across the room, where Agnes Saxby smiled triumphantly.

Susannah turned to Captain Edgerton. "Dr Beasley, perhaps?" she said brightly.

But the words were like ashes in her mouth, and all her pleasure in the evening was gone.

10: Kingfisher

Susannah was determined not to think about Dr Broughton or Agnes Saxby any more. If he were willing to be drawn into Agnes's toils, then so be it, and she would wish them both joy on their wedding day with as much grace as she could contrive. Until that day arrived, however, she would continue to hope and to do what little she could to attract his notice.

On Saturday, he called to visit her stepmother, and had an opportunity to see for himself the improvement in her demeanour. Mama had spent a little time on the terrace or in the garden every day, she had been visited by all of her children and the increased colour in her cheeks and liveliness in her manner was marked.

"I am cautiously optimistic," Dr Broughton said to Susannah when he came to her office afterwards. "This is a stronger change than I had dared to hope for. It may not last, and we must be very, very careful to prevent her from over-exerting herself, but it is promising."

"You may be sure that we are all watching Mama with the utmost attention," she said.

To her pleased surprise, he gave a little laugh. "That I can believe, with Nurse Pett and Miss Matheson on hand. Tell me, what precisely is Miss Matheson's status?"

"She is officially a paid companion, some very distant relation of Mama's, who was taken on to provide company for Mama about six years ago, when she failed to recover well after the twins' birth and began spending a great deal of her time in her room. I took on the task of managing the household, and Miss Matheson looked after Mama. She fusses rather, but she is good-hearted and she never puts herself forward. She chooses to eat in the servants' hall, for instance, instead of with the family."

"Ah, the poor relation," he said. "Yes, a wise choice. The fussing is not ideal, but your stepmother has you, with all your good sense to counter-balance her two over-cautious guard dogs. Your father is good for her, too, I believe. He takes breakfast with her every day, she tells me. Not a man prone to fussing."

"No, although like many men he dislikes the sick room. He is very happy to sit with her when she takes her fresh air every day."

"That is excellent. Is he at home? I shall just look in on him for a moment, if so."

"He is, and will be glad to have a report on Mama's condition."

And that in itself was an odd thing. When had Papa ever spent so much time at home? But three times now he had been in his book room when the physician had happened to call, and he was so subdued these days, even going to church without his usual grumbling. Perhaps he was finally settling down into sober old age. After all, he was two and fifty now, and must surely be beyond the age of unsteadiness.

When her daily chores were completed, Susannah collected her easel and paints and set off for the river. The heat of summer had finally arrived, and the shade of the great trees fringing the water would offer a welcome respite. There might be dragonflies or damselflies, too, as well as butterflies, all to add colour to the scene for her brush to copy.

The path along the riverbank was grown wild with foxgloves and cranes-bill and wild roses and all manner of grasses. She had to lift her skirts to step carefully through the jungle, but her eyes were on the glimmering river, scanning for the iridescent flash of a dragonfly wing. So it was that she was not watching her feet, and tripped headlong over some obstacle hidden in the grass and went flying, her satchel under her.

A very masculine voice cursed loudly close by. Pushing herself up onto her knees, Susannah was astonished to see Dr Broughton's head emerging from between two clumps of foxgloves.

"Miss Winslade! Oh, pray forgive my language... I did not know... Goodness, are you hurt?"

"No... not at all, I think."

"Thank heavens!" he cried, jumping to his feet. "I cannot apologise enough for my stupidity, in leaving my feet so exposed as to cause you to fall. May I assist you?"

"Thank you." Gingerly, she took his proffered hands and allowed herself to be hauled upright again. He was holding her hands! And neither of them wore gloves! Breathe, Susannah, breathe... "So sorry, sir. I was not attending... I should have seen you..."

"It was entirely my fault, Miss Winslade, but I was so engrossed that I did not hear your approach. There was the most amazing bird here just a moment ago. It has flown away now, but such vivid colours! The brightest blue I have ever seen, and all red below… or orange, perhaps. It sat on a low branch for some time, until— Well, it has gone now."

She almost laughed at his enthusiasm, but oh Lord, he was so overwhelming when his face was afire with excitement in that way. "Have you never seen a kingfisher, sir?"

"A kingfisher! Was that what it was? No, I never have. In a town, all birds are drab brown or black or grey, but here… so much colour, Miss Winslade. Oh, are you going to paint something?"

"There is a spot nearby with a charming view of the water, where lilies grow and all sorts of water creatures may be observed."

"Frogs?" he hazarded.

"Sometimes, but I was thinking of dragonflies and water beetles and water boatmen, that stride around on the surface of the water."

"They walk on water?" he said. "That I should like to see. May I come with you? I shall not disturb you, I promise."

May I come with you? Oh yes, a thousand times yes! "By all means," was the only response she could manage. Did her voice sound normal? Heavens, was there ever a greater fool than a woman in love with a man who cared nothing for her? She was an idiot, but she was quite helpless in Cupid's grip, and in her saner moments, she told herself it was as well to have experienced the emotion just once in her life, for the memory would warm her as she declined into confirmed spinsterhood, and then middle age and beyond.

But for now, she would enjoy his company, freely offered, and make of it whatever she could.

He carried her satchel for her as she led him a little way further along the path and found the spot she had in mind. She had a small stool to sit on, but she carefully chose a position with a fallen tree trunk nearby, so that he would be able to sit close to her, where she could see him. He spurned this convenient seat, however, sitting cross-legged on the ground beside her.

"This is indeed a beautiful spot, Miss Winslade. You must tell me what to look out for. Or is it best to be silent? Might my voice disturb the very creatures you hope to paint?"

An hour of silence was not at all what she had in mind, so she said quickly, "No, no! Water creatures are not so timid that a little conversation will deter them."

"But I do not wish to disturb your concentration."

"I can paint and listen and talk all at the same time, Dr Broughton. I had no opportunity to talk to you on Thursday evening, so I can ask you now the question in my mind, which is — are you pleased with Shropshire now that you have had a little time to get to know its inhabitants?"

"I like it very well," he cried, and his sincerity was obvious. "The beauties of the country I am only beginning to appreciate, but of the society in which I now find myself, I have nothing but the highest praise. Dr and Miss Beasley have been kindness itself, and everyone I have met has been affable and welcoming. I could hardly have expected to be received with such open-hearted friendliness. I can honestly say that the people of Shropshire, that small number which it has been my good fortune to meet, rank amongst the most agreeable I have encountered anywhere."

"Such praise will puff us up enormously in our self-consequence, sir. But you should perhaps consider that your own nature plays a part in it, too. Those who are themselves open-hearted and kind meet with friendliness everywhere, while those who are discontented and cross are less welcome guests."

His lips twitched and he allowed that he had arrived in the county disposed to be pleased with it, and went on to tell her something of his life in Edinburgh. He had made friends there, he assured her, but he had always known that he would one day have to leave the city. "I was there only to study under the greatest medical practitioners and teachers at the university," he said. "I had the opportunity to conduct a few demonstrations of my own, too, which was a great privilege. You cannot imagine, Miss Winslade, the thrill of examining the human body in every detail, down to the very heart and vessels that convey blood around it. That was a wonderful experience, but it was only ever intended to be a transitional phase. This is my home now, and this is where my future lies. I hope to build a practice as solid as my father's was, in Chester. That is a fair city, too, although very different from Edinburgh. The Romans had a camp there, did you know that? The very name means *'camp'* in Latin, and the Roman walls still exist in places."

He talked of Chester for some time, and then again of Edinburgh, but nothing of London. It was as if that part of his life had never existed, and yet she knew he had been there, and had studied under the great man whom her stepmother had consulted. Almost he made it sound as if his career as a doctor had begun in Edinburgh, yet she knew it was not so. But she could hardly question him about it. No doubt Dr Beasley knew his complete history and was satisfied with it, and there was no need at all for Susannah to be curious about it. She was, though. Naturally she wondered.

There was an interlude while she pointed out a group of dragonflies, and he became excited all over again. He was such a delight to be with! How could she bear to see him married to Agnes — or to anyone who was not herself?

After that, he began to describe the house at Market Clunbury, and the little family he had discovered there. It was an odd tale, with the smuggled wine and the mysterious night-time comings and goings, and now the disappearance of the children's uncle.

"You do not know any Renshaws, I take it?" he said to her.

"No, although there is a farm out Overbury way— But no, that is Renfrew, I think."

"I will mention it to Captain Edgerton, anyway."

He lapsed into thoughtful silence. Her painting was finished, apart from a little touching up to be done at home, but she had no wish to bring this glorious afternoon to an end, so she told him about the strange visit from Mr Kent and the bag of money.

"What do you think I should do about it, Dr Broughton?" she said. "It has put me in a very awkward position, and makes me feel rather uncomfortable." He was silent for such a long time that she feared she had offended him, or breached some code of protocol. "I beg your pardon, sir. I should not have mentioned it."

"I am honoured by your confidences, Miss Winslade," he said. "It is indeed an awkward position. You cannot talk to your stepmother on such a matter but — forgive me, but is not your brother the best person to advise you?"

"I would not ask Henry's advice on any subject except that of horses," she said crisply. "He has not the least idea of money, takes no interest in the estate and has been away doing who knows what with Timothy Rycroft for most of the summer. But if ever you want a new horse, Dr Broughton, he will tell you exactly where to find one, and get it for a good price, too."

A fleeting smile crossed his face, and he said, "Very well, Miss Winslade. Here is what I should do, if I were in your position — I should tell your father everything."

"Oh." Her eyebrows rose. "Everything? Even about the hundred pounds I kept for myself?"

"Hardly for yourself. That was for essential household expenses. But yes, I would tell him everything, holding back nothing, just as you have told it to me today. Then the matter passes to him, and your conscience is clear. There is no substitute for a clear conscience. When the storm clouds break, that may be the one thing that allows a man to keep his hold on sanity, knowing that he did nothing wrong."

She stared at him, wondering how he had spun her little domestic dilemma into a matter of storm clouds and sanity. Perhaps he saw her confusion, for he went on quickly, "Such considerations are not applicable in this case, but you will still feel more comfortable if you conceal nothing from your father. This Mr Kent was mischievous, I think, to involve you in a matter of business between himself and your father, knowing, as he surely must have done, how torn you would feel."

"You think it was wrong of him?" Susannah said. "Yet he meant it for the best."

"I am sure that he did. Yet I do not think it was proper for him to create such a barrier between father and daughter. But forgive me, I believe it is time for me to leave you. I have been distracting you to such an extent that your brush has not touched the paper for several minutes now, and for that I apologise."

"I stopped painting because my work is finished," she said. "Will you see it?"

He jumped to his feet and came to look. "A kingfisher! Was there a kingfisher on that branch and I never noticed?"

She laughed, as she began to pack away her things. "No, no! That part is all my imagination. The rest of the painting is just as I saw it, but I added the kingfisher to remind me of a very pleasant afternoon. I thank you for your company, sir."

"The gratitude must all be on my side, Miss Winslade, for the privilege of watching your talent at work. The painting is beautiful, and I hope you will have it framed and hung in some prominent position where I might admire it whenever I visit the Manor."

"You are too kind to say so, sir." She closed the satchel and fastened the straps. Now that the moment had come, she could hardly bring herself to say the words of farewell. Even knowing that she would see him again tomorrow at church, she knew that she might never again recapture this wonderful intimacy. His presence brought her an awareness of the world around her that she had never experienced with anyone else. Every sense was enhanced, every colour richer and more luminous, every breath of air filled her with energy and life and a hope for the future. It was all illusion, but she savoured it while it lasted.

While she hesitated, he said, "Miss Winslade, you have honoured me by asking my advice on a matter which troubles you. I wonder if I might presume to take the same liberty with you?"

"Of course, sir. I will advise you if I can."

"I do not know what to do about Agnes Saxby!" he burst out, and she could have leapt for joy. "I do not mind her hanging on my sleeve on social occasions, for I know how to deal with that, I hope, but she keeps coming to consult with me on some spurious medical issue or other, and I cannot refuse to see her as a patient. She brings her maid with her, so it is perfectly proper, but I do not like it. Is there any way of... diverting her from what I presume to be her object?"

"Poor Agnes!" Susannah said, almost gleeful in relief. "She has been trying to get herself a husband for years. Just this year, she has set her cap at Mr Truman, Mr Chandry and Mr Gage's brother, and having failed there, she is now trying her luck with you. But Agnes is a very straightforward girl. She will never try to trick you into a proposal, nor is she ever offended when her overtures are rebuffed."

"Ah, that is a relief. She is not... in love, or anything of that nature? I should not like to break her heart, but I cannot marry her."

"Cannot?" she said, with a frisson of alarm.

"No, for Mr Edser is deep in love with her and I could not possibly take another man's cherished love. It would not be honourable."

Susannah could not find an answer to that. She knew perfectly well that Agnes would never be allowed to marry an apothecary, but she did not wish to give Dr Broughton the least hint that Agnes might be available. Cautiously, she said, "If you wish to escape Agnes's importunings, you have only to tell her openly that you have no thought of marriage just now."

"But that would not be true," he said. "I want very much to marry, just not Agnes. In fact, I shall marry just as soon as I can find another woman who is willing to have me, one who is *not* Agnes."

'Willing to have me...'

The world shifted under Susannah's feet. Did she dare? She was on quicksand, she knew it, but there was a clear path before her and she *had* to take it. There would never again be such a perfect confluence of events with her own desires.

"Then look no further, Dr Broughton, for *I* would be willing to have you. We get on so well that we should deal charmingly together, and you would never need to worry about Agnes again. There! Both your problems solved at a stroke."

So saying, she picked up her satchel and walked away from him as quickly as her shaking legs would allow.

11: After Church

Samuel watched Miss Winslade depart in bemusement. What had just happened? Had she taken his words as a declaration? No, she had just taken his words literally, and responded in her usual straightforward way. Her tone had been teasing but... what if she were serious? Was she truly saying that she wished to marry him? Or rather, that she was *willing* to marry him... not quite the same thing. He had said, very prosaically, that he would marry the first woman who would have him, and she had responded just as prosaically. A practical matter, then. Just as he had decided that it was time to settle down, so it was for her.

Long after she had disappeared from view, he stood pondering, before eventually recollecting himself and turning for home. He found Miss Beasley alone in the house.

"Do come into the parlour, Dr Broughton," she said. "I have just sent for some tea, but if you prefer port or Madeira, help yourself from the tray in the drawing room."

"I will have a little port, I think," he said, feeling that tea was not quite fortifying enough for him to recover his wits after Miss

Winslade's disclosure. Susannah, he remembered. A soft, gentle name, not harsh-sounding, like Agnes.

When he had carried his port through to the parlour, Miss Beasley said in her soft voice, "Have you had a pleasant walk? It is very hot today, so I hope you did not walk too far."

"Only to the River Wooller. It was refreshingly cool under the trees." And then, because he could not get her out of his mind, he added, "I met Miss Winslade there. She painted a very pretty view of the water, with all the tiny ripples over the stones, and the way the sunlight sparkled. She is very clever."

"Ah yes, she is indeed. We have several of her paintings here — two in Roland's book room, for they were given to him in gratitude for his care of Mrs Winslade, and one over there of this house, beside the one of St Mary's church."

He jumped up to look at it, and could only admire the artistry. "It is very well executed. I am no expert on art, but I find such delicate paintings more pleasing to the eye than heavy oils."

"So do I," Miss Beasley said. "Was Susannah alone?"

"She was. Oh, do you think it was improper for me to sit and watch her paint?"

"No, no! She is well past the age of needing a chaperon."

"How old is she?" he said, suddenly curious. "Four or five and twenty? And how is it she never married?"

The manservant came in just then with the tea things, but when he had gone, Miss Beasley said, "Let me see… I think she must be six and twenty now. As to marriage, it is a problem living in such a remote part of the country. It is such a pity, for she would make any man a fine wife. Susannah attends her share of balls, of course, but there is not such a great number of eligible gentlemen hereabouts. If the squire were in a position to go to London for the season and give her a proper dowry she might do better, but he is not so well circumstanced as he once was, and his wife— Well, she has no connections that would be of any use to Susannah."

"Mrs Winslade told me she is the daughter of an apothecary," Samuel said. He had never heard Miss Beasley so chatty, but he was not averse to finding out more about Miss Winslade... Susannah.

"Exactly so. The squire has made some odd choices in matrimony. His first wife was a yeoman's daughter, and the second was barely gentry, although she had a little money. But there, I suppose a gentleman has the same limited range of options as ladies. It is the destiny of many of us in the parish to embrace spinsterhood, unfortunately. Viola Gage, Lucy Cokely and myself — and I daresay Susannah will suffer the same fate, and Agnes Saxby, too, poor child. Now Cass Saxby — I should have said she was bound on the same path, for her father never lifted a finger to help her marry, but she has a great fortune now. She will be snapped up as soon as she is out of mourning, I wager, or perhaps sooner, if one is to believe the servants' gossip about Mr Truman paying her secret visits. Although if there is an understanding between them, they conceal it admirably. As for the younger girls, if the new Lord Saxby, whoever he is, should do his duty and take them off to London, they will soon be settled."

"How is it not known who the next Lord Saxby is?" Samuel said. "Is there some mystery to it?"

"Only an unfortunate set of circumstances," Miss Beasley said. "Lord Saxby only had one son, and they both died after a dreadful accident in January. Their curricle smashed all to pieces on the Astley Cloverstone road. Now the lawyers are delving back into the family tree to find an heir. They are tracing descendants of the Second Baron now, and may yet have to go even further back. Ah, Roland, there you are! Was Market Clunbury very busy? How hot you look. Will you have some tea? It is quite fresh."

Samuel left them to their tea and retreated to his bedroom, where he sat cross-legged on the floor beneath the open window and pondered his future, a future that perhaps contained Susannah Winslade. He could see all the advantages of the match. She was practical, used to managing a household economically. Her down-to-earth manner made her easy to talk to, an important consideration. She was no beauty — that was a distinct advantage, for a beautiful woman would attract other men and that would be too dangerous. But she was not exactly an antidote, either, unlike Agnes Saxby, poor girl. Susannah had a delightful smile and lovely grey eyes, a trim figure and abundant dark hair which it would be a pleasure to let fall through his fingers.

If not Susannah, then who else? Not Agnes, certainly. He did not dislike her, but if Edser wanted her, then he could have her with Samuel's good will. Her two younger sisters were vapid, silly creatures, and too pretty to suit him. Cass Saxby had seventy thousand pounds, so was quite out of his reach. He had met no one else yet, and that was perhaps the most obvious advantage of Susannah — she was willing, here and now, without any tediously prolonged courtship. They could be married by month's end, and perhaps be admiring their first child by the spring.

He shivered. A child...

Dinner with the Beasleys was not an elaborate affair. It was not always on time, and sometimes a promised dish would fail to appear, but the single course was always enhanced with one or two removes, and a decent wine. Samuel was no connoisseur, but he could recognise a good claret when he tasted it.

When the covers had been removed and Miss Beasley had withdrawn, Dr Beasley said, "You are very quiet tonight, Broughton. No trouble, I hope?"

"None at all, sir. Quite the reverse. I am taking thought for my future, now that I am settled."

"Ah! Matrimony?"

"That is where my thoughts lead me, yes. I have had it in mind ever since Edinburgh, for it would surely add to my happiness and comfort, so I determined that I would look for a wife as soon as I should have the good fortune of a steady income. Do you approve, sir?"

"Very much. Although my path never led me in that direction, and I have never felt the lack, it is a sensible step to take for a young man in your position, who has no sister to run his household. You will want to be careful about money just at first, unless you plan to swoop down on Cass Saxby and her fortune." He chuckled.

"She is a little above the touch of a humble physician," Samuel said with a smile. Then, hoping to divert any further speculation on likely candidates, he said, "My principal concern at present is with the very great costs attached to setting up my own establishment. It will prevent me from early marriage, I fear, unless, perhaps, I might be permitted to bring my bride to live here? It would be a very great imposition, I realise, but—"

"We should like that very much," Beasley said at once. "Phyllida and I have long lamented that only the two of us rattle round in this house, which is very well suited to a family. Why, we said only the other day that there is a room on the top floor ideally suited to a nursery, and hoped you might fulfil.our hopes in that regard."

"That is very generous, sir. Naturally it would only be a temporary arrangement, just until—"

"Nonsense. Consider my position, Broughton. I have no heir, no one to whom I might leave this house and the little nest egg I have secreted away. And here you are, like the son I never had, taking over my medical practice. Why should you not take over everything, in time? I may leave my money where I choose, I hope. Now, I make no promises! We may yet quarrel, who knows." He chuckled. "But that is how my mind is working, you see. I do not know how long I may have on this earth, now that my heart has given notice of its ill intent, and it would delight me beyond measure to have a young family here to enliven whatever time is granted me. And it would be a great comfort to me to know that, whenever I am called to the Lord, I have someone to whom I might safely leave my worldly goods, someone who will take good care of Phyllida for me, for she will never find a husband now. So when you find your wife, by all means bring her here to live."

Samuel could hardly find the words to express his gratitude for such unlooked-for generosity, and his hopes to be worthy of such trust.

~~~~~

Susannah almost cried off church on Sunday. How could she possibly face Dr Broughton after so wantonly throwing herself at his head just a few hours earlier? Yet it would surely be easier in the big crowd outside the church than in the more intimate atmosphere of the Gages' card party on Tuesday, where it would be impossible for him to avoid her. And if she had so disgusted him that he wanted no more to do with her, it was better to know it at once.

So to church she must go, but all the way there in the carriage her stomach churned and her legs felt like jelly, and even Mr Truman's short sermon felt interminable.

Outside, she waited distractedly for him to emerge from the church.

"Susannah, are you quite well?" Cass said. "You seem to be agitated. There is nothing wrong, is there? Not your mama?"

"Oh, no, no... nothing of the sort. I am perfectly well, I assure you."

"You do not look it. How pale you are, and if you clutch that reticule any tighter, you will surely crumple it beyond repair. Good day to you, Dr Broughton."

"Miss Saxby. Miss Winslade." He bowed, his face solemn but his eyes sought Susannah's. "Mrs Winslade continues to improve, I trust?"

Susannah hardly knew how she answered him, acutely aware of her own churning emotions, his nearness, and Cass watching them both. She wondered if Cass understood anything of what she was seeing. They made laboured conversation for a few minutes before Cass moved away, to Susannah's intense relief. For a moment, briefly, she was alone with Dr Broughton. The entire parish was gathered outside the church doors, but in that instant she could speak freely.

"Dr Broughton—"

"I should like to talk to you," he said in a hurried undertone. "About the matter we discussed yesterday."

Oh, thank goodness! He was not disgusted with her, in fact he wanted to pursue it...

"If, that is, you were in earnest and not merely joking me."

She nodded quickly, but before she could speak, he went on, "When next I visit your stepmother on Tuesday, I could—"

"I cannot wait until Tuesday!" she burst out. "Let us have it out today, whatever the outcome."

He chuckled then, and Susannah's spirits lifted a little. It could not be the outcome she dreaded if he could laugh at her eagerness.

"By all means," he said. "Shall I call at the Manor?"

"No, no, too public. I shall set out to walk home with the servants, but stop by the river. Can you find the place again, where we were yesterday?"

Miss Gage came over to talk to them just then, her eyes burning with curiosity, so he merely nodded, and after a few more moments, walked away.

Now Susannah was in even worse terror, if that were possible. He wanted to talk... what did that mean? A proposal, or merely a sounding out of the possibility? What if he expected a dowry? Then it would all fall through. Yes, better to meet at the river, so that no one would know of her humiliation.

She waited until most of the servants and farmers and millers had set off before following them. Once clear of the village, the lane was shaded by enough trees to keep her cool, but even so, she walked slowly, to allow the gaggle ahead of her to disappear from view. She half hoped that Dr Broughton would catch up with her, but although one or two stragglers passed her by, she did not see him.

Only when she reached the river did he come up to her at last, and they set off on the riverside path side by side.

"I must thank you for making things so much simpler, Miss Winslade," he said.

"Have I?"

"Indeed you have. It is clear that you approach matrimony in the same pragmatic manner I do myself, and therefore we may dispense with the awkwardness of a formal courtship, or any pretence of violent affection. After a mere ten days' acquaintanceship, that would hardly be convincing."

This was rather alarming. "Affection will grow, will it not?" she said, tentatively.

There was that smile again. "Of course. We shall go on very comfortably together, I am certain, but we need not try to convince the world that after one glance we were swept off our feet by love. No one would believe it, would they?"

Since this was almost exactly her own circumstance, she could find no answer. They reached the opening in the trees where they had sat the day before, and halted.

"You cannot sit on the grass," he said frowning.

"I shall sit on that fallen tree trunk over there," she said.

"Then should you object if I remove my coat? I can place it for you to sit on, to protect your gown against dirt."

She could not refuse such a gallant offer, especially when it brought her the sight of Dr Broughton in his shirt sleeves. Such informality suited him, and she would have many years, she very much hoped, to enjoy seeing him so.

When she was settled, he sat at her feet, crossing his legs neatly. "Miss Winslade, let us get straight to the heart of the matter. My medical practice has a potential income of some four hundred pounds a year, which I am sure I can achieve in time and build upon handsomely, but it may take some years. In addition, I must pay something to Dr Beasley as a partner, and for my board. The remains of my savings amount to twelve hundred pounds, which brings me an additional income of some fifty pounds a year, and I have a home, for the Beasleys are quite happy for me to bring a wife to Whitfield Villa. It is not a great deal to live upon, just at first. I shall be comfortably off eventually, but there can be no extravagances for a while. I lay all this out before you so that you are under no illusions. I have no fortune tucked away in the consols, nor any expectation of a great estate or title or anything of that nature. I must make my own way in the world, as do most men. If this prospect does not appeal to you, then we may shake hands and walk away from this without any ill-will. What do you say?"

It was not at all what she had expected, but she saw the point of it, and if he could be business-like, so could she. "I have no dowry," she said.

"That I suspected," he said. "It is not an obstacle for me."

"I have a hundred pounds a year from my mother," she said. "Up to now I have mostly spent it on myself, but Papa will buy my wedding clothes, which with care will last me for two or three years, so it will be extra income. And we could live at the Manor, and not have to pay board to the Beasleys."

He frowned. "It would not be right to live at your father's expense. I must support my own wife."

"Then a cottage on the estate, free of rent, with gifts of game and meat and vegetables."

"We should need servants, then, and a gig, perhaps, and extra horses. I cannot afford it. Money will be difficult enough just at first, but I know you to be a good manager, and capable of living within a budget. It will just be a smaller budget than you are used to."

"I know how to economise," she said, with a wry smile. "Heaven knows, I have had enough practise. But I think you are trying to deter me, Dr Broughton."

He smiled too. "I shall be more comfortably situated one day, but I want you to understand what you may be taking on if we go through with this."

"I do understand, and I am not holding out for a wealthy husband, I assure you."

"And… I shall want a true marriage. With children," he said, his eyes locked on hers.

"That is in God's hands, but I shall do my very best."

"Then Miss Winslade… Susannah… will you marry me?"

"I will."

"Thank you!" His smile warmed her deliciously. "I shall speak to your father today, and then we shall go to Mr Truman to see about the banns."

12: A Betrothal Is Announced

"You want to marry Susannah?" the squire said incredulously. "But you hardly know her!"

"I know her quite well enough to be sure that she will make me an excellent wife," Samuel said. "She is sensible, hard-working, efficient and nothing ruffles her."

"You make her sound like a housekeeper," the squire grumbled.

"She also plays an excellent game of backgammon," Samuel said, amused.

"And she has accepted you? When she has only met you two or three times? It all seems very havey-cavey to me, Broughton."

"There is nothing untoward about it, sir. We have met on a number of occasions, including here in this house. Yesterday we met by chance when Miss Winslade was out painting, we fell into some deep discussion and discovered we were of like mind on the question of matrimony. Neither of us is romantic by nature. Today after church it was settled between us. We should like to be married as soon as the banns can be read."

"Well, at least you are not rushing about with licences or haring off to Scotland," the squire said. "Is she waiting outside? Let us have her in, and I shall hear what she has to say about all this."

Samuel went to the door, where Susannah was indeed waiting outside, and brought her into the room.

"Well, daughter, this is a sudden start," the squire said, as she curtsied respectfully. "Are you so desperate that you will take the first man who offers for you, eh?"

She laughed, but there was a hard edge to her voice as she replied. "You are wrong on both counts, Papa. I am not at all desperate, and this is not the first offer I have ever received. It is the first I wish to accept, however."

Samuel found that interesting — she had had offers, but she had turned them down. That made her choice rather more flattering.

"He is not putting undue pressure on you, is he? Nothing shameful going on?"

"Nothing at all, Papa. This is my willing choice."

That word again — willing. A pragmatic word, like Susannah herself.

"Off you go, then. Let me speak to my future son-in-law alone." When she had gone, he poured brandy for them both, and sat Samuel in a leather armchair, a pair with his own. "Now, Broughton, I only want to know two things. Is your family respectable, and can you support a wife?"

Samuel took a sip of brandy, then carefully set it down on a side table. "My father was a physician also, in Chester. My grandfather was a clergyman, who rose to become a canon at Chester cathedral. His father owned a modest estate in Cheshire, but being a younger son, my grandfather had to make his own way in the world, although his wife was the daughter of a viscount. As to money, I would not have proposed to Miss Winslade if I had not believed I could support her. Not in such splendour as here, naturally, and we shall have to be thrifty for a while, but once the practice has been built up a little, I shall have a good income."

The squire grunted. "That is an honest answer, anyway. And what do you expect me to do for you?"

Samuel's eyebrows rose in surprise. "Why, nothing at all, sir. I understand that there will be no dowry, so—"

"Oh, I shall do something for her, naturally. I cannot say what, just yet, but there will be something, and you will live here, of course, until you get on your feet."

"I do not think—"

"No, I insist. Heaven knows, we have enough room. Half the place is under covers these days, so you could have a whole wing to yourselves, if you wish. Her mama will not want Susannah to go, and nor do I, truth to tell. She keeps us all straight. So that is settled, but one thing I insist on — you must wait a month before calling the banns. That is not a long time when you have your whole lives before you, but I want to be sure that her mind is quite made up. Women can be flighty sometimes, and if she feels she has made a mistake, better to find it out before the wedding than after, eh? Are we agreed?"

He held out his hand, and Samuel found himself obliged to shake it, but he was determined not to live at the Manor if it could be avoided. He would need to ensure that Susannah was on his side over that.

The squire got to his feet, and went to a desk littered with papers. He pushed the heaps this way and that, lifting handfuls of them here and there, until he found what he sought. "Here, give her this," he said, placing a heavy cloth bag in Samuel's lap. "She will laugh, I daresay. That is for her wedding clothes, and whatever else she needs. But a month, mind, before you go calling the banns."

"It shall be just as you wish, sir, but we may tell our friends, I presume?"

"Oh yes, no reason not to, and I shall send a notice to the London *Gazette*, too. We must do everything the proper way. Now off you go. Take your brandy, and tell Susannah what I have said, and give her that bag. She will find it very funny, for she only gave it to me yesterday, but I had sooner she had it. It is hers by rights, after all. She will understand."

Samuel understood it too, but he said nothing, and bowed himself out of the room. He found Susannah pacing about outside the door, with a footman lurking nearby. Wordlessly he led her to her office, for he was getting to know the way quite well now, and shut the door on the footman who had followed them all the way.

"Why is that fellow trailing all over the house after us?" he said crossly.

"Silas? He always does that. He says he wants to be instantly available in case we should need him, but he just wants to know everything that is going on. There is no escaping inquisitive servants in a house of this size. Is it settled?"

"It is. He will provide a dowry, too, although he cannot say how much."

"Every little extra helps," she said.

"True. Also, he wants us to live here, but I shall talk him out of that."

"Oh?" Her eyebrows rose a fraction. "It would be more practical."

He had no wish to quarrel over the matter, so he said only, "We shall have time enough to work out the details, for your father insists the banns not be called for a month."

She expressed a pleasing amount of disappointment, and altogether he considered that the day had passed off very propitiously.

~~~~~

Susannah's unexpected betrothal caused general amazement. She spent the rest of the day receiving the congratulations, accompanied by varying degrees of astonishment, from her stepmother, from the children, from Henry, who was miraculously at home for once, and from the servants. She wrote a note to Cass, who sent an instant reply.

'My dear friend, What happy news! I suspected something was in the air by your demeanour outside church, but had no idea matters were so far advanced already. How sly you have been not to give me the least hint! We are all agog to hear about it and will call on you at the earliest opportunity to wish you joy in person. Your affectionate friend, Cass.'

Dr Broughton had been invited for dinner, so Susannah had the pleasure of his undivided attention all evening, for no one would be so cross as to steal a man away from his future bride. She sat beside him at table, and then played backgammon for the rest of the evening. He was serious, as he so often was, and displayed no lover-like symptoms, but as she had not expected it, she was not disappointed.

Now that she had, against all her expectations, achieved her object, she could not at all determine what her feelings were. Delight and excitement, of course, that went without saying, but somehow the very prosaic nature of the entire process robbed it of some degree of higher emotion. She sat in her room that night reflecting on all that the day had brought. How swiftly had her life changed! She had scarcely begun to acknowledge the hopes she cherished when they were fulfilled in full measure, and she could hardly grasp it. She would be married, and to the man who had sat in her heart for twelve years, little thought about of late, but always ready to be brought to mind when she was in low spirits for any reason.

He was the source of the shining moment of her life, and now he would be there every day, would order her entire life for her, and yet she knew very little about him. His life in London, for instance, about which he never spoke. He had been there twelve years ago, and he had been in Edinburgh lately, but between the two was a gap of ten years and she had not the least idea where he had been. In London? Abroad? In prison, even... Surely not! Yet how could she be certain? It was unsettling to have such thoughts. It did not cause her to regret her decision, but she would like to know. More than that, she would like him to tell her of his own free will, and not by her questioning. Surely he would, before they married.

~~~~~

The next morning, the Saxby carriage bowled up to the front door while Susannah was still at breakfast with her father and stepmother. Lady Saxby and all four of her daughters swept imperiously into the house, and not five minutes later Dr and Miss

Beasley arrived in the wake of the Gages' carriage, so that the Summer Drawing Room was quite full.

"Where is Dr Broughton?" Lady Saxby said, gazing around as if she expected him to be hiding behind the curtains. "Why is he not here paying court to you?"

"Monday is one of his consultation days in Market Clunbury," Susannah said.

"I should have thought he might make an exception today. But this is very sudden, Susannah. What is the meaning of it?"

The question was an inevitable one, and she had had a little time to consider her answer. "We are both of an age to know our own minds, Lady Saxby. There is no reason to delay."

She caught Cass's eye as she spoke, and saw the pain in her friend's eyes. Cass had been betrothed for months, yet it was still unacknowledged, with many more months to wait until her marriage, whereas Susannah's betrothal had come from nowhere and was proceeding with all haste.

When two more families arrived to offer their congratulations, the room, which was not large, became rather heated. The French doors were thrown wide and the gathering drifted onto the terrace and thence to the shade of an arched walkway covered in roses. Susannah and Cass let the others go ahead and sat on a marble bench.

"Everyone is shocked by the speed of it," Cass said with a little laugh, "but I could see at church that there was something between you, on your side at least. Gentlemen are so good at concealing their true feelings, are they not? No matter how agitated they are inside, no matter how tightly bound by love they may be, honour dictates that they show none of it. Theodore is just the same. But I cannot tell you how happy it makes me to know that you are as loved and cherished as I am, my dearest friend."

Such talk naturally made Susannah very uncomfortable, but she had no need to speak, for Cass was overflowing with joy for her friend and she ran on for some time before there was any break in the gush of congratulations.

"Perhaps this will inspire Mr Truman to overcome his delicate scruples and permit your engagement to be made known," Susannah said.

Cass's face immediately fell. "I do not think it likely. In fact— No, I am over fanciful, I think."

"What is it? You are not beginning to doubt his regard, surely?"

"No... no..." She sighed, pulling at a loose thread on her gloves. "Oh, Susannah, I *will* tell you, I think, and then you must give me your opinion of it, for something happened... You remember me telling you that he calls upon me every Saturday morning? Well, when he came last Saturday, he was very down and said that his conscience was troubling him, because he felt he had been too presumptuous in pressing his suit on me so soon after Papa's death, when I was overwrought. And then, he does not wish it to be thought that he is a fortune hunter. He actually asked... oh, he has the most delicate sensibilities! He suggested that my fortune should be bound up in a trust so that he could not benefit from it. He wished me to write to my trustees to that effect. You may imagine what I said to that! But... I do wonder... Susannah, does it seem to you that he is creating obstacles to our marriage? That perhaps he is cooling in his desire to marry?"

Susannah hesitated to answer, for there was no honest response that sprang to mind that might alleviate her friend's anxieties. A man who found constant reasons to keep a betrothal secret and seemed to draw away was not one who was fully committed to the marriage. If he loved Cass, truly and deeply, then he would want nothing more than to make her his wife as soon as may decently be contrived. But she could not express such thoughts.

Instead, she remembered Dr Broughton's words to her when she had asked his advice regarding the bag of money from Mr Kent. "I think you should talk to Mr Truman," she said, "and tell him exactly what you have told me, holding nothing back. Tell him that such talk distresses you, that the secrecy of your situation upsets you and that, while you do not mind waiting to marry, you see no reason not to announce your engagement to the world. That is my advice. And if he continues to prevaricate, and gives you more reasons not to proceed... well, you will know how to interpret that, I imagine."

"That is exactly what I should advise myself, if I were not involved," Cass said, with a wry smile. "It is just that... if I push him, then I might lose him, and what would I do then?"

"If he breaks away for such a reason, then he is not the man you thought him, and would make you a very bad husband, Cass. If there is reluctance at this stage in your lives, how will he be after ten years of marriage, or twenty? I speak to you honestly as your friend, as I hope you know. More than anyone I want you to be happy, but there is no reason for this prolonged secrecy, none at all, and I cannot be easy with a man who insists upon it."

"That is what I thought," Cass said, but her face was troubled all the same.

Later that day, Susannah had the one interview she was dreading above all others. Jeffrey's thunderous face told her at once that he was in a difficult mood.

"What nonsense is this, Sue?" he said, striding about her painting studio, angrily thrashing his riding crop against his thigh.

"This fellow has been here for all of five minutes and now you are betrothed to him? It is ridiculous!"

"Nevertheless it is true," she said quietly.

"For God's sake!" he burst out, before visibly forcing himself to be calm. "What is the attraction? Why him and not me? For you cannot pretend that you are in love with him or any such foolishness, for you barely know the man."

"But I do know him," she said softly. "I have known him for many years. Do you remember me telling you of the man I met in London who entertained me for a whole evening, although I was but fourteen and below his notice? That was Dr Broughton. And here he is again, he is looking for a wife and his eyes happened to fall on me." There was no need to mention that she was the one who had first put herself forward as a potential marriage partner.

"That is madness, surely you know that? To be mooning about over this man for years and then fall into his arms as soon as you set eyes on him again — that is foolishness beyond permission. It is no basis for a lifetime together. You cannot know what sort of man he is on such a brief acquaintance. Why him and not me? What have I ever done to so disgust you that you will throw yourself at the first stranger who comes along?"

"Nothing at all," she said at once. "I agree it is madness, but it is what I wish and if I am making a mistake, then so be it. I shall have many years in which to repent it."

"Is it because he has a career? But I am trying, Sue! I will have Melverley again one day, if you will just give me a little time, and then—"

"*No!*" she cried, with such force that he took a step back in surprise. "Jeffrey, you must accept what I have already told you many times — that I will *never* marry you. You are obsessed with Melverley, but it would not matter if you were a great lord with ten thousand a year, I should still not marry you, and I cannot even tell you why. You are everything any rational woman should want in a husband, and yet I am not rational at all. I have known you since you were a grubby little boy in torn trousers, and I cannot *ever* see you as an eligible man, no matter how hard you try." The pain in his eyes took her by surprise. "Forgive me, but you must accept this. Will you not shake my hand and wish me joy?"

"With him? *Never!* But you are right in one thing — you are not rational, not rational at all. But perhaps your physician will be more sensible when I lay all the particulars before him."

"Jeffrey—"

But he was gone, whisking out of the room and slamming the door behind him.

13: An Evening At Maeswood Hall

Samuel was rather late in arriving at the Market Clunbury house. Two patients had arrived at the Villa just as he was about to set off, and then it had come on to rain, necessitating a search in his saddle bag for his cloak.

"There's four people waitin', two at the front and two in the kitchen," Charlie said, as he stripped off the dripping cloak in the kitchen. "One lady's been here since eight o'clock. I let her into the waitin' room early, because it looked like rain. I hope I did right."

"Quite right. I will see her first. Any requests for visits?"

"The list is on your desk."

By the time he had seen the early patients, whose numbers swelled as he worked, visited the gentry and then attended to another cluster of patients, and finally endured a sticky interview with the fat apothecary, who believed Samuel had been sending business to his rival, he was more than ready to make his way home.

As he closed up the consultation room, he found Captain Edgerton and Mr Chandry awaiting him in the kitchen.

"Do you remember this, Broughton?" the captain said, throwing a notebook onto the kitchen table.

"Why yes, it is the book you found in the mattress." He flicked through the pages looking at the addresses written there, then frowned. "Or is it? The hand looks different."

The captain smiled broadly, his teeth gleaming. "Ah, very good, sir! It is indeed a different book. We copied the contents of the notebook we found last week and replaced it. Today, when we looked again, it had gone but this one was here in its place, with a different set of addresses."

"How strange! And these markings below — letters and numbers, some crossed out. Orders, presumably?"

"Exactly so, although we have not yet worked out the code."

"But is there any word of Lucas Renshaw yet?"

"Not yet, but we are obliged to be discreet in our enquiries. If, as we suspect, he is engaged in some illicit operation—" He broke off, with an apologetic look at Charlie, who was rolling out pastry at the other end of the table.

"You can say what you like about him, Captain, sir," she said. "Nothin' would surprise me now."

"Well, we have to move carefully, let us say. But Mr Chandry and I have been investigating some of the places listed in the first book we found. Not the private houses, just the inns and hotels. Easy enough to walk in, order a bottle of wine and then say, *'This is very good wine. Where did you come by it?'*"

"And did they tell you?" Samuel said.

"Some of them did, yes. Most were close-mouthed, but enough talked to give us an idea of how it works. A man comes every two months or so, a gentleman, mind, not a ruffian. No name, of course. He takes orders and half the money, then returns a few days later with a cart and collects the rest of the money. It has been going on for several years, seemingly."

"But it is not necessarily illegal, is it?" Samuel said. "Selling bottles of wine is not unusual."

"For a wine merchant, no. For an individual, a nameless one at that, who has no card, no premises, no evidence of duties paid — one has to be suspicious. And the prices are surprisingly cheap."

"Ah, that is very telling."

Edgerton nodded. "Indeed. Another interesting discovery is that the supplier, whoever he is, is offering other goods in addition to wine now — candles, tea, that sort of thing. Perhaps the business is branching out."

"But why is there another book? Are the addresses the same?"

"They are not," the captain said, in a tone of great satisfaction. "We have another list of places to investigate, and we also know something else — that there are *two* gentlemen involved in this scheme, as well as Renshaw and the people who cart the wine about."

"But how did this second book get into the mattress? Unless your uncle came back?" Samuel said, looking at Charlie.

But she shook her head. "No sign of him. Someone must have snuck in at night, because there's always someone in the kitchen in the day, and Uncle Lucas's bedroom is only curtained off, so I'd hear anyone pokin' around in there."

"There is a small window with a loose latch facing the back lane," Edgerton said. "Not difficult for an agile man to climb in or out. Charlie, if you are agreeable to the idea, I should like to leave Mr Chandry with you to keep watch at night."

"To stop anyone sneakin' in, you mean?"

"Not to stop them, no. To see if there is a pattern to the comings and goings with the books, and in the cellar. He will sit here in the kitchen, where he will hear any activity in the yard, or in your uncle's bed chamber. He will take lodgings in the town so that he can sleep during the day."

"He can sleep here if he likes. There's a tiny box room upstairs that we could fit a pallet into with a bit of shiftin' around. It's got a skylight for air, and the little ones are at school all day so they won't be racketin' around keepin' him awake."

"I can sleep through the Last Trump," Chandry said cheerfully. "If anyone asks, I'm your long-lost cousin from Cornwall."

"Are you really from Cornwall?" Charlie said, lifting the pastry onto her pie. "You talk a bit funny."

"I really am, and my sister is a duchess, so you'll have to mind your manners or she'll chop your head off."

Charlie's expression was a picture, but then she laughed. "Oh, you're teasing me, Mr Chandry."

"Ah, but am I, though?" he said, grinning at her.

"It is you who will have to mind your manners, Chandry," Edgerton said. "You will be a guest in Charlie's house, so you must be on your best behaviour, understand?"

"Of course!" he said, his eyes wide with innocence. "I am always on my best behaviour when there is a beautiful young woman in the house."

Charlie blushed scarlet, and Edgerton said with a sigh, "That is precisely what I am afraid of."

~~~~~

Samuel returned to Whitfield Villa very close to the dinner hour, and with his head full of patients and smuggled wine and flirtatious young men, so he was unprepared for Miss Beasley to greet him with, "Mr Rycroft is in your study, Dr Broughton." She seemed oddly agitated.

"A patient? At this hour?"

"Not a patient, I suspect. Take your time. We will hold dinner for you. There is nothing that will spoil."

Rycroft was pacing up and down the room, with a face like thunder. "Where the devil have you been, Broughton? I have been here for more than an hour."

"I beg your pardon, but I was not expecting you so I—"

"Well, you should have been! You cannot expect to steal Susannah away without consequences."

Samuel was very tempted to say that he certainly hoped there would be consequences, and far more pleasant ones than Rycroft's scowling countenance, but he restrained himself. "Will you take a seat? Have you been offered refreshments?"

"No, I will *not* take a seat, and I want nothing from you except what is rightfully mine."

"And what is that, Mr Rycroft?"

"Why, Susannah, of course," he said, as if it should be obvious.

That was a little unsettling. "You have an understanding with the lady?"

"I should say so! For years it has been understood… well, not formally, but eventually… I should have won her round, if you had not interfered. Just because she met you years ago in London, she thinks you are all that is wonderful, but she was just a child, she was open to any kind of falseness and—"

"Just a moment," Samuel said, puzzled. "She met me in London? When was this?"

"How should I know? Years ago, that is all I can say. What has that to say to anything? You will give her up, then? You must, now that you see how it is."

Samuel was more flummoxed by the revelation that Susannah had met him in London, and yet had never mentioned it. Why would she say nothing? It was strange to be secretive about such a thing. And yet how could he ask her outright — it would seem as if he did not trust her. He could only hope that she would tell him freely.

"Well, Broughton?" Rycroft's anger had dissipated, and he looked rather lost, his expression one of desperate misery. "I… I love her, you see. I could not bear it if…"

It was an odd thing, but whereas Samuel had been quite sure that he could not marry Agnes Saxby because she was loved by another man, yet somehow the same constraint did not apply to

Susannah. He pitied Rycroft, certainly, but he was not about to meekly surrender to him.

"Mr Rycroft," Samuel said gently, "I have not the least wish to come between two people united by strong affection, but I must tell you that I have seen no sign that Miss Winslade returns your regard. She gave me reason to believe that my suit would not be unwelcome, I offered for her and she accepted. We are betrothed, and you must be aware that I cannot honourably withdraw. If there is something between you, then it is to her that you should apply, not to me, but I am not confident of your success."

"But if I can talk her round, you will let her go? You will not fight it?"

"Really, Rycroft, this is all hypothetical. Talk to the lady and see what she says."

He seemed to shrink, appearing suddenly very young. "I have already done so," he said in a small voice.

"Then you have your answer," Samuel said, in the voice he reserved for sick children. "I am very sorry for your disappointment, but Miss Winslade must be the best judge of where her happiness lies."

But after Rycroft had taken his scowl away, Samuel could think of nothing but the odd fact that Susannah had met him in London, yet had said nothing at all about it. Why would she hide it? She seemed to be so open, yet was keeping things from him. What other secrets was she concealing? It was deeply troubling, and the more he thought about it, the angrier he became.

~~~~~

Wednesday saw a formal dinner at Maeswood Hall, the first such occasion since the death of Lord Saxby six months earlier. The Saxby ladies would appear in half-mourning for the first time, and there would be general rejoicing at their return to society again.

Susannah dressed with more than usual care. She had not had time to make a new gown, but she was able to modify one from last year that had seen but little wear, adding some new trimmings to spruce it up. In addition, she had a betrothal gift from Dr Broughton, a necklace and bracelets of topaz, which she was rather pleased about. She had not expected anything of the sort, for he had but little money to spare, but he had arrived that morning with it, handing it over with surprising shyness.

"It is nothing... mere trumpery. One day I shall be able to afford better," he had said, rather gruffly. "Do you like it?"

She had said all that was proper, not liking to overwhelm him with effusions, but at odd moments during the day, whenever she had cause to go to her room, she had unlocked her jewel box to admire it afresh.

Owing to a suspicion of croup in little Edward, Susannah had not attended the Gages' card party the day before, so this would be her first public appearance as a future bride, and an awkward one, for Susannah would be stealing the glory that should belong to the daughter of the house. How must Cass feel to be so overshadowed? Or was she perhaps glad that the attention of the company would be drawn elsewhere?

Papa was a little slow to ready himself, so the Manor party was amongst the last to arrive. Lanterns, as yet unneeded, lined the long carriage drive to Maeswood Hall, liveried footmen waited on the steps to greet them, and grooms loitered to attend to the horses. As

Susannah stepped carefully down from the carriage, voices mingled with bursts of laughter emanated from open windows.

They were relieved of cloaks and hats in the entrance hall, from where the butler led them to the Italian Room to be supplied with drinks and then to the ornate splendour of the Gold Room, already hot, crowded and noisy. Lady Saxby and her daughters stood in line to greet them. Susannah looked carefully at Cass, but she showed no sign of disappointment, in fact, quite the reverse.

"Cass? You are looking well," Susannah said cautiously, hoping she was not walking into trouble.

But her friend practically bounced with excitement. "I am — very well!" Then she added in a whisper, "It is to be announced. But say nothing! Mama wishes me to be ladylike and restrained, and if you say a word I think I shall explode with joy! We will talk later."

Susannah nodded, and moved swiftly on, but curiosity stabbed her. Why the sudden change of heart? It was odd, but very good that everything would be out in the open at last.

She greeted friends as she passed them, but hardly saw them, as her eyes sought one particular face in the crowd, and that familiar honey-coloured hair. "He is beside the nymph," Miss Beasley said as she passed by, with a knowing smile. And there he was, his back to her, talking to some of the Gages, and tonight she did not have to will him to turn and see her. She weaved her way through the prattling groups, and touched him lightly on the arm. He turned, he saw her... he did not smile. In fact, he looked positively forbidding.

"Miss Winslade." His bow was punctiliously correct, but no more than that.

A cold spasm washed through her as she made her curtsy, but then he saw the topaz necklace and that brought a smile at last. Not his relaxed, open smile, but still, anything was better than studied coldness.

"You look delightful tonight," he said, but again it seemed politeness rather than enthusiasm.

"What a pretty necklace," Miss Gage gushed. "Is it new? A *special* gift, perhaps?"

"A betrothal gift," Susannah said, and naturally that set her off even more. Susannah liked Miss Gage, for she was a well-meaning woman and had taken good care of her brother and his motherless children, but sometimes she was a trifle too fulsome in her effusions.

Before long they proceeded to the gallery where they were to dine, no other room being adequate for the forty persons invited. Dr Broughton offered his arm, and they went through in their proper place, below the Saxbys but well above the Platts and Whittels, there solely from courtesy.

To her surprise, the squire was invited to take the place of the host at the foot of the table, and he waved Susannah and Dr Broughton to sit beside him. Cass and Mr Truman sat at the top of the table beside Lady Saxby, and the rest of the guests disposed themselves as they would. Once all were settled, but before the soup was put out, the squire rose and tinged a wine glass with his knife.

"Lady Saxby, ladies, gentlemen, may I beg your indulgence for a moment," he began. "Lady Saxby has asked me to make two very special announcements to you tonight. The first is of particular pleasure to me, and a matter that is no secret to most of you. I am very pleased to tell you that my eldest daughter, Susannah, is engaged to be married to Dr Samuel Broughton." There was a murmur of approval, but clearly it was not news to most of those there. "The other announcement should by rights be made by Lord Saxby, but since, to our very great sorrow, he cannot be here with us tonight to enjoy this moment, it falls to me to impart the very happy news that his eldest daughter, Cassandra, is to marry our very own clergyman, Mr Theodore Truman. I am sure you will join me in wishing all four young people great joy in their lives together."

There were little cries of excitement up and down the table, Cass blushed very charmingly, Mr Truman rose with a smirk and took a bow, and the excitable Platts broke into spontaneous applause. Lady Saxby frowned at such unseemliness, signalled to the butler to set out the soup tureens, and the meal began.

Dr Broughton was pleasingly attentive throughout the meal, to the neglect of Mrs Drinkwater on his other side, and his frighteningly stern countenance melted a little with each course, until by the time the covers were removed and the sweet dishes laid out, he was all that Susannah could wish for in a future husband. She was not so foolish as to expect professions of affection which he could not possibly feel, but his unsmiling face had struck terror in her heart, and his better humour warmed her inside.

They talked of nothing in particular — the food, the room, the many paintings on the walls, a subject on which he was very knowledgeable. He asked a flattering number of questions about her, too — could she ride, did she play or sing, did she like to dance, had she enjoyed her season in London?

"I was never so fortunate as to enjoy a season, sir. The assemblies at Market Clunbury and Shrewsbury were my season, and I never wanted for more."

"You never longed to attend Almack's, and beg leave of the patronesses for the right to sup on bread and butter and lemonade?" he said, with a teasing smile.

She laughed, and said, "I doubt I should ever be admitted there, nor at any of the grand balls I read about in the London newspapers. A thousand people at some of them! The heat and noise must be unbearable. I have no wish to return to London. It is endlessly fascinating for a short visit, but I should not like to stay there for long."

"You would miss the river and your frog orchids and the water creatures that walk on water."

"Indeed I would! There is so much in nature to enchant the eye and soothe the soul. London is all bustle and haste and confusion, but the country, and especially my own little corner of it, brings me peace and tranquillity."

"There is much to be said for peace and tranquillity," he said thoughtfully. "May we both enjoy your little corner of the country for many years to come."

He smiled — oh, that smile! — and raised his glass to her in a toast, and in that moment she loved him with all her heart and soul.

14: Hot Milk At Midnight

All too soon, Lady Saxby rose to lead the ladies away to the saloon. It was a warm evening, the French doors had been thrown wide for air and there was still some light in the sky. It was inevitable that many of the guests should wander onto the terrace, or walk on the several paths lit by colourful lanterns.

"Come, let us slip away for a quiet coze," Cass said, sliding her arm around Susannah's.

"I hope you will tell me all about it," Susannah said, "for the last time we talked, which was all of two days ago, you were in fear of his regard waning, and here you are with everything settled. Are you to marry soon?"

Cass's face fell. "Not before January. Theodore is determined that we shall all be completely out of our blacks. He hopes, too, that the new Lord Saxby will be here to give me away, but Mama is not keen on *that*, as you may imagine. She is convinced he will be a chimney sweep or a coal miner, or some other filthy occupation." She giggled. "Poor Mama! I think he will be an attorney or a clergyman, or something equally dull. But let me tell you about Theodore. I took your words to heart, you see, about telling him just how I feel. I sent him a note asking him to come and see me, and then I simply told him that it was distressing to have everything secret and I did not mind when we marry, but I wished we could at least announce the engagement. I may have cried a little bit as well, and gentlemen never like tears, do they? Honora can cry whenever she wants, you know, and very useful she will find it, I imagine, when she wants to bend a gentleman to her will. It never worked with Papa, but then he was particularly resolute. But Theodore is not so resolute, and although I did not at all intend to cry, for I am not a watering pot as a rule, it had the proper effect on him. He was quite mortified to have caused me pain, and agreed at once that everything must be put on a proper footing. He was... oh, Susannah, he is such an affectionate man! I am so very fortunate!"

"Indeed you are, and I cannot tell you how pleased I am that it is all out in the open at last, and there is no more secrecy."

"Oh, it is wonderful!" Cass said. "There should never be secrets between two people who love each other, should there?"

Even as she voiced her agreement, Susannah reflected on Dr Broughton's secret — his time in London, of which he had not yet spoken a word. He was the one who had urged her to be entirely open with her father, but he had not yet been open with her, and she had no idea what to make of that.

They did not walk far, for Cass's misshapen leg troubled her if she overdid her exercise, and as soon as they returned to the terrace, they saw the gentlemen emerging to join them, at least the two of particular interest to Cass and Susannah. Mr Truman soon led Cass away down one of the paths, but Susannah was not left alone with her betrothed for long, for Agnes scampered over to them, her face shining.

"Dr Broughton, Dr Broughton!" she cried as soon as she was within hailing distance. "May I offer my congratulations and wish you joy? Such wonderful news. I cannot tell you how pleased I am."

"Thank you, Miss Saxby," he said.

"I wanted you to know that I am very happy about it, because you might have thought I would not be, but I assure you I am."

His lips twitched, but he answered gravely, "I am very glad to hear it, and I trust that your happiness will cause an improvement in your health, so that you will not need to call upon my services quite so often."

She did not blush, for Agnes was not constrained by great delicacy of feeling. Instead she said solemnly, "I think it very likely, sir. Oh, I am so pleased for Susannah, for we all thought she would never find a gentleman who would appreciate her as we do, yet here we are and is it not romantic? You arrive, sir, a stranger in our midst, and within days Susannah has quite swept you off your feet, and it is the same with Susannah. You both knew how it would be at once, perhaps in the first moment you met." She sighed. "Such instant attraction is a charming tale."

"That is one of the advantages of being a little bit older and perhaps wiser," Susannah said, trying not to laugh. "One is a little more familiar with the world, so that one knows just what would suit one best."

"Older and wiser... is it so? May one not know one's own mind when one is sixteen, but only when one is six and twenty?"

Susannah understood her reference to Mr Edser. "One does not always understand all the consequences of one's actions at sixteen as well as one might at six and twenty," she said gently. "There is a husband who suits each of us perfectly, if we are patient and wait for him to appear, Agnes. Look at Cass, too, for the proof of it. It is not always sensible to rush into matrimony with the first man who offers."

"I am sure you are right," Agnes said sadly. "It is better to heed the advice of others in such cases."

"In extreme youth, that is so," Dr Broughton said with surprising firmness. "When a lady is a little older, however, in particular when she is of age, she has gained enough wisdom to decide for herself. Would you not agree, Miss Saxby?"

Agnes looked at him thoughtfully. "When she is of age?"

"I would say, from my own experience, that is the point at which a lady may confidently determine her own future, without regard for the opinions of others, however well-meant. The law agrees with me, in fact, for is not that the precise time when a lady no longer needs permission to marry?"

"It is," she said. "Indeed it is, Dr Broughton. Then I need only wait and... I may confidently decide my own future." Slowly, a smile spread across her face. "Thank you, sir! Your words are most welcome."

She almost skipped away across the lawn and up the steps to the terrace, where quite a crowd was now assembled, awaiting the commencement of the dancing.

"Lady Saxby will not thank you quite so enthusiastically for that piece of advice," Susannah said. "She has been trying to steer Agnes away from any lingering regrets for Mr Edser for years."

"But I think she has not succeeded," he said quietly.

"It would be a most unequal match. A baron's daughter and an apothecary? It is unthinkable."

"Yet she *does* think about it, and so does he, and I believe that what was unacceptable at sixteen may be less so at one and twenty. You may find that Lady Saxby will be very glad to have both her eldest daughters safely married, to leave the way clear for the younger two."

"In truth, that is a very good point," she said. "Two daughters will be much easier for a widow to dispose of, and it has to be said, in all honesty, that the likelihood of Agnes attracting a more acceptable suitor is slim at best."

He chuckled and said, "You will make an admirable wife, Miss Winslade, when you are so readily disposed to accept my opinion."

"I concede the point on this occasion, sir," she said demurely. "I cannot guarantee always to do so, however."

He laughed out loud at that, and she was thrilled by this trivial success. If only she could always turn him to such good humour. He had started the evening quite out of charity with her, although she had no notion why, and now they were on the best of terms.

Hearing the music striking up, he gave her his arm and they returned to the house to open the dancing.

~~~~~

As Mac was readying Samuel for bed that night, the Scot said, "Ye like her, dinnae ye?"

Samuel did not pretend to misunderstand. "I would hardly have proposed marriage if I did not like her."

"Aye, but it's a wee bit mair'n likin' her, I'm thinkin'."

Samuel chuckled. "I *do* like her, and the more I get to know her, the better I like her. There now, does that make you happy? I have no idea why I tolerate you, impertinent Scot that you are. Get along with you."

Mac laughed, gathering up the discarded clothes and backing out of the room.

In truth, Samuel reflected on the evening with unalloyed pleasure. He had started in the worst of ill-humours, knocked off-balance by Rycroft's revelations. He had been disposed to be angry with Susannah for not telling him that she had previously met him in London. His greeting to her had lacked warmth, and he regretted that. He should not have allowed his irritation to affect his manners. But then he had noticed that she wore his gift to her, and when he had paid her some meaningless compliment, she had coloured up in the most charming way. And her eyes! She had the loveliest eyes, and when she had looked at him... he had been aware of a warmth inside him that took him a little by surprise.

Whatever her reason for concealing their previous meeting, he could not believe it to have any underhand motive. When he had raised the subject of the season, the perfect opening for her to mention their previous acquaintance, she had talked easily about London without a hint of consciousness. Besides, he could hardly fault her for such reserve when he had told her nothing of his own history. He would have to do so, of course, but not yet. Her father had given him some breathing space.

It was odd that he could not recall her at all from London, and surely if they had been introduced he would have done so? She had not participated in the season, but perhaps she had been a patient? No, he would have remembered her, surely. He remembered every one of his patients. He pulled on a robe, picked up the candlestick and padded barefoot down the stairs to his study. Lighting a candelabrum, he pulled a box from a cupboard and slowly began to leaf through the contents.

He had not been long at his task, when the door opened and Miss Beasley's cambric-swathed head appeared in the flickering light of her candle.

"Dr Broughton? I heard your door open. Is anything amiss?"

"Nothing at all, ma'am, although I might ask you the same question. Could you not sleep? Would you like a powder? I have some of my own formulation."

She smiled, but shook her head. "I never take anything of that nature. A cup of hot milk and a few verses of the Bible usually does the trick. Would you like some hot milk yourself?"

"Thank you, that would be a kindness."

Hot milk! It was almost like being back in the nursery. He would rather have had a brandy, his habitual nightcap for many years, but he could not justify the expense of a bottle. No, it was more than that, he knew. He could not deceive himself. Perhaps he would never be able to drink a bedtime brandy again.

She returned a little while later carrying a tray, with two cups and the candlestick balanced on it. "May I sit with you for a while?" she said, setting his cup down on the floor beside him. "I have no wish to disturb you, but a little conversation would be just as effective as the Bible."

"Of course," he said at once.

"It is so pleasant to have another gentleman in the house to talk to," she said in her gentle tones. "Ladies are not at all the same, forever talking about servants or meals or fripperies, but gentlemen are so interesting."

"Do you think so? So many of them only want to talk about horses and shooting things and dogs, or medical matters in my case."

"But that is exactly what I mean!" she said. "Everything about medicine is fascinating to me."

"As it is to me too," he said. Then, because he knew that she would be far too polite to ask directly, he said, "I am looking through my sketches of previous patients." He did not explain that he was looking for Susannah's face amongst them, for that would involve mentioning London and he was not yet ready for that.

"You sketch your patients? How interesting! May I see?"

He laid some of them on the desk where she sat. "That one had a weak heart. Now, she had severe dropsy, poor lady. This one had the most troublesome digestion. And this one had nightmares."

"All of them are women," she murmured.

"I do have one or two gentlemen. This is a very distinguished naval man, an admiral now, I believe. And… let me see… here is a viscount. Ah, now this is another one of my lonely ladies… and this one. There were quite a number of those."

"Lonely ladies — do you mean widows? Or spinsters?"

"Sometimes, but many were married and would be accounted successful members of society, except that they had nothing to occupy their hours. Their children were looked after by nursemaids and governesses and schools, their servants ran the household and their husbands had mistresses and government duties to occupy them. At their country estates, they had their charitable works but in town they were expected to enjoy themselves. If they did not… they discovered themselves to be suffering from a malaise, so they visited a physician. Inability to sleep, headaches, lassitude, loss of appetite, odd pains in the legs... I have seen all of these, vague illnesses that come and go. When they came to see me, I sketched them, and while my charcoal was busy, they talked and I listened and they went away feeling better."

"Now Roland would prescribe an emetic and send them on their way," Miss Beasley said softly. "He has no patience with women who have nothing much wrong with them. What do you prescribe for them?"

"Sleeping powders and tonics, if they want them, but I also advised them to go out for a walk every day, and not to avoid the sunshine. Red meat and wine are beneficial, too, but sunshine is my miracle prescription, Miss Beasley. Exercise and sunshine. There is a reason peasants enjoy such rude health."

"Then you would have us all throw away our parasols?" she said mildly.

"I would," he said, then chuckled. "No, perhaps it would too greatly shock society if every lady of quality were to sport brown skin from exposure to the sun, but she should at least take her exercise in the air, and not stay cooped up indoors."

"You have some interesting ideas, I can see. We will talk more about this at another time, but my milk is finished, so I shall leave you to peruse your lonely ladies, Dr Broughton. Thank you for allowing me to see them. I am sure I shall sleep now."

So saying, she slipped out of the room, having delicately refrained from asking him why on earth he was looking at such things in the middle of the night. He was not sure what he would have done if she had asked. Told the truth, he hoped, but there was a sliver of uncertainty at the back of his mind.

A few more minutes brought him to a conclusion — however he had met Susannah in London, it was not because she had consulted him as a patient. Dissatisfied, he boxed up the sketches again, blew out all but one candle, and went to bed.

~~~~~

Samuel was inspired by seeing his sketches to begin the habit with his new patients. Almost every day saw him adding to his collection. Lady Saxby at the Hall, who had a strange pain in her stomach. Mrs Drinkwater, who was suffering from sleeplessness. Mrs Cokely, even though she refused to be a patient, telling him roundly she required no medical services.

"I am as fit as a pig, thank you very much, apart from a little creaking of the joints, and there is nothing anyone can do about that, is there?"

He agreed there was not, but even so, he stayed for half an hour, drawing and listening to her tales of events long past and people long dead, although she spoke of them as though they were very much alive.

On Sunday after church he walked back to Cloverstone Manor with Susannah, and spent the whole day with her, walking in the grounds with the children around them, talking and laughing and utterly content. He had never before felt himself to be a part of a real family, and he was enchanted.

He visited the Manor often to see his patient. On one such visit, he managed to take Mrs Winslade's likeness, watching with satisfaction as she cuddled her youngest child on the terrace, while the others played on the lawn. When the smallest of the girls fell and hurt herself, Samuel could not resist laying down his sketchbook and scooping her into his lap, to be petted until she felt better.

"Your stepmother is coming along well," he said to Susannah as she walked with him back to the stables after the visit. "I confess, I had no expectation of so great an improvement."

"It may be my fancy," Susannah said, "but it seems to me that her breathing is a little easier, too. Do you think… dare we hope for a complete recovery?"

"As to that, consumption is a cruel illness, and so protracted that there may be periods of improvement even in the worst cases." He hesitated, then added, "I do not want to give you false hope, Miss Winslade. When the benign summer weather gives way to winter, we may see another downturn. Nevertheless, whatever happens in the future, even if the outcome is the one we all dread, at least your stepmother has had the great joy of her children's company."

"And they of hers," she said. "If she is lost to us, they will remember her now, and that is a very great boon."

"Shall I see you at the card party tonight?" he said, and her answering smile was warm, those grey eyes lighting up. Such lovely eyes!

"I certainly hope so. Henry is off on his travels again, but Papa loves the card table, so I shall be able to go if the children can spare me."

He frowned a little. "So you do not go unless your father goes?"

"Or Henry. I should not like to call the carriage out just for me. That would be shockingly indulgent."

"You place too low a value on yourself sometimes," he said. "You are a daughter of the house, after all."

"It would hardly be appropriate to place myself on too high a form just when I am about to become a humble physician's wife," she said, and her teasing countenance made him smile too.

He lifted her hand to kiss it. "You will be a delightful physician's wife." He was enchanted to see her blush fulsomely, and lower her eyes in the most maidenly manner. "I shall see you tonight, I hope."

"Oh yes... I do hope so... if I possibly can." And, all delightful confusion, she scurried away.

He turned to see Mac watching him with a wide grin on his face. "Yes, yes, yes! I know. Let us go, shall we?"

Susannah did come that evening, and the numbers were such that they were not needed for the card tables, or perhaps the others kindly left the betrothed couple to themselves. Whatever the reason, they were able to play backgammon quietly in a corner for hours, talking about anything and almost everything. She was so easy to talk to that Samuel felt he had known her for years. And perhaps he had. Perhaps they had met long ago, and even though he could not recall the occasion, some shadow of it remained to strengthen the bond between them. He went to bed that night entirely content in his new life. He had been in Great Maeswood for just three weeks and already it felt like a comfortable and pleasant home.

Samuel woke to the sound of shouts, and frantic hammering on the front door. Scrambling into a robe, he rushed down and wrestled with the multitude of bolts on the front door. Outside, the Cokelys' young maid, her face blotchy with tears.

"Please, sir, 'tis Mrs Cokely, sir. She be dead in 'er bed."

15: The Grassy Meadow

Samuel walked along the road, unnaturally deserted at this hour, with Dr Beasley and Miss Beasley at his side. The front door of Bramble Cottage stood open wide.

"Miss Cokely?" called Beasley. "May we come in?"

She was still in her nightgown and robe, her hair in curling papers and covered with a voluminous cap, her cheeks wet with tears. "Oh, yes, do come in. Thank you so much... so sorry to call you at this hour but..." She buried her face in a handkerchief with a little sob.

"There now, Lucy," Miss Beasley said. "Let us leave your mama to the gentlemen, and do you come upstairs. Is Sarah back?"

"I sent her to fetch Mr Truman. To say a few prayers. I cannot be easy until he has said a prayer for her soul. Such a shock, you see. So sudden. Never expected it, and for her soul to be cut adrift so abruptly..."

"Of course, of course, but you will want to be dressed for that, I daresay. Let me help you. Come along now."

The two men went into the downstairs bedroom where Mrs Cokely lay peacefully in bed, seemingly asleep but for the greyish hue to her skin.

"Well, she had her allotted years and a few more besides," Beasley said. "Not exactly an untimely death."

"Yet she did not seem close to death when I saw her only yesterday," Samuel said.

"There is no knowing with creatures as frail as she was," Beasley said. "The heart can give out at any moment, without the least warning. When Sarah comes back, she can run up to the farm for Mrs Vale. She does the laying out these days. Truman will arrange the burial, whenever he comes. I doubt it will be soon. He is not a man who hurls on coat and boots to be out of the door in five minutes. It must take him half an hour to get his cravat just so. Let us wait for the ladies in the other room. I expect there is somewhere to sit, amidst all those hats."

Miss Cokely appeared in a remarkably short time, dressed in a sober gown of dark blue, her hair neatly tucked under a linen cap, far more composed than before.

"So sorry," she murmured. "So kind of you to come. I know there is nothing you can do, but... but..."

"Of course, Lucy," Miss Beasley said. "Naturally we came. We would have been very upset if you had not sent word to us. What else are friends for?"

"Thank you, dear. How kind you all are, even Dr Broughton, who barely knew Mama. She had such a happy day, yesterday, thanks to you. Phyllida, Dr Broughton came again and sat with Mama for such a long time and listened to all her ramblings about times long gone. She never remembers what happened yesterday or last week, but thirty years ago is completely clear in her mind. *Was* clear, I mean. And then Mr Truman came later and administered the Holy Sacrament to her, and that made her so happy, you cannot imagine. Such a long time since she was able to attend church, so to have the church come to her was a great boon. She was so cheerful yesterday evening. A little tired, but no worse than usual. And then this. Poor, poor Mama, and I not by her side when she went. I do hope Mr Truman comes soon. A little prayer, just to speed poor Mama on her way, and I shall feel such a lot better."

Mr Truman eventually arrived, and Dr Beasley and Samuel felt able to leave. When he reached the house, Samuel found the sketch of Mrs Cokely, and took it to the smith's eldest son, who was handy with wood, to have a frame made for it.

~~~~~

Susannah's day began auspiciously, with her stepmother out of bed and dressed for breakfast, for the first time in months.

"This is a good sign, daughter, would you not say?" her father said, following her to her office after they had eaten. "She is improving every day, I believe."

"True, but Dr Broughton warns that we should not become complacent. This change may be only temporary."

"I daresay that is sensible." His face fell. "I cannot help hoping, though. I so much wish her to be *well* again, as she used to be. Do you remember her when she first came here? Such a lively little thing, so happy and smiling and full of life! I loved to watch her dance, you know. Sometimes I never danced with her at all myself, just for the pleasure of watching her."

"I remember, Papa."

"And now…" He rubbed his face tiredly. "Ah well. No point railing against such things, is there? I have brought trouble to all my wives, one way or another. Jane… she was a lively one, too. Rode as hard as any man, jumping every hedge and ditch right alongside me. I never had the same pleasure in the hunt after she fell. And poor Philippa! All she ever wanted was a child of her own. Not that she loved you and Henry one bit the less, but she so badly wanted her own. And now Lilian, who has too many. I always seem to get things wrong."

"You loved them all dearly, Papa," Susannah said. "You loved them and cherished them, always, and that cannot be wrong."

"That is true," he said, "but perhaps it is better to love a little less, then it would not hurt so much. Your way is better, I think, with Dr Broughton, a simple practical arrangement. He is a personable young man and will make you an agreeable husband, daughter, and you are not merely blinded by a handsome face and pretty manners, like Cass Saxby."

"You disapprove of her betrothal to Mr Truman?" Susannah said, surprised.

"Well, if she likes him, I suppose there is no harm in it, but I can tell you this — he never looked at her until she had seventy thousand pounds in her pocket."

Susannah said nothing, for the same thought had crossed her mind, too. When he had first arrived in Great Maeswood, Mr Truman had seemed to favour Agnes. But then Lord Saxby had died and the dowries of fifteen thousand apiece for the younger girls had been replaced by ten thousand between them, and Cass had learnt of her great fortune. The next time Susannah had seen Cass, there had been an understanding with Mr Truman. A swift courtship indeed. And then there was that strange business of telling Cass that he loved wildflowers, and especially orchids, yet when Susannah had told him of the frog orchid, he had seemed to know nothing of such things, and showed little interest. It was very odd. He was a strange man, no doubt about it, and not quite the uncomplicated, charming man he appeared to be. Still, no doubt he would settle once he was married to Cass.

For her walk that afternoon, Susannah took her painting equipment to the meadow above the river. The frog orchids were still there, although all but buried in the rising summer grass, which swayed like the waves on the sea at the slightest breeze. She hoped to capture that movement with her brush.

She had not been painting long when she heard herself being hailed. Dr Broughton! He and his groom were just crossing the river. As she watched, he dismounted, handed the reins to the groom and walked up the hill towards her.

"Another view of the frog orchids?" he said cheerfully, tossing aside his hat and gloves, and throwing himself to the ground.

"Just the grasses, today. Are you on your way back from Market Clunbury?"

"I am. I thought to ride this way in the hope of seeing you out with your easel. Have you heard the news? Mrs Cokely has died."

"No! Oh, poor Miss Cokely! How she will feel it. I daresay she has never lived alone before, and how she will manage for money I cannot imagine without her mama's little pension. I am sure she makes very little from her bonnets. What happened? Did the old lady have an apoplexy?"

"She just passed away peacefully in her bed sometime during the night," he said. "Miss Cokely was most distressed that she had not been with her mother when it happened."

"I imagine she would be. How dreadful for her. She must be distraught, and it is too late to call on her today, for she will have had her dinner. I shall go first thing tomorrow, and take her a length of black, for I am sure she has none to hand. But let us talk of more cheerful matters. How is your practice going?"

"Rather well, I think, although it is early days yet. There is bound to be great curiosity about a new physician, so initially there will be a great many patients trying me out and finding out what I charge, and whether they can afford my services."

"Are you very expensive, sir? Perhaps I should send for the apothecary to treat Mama."

His lips twitched slightly, which she was coming to recognise as a sign he was amused. "Be assured that my rates are not excessive, but I must charge according to my training and experience. That is why it will take some time to build the practice. In a year or two, I shall hope to have my income on a stable footing, and then I may begin to build… develop a reputation, draw in people from further afield. Who treats the work house residents?"

"The master's wife, I believe."

"Then there may be a call for a qualified physician to attend. I should also like to find a generous sponsor who would allow me to start a travelling consultancy."

"Whatever is that? Something like an itinerant preacher?"

The lips twitched again. "A little, perhaps. It involves riding round the outlying villages and farms on a set day, to visit those who cannot afford regular fees. My father had such a scheme, and I helped to set one up in Edinburgh, although there were several of us who shared the duties, so it was not arduous."

Susannah thought it a wonderful idea, and said so. She loved to listen to him talking so, his face alight with enthusiasm, full of ideas for the future. *Their* future, now. Her fate was inextricably bound with his. If he was successful and earned a good income from his work, then she would be wealthy and live in some style. And if he did not... then she would economise. She was very good at economising.

"I had better be on my way," he said, rising in one fluid motion to his feet. He was not a small man, so his elegance of movement was all the more attractive. He was a graceful dancer, too, she had discovered. "You will not stay here too long? The breeze has an edge of coolness to it, I believe."

Such concern for her wellbeing was pleasing. "Not long, no. I have almost finished."

"Miss Beasley wishes me to invite you to dinner one evening. Would tomorrow suit you, if you have no other engagement? They will send their own carriage for you."

"That is very kind. Thank you, I should like that."

"She would like to show you over the house, so that you may decide upon the room you wish to have."

"Room?"

"A bedroom, furnished and decorated however you wish it. And you will want to look over the nursery rooms, too."

"But... we are to live at The Manor!" she cried. "I already have rooms in mind."

He frowned, the cold visage sending chills down her spine. "That is your father's idea, not mine. It will suit me much better to be settled in the village, rather than out in the country, miles from anywhere."

Was he to rip her away from all that was familiar? She jumped up from her painting stool, spinning round to face him. She could not live with the Beasleys, she could not! "But I cannot leave Mama!" she said with passion, suddenly terrified.

"Your stepmother has two people whose sole function is to attend to her every need, as well as a husband and a houseful of servants. You are hardly indispensable."

"No, but... paid nurses and servants are not the same, and Papa has other matters to attend to. She needs her family about her, and I am the only one who is able to fill that rôle."

"You can visit her every day," he said brusquely. "You can ride over every morning, and return in time for dinner. I would not deprive her of your company, but she does not need you in the evenings, after all."

"But the Manor has so many empty rooms, and there would be very little additional cost to add you to our housekeeping." She knew she was beginning to sound desperate but the prospect of moving from the spaciousness of the Manor to the comparatively cramped quarters of Whitfield Villa frightened her.

"Miss Winslade," he said, with icy formality, "you must allow me to know what is best for myself, my career and my family. There are considerations of which you cannot be aware—"

"What considerations? Do my wishes count for nothing?" she said, panic rising in her breast.

"Of course, but there are benefits to beginning our married life with the Beasleys of which—"

"What benefits? How can it be better to live there, in subservience to Miss Beasley, when I might live at the Manor and be to all intents the mistress of the house?"

"I understand," he said, wrapping one hand in both of his, with a sympathetic expression. "You want your own establishment and that is perfectly natural. It is to my shame that I cannot yet provide that for you. But— No, I must be completely honest with you. The situation is more complicated than you might have supposed. Dr Beasley has no heir to whom—"

She snatched her hand from his grasp. "That is perfectly horrid! You think he will leave you the house, so we must insinuate ourselves into his good graces, is that it?"

"No! He has—"

"I will have no part of it, do you understand? I want nothing to do with so vile a scheme! Go away! Please go away." She turned and began to gather up her painting things, and only succeeded in scattering them on the ground.

When she turned round, he had gone, striding away down the hill.

Hot tears scalded her face as she stuffed everything back into her satchel, all pushed in anyhow, for she could barely see what she did. For every step of the long walk home, she berated herself for her foolishness. To quarrel with him over such a matter! What if he should cast her off because of it? She would be devastated... utterly bereft... heart-broken. So many times she had scoffed at some friend or other who had declared her heart to be quite broken, but now she understood it completely. There was a pain, a real pain, in her heart at that moment as she faced the prospect of a future without Dr Broughton. Samuel. She had had him within her grasp and now perhaps she would lose him.

As soon as she reached home and the safety of her room, she sat down at the writing desk in her room, not even bothering to remove her bonnet in her haste, and reached for pen and paper. But the pen was motionless in her hand. What could she say? And how could she send a groom hurtling off to the village with a note for her betrothed without arousing comment? It was awkward indeed.

The maid came in just then to lay out her evening gown, and the moment was lost. He would come tomorrow to see Mama, most likely, and she could apologise to him then, in person.

Relief arrived shortly before dinner, in the shape of a neat little note from Miss Beasley, expressing pleasure at the prospect of entertaining her to dinner the next day, and informing her that the carriage would collect her at four, since they dined at five, and would return her at whatever hour suited her. She had forgotten the invitation, and he was not so ungentlemanly as to have withdrawn it. So the breach was not yet beyond repair. That cheered her a little, enough for her to appear downstairs tolerably composed.

Two of Papa's card-playing cronies had been invited to dine, so with Henry they had a four for their games, and Papa was kept happily entertained all evening. After Mama had become so ill and taken to her bed, he had gone through a long spell when it seemed his sole purpose in life was to drink the cellar dry. There had been whole days at a time when he had been too inebriated to leave his room, and Susannah had tended to him herself to keep the servants from seeing him in such a state. The only event which had given him any pleasure was the weekly outing to Market Clunbury with Lord

Saxby. Since his friend's death in January, the squire had stopped drinking so much, but had taken to spending whole days away from home, and not on estate business, either. Lately, though, he had seemed calmer, staying at home, attending church and inviting friends for the evening. It was bad for the victuals budget, but far better than sitting alone with a bottle.

Susannah sat quietly with her sewing. It was a peaceful, pleasant evening, and only the worry at the back of her mind regarding her quarrel with Dr Broughton could mar it. She went to bed tolerably content.

She woke early, roused by some indefinable sound — running feet in the distance, and then the unmistakable sound of sobbing. Pulling on a robe hastily, she opened her bedroom door.

"Oh Miss Winslade, Miss Winslade!" It was Miss Matheson, skidding to a halt outside her door, her face blotched with tears. "Come quick! It's Mrs Winslade — we can't rouse her!"

Susannah's light feet carried her swiftly down the corridor, where the door to Mama's room stood wide open. Inside, her maid, white-faced, and a housemaid, screaming. Nurse Pett bent over the bed, hiding the figure within.

"Let me see," Susannah said, crossing the room with quick strides.

But one glance told her the dreadful news. Mama was dead.

16: Coincidences

Samuel could hardly believe it. Two deaths in two successive days was an astonishing coincidence, and the second of the two was far more concerning. Mrs Cokely had been a very old lady, her death sad but hardly untimely. Mrs Winslade was another matter. Her illness, if it was indeed consumption, was typified by a long, slow and painful process, not this sudden catastrophic outcome. What could have happened?

Dr Beasley rode with him to Cloverstone Manor, his expression sombre. "A bad business," he said, more than once. "The squire will feel it extremely, for the reports were so promising. Still, one can never tell with these illnesses. There is just no knowing when the end will come, early or late. Such a bad business for the squire."

"You do not find it strange that Mrs Winslade should die so unexpectedly?" Samuel said.

"Strange? Not at all. When one is as grievously sick as Mrs Winslade, why, one lives on the edge of a knife. Death may strike without the least outward sign of trouble. Her heart gave out, no doubt, or something of the sort. Nothing unexpected about it, Broughton."

When they arrived, they found the knocker already swathed in crêpe and the shutters closed, but the door opened as they approached. The butler, barely controlling his tears, admitted them and a footman led them directly to Mrs Winslade's room, where the mourning candles were the only light in the room.

Beside the bed, the squire wept quietly, and Beasley quickly crossed the room to sit by him, talking in a low voice. Susannah rose from a chair in a gloomy corner, so dark that she was invisible until she moved, and the lace of her fichu caught the candlelight. She was very pale, her eyes huge in her distressed face.

"I am so very sorry," Samuel said to her quietly.

"Yes... thank you."

"How did it happen? Was there a sudden crisis?"

"Nurse Pett came in at the usual time and found her lifeless."

That was puzzling. "There was no warning? No gasping for breath? She did not summon help?"

"No. She has a bell beside the bed, and Nurse Pett sleeps lightly so would hear her if she called out. She checked on her at midnight, and she was soundly asleep at that time, and very peaceful. This morning at six she was dead."

"Did she take laudanum last night?"

Susannah nodded. "The usual dose from the bottle you gave her. Nurse Pett recorded the time and the dose in her book. She is very methodical. Do you wish to see her records?"

"If you please."

She lit another candle, and carried it to a large cabinet against the wall. From within, she withdrew a notebook, and a small bottle.

"Nurse Pett is very competent. I do not doubt that she gave the correct dose."

He put the notebook back, and took the bottle from her. "Where is Nurse Pett?"

"In the dressing room next door, where she sleeps."

"May I speak to her?"

"Dr Broughton, what do you suspect?"

"Suspect? Nothing, nothing at all, but... it is odd, that is all. She was so well last time I saw her, so much improved. And now this. I cannot fathom it."

"She was very ill," she said. "It is hardly a great mystery why she died."

"But it *is!*" he said, loud enough that Beasley and the squire turned to look at him. More temperately, he went on, "Her death was sudden and I need to know *why*, that is all."

"I believe you refine too much upon it," she said, her eyes bright in the gloomy bedroom. "There is nothing untoward about this, and people die all the time. As a physician you must be used to it."

"And every death must be explained," he said. "There is always a reason for it. I should like to be sure that there was nothing amiss with the medication, that is all."

She made no further protest, and led the way through to the dressing room. It was very tidy, even the small truckle bed neatly made. One shutter was ajar for a little light. Nurse Pett and Miss Matheson both rose and curtsied politely.

Samuel held up the bottle. "This is the bottle from which you dispensed Mrs Winslade's last dose of laudanum last night, Nurse Pett?" She nodded. "And you have been drawing from this bottle for some time, clearly, for it is about half full. Would you say that this is about the same level as when you last saw it?"

"Oh, sir, Mrs Winslade would never—" Miss Matheson began.

"I am merely considering all possibilities, Miss Matheson."

"It is the same level as last night," Nurse Pett said, triumphantly, clearly expecting the question. "First thing I checked, sir. And the cupboard was locked anyway, so she couldn't have got to the bottle, even if she'd a mind to. I always lock the medicine cupboard at night. I'm very careful about things like that."

"Indeed you are, and that is a relief to my mind," Samuel said. "We can now say with certainty that Mrs Winslade did not accidentally take too much laudanum. Miss Winslade, may we talk in private?"

She led him silently to her office next door, throwing open the shutters for light. Now that he could see her clearly, he was appalled by her haggard and anguished countenance.

"You are very composed, but this has been a dreadful shock to you," he said in a low voice. "Will you take a little brandy?"

She shook her head, pulling her shawl closer about her body.

"You must not be alarmed by all this questioning," he said. "In the event of a sudden death, there are always enquiries to be made. The coroner will certainly want answers to the same questions. Who is the coroner here?"

"Dr Beasley."

"Oh. Well… in that case, I shall inform him of all that I have discovered. Miss Winslade, will you not sit down? You do not look well."

There was a glimmer of a smile, barely there, but she sat in the chair he held for her, her head drooping. Then he drew up another chair and sat facing her. It was hardly the time for personal discussions, but their quarrel had eaten away at him. That she should imagine he would ingratiate himself with Beasley for gain! He could not bear her to think so ill of him.

Unable to leave matters as they stood, he said, "May I talk to you… explain something? For we parted yesterday on bad terms, and I am very sorry for it." Her head jerked up, and there was something, some expression in her face that gave him hope. He went on, "I should have stayed… explained a little better, for I think you have a wrong impression, and I would correct it, if I can. If you will be so generous as to permit it, I should like to tell you all that has transpired between Dr Beasley and myself regarding… the future."

She nodded her approval, so he went on, "It came about the evening after our discussion at the river, when you surprised me by telling me that you were willing to marry me. My abstract plans to marry at some unknown point in the future suddenly became much more immediate, and so I mentioned to Dr Beasley that I contemplated matrimony. Knowing that I could not afford to set up my own establishment for a year or two, I asked if he would be willing to consider housing my bride at Whitfield Villa also. That was all my concern, I assure you — a temporary arrangement, to permit us to marry at once. He not only agreed to it, he told me that he and Miss Beasley had hoped for just such an outcome. And then he told me that he had no heir, and would consider leaving everything to me. I give you my word, I had no thought of such a thing until that moment."

"I should have known that you would not scheme in such an odious way," she said, with a rueful smile. "I beg your forgiveness for ever thinking such a thing."

"There is nothing to forgive," he said, with cautious optimism. "I raised the subject clumsily, and it was a natural conclusion to reach. The snag with Beasley's offer — and there is always a snag, is there not? — is that he wishes us to live there, so that he might have children about him in his declining years."

"He should have married himself if that was so important to him," she said, but she smiled as she spoke, so he knew she was not displeased with him.

"Very true! But such considerations are immaterial now, for we cannot marry while you are in mourning." He hesitated. "May I take it that you still wish to marry, despite my ineptness yesterday?"

"Do you?"

He caught his breath at the evasion. Was she looking for a way out? For an instant, his future crumbled before his eyes and he was swept by fear. Surely she could not—? But her eyes, those clear grey eyes, were gazing at him steadily. He must compose himself, and answer her. "I do... I do wish it, yes. Very much. And you?"

She nodded firmly, and her expression shifted slightly. She had been nervous of his answer, he realised with exhilaration. It was more than merely being willing, she truly wanted to marry him.

"Then that is settled," he said. "But we will not decide where we are to live until nearer the time." Again she nodded, and there was a little smile on her lips that pleased him greatly. "I suppose you cannot now dine with us tonight," he said, with genuine regret.

"No, I cannot leave the house for a while, but you may dine here sometimes. I should like to see you now and then."

The anxiety in her eyes was touching. He could not bear to think of her trapped here in a house of mourning, with only her father and brother for company. "I shall come and see you very often," he said, and her relieved smile warmed him.

He was very fortunate in his choice, very fortunate indeed. She would make him an excellent wife. He breathed deeply, aware that he had stood on a precipice for a moment, yet had managed to draw back from it. It had mattered to him, he realised with surprise. This strange, almost casual, betrothal mattered dearly to him. He would have been very grieved to see it slip out of his reach.

~~~~~

On the ride home, Samuel told Beasley all he had discovered, but the older man waved it all away without interest. There was no doubt in his mind that Mrs Winslade had died a natural death, however sudden. Samuel was not so sure. He had never heard of a consumptive patient who had not lingered on to the point where death was a welcome release, and Mrs Winslade had been well short of that point.

Having seen his horse safely in Mac's care, he walked down the road to the apothecary.

Mr Edser was already aware of the news. "This is very unforeseen, Dr Broughton," he said, his round face filled with concern. "I thought she had a little more time yet."

"So did we all, Mr Edser. I am checking all the possibilities, purely as a precaution, you understand, but might I see your notes for the most recent medicines you made up for Mrs Winslade?"

"I have the book ready for inspection, sir, in anticipation of just such a question, but I am sure you will find all in order. Come into the mixing room. There now — here are your written instructions, sir, and here is the record of what I prepared. You will remember that I queried the laudanum with you, as being a lower dose than Dr Beasley was accustomed to prescribe. But I followed your instructions to the letter, I assure you, sir."

"I never doubted it, Mr Edser." He sighed. "It must be that Mrs Winslade's illness was more advanced than we thought."

"Or perhaps she had some other condition," Edser said. "It is such a pity we cannot see inside the body, to see what part may be in worse condition than we suspect."

The bell over the outer door jangled, and Samuel followed Edser back into the shop, where an agitated Miss Gage stood, clutching her reticule.

"Oh, Mr Edser! Such terrible news — have you heard?"

"About Mrs Winslade? Yes, I—"

"The *second* death! Two deaths, you see, so now there will be a third. It is always so. I am warning everyone to be careful. Horses — we must all stay well away from horses and carriages. Dr Broughton, do not ride anywhere, I beg of you! And you, Mr Edser — although you are so careful, always, I know that, but you must use extra vigilance now. Every preparation, you must check and check again, in case — oh, how dreadful it is! Two deaths so close together, so there is bound to be a third, you see. Bound to be."

"Miss Gage, I don't think—" Edser began.

"I am advising everyone to avoid all risk," she went on, oblivious. "Stay at home, if possible, or undertake only quiet activities. No saws or hammers! Keep away from the river, and— Oh! The bull! Where does Mr Vale keep his bull? Are the fences secure?"

"Miss Gage, I am sure there is no possibility of a third death," Mr Edser said, but Miss Gage groaned and shook her head.

"Would that it were so!" she cried despairingly.

Samuel was amused, but the poor woman was truly anxious about the possibility of a third death, and rational argument would not sway her.

"Miss Gage," he said cautiously, "you are very brave to warn us all in this way, but may I now escort you home? You must not take any further risk yourself, you know. You are too valuable to your family and the whole village."

"Valuable? Me?" she said, in surprised tones. "Do you think so?"

"Of course. You are quite indispensable, and I shall not rest until you are safely at home."

"Indispensable... oh, how kind you are to say so, Dr Broughton. Thank you, your arm would be most reassuring."

They walked slowly through the village, Miss Gage uttering a little squeal and shrinking towards him every time a horse or farmer's cart passed by. They had just turned in through the gates of Lower Maeswood Grove when Mr Gage came flying down the drive.

"It is all right, Vi! It is one of the dogs — no need to worry any more," he cried as he approached.

"Oh! One of the *dogs!* Oh, such a relief!"

"Yes, Ian, poor old fellow. He was getting very long in the tooth, so it is no surprise. There now, you see, all is well after all, and no one else will die."

"Oh, thank goodness! Not that I am not very sorry about Ian, for he was a pleasant sort of dog, not so *bouncy* as some of yours, and it is always a sad time when any creature dies, but I am very glad it is not a person. Very glad indeed. Thank you so much for your arm, Dr Broughton. I shall do very well now, for Laurence will see me the rest of the way home."

Samuel turned and began to make his way home again, but once more he was hailed, this time by Captain Edgerton, with Mr Chandry at his side.

"There you are, Dr Broughton!" Edgerton said. "We have been following you all around the village. When you were not at home, we were directed first to the apothecary and then to the Grove."

"Here I am, Captain, entirely at your disposal."

"Excellent. May we have a word — in private?"

Samuel led the two men back to the Villa and into his study, and poured Madeira for them all. "Now, gentlemen."

"Dr Broughton, I am a suspicious man by nature," the captain said. "When I hear of one death, that does not worry me. With a second death, only a day later, I begin to wonder. And when a third event occurs, all my instincts are aroused."

"If you mean the third death that so agitated Miss Gage, that matter has been resolved by one of Mr Gage's dogs," Samuel said.

"Ah… that is good news for Miss Gage, if not for the poor animal. However, that was not the third event to which I referred. Chandry has been patiently awaiting a night-time visitation at the house in Market Clunbury, and last night his patience was rewarded. At about two in the morning, a man climbed through the window from the alley, and placed some items in Renshaw's mattress. Chandry watched from behind the curtain separating Renshaw's sleeping area from the kitchen. We had agreed that he would not tackle any intruders single-handed, but unfortunately the man decided to enter the kitchen — perhaps he thought to obtain some food, who knows."

"And he encountered Chandry?" Samuel said.

"Smashed right into me," Chandry said, with a grin. "I tried to seize hold of him, but he was too slippery for me. There was a brief exchange of fists, he pushed me over, then he turned and fled. By the time I'd got to my feet he was gone."

"Not your fault, Michael," Edgerton said. "He took a nasty blow to the ribs, Broughton. It would have taken the wind out of his sails and no mistake."

"Let me have a look," Samuel said.

"Oh, it's all right. Charlie patched me up," Chandry said with a grin.

"Who would you rather have patching you up, an untrained girl of seventeen or a qualified physician?" Samuel said.

"To be honest, unless I was at death's door, I'd far rather have Charlie. She's devilish pretty."

Edgerton snorted with laughter. "You are an incorrigible rogue, Michael. Behave, or I will send you back to Cornwall."

Samuel pointed to the chaise longue. "Shirt off, Mr Chandry, if you please." Chandry grinned, and did as he was bid. "While I examine the damage, you may tell me, if you wish, what it was that the fellow placed inside the mattress."

"The original book was returned," Edgerton said triumphantly. "However, at the moment, that seems a little less interesting than all these deaths of yours, Broughton."

"Not my deaths!" he said sharply. Then, in more moderate tones, he went on, "I know you are trained to sniff out murder and mayhem, Captain, but I fear this one is a lost cause. Mrs Cokely was four and eighty, and very frail. Mrs Winslade's death was unexpected, it is true, but I can find no sign of mischief in it."

"Ah, you have looked, have you?"

"Naturally I have looked. Whenever a patient of mine dies, I like to know the cause of it, if at all possible." He explained all his findings with the laudanum. "Besides, I cannot see that an intruder at the house at Market Clunbury has any connection to either of the deaths."

"Nor can I," admitted Edgerton.

"Then it is just a tragic coincidence."

"It may be so, but I do so *dislike* coincidence, Broughton. It feels as if something is misaligned, like the pattern on badly-matched wallpaper."

Samuel chuckled. "I cannot help with that, but at least I can say beyond doubt that Charlie Renshaw is my equal in this instance. I cannot improve on her patching up. You may put your shirt back on, Mr Chandry."

He was showing the two out when a carriage, coated with the dust of much travel, turned into the drive. Samuel knew it at once. His whole body washed with cold fear. As quickly as civility allowed, he made his farewells and slammed the front door.

Then he retreated to his study and waited for the disaster to reach him.

17: Information

Samuel sat at his desk, head on his folded arms, listening. The door knocker first. Then the rat-tat-tat of Thomas's footsteps briskly crossing the hall. The slow creak of the door opening. Voices, two male voices, one confident, patrician, the other the low murmur of the servant. Thomas's footsteps again, and another door opening. Dr Beasley's voice in the hall. The other voice... the tones so familiar, so much dreaded. Samuel's stomach churned merely at the sound.

Then a long, agonising silence.

There was no clock in the room, so he pulled out his pocket watch. A quarter hour. A half hour. Another quarter. Almost an hour before they emerged, with low voices in the hall, then the front door opened again and the voices faded. Eventually there was the sound of carriage wheels crunching over the gravel, and the front door closed again.

More silence.

A fly wandered in, bumbling noisily around the room, then banging with a bzzt-bzzt-bzzt against the glass before finding an opening and disappearing into the garden again. Samuel envied the creature. If only he could simply fly out of the window to freedom, and escape the doom that was bearing down inexorably on him.

A soft tap on the door. Samuel laid his head on his arms again. Here it came.

"May I come in?" Beasley's voice was gentle, concerned. "I can see that you know about my visitor, and I imagine you know what he has said to me."

Samuel raised his head enough to nod.

"Will you tell me about it — give me your side of the story?"

He shook his head.

"Why ever not? It is hard to believe of you — there must be *something* you can say in your own defence, some reason, some extenuating circumstance? Tell me what actually happened."

Slowly Samuel raised his head. "I never have, and never will, speak of it."

"But why?"

"Because whatever I say, no matter how plausible, you will never, ever know whether I am telling the truth. No one can. There will always be that tiny little niggle of doubt at the back of your mind. A man can be as honest as the day, or the worst scoundrel in Christendom, and no one alive can tell the difference."

A long silence.

"Does Susannah know of this?" Beasley said.

He shook his head.

"Well, she will know soon enough for the news is on its way to her even now. For myself, I need to think long and hard about this. I must tell Phyllida, too, and we shall pray for guidance together. Then... we shall see how we may proceed from this point."

He quietly left the room.

Samuel laid his head down again and closed his eyes. He was in no doubt of the answer. It was over. Everything was over.

~~~~~

Susannah had no time to grieve. There was so much to be done — Mama's room to be swathed in black crêpe, the children to be told, mourning clothes to be organised, armbands for the footmen, black caps for the women, all the clocks to be stopped. She had not even begun on the letters. It should be Papa's job, of course, but when she had tentatively suggested that he might like to make a beginning, he had burst into fresh tears. He sat, even now, at Mama's side, as if he expected her to wake and ask for her breakfast.

Even the servants had gone to pieces. Binns had had to be helped away to his quarters, Mrs Whiteway had succumbed to hysterics in the kitchen so there was no knowing when anyone would next eat, and Susannah kept coming across little clusters of weeping maids. Only Mrs Cobbett, the housekeeper, seemed to have retained her ability to function. And Silas, the first footman, of course. Nothing seemed to disturb his air of assurance.

It was Silas who found her now, in the box room looking out lengths of black material for the children. "Beg pardon, madam, but there's a Sir James Strickland to see you." He held out the card, but it contained nothing but the name and a Hertfordshire address she did not recognise.

"Strickland? I know no one of that name, and I cannot see anyone today. Tell him to call again some other time."

"He did say it were urgent, madam."

"I do not care how urgent it is, a family death takes priority, and I wonder he calls at all when he sees the knocker wrapped in black. It is very poor form." Strickland... something about the name was familiar. "Wait... ask him how he knows me, Silas. No... I remember it now."

He was the eminent physician whom her second mama had consulted in London. It was Strickland's house where she had met Dr Broughton, all those years ago. She had little memory of him — an older man in a large wig with a distinguished appearance, but nothing more specific than that. She doubted she would recognise him if she passed him in the street.

But when she entered the East Ante-room where he waited, she knew him at once. The wig had become a much smaller affair, with three neat rolls each side, but the air of aristocratic hauteur was the same. The bow was little more than a nod, and the smile... she thought it supercilious. Dr Broughton rarely smiled, but when he did his whole face lit up with a glow that left the observer in no doubt of its genuineness. With this man, one felt no such certainty.

For some reason she could not quite explain, she mistrusted him. Whatever his purpose in coming to see her, let him say what he had to say and be gone.

She made him a respectful curtsy. "You wished to speak to me, sir."

"Miss Winslade, a thousand apologies for this unseemly intrusion upon your tragedy, but I trust you will forgive it when you understand the importance of what I am about to say. I would not dream of commandeering your attention at such a grievous time, except in the most urgent wish to be of service to you and your family, and put you in possession of some information which I believe to be of the utmost pertinence to your present situation."

She had no patience with such garrulity, but she sat and waved him to a chair. He chose to remain standing, however, striding back and forth across the room as he gave vent to his oratory. He begged her forgiveness a dozen times, at least, so that she was forced to say wearily, "What is it you wished to say to me, Sir James?"

He looked at her speculatively. "You are betrothed to Samuel Broughton."

It was a statement, not a question, but she said, "I am."

"Then I—"

The door opened, and Henry rushed in. For the first time, Sir James's smooth composure was ruffled, and Susannah could well understand it. Henry was a careless dresser at the best of times, but today he looked as if he had just rolled from his bed and stepped into whatever clothes he had discarded the day before. And perhaps he had, at that, and his hasty entry spoke of a belligerent nature.

Sir James took a step back. "Who are you, sir?" he barked.

"Sir James, may I present to you my brother," Susannah said. "Henry, this is Sir James Strickland, who used to physic our second mama in London."

Sir James looked surprised, but perhaps he had forgotten a patient from so long ago. He made a slight bow.

Henry had no interest in such formalities. "What are you about, coming here at such a time? Who let you in, and why would you so disturb our grief on such a day? Are you not aware that our mama is this very day lost to us? Begone at once, sir!"

Sir James immediately began his apologies all over again, but Susannah could not listen to it. "Henry, Sir James is here to speak to me, and the sooner he is allowed to do so, the sooner he will be gone. Pray continue, Sir James."

Henry grouched to the window seat, and sat down, arms folded, with a huff of disapproval.

"Thank you, madam," Sir James began, although with a wary glance at Henry. "Let me be brief. The man to whom you are betrothed, Miss Winslade, has a dark history. Although to all outward appearances he is a fine young man and an accomplished physician, and no doubt is accepted as such in his new setting, there is much about him that may be told that casts him in a different light. It gives me no pleasure to say such things of one whom I regarded in the light of a son, but—"

"For heaven's sake," Henry muttered, rolling his eyes, and Susannah could only agree with him.

"If you would kindly get to the point, Sir James," she said stiffly, "for I have much to attend to today."

He gazed at her, as if trying to gauge her mood, but all his suave assurance had returned, so he made a slight inclination of the neck which might have been a bow. "I wished only to soften the impact of my words, but perhaps nothing can do so. Madam, it is my sad duty to inform you that two years ago, Samuel Broughton was tried for the murder of his wife, and her child not yet born."

The silence was absolute.

It was as well that Susannah was sitting down, for the terror that roiled at her insides would surely have brought her to the point of collapse otherwise. Murder! Yet he had not been hanged for it, or transported, so by some means it was behind him now, and naturally he would not mention such a thing in society. *'What pleasant weather we are having, and by the way, I was once tried for murder.'* No, it was understandable that he would want to leave that part of his life in the past.

But his *wife!* He had been married, and he had never told her *that*, and in some ways that disturbed her more than anything else. For a moment she was speechless, and it was left to Henry to formulate a response. He was shocked and outraged and said so, volubly and at length, and for some time Sir James allowed him to rant unchecked.

This was fortunate, for it gave Susannah time to get her disordered wits under control. By the time Sir James continued his tale, she was icy calm, and able to listen to it with every sense alert.

Sir James's only daughter, it seemed, was the lady in question, and he gave all the circumstances of her death, of how it had been assumed that it was a tragic accident when she was found dead in her bed one morning. Such things do happen, he said. But then, somehow, suspicions had been aroused... a large quantity of laudanum unaccounted for... the jealous nature of the husband... a fierce quarrel the day before. Samuel had been arrested, and brought to trial, but the jury had been inclined to be generous and he had been acquitted.

"After that, he ran away from society," Sir James said. "I lost all trace of him until just a few days ago, when I read the notice of your betrothal in the *Gazette*, Miss Winslade. Naturally, I came at once to apprise you and his benefactor of all the circumstances. You may imagine my horror on discovering that history is repeating itself, and here is another woman found mysteriously dead in her bed with no obvious cause."

That was too much for Susannah. She got to her feet and calmly smoothed her skirts. "So you think that my stepmother was murdered, do you? For what reason, sir? Why would Dr Broughton wish to murder his future mother-in-law?"

"As to his reasons, I cannot say, madam, but a man who has murdered once may the more easily turn to foul means a second time."

"You have said yourself that Dr Broughton was acquitted of murder. That makes him innocent in the eyes of the law, sir, without any stain upon his character."

"You defend him," Sir James said with a supercilious little sneer. "Your loyalty is commendable, my dear, but you may wish to consider that he never denied the charge, or made the least push to explain himself. I have wondered often why he would do so, when his life hung in the balance. I wished only to convey this information to you before you take an irrevocable step after which Broughton's disgrace would become yours and your family's, too."

"And we appreciate it," Henry cried. "Susie, you cannot marry the fellow now. It is impossible. We are deeply grateful to you, sir, for coming all this way to rescue us from disaster."

"It was the least I could do," Sir James said, with a little bow.

"Not really," Susannah said contemptuously. "You could have achieved the same effect, and more discreetly, by staying quietly at home and writing to my father, could you not?"

"Letters go astray, and one would not wish to commit such deleterious information to the mail."

"Deleterious... yes, indeed," she said, shaking with anger. "In that you are correct. Such a tale, giving only one side of the story, would indeed be harmful to the reputation of an honest professional man. And in order to ensure such information did not go astray, you leapt into your carriage and drove all the way from Hertfordshire to Shropshire, and to tell me what? That a man was accused of a crime and was subsequently acquitted of it. By what authority do you take it upon yourself to disseminate such information? Why should you assume that I am not already fully informed of all the circumstances? And you certainly have no right — not the least right in the world — to suggest that my stepmother died of anything but natural causes. You are neither her physician nor a relation, nor are you the coroner or magistrate or constable. You have no standing in Shropshire, sir. Your opinions are not welcome here, and I suggest you take yourself back to Hertfordshire immediately and meddle no more in matters that are not your concern."

The sneer strengthened. "My only concern was for your welfare, my dear. It was kindly meant, I assure you, but, having discharged my duty, I will stay no longer. Good day to you."

He strolled out of the room, shutting the door quietly behind him.

"Insufferable man!" Susannah cried.

"The fellow was a bit poker-faced, I grant you that," Henry said. "Still, Susie... *murder!*"

"He was acquitted."

"But he might still have done it, you know. People get off scot-free all the time after the most heinous of crimes."

"And he might equally well be entirely innocent, and wrongly accused. *That* happens all the time, too. Look at poor Victor

Hutchison, who was accused of murdering Lord Saxby and it was no such thing. He was nowhere near the place."

Henry shrugged. "Perhaps but still... I shall have to tell Father, Susie."

"Of course, but not today. For pity's sake, say nothing until he is more himself. Let him grieve in peace. There is no urgency about the matter, after all, for there is no question of marriage until I am out of mourning."

"There is no question of marriage at all!" Henry said sharply. "You are deranged if you still plan to marry the fellow after this. I always thought there was something havey-cavey about the business. I mean, you hardly know him, and it is not as if you are in love with him or anything of that nature, yet now you are clinging on to him for dear life, even though he murdered his wife— Yes, yes, acquitted, I know. I was not even aware he was married. It just goes to show — one can never really know a man who arrives out of nowhere."

Fortunately for Susannah's state of mind, her brother said no more on the subject and she was allowed to escape without further scrutiny. She was not sure she could hold her shattered nerves together for much longer, and if Henry had interrogated her too closely he would certainly have discovered that she knew as little of Sir James's revelations as he did.

She retreated to the safety of her studio, not to paint but to find a few minutes of solitude to recover her composure. On a normal day, this would be one of the most obvious places she would be looked for, but today was not a normal day and no one would expect her to be painting at such a time. The easel bore her most recent effort, with the bowl of fruit she had been attempting to immortalise still sitting forlornly on the table. She had never had the same success with artificial composings as with the natural world. It was so easy to sweep paint across the paper in fluid streaks — sky, clouds, the ever-shifting colours of the trees or the river. The transient beauty of a dragonfly or a ladybird could be fixed with a few dabs of the brush. But a bowl of peaches and oranges stared balefully at her, defying her to reproduce them.

There was a chaise longue under one of the skylights, and here she lay, gazing up at the clouds scudding past far above. His wife… what had she been like, his wife? Was she anything like Susannah? Had he loved his wife so much that he chose a replica for his second marriage, or had he chosen someone as unlike her as possible?

It did not matter, she decided. He was betrothed to Susannah now, and everything else was in the past. If he did not want to tell her about it, so be it. Let him keep his secrets. No one should be forced out into the open unless he wished it, and Sir James Strickland had no right at all to spread such tales about. She would not allow his malice to spoil her future.

She would marry the man she loved, and no tale from the past could stop her. She rose, straightened her spine and went downstairs to take up the reins of the household once more.

18: Beside The River

Samuel sat unmoving at his desk, just as when Dr Beasley had left him. Lassitude and despair had him in their icy grip, and he waited without impatience for his world to end. He was not sure how that would manifest itself — it might be Beasley returning to ask him to leave, or it might be a note from Susannah ending their brief engagement — but one way or another, his life here in Great Maeswood was at an end.

But nothing happened. Occasionally he caught the sound of voices, or footsteps passing his door. Once the knocker sounded and Thomas answered the door. But then the door closed and Thomas went away again. Gradually the house descended into its afternoon somnolence. The fly returned, or perhaps it was another fly, bashing itself against the glass time after time, even though just six inches lower the route to freedom could be found.

Bzzt-bzzt-bzzt.

Samuel rose, and pushed the sash window a little higher. The fly buzzed momentarily, then found its way outside again.

Escape...

Impulsively, Samuel climbed over the sill, ducked under the raised sash and jumped down into a bed of small shrubs. Within moments he was hidden by taller shrubs and could make his way unseen to the gate at the bottom of the garden. And beyond that was the path to the river and freedom.

Unlike the Sunday before last — was it really such a short time ago? — when he had followed Susannah to the river after church, there was no one else on the path today. The labourers were all hard at work tending their fields or pigpens or lathes, their wives gossiping together as they spun their wool or fed their babies. The gentry were lazing under trees, sipping lemonade. He was alone. He would always be alone, he realised. His dream of a quiet country practice, of riding about to far-flung farms and mills, with a wife and a cluster of children waiting to welcome him home each evening, was gone, the flames of his hopes doused by the cold rain of history. What would he do now? What *could* he do? Nothing... for there was nowhere he could go that was out of reach of Sir James Strickland and the story he told.

Samuel came to the place he sought, the little opening in the trees where he had sat watching Susannah bring the river alive with her paint brush, and a day later they had agreed to marry. The river was lower today, for there had been no rain, but it burbled cheerfully over the stones, running on to its inevitable destiny, to become one with the sea. Samuel's destiny was just as inevitable, it seemed. He had fallen into a dark pit, and no effort of his was sufficient to enable him to climb out again.

He was resigned. There was nothing to be done about it, so he would do nothing. He sat down, crossing his legs, and watched the river. Perhaps, if he were lucky, he would see a dragonfly or a creature walking on water, or perhaps a flash of brilliant colour would herald the kingfisher. He would like to see another kingfisher.

At some point, hours or minutes later, he could not tell, Mac found him.

"Sam, are ye—?"

"Go away," he said tiredly.

"Will ye no—?"

"For the love of God, leave me alone!"

Mac went away, and there was blessed peace again, the only sound the never-ending murmur of the river and the susurration of the trees above and behind him. That was one comfort, that the trees hid him, keeping him invisible from the path. No one would disturb his solitude who did not already know the place.

It seemed a long while later when Susannah came, but by then he had lost all sense of time. One moment he was alone, and the next she was there, sitting beside him, her arms around her knees, gazing out at the river just as he had been. She was without bonnet or gloves, as if she had simply run out of the house. And she said nothing. That was a mercy at least. So he said nothing, too, and for a long, long time they sat thus side by side, unmoving, unspeaking, like two statues.

But still her presence was an intrusion. He could not think his thoughts in comfort while she was there. Somehow, even though she said nothing and never even moved, she was a distraction, dragging him back into the miserable world against his will.

"Why are you here?" He had grown so accustomed to the silence that his voice sounded harsh.

"Because Mac asked me to come," she said. That took him by surprise. No sympathy, no accusations, no spurious attempt to justify herself. "He told me you shouted at him, and he thought perhaps you would not shout at me. Frankly, I do not care if you shout at me or not."

She was not looking at him, her gaze still fixed on the river, but he could see the smile playing about her lips. He could not make her out. Perhaps she did not yet know…

"Did Strickland come to see you?"

"Oh yes." She turned now to face him, and those clear grey eyes took his breath away. "He regaled me at tedious length with some history of yours, but why he should take it upon himself to do so is more than I know."

"He plans to destroy me," Samuel said despairingly.

"And do you plan to let him?"

"How can I prevent him? He has done it once and he can do it again. He will destroy everything and I will have nothing."

"Not quite nothing," she said fiercely. "You will still have *me*. Not even Sir James Strickland can tear me away from you." While he was still catching his breath from such openness, she went on, "Samuel, I have known what I wanted for a very long time, so that when it came within my reach I was prepared to fight for it. Now I will fight to keep it — to keep *you*. Whatever happens here as a consequence of Sir James's interference, we must stay together. We can start again… move to another part of the country… go abroad, perhaps. America! There must be a need for physicians there."

"My reputation will follow me."

Stranger at the Villa: Strangers Book 3

"Is there nothing you will fight for? What do you want more than anything else in the world?"

"Another child," he shot back, unthinking. The shock in her face stunned him. "You did not know?" She shook her head. "No, I suppose he would not tell you *that*."

"That you had a child? No. A son? Or a daughter?"

He breathed hard to fight down the pain, the unbearable *desolation* that rushed up inside him, threatening to drown out every rational thought. He could not think of her without feeling as if his very heart had been ripped from his body, and the world pressed down on him. His eyes closed, screwed tightly shut. He was in that dark place again, with an entire mountain bearing down on him, suffocating him, choking him... He could not breathe... could not breathe...

Her hand was cool against his cheek. She said nothing, for what was there to say, after all? But the touch of her hand reached something inside him, something leaden and dark, that had sucked all the life from him for years. Her unquestioning faith in him had the power to dissolve it. To his astonishment, he felt scalding tears coursing down his cheeks. He had never cried before, not once, but now that he had started, he sobbed uncontrollably.

Susannah took him in her arms, enfolding him against her breast as if he were a child, stroking his hair and rocking him gently. Gradually he became aware of gentle kisses on his hair, then his forehead, his cheeks. Kisses... how he wanted her kisses!

His lips sought hers hungrily and she melted into him as if she belonged there, kissing him back just as fiercely. Where had that need come from? For himself, he had long yearned for the warmth of a womanly body in his arms again, for softness and the gentle yielding nature of the female sex, but he had never expected passion in return, and not from the practical Susannah Winslade. Her warmth fanned the flames of his ardour and he could not get enough of her.

Eventually, good sense pulled him away from her. "I... beg your pardon. I allowed my enthusiasm to get the better of me."

"Do not apologise," she said, rather breathlessly. "Your enthusiasm was delightful."

Somehow they had fallen onto the grass, so she lay on her back smiling up at him. Her hair had come loose and one stray curl had broken free. It taunted him, that tantalising curl, drawing him closer, daring him to touch it...

He jerked away from her, disgusted with himself and with her. "Do not say such things!" he said, his voice harsh. "You should not— The fault was mine, but— It is not ladylike to behave so... to *enjoy* that."

She sat up, staring at him with those clear, guileless eyes, filled with hurt now. "Not enjoy kissing the man who is to be my husband? Would you have me push you away?"

"Yes! A respectable woman would have more decorum than to behave so."

"Oh, am I not respectable now? May I remind you, sir, that you were the one who began it."

"I was... carried away by my emotions," he said. "I have apologised for my weakness. It was wrong of me, and will not happen again."

"Samuel, what is the matter with you?" she cried. "You have endured the most abominable trials of your fortitude, and survived with your head high. Now all that is threatened. Of course you are emotional! And what more natural than to seek a little comfort? We all need affection in our lives, and that is not weakness but part of what makes us human."

She made it seem so normal, yet every part of him rebelled at the thought. She was wrong... she must be wrong! He could only shake his head in disbelief.

"Why do you say such things?" he whispered. "That is precisely what separates us from the beasts, that we are capable of higher thought and reining in our baser impulses."

"And we are also capable of great love!" she cried. "*That* is what distinguishes mankind, the ability to love another person more than oneself. Samuel, I do not ask for affection from you if that is not in your nature, but you must allow me my own feelings for you. I cannot be — have never been — indifferent to you."

"But you barely know me," he said, bewildered.

"I know you better than you might suppose. When I was fourteen, I went to London with my second mama. She had no children, and it grieved her greatly, so every so often she consulted with an eminent physician in London who specialised in female problems."

"Sir James," he said, lifting his head to look at her.

She nodded. "Sometimes she took me with her, and on the last occasion, when I was fourteen, we were both invited to dine with him. So there I was, on my very best behaviour, in a brand new gown for the occasion and my hair up that evening for the first time ever, trying to pretend I dined in such distinguished company every night. At table, I was seated next to one of the young physicians Sir James was helping to train. He was very kind to a little girl from a distant county, helping me to the best dishes and reminding me, very surreptitiously, which cutlery and glasses to use when I hesitated, and after dinner he taught me to play backgammon. He was very patient, for I confess I was not an apt pupil. I have never forgotten his kindness, nor his honey-coloured hair." She smiled, one hand reaching up to stroke Samuel's hair. "Then there was the way his eyes lit up whenever he smiled — and he smiled a great deal. He became my ideal gentleman, a pattern-card of just the sort of man I should like to marry, if ever such a one should appear in this remote corner of the kingdom. And then one day — there he was. A little older, a little more serious, but just as handsome and kind and gentlemanly. Do you blame me for throwing myself at your head at the first opportunity, Samuel?"

"I do not remember you at all," he said, wonderingly. "I wish I could, but my memory is entirely blank."

"Well, I am very forgettable," she said, laughing. Before he could protest, she said, "So now you know how it was that I knew exactly what I wanted, and why I can kiss you without reserve. I cannot be reserved, Samuel, not with you. You mean too much to me."

Her words moved him. There was something powerful in the simplicity of her position, and the heartfelt openness of her manner. He could not like her passion, for it was hardly chaste, but he could not deny the truth of her ideas. *'That is what distinguishes mankind, the ability to love another person more than oneself,'* she had said, and that was undeniably true, for he had experienced it himself. Could he reach out to her, too? Surely she deserved the truth, or as much of it as he could manage.

"Cressida," he said, his voice no more than a whisper. "Her name… Cressy."

She was alert at once. "What happened to her?"

"He took her. Strickland."

"Oh. I suppose she is his granddaughter."

"I was in prison for almost a month, awaiting my trial. When I came out, she was gone. Everything was gone — my house was stripped to the bare boards, all my books, everything that was not locked away in the safe. And my daughter."

He wanted to say more, to explain her sweet childish innocence, her smiling face, her glowing golden hair... but he could not. Grief and loss overwhelmed him, and he lowered his head and wept softly again.

Susannah understood. She did not press him, but pulled his hand to her lips and kissed the palm, a gentle kiss of sympathy. Of trust. Of love...

He looked up at her in astonishment, this woman who had fallen accidentally into his life. What had she done to him? His grief was still there, for nothing could wash it away, but somehow he could now face the future with... well, not optimism, exactly, but perhaps with resignation. With acceptance. Whatever horror was yet to come, he could accept it because she would be beside him. She had reached out her hand to him, and drawn him back from the abyss of despair.

"I believe I should go home," he said slowly. "Dr and Miss Beasley are considering my future, and it will look very bad if they realise I climbed out of the window to escape."

She laughed. "Did you so? Good gracious, how rebellious of you, although I confess I have often wanted to do the same."

"Why did you not?" he said, mesmerised by these confessions. "Oh, but you are not a coward like I am. You stood your ground and fought your corner, I suppose."

"Not at all, I should have done so in an instant, had not my skirts hampered me. Long skirts are such a trial, you have no idea. Instead, I tend to run away and hide somewhere in the house. It used to be the attics, but nowadays my painting studio is my refuge." He offered her a hand to help her to her feet. As she brushed down her skirts, she said, "Will you be all right? You are not a coward, you know, just a little backwards in coming forwards."

"You do not blame me, then, for not telling you about... well, everything?"

"It is your story to tell or not, as you please, and it is no one else's concern. Naturally I hope you will tell me the full story one day, but I shall never ask it of you. Samuel..." She gazed up at him with limpid-clear eyes. "It is not in your nature to fight for yourself, I can see that, but I hope you will always hold your head high. You have done nothing wrong, after all."

"You cannot possibly be sure of that," he said. "Just because I was acquitted—"

"True, but you told me yourself that your conscience was clear. You said, *'When the storm clouds break, that is the one thing that allows a man to keep his hold on sanity, knowing that he did nothing wrong'*, do you remember? So I never doubted it. Besides, your wife was with child when she died, and you would never, ever have killed a child. So remember that you have done nothing wrong, and that you will always have my love, and let that carry you through whatever trials lie ahead."

Samuel could say nothing, rendered speechless by her indomitable spirit and uplifted by her buoyant optimism. And her love! She loved him, and was open enough to say so to his face, wanting nothing in return. Such unwavering support humbled him. He kissed her hands and then, very gently, her lips, and watched her walk away from him.

When he turned to begin the walk back to Great Maeswood, he found Mac waiting beside his horse, a huge grin splitting his face.

"See? Ye like her. Told ye so."

"You are an impertinent scoundrel, and you may return to Edinburgh any time you wish."

"Nae, ye'd miss me if I went."

"Heaven help me, I probably would," Samuel said, as they began the walk back. "Thank you for fetching Miss Winslade."

"It helped?"

"Yes, it helped, although there was no need to panic. I was not about to do anything stupid, like throw myself in the river."

"Nae, ye'd have tae be awful clever to drown yeself in a foot of water, right enough." The Scotsman chuckled, then said soberly, "Glad ye's all right, Sam. Had me worried again for a while there."

When he reached Whitfield Villa, Samuel went in through the front door, noticing at once that Dr Beasley's book room door stood wide open.

"Broughton, there you are," Beasley called, obviously watching for him. "Come in, will you, and shut the door."

Samuel had prudently asked Mac to straighten his neckcloth for him before they reached the house, but he still felt a trifle dishevelled. He wondered if he had grass stains on his breeches.

Miss Beasley was in the book room, too, her face serious, and his heart plummeted again. This was not going to be pleasant.

"Sit down, my boy," Beasley said. "Yes, sit beside Phyllida there. Madeira? That is your favourite, I think. Now then, we have been talking... discussing it all, you know, and I have apprised Phyllida of everything that Strickland said, for I felt it only fair that she should know, since you both live in the same house. I will not deny, it is a disturbing story, very disturbing. We have talked it up and down and roundabout, and we have come to a conclusion."

Samuel took a sip of Madeira, and then, because he felt he would need it, a second, larger draught.

"Samuel, my dear boy, what a dreadful business for you," Beasley said. "To be accused of murder — and of your own wife, too! It hardly bears thinking about."

"And a child coming, too," Miss Beasley said, her voice high with distress. "How you must have felt it!"

He felt as if all the air had been sucked out of his lungs. Sympathy was the last reaction he had expected.

"I have been trying to remember the case," Beasley went on. "It was extensively reported in the London newspapers, and I followed it with interest at the time, although I had forgotten your name. Every medical man has fears of just such a situation, of being accused of murder, either by commission or omission. It is a risk we all take every day. What struck me at the time were two factors — firstly, that you made no attempt to answer the charges made against you, and secondly, the number of very eminent people who spoke on your behalf. Clearly, you had many friends in society, powerful friends, and that spoke well of your character. In fact, now that we know you, we both felt that the story did not fit you at all. Sir James talked of a violent quarrel, and jealousy, and we cannot see the least sign of that in you."

"No, not at all," Miss Beasley said. "You have such a calm nature, Dr Broughton. Even when Thomas spilt soup on you the other day, you showed not the least vexation with him. You joked about it with him, as I recall, although he was most distressed and offered his resignation the very next day."

"And then McNair's recommendation weighs heavily with me," Beasley said. "I asked for a competent physician and a good Christian, and most particularly the latter, and he sent you, which is good enough for me."

"We can see that you are a good Christian," Miss Beasley said, "for you have no hesitation in saying the Grace when we ask, and you never show the least sign of impatience with my Bible readings. You even said, if you remember, how pleasant it was to be in a household where the proper observances were maintained. That is what weighs with me, Dr Broughton, so for myself, I do not think you can have done anything very wrong, or if you have, you have repented of it, and therefore God has forgiven you."

"And whatever God may say about the matter," Beasley said, "a jury of your peers deemed you innocent of the crime of which you were accused, and that is good enough for me. You have our trust, Samuel, and so we go on exactly as before."

Samuel was so overcome that he could only say, "Thank you, and God bless you both."

19: Dinner At The Dower House

'The Dower House, 15th July. Dr Broughton, I am aware that your day has been a heavy one, and you may wish to remain quietly at home tonight. If so I will completely understand. However, there are some matters which I would very much like to discuss with you at the earliest opportunity. If you would care to dine with us at the Dower House tonight at six, that would be most helpful, and I believe you will not be disappointed in Mrs Edgerton's cook. Yours, Captain Michael Edgerton.'

~~~~~

Samuel would indeed have preferred to stay quietly at home that evening, but he suspected that the captain would quietly pester him until he complied, so it was as well to get it over with as soon as possible. Besides, it would be enough of a distraction to prevent him from brooding. He was no longer gripped by despair, since Susannah and the Beasleys had all declared that they would stand by him, but that did not mean that the affair was over. Sir James would spread his poison widely, and all the patronage he had been so assiduously cultivating amongst the gentry of Market Clunbury would trickle away to nothing. He might yet be ruined, and then the Beasleys' support would avail him nothing. And how then could he marry

Susannah? Her optimism was uplifting but he had to have an income to support a wife.

He was still sunk in gloom, therefore, and very ready to be diverted when he walked the short distance to the Dower House. There were four people awaiting him in the drawing room, for Chandry had gone back to his post at the Market Clunbury house. Mrs Edgerton greeted him graciously, the only lady present. Captain Edgerton was at his most urbane as host. Samuel also remembered Mr Willerton-Forbes, the stylish London lawyer. The fourth was new to him, a small, unobtrusive man by the name of Neate.

"We have not met before, I think?" Samuel said. "Are you new to the village, Mr Neate?"

"No, but I am very pleased you should think so," he said enigmatically, and Samuel was too polite to enquire what he meant.

The dinner was excellent, and considerably more adventurous than the simple roasts and vegetables that the Beasleys' cook produced. Samuel had no hesitation in praising the food effusively.

"Mrs Edgerton's cook trained under a French man-cook," Edgerton said rather smugly. "She is not quite as accomplished as Mrs Gage's man-cook, but Luce is working on that."

"Chambers has very kindly agreed to teach her some of his more unusual receipts," Mrs Edgerton said. "Well, gentlemen, I know you are wishing me away so that you can discuss your little intrigues with Dr Broughton, so I shall leave you to the port. Do not rush, for I have reached a most exciting part in the novel I am reading and will not thank you to be dragged away from it, I assure you."

The gentlemen all rose as she left the room, and then resettled themselves, moving chairs nearer to the captain's end of the table.

"'*Our little intrigues*', indeed," Edgerton said, with an affectionate smile. "We are solving murders and righting wrongs and bringing the wicked to justice, but to Luce, they are nothing but little intrigues, mild amusements to while away the time."

"It is unfortunate," Willerton-Forbes said, "that we are so often obliged to withhold the details of some of our successes. There are times, Dr Broughton, when we cannot reveal the truth, even when we are quite sure of it."

"Is that a matter of discretion?" Samuel said.

"Indeed. Naturally, if we uncover a crime and there is a reasonable chance of obtaining justice, we will follow that course, but sometimes there is no possibility of justice without causing great tragedy for good people. In such cases, we will be discreet."

"It goes against the grain, sometimes, to see villains get away with their wickedness," Edgerton said, frowning.

"But it is for the best, Michael," Willerton-Forbes said gently. "And if one investigation ends unsatisfactorily, there is always another, with the chance of a better outcome."

"You are finding plenty to occupy you?" Samuel said. "Even in a village as small as this?"

"It is astonishing how much wickedness there may be in a small village," Willerton-Forbes said, smiling. "When we first came here in March to uncover the mystery of the long-dead lady in the wine cellar of this very house, we little thought we would still be finding new mysteries all these months later, but so it is."

"Mysteries? Plural?" Samuel said, amused. "So you are not just talking about the missing Lucas Renshaw, then?"

"No indeed," Edgerton said. "There was the French maid, Marie Fournier, first, and then a secret project, which we cannot mention, and then Renshaw, which led us to the mysterious wine business being operated from the cellar of your house in Market Clunbury, Broughton. Oh, and Willerton-Forbes had a notable success with Mr Gage's financial affairs. That was an impressive series of enquiries, Pettigrew."

Willerton-Forbes half rose and made his friend a bow.

"And then... there are my coincidences," Edgerton said.

"I was afraid we would come to that," Samuel said. "I applaud your inventiveness, Captain, but I cannot accept that there is any connection between the deaths of Mrs Cokely and Mrs Winslade, and whatever is going on in Market Clunbury."

"You may be correct," Edgerton said. "But hear me out, Broughton. You asked Neate if he were new to the village. He is not, but you have never noticed him before tonight, and that is precisely his part in the workings of Edgerton, Chandry and Associates. He remains unobtrusive, and has a happy knack of blending into any setting almost invisibly. Even tonight, when he was seated beside you, I daresay you cannot recall of what he spoke."

"Of course I can," Samuel said, and immediately tried to think of a topic. "Well..."

"Exactly so," Edgerton said, eyes twinkling. "He is excessively useful to us, for he can pass equally well as a servant or a gentleman, merely by some alteration of attire and voice."

"This is my normal voice, the one I use when I am being a lawyer," Neate said, "or I can sound like a very superior gentleman's gentleman, like this, or maybe I can be an ostler, straight from the farm."

Samuel laughed at the rapid changes of accent. "That is very impressive."

"But most of all, he can blend in with the locals," Edgerton said. "His job since we arrived here has been to talk to the servants, and make himself known at the inn here, and also at Astley Cloverstone and in Market Clunbury. So it is that he discovered that a man called Wilkinson arrived on the mail coach from London on Saturday last, and put up at the Cross Keys at Astley Cloverstone. Almost a week later, on Thursday night, Mrs Cokely died. On Friday night, Mrs Winslade died, and Chandry bumped into an intruder in Market Clunbury. And on Saturday morning, Wilkinson was found to have vanished, without paying his shot, I might add."

"Coincidence," Samuel said, shaking his head.

"And I might even agree with you on this occasion, except for one small fact," Edgerton said. "When he first arrived, Wilkinson loitered in the tap room for much of each day, buying ale for anyone who would sit and talk to him, and asking a lot of questions. Some of the questions were the sort anyone new to the area would ask — were there any good walks, was it profitable hunting country, what the nearby villages were like, that sort of thing. But he also asked about a physician. He had a sore knee after a long walk, and he wanted it seen to. There's a surgeon-apothecary in Astley Cloverstone, but that wasn't good enough for him. He said he wanted a proper physician, London trained. So he was given your name. You might even have treated him."

"Not by that name, certainly."

"He is a small man, smaller than Edgerton, and wiry," Neate said.

"Still no," Samuel said.

"He asked a great deal about you, seemingly, and about the patients you were treating," Neate said. "He was interested in Dr Beasley, too, and how you came to be working with him, and how long you had been here, but mainly it was about your patients."

"And Mrs Winslade was mentioned, I suppose?" Samuel said, caught up in the story.

"She was. Not Mrs Cokely, that I can find out, but he was very, very interested in Mrs Winslade, and he took off as soon as she was dead."

"Forgive my cynicism, gentlemen," Samuel said, "but it all seems rather a stretch to me. Wilkinson certainly seems like a suspicious character, but why he would wish to murder Mrs Winslade is beyond my ability to fathom, or yours, I suspect."

Captain Edgerton was about to speak, but Mr Willerton-Forbes waved him to silence. "Wilkinson's behaviour is certainly curious, but it is Sir James Strickland who interests me most. Why is he here? That is the question I ask myself. Clearly he felt compelled to come here and tell his story, a story which, not to put too fine a point on it, would blacken your reputation, Dr Broughton. And I wonder very much why he should do that. Can you shed any light on the matter?"

Samuel felt trapped. The room was hot, too hot even though all the windows were opened wide to the evening air. He tugged at his neckcloth. How could he answer? Could he even bring himself to speak of it?

"I beg your pardon for raising what must be a terribly difficult subject for you," Willerton-Forbes said, his voice sympathetic. "You need say nothing if it distresses you. Let me instead tell you what I know of the matter, but you may stop me at once if I step too far."

He paused expectantly, but Samuel was paralysed, unable to speak of it, but equally unable to prevent the lawyer from saying whatever he wished. If he were checked now, he would only talk about it to his friends later — may already have done so, in fact. It was better to know what they were saying of him.

Tentatively, Willerton-Forbes went on, "It was Strickland's daughter to whom you were married and of whose murder you stood accused, and were ultimately acquitted. He, in fact, was the one who pursued the accusation, when the suspicions of the servants were aroused. One might speculate, therefore, that he felt some... resentment, shall we say. That he held you responsible in some way for the death of his daughter and the child she carried, even though the law said otherwise. He may have felt, perhaps that you had got off too lightly."

"Too lightly!" Samuel said, stung into a response. "When I lost everything? *Everything!*"

"Except your life," Edgerton said savagely, "and your ability to make a living. That is what outrages him the most, I suspect, that you are not hanged or transported or, at the very least, starving in a ditch somewhere, but still practising medicine and about to marry the squire's daughter. I know nothing at all of Strickland, but I do not like him coming here in all his pompous glory and spreading malicious tales about you."

"Michael, Michael," Willerton-Forbes said gently. "We must be objective, remember? It is not our place to take sides, only to attempt to understand, to make deductions, and to correct clear injustices, where we find them."

"But this *is* an injustice!" Edgerton said. "To come here and denigrate an innocent man, an *honourable* man, to try to damage his livelihood, is unconscionable. Surely you agree, Pettigrew?"

"Again, you are taking sides," Willerton-Forbes said. "Try to think like a lawyer, Michael. We know nothing of innocence or honour, for we cannot read the heart of any man. Which of us can? All we have are facts, and I do not imagine that Sir James said anything of Dr Broughton that was untrue, only that he was accused of a great crime but he was tried under the law and acquitted. There is no injustice in that, quite the reverse. I remember something of the case, for one of my chamber's most accomplished barristers acted for the defence — Sir Edward Browning. Do you remember him, Dr Broughton?"

"I do. He was most impressive, and I was very grateful for his good offices. I never quite knew how he came to be assigned to me, for I did not know him at all."

"Oh, let us say that you have friends who are well-situated to arrange such matters," Willerton-Forbes said, with a little smile.

Samuel understood the allusion, and said no more. He had no idea who the well-situated friend might be, but he was painfully aware of his existence.

"Even if every word is true," Edgerton said mulishly, "that does not mean it is Strickland's place to tell the world of it."

"It is public knowledge," Willerton-Forbes said. "Anyone may go to the newspaper offices and read the reports of it. Sooner or later, word would have got about. Sir James merely ensured that it was sooner rather than later. His intentions might indeed be malicious, but equally he might wish only to issue a warning, from genuine concern. We cannot tell. But on one point I agree with you, Michael. I do not think it is mere coincidence that Wilkinson and Sir James have arrived here just now. The notice of Dr Broughton's engagement was in last Friday's *Gazette.* Wilkinson would have caught the mail coach on that same Friday evening. Sir James travelled more decorously in his own coach, arriving only yesterday. Both, I suspect, came with the same aim, to blacken your reputation, Dr Broughton, Sir James by rumour and Wilkinson more directly."

"Perhaps they are in league together!" Edgerton cried triumphantly. "Wilkinson is an assassin engaged by Strickland!"

"Michael," Willerton-Forbes said sadly. "You allow your imagination to run away with you. Sir James Strickland is a baronet with an estate in Hertfordshire, and a very distinguished physician. He is hardly likely to engage an assassin, and if he had done so, he would not then come here himself."

"Why would anyone engage an assassin against Mrs Winslade?" Samuel said.

There was a long silence.

"It is irrelevant at this juncture," Willerton-Forbes said, with an airy wave of one hand. "Our first priority, I feel, must be to determine if it was possible that Mrs Winslade was murdered. Dr Broughton, you have helpfully shown that there was no excess of laudanum consumed. We may reasonably exclude poison, for there would surely have been signs of it — vomiting, for instance. There was presumably no sign of injury or it would have been remarked upon. The obvious method that springs to mind is suffocation. A frail lady, perhaps fast asleep under the influence of a modest dose of laudanum, a pillow over the face? What do you say, Dr Broughton? Would such a thing be possible?"

Samuel's mind rebelled furiously at any suggestion of murder, but his medical training bubbled to the fore. "It would be possible, yes. Mrs Winslade was a delicate little woman, and her illness had robbed her of any strength. Taken by surprise while sleeping, she would have been quite unable to put up a fight, so there would be no sign of resistance. Yes, it would be possible. And if you want to expand the conspiracy, Mrs Cokely would have been just as easy to kill by that method."

Edgerton laughed. "Now you are getting into the spirit of it, Broughton! I cannot see any motive for anyone to kill Mrs Cokely however."

Samuel froze. "And you can for Mrs Winslade?"

"Certainly. Mrs Winslade was your patient and not expected to die for a long while yet, so people are bound to wonder at a sudden death, and whether there was something amiss in the treatment you prescribed. A vindictive person might want to kill her purely to make mischief for you. You will be pleased to know that I cannot consider it likely that you killed Mrs Winslade yourself. It would require a plausible reason for *why* you might have murdered your prospective mother-in-law, and I confess myself at a loss there. I would have said, myself, that Squire Winslade had the best motive for killing her, if killed she was. Or even Miss Winslade, perhaps. Not that I think such a thing for a moment, but one could make a case against either of them."

Samuel said nothing. He could devise motives for all three of them, if he set his mind to it. He might have murdered Mrs Winslade to set Susannah free to leave the Manor, or she might have done it herself for the same reason. Or the squire, driven by his wife's lingering illness to seek comfort in the wrong arms might have wished to free himself. If Edgerton knew of the quarrel with Susannah, or of the squire's behaviour, he would not dismiss the possibility so lightly.

"It is unlikely, however," Willerton-Forbes said. "Wilkinson is definitely the most plausible villain, but if his actions are aimed against you, Dr Broughton, then it can only be connected to your life before you came to Great Maeswood. If we are to investigate this affair properly, as we should like, it will mean a certain amount of raking up the past. You may be assured that we will be very, very discreet, but it would help us considerably if you would furnish us with a list of your friends in London to whom we may apply for information."

Raking up the past... He shivered. What good did it do? It would not bring Corinna back, nor Cressy, either. But if Mrs Winslade had indeed been murdered, he owed it to Susannah and all her family to help bring her murderer to justice.

He nodded. "I will help as best I can. Just do not ask me to talk about it, for I cannot. I can never talk about it."

"We understand," Willerton-Forbes said.

Samuel was quite sure that they did not.

20: *Nothing To Say*

Sunday was a blessed day of peace. Samuel was woken by Mac at his normal hour, with no urgent summons to an unexpected death. He set off for church with Dr Beasley on one side of him, and Miss Beasley on the other, like guards. At the Villa gate, they found quite a crowd loitering, with Captain Edgerton foremost among them, but also Mr Edser, several of the Gage family, and a great number of servants. They all crossed the road to the church in a body, surprising Mr Truman, who was used to his parishioners arriving in a steady stream, not a flood.

Susannah was not there, of course, nor was Miss Cokely. It was too soon after their bereavements. But Mr Truman gave a fine stirring speech about the shortness of life and the need to make each moment count, with which sentiments Samuel could heartily concur. He had to seize the opportunities before him, and not allow himself to be buffeted by the vicissitudes of life, although such a resolution was more easily made than kept.

After the service, Samuel found himself surrounded by people who wanted to shake his hand and tell him that they had a game knee or a touch of belly ache or trouble sleeping, and would be calling upon him at the earliest opportunity. No one mentioned

Strickland or London or murdered wives. He was touched by their loyalty to one who was, after all, a stranger in their midst.

Once he could escape his well-wishers, he set off along the path to Cloverstone Manor. Two weeks ago, he had followed Susannah this way to settle their future. One week ago, he had walked by her side and spent a happy day at the Manor, seeing in the squire's large family a glimpse of his own future. But that seemed far in the past now, for it was before he had quarrelled with Susannah. Before the deaths. Before Strickland.

Now he was despondent for the future. No matter that the Beasleys still believed in him, or the whole village for that matter, Strickland's poison would undoubtedly spread. People would wonder about him, and talk, and every little mishap — a wound that failed to heal aright, or fever that could not be abated — would be set at his door, and his patients would drift away from him.

Then there was Susannah. They had patched up their differences, but there was still a gulf between them. Where they would live was not yet settled, and might always be a matter of contention between them. That was the trouble with hastening into a betrothal when they knew nothing about each other. There was always the risk of an unpleasant discovery — such as finding out that one's future husband had been accused of murdering his wife, for instance. She had seemed to accept that with equanimity, but what must she feel inside? Could she ever truly trust him?

As for her unexpected response to his kisses, he was no longer sure what he thought about that. In his mind he was quite certain that a properly brought up young lady should be more demure, but he could not deny that he had enjoyed her passionate response greatly. So much so that he could barely stop thinking about her, and wondering if, after scolding her soundly for her exuberance, she would permit him to repeat the occurrence.

It was fortunate that he had no time to brood on the walk to the Manor, for Captain Edgerton strode along beside him, on his way to make enquiries about the death of Mrs Winslade.

"Very discreet, naturally," he assured Samuel. "We have no wish to add to the family's distress. If Miss Winslade should ask about it, pray tell her that we are ensuring that nothing untoward could have occurred. Just as you checked the laudanum, so we need to check that no intruder might have entered the room."

"But that is not quite true, is it?" Samuel said. "You *do* think an intruder entered."

"I think it possible, yes, but I should be relieved to be proved wrong. We will make some enquiries about the servants, too, although trouble from that quarter seems unlikely. In fact, murder seems unlikely altogether. Still, we have to check every possibility."

"Are your associates not engaged on this enterprise? Mr Willerton-Forbes was not in church this morning. I hope he is not unwell."

"No, no, nothing ever ails Pettigrew. He has gone haring off to London, about the matter we discussed last night. Could not even wait out the Sabbath, which displeased the pious Mr Truman, I believe."

"And Mr Neate? I saw him in church, but he is not here now."

Edgerton grinned. "Ah, but that is because he is walking with the Manor servants up ahead of us. He will sit in the servants' hall and find out if anyone noticed anything odd that night, or in the few days before that. Servants notice all sorts of things that their masters and mistresses would not see — a stranger loitering in the grounds, for instance, or someone asking questions. I assume no one asked you any unusual questions, Broughton? Did anything happen in the past week that seemed odd to you?"

"Nothing at all, but then I have not been here long enough to know what is odd and what is perfectly normal," Samuel said. "I do not have your eye for such things, and thereby assume that everything is normal."

"Ah yes, I see trouble everywhere, and you see it nowhere," Edgerton said lightly.

"Yet it finds me anyway," Samuel said sombrely.

At the Manor they separated, Edgerton to examine the outside of the building for possible points of entry for a murderer, and Samuel to find Susannah. He was diverted from this objective by Binns.

"The master would like a few words with you, sir, if you would be so good."

"Of course."

He followed in the butler's slow, unsteady wake, although he knew the way well enough by now. The squire was, as usual, pacing about his book room, a glass in one hand, as if he could not bear to be still. His desk was always heaped high with papers, but Samuel had never seen him working there, and the piles never seemed to reduce.

"There you are, Broughton. Knew you would be here today. Yes, yes, Binns, you may go away. We shall not need you. Off you go now."

"Good day, sir," Samuel said, with a polite bow. "No recurrence of your trouble, I hope?"

"What? Oh, that... no, no, you fixed me up very well, I must say. Nothing wrong with your skills in medical matters, anyway."

"Is it about Mrs Winslade? I have not yet offered my condolences—"

"Never mind that!" the squire snapped. "I hear the most dreadful rumours of you, Broughton, that you murdered your wife, for heaven's sake! Murdered her, in cold blood! Now I am sure there is no truth in any of it, but I have to consider Susannah. What do you say to all this nonsense, eh?"

Samuel did not pause to consider his reply. "I have nothing to say to it."

"Nothing? *Nothing?* You are accused of murder and you say nothing? An honest man would proclaim his innocence from the rooftops."

"So would a dishonest one."

"Eh? Oh, that is meant to be clever, I suppose. But this is not the time to play with words, Broughton. If you want to marry my daughter, I shall want an assurance that she is not going to be murdered in her bed. Tell me the truth at once, did you or did you not murder your wife?"

"Squire, I have no intention of answering such a question. You are free to believe whatever you want of me, as is Miss Winslade."

"Well, that is not good enough, sir! Not nearly good enough! I will not have it, do you hear? I will not have you marrying my daughter when you cannot even answer a straightforward question like a gentleman."

"It is hardly gentlemanly to ask a man if he committed murder, sir."

"Do you dare to bandy words with me, you young jackanapes? It is intolerable! Get out of my house, and do not come back. I never want to see you again, you impudent scoundrel!"

"As you wish, sir. May I see Miss Winslade before I leave?"

"No, you may not! Get out this minute! Go on, out!"

Samuel bowed, not offended by the squire's bluster, and making due allowance for his state of mind only a day after his wife had died. He would come to a more rational attitude in time, he was sure, and if he did not, it hardly mattered, for Susannah was of age and might marry to please herself.

Finding Binns lurking outside the book room door, Samuel was escorted out, where he at once saw Captain Edgerton, his coat off, surrounded by a little group of grooms and gardeners, all looking up at the ivy-covered wall.

"Now what are you about, Edgerton?" Samuel said.

"Proving that it would be easy to effect an illicit entry," he said, with a grin. "Either that or breaking my neck, one or the other."

And with that, he launched himself at the ivy, and climbed, slowly and steadily, towards an upper floor, where a casement window stood wide open. He got about half way up when a branch detached itself from the wall, and left the captain dangling by one arm, as the watching crowd gasped. Undeterred, Edgerton found some solid footholds and continued up. A branch broke with a loud snap, and this time there was no foothold to be found. Using only his arms, the captain inched his way downwards again. It seemed a very long time before he had both feet on solid ground again.

"Hmm, he would have to be lighter than I am, and very agile," he said thoughtfully.

"Even if you had succeeded, the gap between the mullion and the window frame is very narrow," Samuel said.

"Oh yes, I could not have effected an entry there, I am not slender enough. It was more a question of demonstrating the possibility, but I believe now that only a monkey could do it. What a pity. Still it was fun trying."

"Does Mrs Edgerton know what you get up to during your investigations?" Samuel said.

Edgerton only grinned. "I wonder what the possibilities are at the back of the house."

Samuel left him to it, and walked home.

~~~~~

"Henry should not have told you anything about it," Susannah said, trying not very successfully to keep her anger in check. "We agreed that we would not trouble you at a time when—"

"Not trouble me? When my own daughter is about to marry a wife-murderer?"

"Now, Papa, it is no such thing. He was tried in a court of law and acquitted, which means—"

"Tried, was he? And acquitted? Hmm, I wonder Henry did not tell me *that*. Well, I shall talk to Strickland about it, if he is still here. I have sent a note down to the Boar's Head asking him to call upon me, and I shall see what he has to say about it, for I got nothing out of Broughton, nothing at all. He looked me in the eye, as cool as you please, and told me I was free to believe whatever I liked, but he would never talk about it. He must have talked about it before his trial, so why not say as much to me?"

"But he did not, Papa. He cannot bring himself to speak of it. You can surely imagine how he must feel, to lose his wife and then to be accused of murder. How he must have suffered!"

Her father took a long draught of wine, then recommenced to pace about the book room. "I do understand that, daughter. It must have been a dreadful business, if he were innocent. But if he were not... Do you see my predicament? How can I permit you to marry him when I might be handing you over to a murderer?"

"Papa," she said cajolingly, "remember that I am of age, and free to make my own decisions. It is my choice to marry Dr Broughton, and I have no doubt that he is an honourable man who would never hurt anyone. He is a physician, after all, dedicated to healing."

"You are a woman, swept by emotion, and therefore not rational. It is for me, as your father, to advise you on the suitability of those who would marry you."

"Advise, certainly," she said, giving it up and tackling him head on. "But you have no power to forbid it."

"No, but I can forbid him from coming here with his smooth ways to seduce you, and I have done so. He is forbidden this house, until such time as he can be open with me."

~~~~~

'12 Chester Road, Market Clunbury, 22nd July. My dear Susannah, I hope you are all well, and not overwhelmed by your tragedy. It saddens me more than I can say to be banished from your gentle company, especially at such a time when I might hope to be of some

small comfort to you in your grief. However, your father has not forbidden me from writing to you, so with humble heart I send this missive to you in the hope of raising your spirits somewhat. If I transgress, I beg your forgiveness and if no reply is received shall importune you no further with my unwelcome words. I confess myself optimistic that you will not spurn such an approach. Dare I hope for a reply, and perhaps a few words of encouragement to continue? It would cheer me enormously to know that I am in your thoughts, as you are in mine. I find that my history has not yet reached the town, so I have seen several patients today. If this changes, however, I plan to stroll about the town and look in on the principal establishments, so they will see that I am not ashamed to show my face. You see, I am taking your advice to heart, and holding my head high. If it does not sound too pleading, may I say again how much I long to hear from you? But I shall understand if you cannot spare a thought for me at such a difficult moment. If so, I can only offer my deepest apologies for intruding on your time. Yours in affection, Samuel.'

~~~~~

'Cloverstone Manor, 23rd July. My dearest Samuel, I cannot fully express my delight at receiving your letter. It had not yet occurred to me that we could write to each other! I suppose I had not thought we would need to, but I do not know when I might see you again. Papa is implacable, and we are not even to attend church for a month at least, and there will be no card parties or other entertainments. Not that I wish for such frivolities in the least, except for the chance to meet you, my dear one. Where is the best address to write to you? If I write to you at Whitfield Villa, the Beasleys will know of it and Dr Beasley might feel obliged to mention it to Papa. Not that we are doing anything wrong, but Papa might try to forbid it and it would be most disagreeable to fall out over it. He is such a kindly father as a

rule that I very much dislike being at odds with him. I shall write to the Market Clunbury house, I think, and that will be most convenient, for Holliday, our groom, collects the mail from the office at the Swan Inn every day, and deposits our letters, so he may just as well deliver to you directly and collect any letters from you, and save the cost. Be assured that we are all well here, and Papa is in better heart than he was at first. The uncertainty of Mama's health wore him down, I think, and now that all is resolved, he is determined not to be downcast. Lovingly yours, Susannah.'

~~~~~

Twice in two days the sexton was obliged to take up his spade, and Mr Truman to preside over a freshly dug grave. Although Mrs Winslade's burial naturally attracted the larger number of mourners, Mrs Cokely's was not far behind. In both cases, the refreshments were provided by the Gages at Lower Maeswood Grove, by tradition. Being the nearest great house to the churchyard, they accommodated the funerals of the gentry, while the Boar's Head provided for the lower orders.

Samuel attended both funerals, lurking unobtrusively, not knowing quite what his status was now. Apart from the glowering Jeffrey Rycroft, the goodwill of the parish held, and he was not ostracised or treated in any way differently from before. He was acutely aware of his position as an outsider, however. For a brief moment, he had glimpsed a future where he had everything he had ever wanted — his own family about him, a thriving practice and a position in society, respected and accepted. Now that future hung by a thread. When he looked about him at these men who had their roots deep in the soil of Shropshire, whose families had lived in the county for generations and whose right to be there was unquestioned, he felt even more of an outsider, and a grey gloom settled on him.

There was one person present he had not met before — Timothy Rycroft, a son of Lady Saxby's from her first marriage. He was a younger version of his brother Jeffrey, a little rangier and more restless, perhaps. Samuel took no notice of him after the first introductions, but he discovered that the reverse was not true. Mr Timothy Rycroft sought him in his inconspicuous corner, and took a surprising interest in his work. Had he many patients? Had he opened up the Market Clunbury consulting rooms? Did he plan to live there? Might he move to larger premises if the practice grew sufficiently? Samuel answered where he could, but told him honestly that he could not foresee the future. He was rather pleased with the younger Rycroft, finding him a lot easier to talk to than his more volatile brother.

He left early, thinking that he might yet have time to ride over to Market Clunbury to see if a letter from Susannah awaited him. That would cheer him up!

As he strode down the drive to the road, Captain Edgerton caught up with him.

"You are still received in society, then?" he said cheerfully.

"For the present," Samuel said glumly.

"Ah, your pardon, Broughton," Edgerton said. "My humour is ill-timed."

"How go your investigations, Captain? Have you settled whether Mrs Winslade was murdered yet?"

Edgerton heaved a sigh. "Not yet. All I have been able to determine is that it would not be easily accomplished. You observed the difficulties with entering by a window, and all the doors are bolted at night, with the scullery maid sleeping in the kitchen and a night porter on patrol. Even if one could effect an entry, Cloverstone Manor is a veritable rabbit warren of a house — wings sprouting here, there and everywhere, meandering corridors, rooms within rooms within rooms. How would anyone not totally familiar with the house ever find their way to one particular room?"

"How much time elapsed between Wilkinson's arrival and the death of Mrs Winslade?"

"Six days... oh, you think he had time to scout the place first? Let us suppose he takes a couple of days to identify Mrs Winslade as a possible target. He then has several nights in which to observe the house from the outside, work out where the bedrooms are and then slip in through a window, wandering around until he had identified the correct room. Yes, it could be done," he added thoughtfully.

"You still think Wilkinson murdered her?" Samuel said.

"Well... I would not go quite so far as that," Edgerton said ruefully. "Let us say merely that *if* Mrs Winslade was murdered, then Wilkinson is the most obvious suspect. That is all. But as to why, or whether there is any connection at all to you or Sir James or Mrs Cokely or the business with the wine in your cellar... who can say? Perhaps it is all coincidence after all."

They had reached the road, where Samuel expected them to go their separate ways, but Edgerton said, "Will you come across to the Dower House for a moment? I have something to show you."

The Dower House was quiet, with no sign of life, but Edgerton led Samuel into a study. Unlocking a drawer of the desk, he brought out a letter. "This arrived yesterday. I should be interested to know what you make of it."

'Michael, A quick note, as I am off again at once. I have talked with Dr B's friends, who were most forthcoming, but know nothing at all of what happened. It is a mystery to them, and they say Dr B did not help himself by saying nothing. Even they, who know and respect him, cannot be sure that he did not murder his wife. Try if you can get him to talk about it. Pettigrew.'

Samuel could not breathe... so little air...

"Will you not—?" Edgerton began, his tone gentle.

"I *cannot* speak of it!" Samuel growled. Throwing the letter down, he strode out of the house.

21: No Smoke Without Fire

Once the funeral was over, Susannah began to receive condolence calls. Amongst the earliest were Lady Saxby and her four daughters. Lady Saxby was still in unrelieved black, but Cass, Agnes, Flora and Honora all wore some form of half-mourning. Susannah had already decided that her own mourning would not be so strict. Two months, perhaps, in full black, but then she would go into half-mourning and then, surely, the banns might be called?

The ladies expressed their shock, their sorrow and their well-wishes in the usual form. They moved on to Mrs Cokely, with more shock, sorrow and well-wishes. They enquired after Papa, and on being told that he and Henry had gone to Shrewsbury on some matter of business, Lady Saxby said languidly, "Gentlemen are much better to be busy at such a time, for nothing is more dispiriting than a gentleman kicking around the house being miserable. Whereas we ladies have not the fortitude to face the world, and must seclude ourselves away until the worst of our grief has expended itself."

Susannah wondered just why Papa had found it necessary to go to Shrewsbury at such a time, but said nothing. It might, after all, be nothing but a financial or legal matter. They had progressed as far as the weather and Lady Saxby was looking at the clock on the mantel when Agnes, always the most forthright of them, raised the subject that must be uppermost in all their minds.

"And how is Dr Broughton, Susannah?"

There was a charged silence in the room, but Susannah was prepared. "He is very well, thank you, Agnes. I have not seen him lately, but he writes to me regularly."

There! That satisfactorily answered the unasked question, as to whether the engagement still held.

"You have not seen him?" Agnes said in astonishment. "Then he has not called since—?"

"Since Mama's death? Naturally he called at once, but not since then, for Papa forbade him the house." Let them make of that what they would.

"Quite right, after what he has done," Lady Saxby said, pursing her lips a little.

"What *has* he done, Lady Saxby?" Susannah said sweetly.

There was no recovering the conversation after that, and her ladyship made no effort to do so. "Come, girls," she said briskly, as she rose and prepared to leave. The three younger girls fluttered out of the room after her, but Cass lingered, laying one hand lightly on Susannah's arm.

"I am glad you are standing by him," she said quietly. "That more than anything will serve to squash these foul rumours, for you of all people must know the full story. He would not hide anything from *you*." While Susannah was still trying to formulate a reply, she went on, "And the Beasleys will stand his friend, too, although Miss Beasley said they have been told nothing of the matter by Dr Broughton himself and will not enquire. She said only that he is a good Christian, and they will not turn their backs on him when he is guilty of nothing in the eyes of the law, and all Christians should do the same. She was quite forthright about it. Indeed, I have never heard her speak so robustly before, and seemingly she actually gave Miss Gage a set down over it. Miss Beasley, who would not say boo to a goose! Can you imagine?"

"I should have liked to have seen that," Susannah said faintly.

"So should I, for I only heard of it from Miss Gage herself. She was outraged, as you may suppose! Poor Miss Gage, to be lectured on Christian charity by Miss Beasley. But I must not keep Mama waiting."

She turned for the door, but then turned back to Susannah. "How dreadful for you to be separated from your betrothed. Once you are able to venture abroad again, you may call upon me and we could go for a walk through the village, perhaps? At a time when he is known to be at home?"

"You are very kind, but I should not like to go against Papa's wishes."

"He has forbidden him from the house, which is his right, but has he forbidden you from seeing him?"

"No, not that, and I do not know how he could, since we are betrothed and I am of age. We could call the banns whenever we wish, and there is not a thing Papa could do about it. Still, I do not like to set my will against his, not at such a difficult time. I would not add to his distress."

A footman arrived at a run to inform them that Lady Saxby was ready to depart, and Cass rushed away, but her words lingered in Susannah's mind. Writing to Samuel was wonderful, and she wrote long, chatty letters every day, knowing that he would not have to pay for them, and he wrote back at equal length, funny stories of the Renshaw children, or what he called his 'kitchen door' patients, but oh, how she longed to see him! It would reassure her that he was in good spirits better than any words on paper. He told her he was not downcast, but sometimes a phrase would strike her as not quite so buoyant as she would like. Only the sight of him, and hearing him speak, would banish those fears. Yet however much she longed for it, she could not add to her father's troubles by insisting.

Amongst the stream of callers, there was one she expected sooner or later, and he did not disappoint her. Jeffrey came one day just after breakfast, while Susannah was still at her desk. He bounced in like an overgrown puppy, far too cheerful for a condolence visit, and kissed her hands.

"Well now, Sue, how are you? You look excessively pale, but that may be the gown. Black does not suit you at all, but you will not be in full mourning for long, I daresay. A month or two, perhaps, for she was only your stepmother, after all. Not like a real mother, is it? I was sorry when my stepfather died, for Mother's sake, but I cannot say it grieved me overmuch. Lord, Sue, could you not afford a better gown than that? I should be ashamed to see my sisters in such a worn old thing."

"I had only enough material left for one new mourning gown," she said calmly. "I keep that one for when visitors are expected, and wear this when I am busy with my household duties."

He did not take the hint, bringing forward a chair for himself and sitting without waiting for an invitation. He had done so scores of times before, but somehow the presumption irritated her this time.

"What was it you wanted, Jeffrey?" she said. "I must tell you that I have much to do and less time than usual in which to do it. If this is just a morning call, you would do better to come at the proper time, when I am at leisure to receive you."

"That is not very friendly," he began huffily, before thinking better of his words. "But let us not quarrel, not today, for there is such good news."

"I am glad to hear it."

"Well, you do not look very pleased, but then I suppose you do not yet know. Your father did not tell you? He is to put up ten thousand for you. There! Is that not wonderful?"

It would be wonderful, of course, if it were true, but Susannah's first thought was that it could not possibly be so, for where would Papa obtain ten thousand pounds? He had said he would give her some sort of dowry, which she had supposed might be a thousand or two, raised by extending the mortgage or selling off a parcel of land, but ten thousand? It was impossible.

She was assailed by another thought. "Why would he tell *you* such a thing?"

Jeffrey raised his brows in astonishment. "Naturally he would tell me. We have talked it through and it is all settled between us."

"But why on earth should you be talking to Papa about my dowry? It is Dr Broughton to whom he should be talking."

"Good Lord, Sue, *that* is all finished! Surely you realised that? You cannot possibly marry a man like that."

"A man like *what?*"

"A murderer," he said, with a shrug of his elegantly clad shoulders. "It is out of the question. Your father will never countenance it, and so he came up with this scheme to make it possible for you to marry me."

Susannah jumped to her feet so rapidly that her chair crashed over behind her. "How *dare* you—?" she began, before realising that she was directing her rage at quite the wrong person. Flinging open the door, she almost bumped into Silas, lurking just outside.

"Where is my father?" she demanded.

"In his dressing room, madam."

"At this hour?"

"He is preparing to go to Shrewsbury with Mr Henry, madam."

Shrewsbury again? That was odd, but Susannah had no time to waste.

"Sue—" Jeffrey began.

"Go *away*, Jeffrey. Never raise this subject with me again, do you hear?"

With that, she picked up her skirts and ran, to catch her father before he left. She need not have rushed, for when she rapped on the dressing room door, it was opened by Trent, the valet.

"One moment, if you please, madam," he said. "We are just at a delicate stage with the cravat, and cannot be disturbed."

He shut the door again, and Susannah was left to fume impatiently in the corridor, pacing back and forth. Silas crept round the corner, loitering in his oily way. Whenever there was anything going on, there he would be, lurking, watching. There was no point sending him away, however, for he would only shift out of sight and reappear again as soon as her back was turned.

After what seemed an unconscionably long wait, she was finally admitted to her father's sanctum. He was standing before a full-length looking glass in his shirt sleeves.

"What is the crisis, daughter?" he said with a cheerful smile, as Trent carefully manoeuvred him into his coat. "Be quick, for I need to be off."

"Trent, please leave us."

Without haste, the valet scooped up some discarded neckcloths and bowed himself out.

"This sounds serious," Papa said with a chuckle, turning this way and that to admire himself, and making a minute adjustment to his waistcoat. A new one, she thought, for she had not seen it before. He was very dressed up for his business in Shrewsbury.

"Papa, what are you about to discuss marriage and dowries with Jeffrey, when you know that I am betrothed to Dr Broughton? And ten thousand pounds? You cannot possibly have such a sum."

"But I might have, daughter," he said, regarding her in the mirror with a smug grin. "I very well might have, and quite soon, in fact. So you see, it will all work out very satisfactorily."

Suddenly, she understood. The new waistcoat, the visits to Shrewsbury, the contented demeanour... "You are planning to marry again."

"Hoping, certainly," he said, turning to face her at last, a smile on his face. "The banker's youngest daughter. Do you remember her? Pretty little thing, and her father has promised me thirty thousand. What do you think of that? It will set us all to rights, and you can have ten thousand for your dowry, but only if you marry Jeffrey, mind. I will not have you throwing yourself away on this physician, who comes here with his smooth ways. He must have cast some kind of spell on you, for you were never so irrational before."

"I am betrothed, Papa. It is quite settled."

"Betrothals can be broken. I always knew there was something havey-cavey about the whole business. Well, it will not do. I shall not let you marry a man who would murder you at the first wrong step. You must be mad even to consider it."

"But he was acquitted!" Susannah cried. "A jury considered the evidence and found him not guilty of any crime."

"There must have been something suspicious or they would never have arrested him. There is no smoke without fire, as they say. No, you had best give him up, daughter. I will not have him in this house, and if you marry him, then the same will apply to you. It will be as if you were dead, for I cannot acknowledge the wife of such a man, you know. I should be obliged to cut you, however much pain it might cause me. And now I must run, for I cannot keep a lady waiting, you know."

He swept out of the room, leaving her seething with impotent rage. But not for long. The heat of her anger soon turned to something much more coldly implacable. She would not be bullied! And if Papa could set aside his grief so easily, then she need not regard his sensibilities in determining her own behaviour.

She went below stairs to seek out the housekeeper.

"Mrs Cobbett, your mother lives in Market Clunbury, I think, does she not?"

"Yes, madam, she does."

"And how does she keep?"

"Oh, not too bad for her age, madam. Not so good on her pins, nowadays, and she doesn't see too well, but otherwise she is not so bad. My sister looks after her."

"Nevertheless, you must worry about her," Susannah said. "I am sure it would reassure you if you could pay her a visit. I need to make some purchases at the drapery on Chester Road so I can make up some more gowns, so we shall have an excursion to town. Have the carriage brought round in one hour."

Mrs Cobbett smiled as she curtsied. "Very good, madam. I'll be ready."

~~~~~

Samuel quickly learnt that fierce loyalty to one of their own was a trait only applicable in Great Maeswood. Where the villagers had rallied round him and gone out of their way to show that they took no notice of rumours, the townsfolk of Market Clunbury were less friendly, once the rumours had reached them. At first there had been, if anything, an increase in patients, no doubt drawn by curiosity to see what an alleged murderer might look like, but once the thrill of seeing a possible criminal had turned to disappointment that he looked just like any other man, they had drifted away. One or two persisted, however. The shy Mrs Tilford came to the consultation room herself.

"You will not tell my husband, will you?" she said, clutching her reticule and a parasol and several parcels.

"I do not know your husband, Mrs Tilford," Samuel said, "but even if I should meet him, I would never disclose anything about the confidences you have shared with me."

"You see, he has forbidden me from sending for you... will not have you in the house, he says, but he did *not* forbid me from calling here. So I thought, if I were to do a little shopping and then call in here, he need never know, need he? And talking to you is so good for me, Dr Broughton. I feel so much better afterwards. You do understand me so well, and you were right, I did not need the sleeping powders at all. Not once!"

Only after Mrs Tilford had left did Samuel let his laughter bubble to the surface. Women were such ingenious creatures! Anyone who claimed that men had the superior intellect was patently misguided.

He was still laughing when he heard the outer door open again, and the bell ring rather gently. He schooled his features to solemnity again and opened the door to the hall, only to encounter the last person he had expected — Susannah was gazing up at him, her face filled with an endearing mixture of hope and nervousness.

A rush of joy burned through him, and with a laugh of delight, he swept her into his arms and kissed her with an urgency that took him utterly by surprise. Lord, how he had missed her, this odd little creature who seemed so practical, yet was filled with passion. She filled him with passion, too. Oh, the warmth of her, the way she leaned into him, moved with him, yielded herself utterly to the moment. All the disquiet he had felt over their first kisses was drowned in a tidal wave of joyous bliss.

He was vaguely aware that Charlie had peered round the kitchen door then gone away again, and still they stood in the hall, locked together, lost in their own secret world. When, after a very long time, he raised his lips from hers, she smiled up at him enchantingly.

"I need not have worried, then," she said, with a little laugh.

"What were you worried about?" he murmured. Her bonnet had gone askew, and he could not resist pressing kisses along her cheek, then her ear, and down the curve of her neck. She exuded such warmth and he drank it in like honey, but he was ashamed of himself, too. To lose control in this way! It was despicable, and yet he was helpless to resist her.

"I was afraid you might not be pleased to see me," she whispered. "But I think you are. Very pleased."

He leaned down to pat butterfly kisses over her throat. "I *am* pleased, although…"

"Although?"

"I wonder if I am not making a terrible mistake in marrying you," he said softly. "It is my gravest fear that you may be too much like Corinna."

Terrible mistake? She froze in his arms, looking up at him with wide eyes, suddenly alert. "Corinna? Your wife?"

He nodded.

"She was… like me?"

He realised then what he should have understood far sooner. "You are curious about her."

"Of course, but you need not talk about her if it pains you."

He shook his head again. "Corinna… she does not pain me. Only her death… I cannot talk about that, but… Do you want to know about her?"

Mutely she nodded. *Terrible mistake?* Please God, let him not cry off!

"Then come inside and I will tell you."

22: Of Marriage

A terrible mistake... He could not mean it!

Susannah allowed herself to be ushered into the consultation room. To compose herself, she walked about pretending to examine the room. The furniture had a slightly faded air, but it was comfortable enough, with a reassuring smell of beeswax polish. After three circuits, her tumultuous pulse had calmed a little, but she could not entirely hide her distress.

"What is it?" he said. "Have I said something to upset you?"

How could he possibly not know? "I..." There was no way to dissemble, so she blurted, "You will not jilt me, will you?"

His eyebrows shot up. "Of course not! Whatever made you think such a thing?"

"You said it was a terrible mistake!"

"Oh... no, I did not mean... I would never..." Then, more softly, "Susannah, I shall not cry off. I look forward to our marriage very much, but you should perhaps understand my fears for you, so that you may be on your guard. Let me tell you of Corinna and my marriage, and then you will see. Will you sit down?"

She removed her bonnet and gloves, and sat hopefully on the leather sofa. Would he sit beside her? Surely he would.

"A glass of Madeira?" he said, his hand hovering over the decanter. "Or Charlie can make tea, if you prefer."

"Madeira, please," she said rather breathlessly, although she was not sure her shaking hands could hold the glass steady. The blood was still pounding in her veins, and she was glad that she could sit down, for her legs seemed to have turned to blancmange.

He set her glass on the edge of a cabinet within her reach, and his own on a low table, then, to her disappointment, took the chair facing her.

"It is good that you came today," he said. "There is so much that cannot be conveyed in a letter, but to see you here was beyond my expectations. How did you manage it?"

"I needed some lengths of black for new clothes, and you happen to be next door to a drapery so…"

"How clever you are," he said, with a smile that warmed her inside. It was all right! He was not angry with her. He went on, "After all, your father cannot possibly object to the purchase of mourning clothes."

"I do not care what Papa thinks," she said bitterly, straightening her spine. "Mama is barely in her grave, and he is courting again already. I should have expected that, for he has never been alone for long. He always has someone in mind. The banker's daughter this time, who cannot be a day above eighteen, and will bring him thirty thousand pounds, if you please! And he will give me one third of that, but only if I marry Jeffrey Rycroft. So generous of him! It is bribery, pure bribery. As if I would be tempted, even for a *hundred* thousand."

"Would you not?" he said softly, his eyes twinkling. "I had thought you more practical than that. A hundred thousand would compensate for a great many bad habits, I should have supposed."

She laughed, her anger dissipating at once. "Oh yes! And Jeffrey has not many bad habits, in truth, merely a certain laziness and an inability to settle to a career. Had he inherited the fortune that should have been his and been able to live as a gentleman, he would have been very eligible. He is very good-humoured, when the mood takes him."

"And he is fond of you," Samuel said. "He has remained faithful for many years."

"That is true, and is in his favour, I suppose."

"In addition, he is handsome and gentlemanlike and thoroughly agreeable, and with ten thousand pounds—"

"And despite all these attractions, I still do not wish to marry him," she said quickly. Then, in sudden anxiety, "You sound as if you are trying to get rid of me."

"No, no. That is not what I want at all, but I do have concerns. When we first discussed the matter, it seemed to me that we both wanted the same thing — a pragmatic arrangement without high drama, a mutually agreeable but pleasant companionship."

"Pleasant companionship?" she murmured, appalled.

"Now I think that perhaps you see it differently." Before she could think of a sensible response, he went on musingly, "It is a matter of curiosity to me how one chooses a matrimonial partner. I do not fully understand why you prefer me to a man far better known to you, and no more impecunious than I am myself, especially now, when my career is so precarious. I certainly never understood why Corinna chose me."

"I daresay she fell in love with you, just as I did," Susannah said, puzzled. What other reason could there be?

"Not a bit of it," he said, shaking his head in bewilderment. "Love had nothing to do with it, not on her side and certainly not on mine. I would never have dared to think of her. She was a baronet's daughter with a dowry of thirty thousand pounds, fêted wherever she went, and I was nobody, at the very beginning of my career. One day her father summoned me to his study and told me that she wanted to marry and I was the man she had chosen, and to this day I have not the least idea why."

"She must have felt some affection for you," Susannah said. "In her position, she hardly needed to marry for security, so why marry at all, unless she preferred one man above all others?"

"Now that part I understood — why she wished to marry at all. She had no choice about that."

"Her father forced her?"

"Not exactly. Let us say merely that marriage was forced upon her." Susannah frowned, puzzling over that, so he added quietly, "She was with child."

"Oh!"

"That was another mystery — who her lover was," he said.

"Oh!" Susannah said again. Then, working it out, she said, "That was Cressy?" He nodded. "Then... she is not yours!"

"Not my blood," he said at once, his breath ragged. "My daughter... in every way... that matters."

He fell into silence, and Susannah was too shocked to speak. It was too much to take in all at once. Such a strange marriage! To be called upon to rescue a high-born woman from her own folly, and accept her unknown lover's child. Yet he had done it, and grown to love the child with a father's fierce pride.

But there was one comfort that leapt out at Susannah — he had not loved Corinna. She had not that pain to cope with. Not that she had any illusions — despite the warmth of his kisses, she knew he was marrying now for pragmatic reasons, not love. To be the unloved second wife was a rôle she would gladly accept, but to be the successor to an adored first wife would be hard to bear.

Samuel still said nothing, absently sipping his Madeira. She did not want to press him to talk, especially when any mention of Cressy brought him distress, but the silence was beginning to oppress her.

"I should like to know more of Corinna," she said tentatively, "but not if it would upset you."

He gave her a small smile. "No, I do not mind. What shall I tell you of her? What do you want to know?"

"Everything!" she cried, glad that he had been drawn out of his pensiveness.

He nodded. "Very well then. She was fourteen when I first met her, on one of her frequent visits from Hertfordshire. Her mother lived in the country and was trying to instil some decorum into her, but she preferred London and the largely masculine society gathered around her father. She was allowed to join us at table, where she mesmerised the company. Everyone doted on her, even then, when she was a mere wisp of a girl, but so lively and amusing."

"But not you," Susannah said, catching the flatness of his tone.

"No. I thought her a sad figure, if you want to know. It seemed to me that she craved attention, especially from men. She responded to it as a plant responds to sunshine and warmth. She unfurled her petals and blossomed under their admiration. That is a major difference between you — she expected, nay, demanded, it, whereas you have a self-assurance that is sufficient unto itself. You need no man to bring you to life, but Corinna did, and all her society gloss was brittle, ready to break at any moment. Or so I thought, anyway, which is why it was such a surprise when she chose to marry me. But then, that is a similarity between you — both of you knew exactly what you wanted, and had no hesitation in asking for it."

"Was it a difficult decision — to marry her?"

He smiled ruefully. "It took me about two heartbeats. I had always planned to marry, just as I had planned to set up my own medical practice one day, but it had all seemed to be no more than a dream. When I was a boy, my father had intended me to take over his practice, in time, but he died before I was fully qualified and it was sold to pay for my training. At the age of five and twenty, my ambition seemed unlikely to be achieved for many years. And here it all was, everything I had ever wanted — a wife and child, a dowry of thirty thousand pounds and my father-in-law's help to establish myself. Of course I leapt at it. Do you think I should have turned her down?"

Susannah raised her eyebrows. "How can I possibly answer such a question? Whatever decision you made must have seemed like the right one at the time."

"It did, yes, and I never regretted it. Strickland found us a house, furnished it, put servants in place and had us married in ten days. Then he helped me establish my medical practice. I shall be forever grateful to him for that. Whatever happened afterwards, he was more than generous towards me then."

"Did you—?" Susannah stopped, realising that her curiosity was becoming intrusive.

"You may ask anything, although..." His voice dropped to a whisper. "I may not answer."

"I wondered if, in time, you grew to love her? Or to feel *something* — some affection for her."

There was a change in his face as his expression became one of surprise. "For Corinna herself, I felt neither liking nor dislike, and certainly not love. She was always far above my touch, someone whose life intersected with mine but only on the most mundane level. When we met, which was not often, we were perfectly polite, but never more than that. I was necessary to allow her to maintain her reputation, but otherwise she did exactly as she pleased, as she had always done. Are you shocked? Do not be, for that was the way everyone of her set behaved. The men had their mistresses and the women their lovers, and they flitted through the drawing rooms and ballrooms and saloons of London like gaudy butterflies, sipping their nectar and living their charmed lives, existing only for pleasure and never stringing together a single coherent thought. Ha! Do I sound cynical? I do, I think, but I never cared. I had my work and my own friends, more serious types, who spoke of politics and philosophy and the changing world, and held myself true to my own principles, and let Corinna do as she pleased, even as I despised her behaviour. That was my life for seven years."

"I wonder that her father never tried to rein her in," Susannah said. "He seemed a proud man to me, not someone who would condone such behaviour in his daughter."

"He loved her dearly, as any father would," Samuel said. "He was too fond of her, perhaps, and over-indulged her, for I never once saw him reprove her, but he watched over her most attentively. Before I married her, he made it clear that he would tolerate no usurpation of his position. *'You may be her husband,'* he told me, *'but I am her father, and I shall take care of her, as I have always done.'* Corinna adored him in return. They were very close."

"And you never grew close to her yourself? Surely when you escorted her about town—"

"But I never did so," he said. "We were never invited anywhere as a couple. She had her life and I had mine. Occasionally our paths crossed in society, but Corinna always had a man with her. I neither knew nor cared who they were. She joked about them sometimes, when she was at home. Sundays — that was the one day we were together, attending church and then dining quietly alone. She used to tell me of the places she had been to, the people she had seen, but always in a sort of code. *'Lady B is with Sir A now,'* she would say, or, *'Lord D has a new mistress, a very pretty opera dancer.'* And she talked of her own lovers the same way, as *'Mr T'* or *'Lord C'* and latterly just by the description *'a most superior gentleman'*. I am not sure what that meant, but she gave me to understand it was someone very high ranking. Perhaps royalty, she seemed to imply. Someone very important, anyway. And she seemed to care for him, whoever he was, although in her own eccentric way."

He reached for his wine glass again, then, finding it empty, set it down with a sigh.

"She sounds an oddity," Susannah said, sipping her own wine. "I should think she would be an uncomfortable person to live with."

"I never found her so," he said pensively. "Besides, she told me before we married how it would be. *'I shall have my own life and my own friends, and you will not be a part of that,'* she told me. *'I shall have lovers and you will not be jealous, or interfere in any way.'* And I did not. Her way of life disgusted me, but I minded not at all, for I had something more precious to me than anything in the world, for I had—"

He stopped, his breath rasping, unable to say more.

Susannah finished the sentence for him. "Cressy."

He nodded, his eyes closed, his face anguished.

Outside in the street, a carriage rattled briskly over the cobbles, and somewhere a hawker called, touting his wares. Inside, there was only Samuel's pain, and Susannah was helpless to assuage it. If only he were sitting beside her, she could offer him some comfort. Was this how their marriage would be? Would he hold himself aloof from her?

Impulsively, she jumped up and knelt at his feet, taking his hands in hers. His eyebrows shot up in surprise, but he made no move to pull away from her.

"Samuel, have you never thought of claiming her back? Cressy is your daughter, so—"

"*No!*" he cried, his expression anguished. "I cannot! In law, she is mine, but..." He took several heavy breaths, calming himself, then continued more quietly, "After my trial, I had nothing — no home, no income, nothing, and my reputation was tainted. It was clear to me that Cressy was better off with her grandparents in

Hertfordshire, where at least she had family about her, and a great estate to run around in."

"But now—"

"I still have nothing," he said quietly. "No home of my own, and a career that hangs by a thread."

"Does it?" she said. "Not everyone will believe Sir James's rumour-mongering."

"Enough will. Look around you. This is my consultation room, in the middle of my hours of attendance. Do you see any patients? Oh, there are still a few, but mostly my hours are empty."

"But you will not give up?" she cried. "You must not give up! People will come back to you, if you give them time."

He smiled. "You lift my spirits, Susannah. No, I shall not give up, but I fear it will take me longer to establish myself than I had hoped, and so our marriage cannot be soon."

She released the breath she had not been aware she was holding. "I care not how long I have to wait, so long as we are wed in the end. I am very glad that Corinna has not deterred you from matrimony altogether."

He shook his head, and thrilled her by lifting her hands to be kissed. "I rather enjoyed my marriage, in fact, so much so that I was quite ready to enter matrimony again as soon as the opportunity arose."

Susannah had no idea what to make of such a statement, but fear gripped her. "Is that what you expect from me?" she cried distressfully. "The same sort of marriage you had with her? That we will never be more than polite to each other? That we would have our own lives and hardly ever see each other? For I tell you now, such an empty marriage would make me very unhappy."

"Empty?" he said, sounding startled. "Is that how you see it?"

"Do you not? Yes, to me it sounds very empty. You were two people who happened to live in the same house, like... like *lodgers*. You had almost entirely separate lives. Were you not lonely?"

He frowned, as if he had never even considered the question before. "Lonely? I was not aware of it. I had my work, my friends, much to occupy me. I never felt any lack."

"But there must be affection in a marriage!" she cried. "Not necessarily romantic love, but a fondness, certainly. Husband and wife must reach out for each other... must *touch* each other." She lifted one of his hands to her face and held it against her cheek. "Do you not feel it? The warmth of another person, someone who cares for you, who wants to make you feel better? Is it not wonderful? You enjoy it when we kiss, I know."

"Of course I do," he said shortly, "because I am a man, and men have that weakness in them, to enjoy such physical connections. A woman should have better control of her impulses, for if she does not, she inevitably descends into wickedness. Corinna was a degraded and sinful woman, and I would not see you follow the same path."

Susannah rose and moved to the window, standing with her back to the room as she blinked away tears. It was true that she had never expected love from him, for that was all on her side, but she had hoped for something, some gentleness, perhaps. But this! Such a bleak kind of marriage lay before her.

Numbly, she stared out of the window, wondering despairingly how she would ever manage to convince him that a display of affection was not the first step on the road to ruin. But she was an optimist, reminding herself that they had the rest of their lives to reach an accommodation. No wonder he was so withdrawn, after such a strange marriage, to a cold and uncaring wife! But she would draw him out, she was certain of it. Surely, in time, she could soften him a little. One day, he would appreciate that his wife loved him with every ounce of her being, and be glad of it.

23: Stout-Hearted Burghers

Samuel picked up his wine glass and got to his feet. "Do you want some more Madeira?"

Without turning away from the window, she shook her head. Was she angry with him? He had been fairly blunt with her, but it was as well for her to understand him. She needed to know his fears for her, so that she might draw back from wantonness.

He crossed to where the decanter stood on a tray, picked it up and drained the last drops into his glass. "Hmm. We will need another bottle." Opening the door to the kitchen, from which cooking smells emerged, he said, "Charlie, will you bring another bottle up from the cellar, if you please."

Charlie returned in a few minutes with the new bottle, and Susannah turned to watch him open it.

"Wait," she said suddenly. "May I see that?"

"What, the bottle? I have no idea what it is, for nothing in the cellar is clearly labelled."

She picked it up and gazed at it, puzzled. "Where did you get this?"

"From the cellar here. Lucas Renshaw must have bought it."

"But not legally," she said at once. "You see this mark on the bottle? It is meant to be a cockerel, with the 'W' for Winslade. This bottle was specially made for Papa's wine, and should never have left the Manor. This is *Papa's* wine, Samuel. You appear to have bottles of stolen wine in your cellar."

"Good grief! Let me find a light, and we will have a look below stairs."

Samuel held the lantern aloft as Susannah examined the wine racks in the cellar. Every bottle bore the same mark, that of the squire.

"Binns orders these from a supplier in the north of England, and then bottles the wine himself," Susannah said. "Samuel, every one of these came from Cloverstone Manor, and should never have left there."

"There are more," he said. "Follow me."

He led the way to the main part of the cellar where the multitude of straw-filled boxes were stacked high, each filled with more bottles. A quick sample of the first few boxes showed that the bottles were the same, showing the Winslade mark.

Holding the lantern high, he walked beside her as she moved from box to box down the full length of the cellar, lifting a bottle from every box she could reach. Each and every one bore the same mark.

"I do not understand," she said, gazing around at the boxes piled high. "There is so much of it. A bottle or two, maybe a dozen here or there, but *this!* I cannot see how it could happen. And yet... our requirements for wine have crept up in recent years, it is true.

We are ordering perhaps twice the number of barrels of five years ago. I thought it was just Henry and his friends drinking more than before. Look, there are candles here, too, and these are from our supplier, so I would guess they came from the Manor too. Someone has been stealing from us for years, to accumulate so much here. Yet why? What is the point? There is far more than anyone could drink."

Samuel could not hide the truth from her. "This is not the acquisition of one man with a thirst, Susannah. This is a business. The wine arrives, usually in March or October, to fill this cellar, and then it is gradually sold on to inns and hotels and a few private individuals. Captain Edgerton and Mr Chandry are investigating the matter, but have had no luck in finding the source, until now. But if all of this came from the Manor, then they will have a place to begin looking."

She sighed. "They will have to start with Binns. As butler, he has the sole responsibility for the wine cellar, including bottling, and yet, he has been with us for so many years! He was born on the estate, and has never given a moment's concern before. And this is such a vast enterprise, too. All the upper servants make a little money on the side from selling surpluses, or accepting gifts from tradesmen in exchange for our custom, but this is on a different scale altogether. But it could be no one else. The wine cellar is his domain. I shall ask Captain Edgerton to call upon me, and we can talk to Binns together."

Susannah left soon afterwards, leaving Samuel to brood. His straightforward marriage was turning into something much more complicated before his eyes, and he was not sure what to make of it. He had anticipated a gentle companionship, but it seemed that Susannah had no wish for that, and he was not at all sure that he wanted it himself. He loved her passion, for it awoke fires in himself that he had never suspected. And yet... his experience with Corinna had taught him that a passionate woman was also an unfaithful one. He did not want another marriage like that. How could he be sure that Susannah would never betray him?

If only his father were still alive, for who better to advise him? There were men who had acted in a father-like way towards him, such as Dr Beasley, and Dr McNair from Edinburgh, but neither had married. His friends in London were either bachelors, or had the sort of detached marriage he had had with Corinna. He could think of no one of his new acquaintances who might provide some guidance for him.

He was not much given to introspection, so he soon drained the last of his Madeira, and determined that he would do something — anything — to keep himself busy. Activity was the best cure for a fit of the blue-devils. If his patients would not come to him, he would walk about the streets and see whom he might bump into. In one matter, he was in perfect accord with Susannah — he needed to hold his head high.

No sooner had he made this resolution and jumped up to put the plan into effect than the bell in the hall rang. On opening his door, he found both the town's apothecaries waiting there, hats in hands, their expressions belligerent.

"Might we have a word, Dr Broughton?" the fat one said. "If convenient, of course."

With sinking heart, he ushered them into the consultation room. "I am quite at leisure," he said. "Madeira, gentlemen?" With the formalities out of the way, and the pair seated, he said, "And how may I be of service?"

They exchanged glances, then the thin one nodded encouragingly to his colleague, who cleared his throat noisily. Samuel waited without impatience for the blow to fall. He knew how it would be — *'much regret... unforeseen circumstances... unable to do business... obliged to sever all connections...'* Strickland's rumour-mongering had spread far and wide.

"You see, sir, it is thus-wise," the fat apothecary said. "Generally speaking, I and my fellow townsman here have little agreement between us. That's natural, with two persons pursuing the same profession in the same town, not a hundred yards apart. There's bound to be a tiny amount of what you might call occupational rivalry, isn't that so, Bob?" The thin man nodded vigorously. "Best of enemies, that's what we are — ha ha ha. But on this matter — on this one matter alone — we speak as one, don't we, Bob?" Another nod. "No dissent between us at all. We are entirely agreed on it. Not the slightest hint of any dispute."

Samuel nodded encouragingly.

"You see, we don't like it, we don't like it at all."

"No, we don't," said the thin man, finding his voice at last. "Not at all."

"Indeed we don't. We don't like a man coming here and stirring up trouble. It's not right."

"Definitely not right."

"And it makes no difference him being a baronet, it's still stirring up trouble and we don't hold with it, not when we can see for ourselves that you're an honest physician, as has dealt fairly with us right from the start."

Samuel said nothing, but perhaps his face registered his incredulity, for the fat apothecary went on, "Ah, sir, you think that everyone will listen to this baronet and believe you to be a no-good scoundrel, but you will find that in this town, at least, we think for ourselves and don't take the word of any man, just because he says so, be he the highest in the land. And what was he about, that's what we want to know. Why should this man come all the way from London to our humble town, and take the trouble to enter every shop and tell tales about you, sir, what's done no harm to a soul. And he even admits it himself — that you was acquitted of all crimes, sir. I don't know what the law says in London town, but here in Shropshire, if a man is accused of a crime and acquitted, then he's accounted as innocent as a new-born babe and that's an end to it. So we thought to tell you to your face, sir, that we listen to no foul rumours about you, and everyone who comes to us will be told the same."

Samuel smiled and shook his head. "Gentlemen, I thank you both with all my heart. I confess, I had almost despaired when I discovered that Sir James was here, for there are many who will delight in believing the worst of any man. I felt sure my brief career as a physician in this town was at an end. But your support will encourage many to take a more lenient view, and I can never sufficiently express my gratitude. There is no doubt that the burghers of England's provincial towns have hearts as stout as anywhere in the world."

"Why, stouter, sir," said the fat apothecary. "There's no *Londoner* going to tell us how to think, baronet or no."

Samuel chuckled. "And that is entirely as it should be. A little more Madeira?"

"I don't mind if I do, and perhaps while we're here, you could enlighten us about this new treatment you have for certain gentlemen's complaints, for we've heard of several cases, but the gentlemen concerned were mystified as to the particular constituents of the ointment."

"It was something I heard of in Edinburgh, that came from some country folk — a traditional remedy. It seems to help. Shall I write out the receipt for you?"

After that, it was almost an hour, and a second bottle of Madeira, before the two apothecaries shook Samuel's hand with provincial energy and left him to himself. He rode home bemused but well pleased with the day.

~~~~

Susannah dispatched a groom with a note to Captain Edgerton as soon as she returned to the Manor, but it was not until the next day that he called in response. Silas showed him into Susannah's office, leaving the door ajar as he withdrew, but Susannah closed it behind him.

"He is always listening at keyholes, that one," she said, pulling a rueful face. "If we speak low, he will not overhear us."

The captain laughed, and opened the door again. Silas jumped away from it, his face assuming a blank expression. "Ah, good, you have not yet disappeared," he said brightly. "Be so good as to run down to the stables and ask one of your grooms to have a look at my horse. I forgot to mention it earlier, but I noticed a very slight lameness as I rode over."

Silas could do nothing but bow and walk away down the corridor. The captain watched him go.

"There, we are safe for a while, at least, but you really should get rid of him, you know. Listening at keyholes is very bad form in a footman. That is a privilege reserved for the butler. I beg your pardon for not calling at once, Miss Winslade, but I was out all day yesterday and only returned home shortly before dinner, and dared not keep Luce waiting. One should never disrupt one's wife's culinary arrangements, for fear of being spit-roasted oneself."

Susannah could not help but laugh. "I am sure Mrs Edgerton must be used to the irregular hours involved in your activities, sir. She would hardly fret over a little lateness."

"Ah, but you cannot imagine how out of temper Luce gets if a meal is late. She is a positive termagant, I assure you." But his complacent smile belied his words.

"What you mean, I am sure, is that you are too fond of your wife to miss a meal in her company."

"Fond of my wife? How *outré* that would be!" He laughed, and went on, "Shall we have a look at your cellar, Miss Winslade?"

Susannah took the spare set of keys from their hook and led the way, relieved to see no sign of Silas.

"Who has access to the keys?" Captain Edgerton said.

She frowned, thinking about it. "Almost anyone," she said at last. "My office is locked when I am away for any length of time, but during the morning hours I come and go, so anyone could walk in. Binns has the other set of keys, naturally. They are kept in his room below stairs, but I doubt it is ever locked."

There were six service stairs at the Manor, and Susannah chose the one that avoided the front of the house, where Binns might be. The wine cellar occupied the whole of the basement below the west wing, the racks of barrels and bottles stretching into the darkness beyond the reach of the two lamps they had brought.

"This is quite a big operation," Captain Edgerton said thoughtfully.

"Papa loves to entertain," Susannah said. "When we hold our Easter and Michaelmas balls, half the county enjoys our hospitality. Many of the bottles were laid down years ago, when Papa had more money. I have to say, Captain, that this looks perfectly normal to me. The number of barrels, the racks of bottles — there are no gaps to suggest anything missing, and the quantity looks much as usual."

"That is surprising. One would suppose that the sort of quantities that have found their way to Dr Broughton's cellar would be noticed." The captain lifted one or two bottles to inspect them. "These are of the same style. There is no doubt that the bottles, at least, came from here."

"Oh? You think the wine came from elsewhere?"

"It is a possibility. How do these barrels get in and out? Not by way of that narrow stair we came down, I wager."

"There is an outside door."

She led the way to the far end of the cellar, and unlocked one side of a double door. Outside was a level space of beaten earth large enough to turn a wagon and four horses, and screened all around by tall bushes.

"Well, this is very convenient," Captain Edgerton said, with a grin. "No doubt there is a quiet way to come and go without using the carriage drive."

"The lane to the Overbury road," Susannah said. "Also, this wing is very little used except when we have guests. Any one could move about without attracting attention, even in the daytime. So

Binns has been carefully bottling our wine, and then allowing his cronies to sneak scores of bottles out of the back door."

"More than scores — hundreds," Captain Edgerton said sombrely. "Yet all looks as usual to your experienced eyes. So how are they doing it? May I see the cellar book?"

"Here it is. You can see that it is up to date. Henry checks it every week, and initials it."

"Not your father?"

Susannah smiled. "Papa is... not very good at keeping records, so the cellar was in some disarray at one time. Henry took over the cellar book a few years ago. Timothy Rycroft devised a system for him, and Henry follows it meticulously. Do you want to talk to Binns now?"

"No," the captain said slowly. "I have a better idea. Mr Chandry has been making progress on understanding the notations in the two notebooks we found. If he is able to deduce when a delivery or removal will take place at the Market Clunbury house, we shall be able to catch the thieves in the act, which will be much more satisfactory."

"That sounds like a risky endeavour," Susannah said.

Captain Edgerton chuckled. "The very best kind, Miss Winslade."

~~~~~

Samuel's Market Clunbury patients may have been thin on the ground, but the inhabitants of Great Maeswood, Astley Cloverstone and Woollercott were determined to show their loyalty to one of their own. On Mondays, Wednesdays and Fridays, therefore, he sat quietly in his consultation room in Market Clunbury, almost untroubled by calls for his professional services. On Tuesdays, Thursdays and Saturdays, in contrast, Whitfield Villa saw a steady stream of arrivals all morning from the lower classes, although not the gentry, who seemed to have taken Strickland's rumour-mongering to heart.

One exception was Maeswood Hall, where he was summoned to treat Cass Saxby. He found her propped up in bed, very pale, with Susannah quietly sewing beside the bed.

"I shall not apologise for sending for you on false pretences," Miss Saxby said to him with a smile. "I am quite well, or at least, not at death's door, and have been much improved these last two days, but I waited until Susannah called so that you might enjoy a walk together, since you may not go to the Manor."

"Cass! Such deceit!" Susannah cried. "Even so, I hope you will allow Dr Broughton to advise you, for it is not at all like you to be ill in this way."

"I have no intention of leaving until I have heard all about it," Samuel said. "You are very pale, but not feverish, I think. May I examine your pulse? And then you may tell me everything."

"Oh, it is nothing — just something I ate that disagreed with me, I daresay. I was very sick for a few hours, but I feel a great deal better now, I assure you."

Gradually, Samuel drew the story out of her, and gave her the usual bland advice he gave all his patients, for he could see that she was already well on the road to recovery.

"What do you think is the matter with her?" Susannah said, as they set off on the path towards the Manor, Samuel leading his horse. "Apart from her childhood, she has never suffered a day's illness in her life. I was so relieved when she agreed to send for you."

"I suspect she is right, in that it was something she ate," Samuel said easily. "In this hot weather, it is all too easy for meat to spoil, but she is young and healthy and will recover very quickly. I am glad she called me in, though, for it is always concerning when a healthy young woman succumbs to illness unexpectedly."

"Unlike Lady Saxby and Honora, who call you in repeatedly without cause," Susannah said, smiling.

"The cause is real enough to them," he said. "And the fees are real enough to me."

Susannah burst out laughing. "Very true! But that will not be enough to keep us afloat, will it?"

"No, and I have noticed that they have not sent for me at all since Strickland was here." He sighed. "Ah well, perhaps in time they may relent. But if I am underemployed as a physician, Captain Edgerton is finding ways to keep me busy. There is to be an amusing little adventure tomorrow night."

"He has recruited you to this business of catching wine thieves, has he?"

"And Mac, my groom and valet, and Spencer, the groom from the Grove. Do you know him? I expect young Renshaw will be up for a bit of action, too, so between the lot of us, we should be able to secure the scoundrels."

"Be careful!" she said, turning to him with huge, frightened eyes. "Do not take any unnecessary risks."

"No need to worry," he said. "With Edgerton in charge, it will be as easy as falling off a log."

24: A Night-time Adventure

Seven of them congregated in the kitchen of the Market Clunbury house just as the sun was setting, for Captain Edgerton to make his dispositions. The first task was to persuade Charlie and the Renshaw children to go upstairs to bed, out of harm's way.

"No, you cannot watch, and no peeking out of the upstairs windows, either," Edgerton said. "If the miscreants see anything odd, they may bolt and then we shall never catch them. Up you go, and all lights out, if you please, and if you hear noises — stay exactly where you are, you hear?"

"I can help," Charlie said mulishly. "I won't get in the way, I promise."

It was Chandry who spoke up. "Charlie, you are the world's most intrepid girl, but a mill is no place for the fairer sex. All the men would feel the need to protect you, and that would be a distraction. We can only do what needs to be done if we know that all the women and children are safe. Do you see?"

Slowly, two spots of colour on her cheeks, she nodded, and led the children away up the stairs.

Edgerton gathered his troops around the kitchen table. "The usual time for these people to appear is around three of the morning," he said. "They will arrive by way of the alley at the back, which is uncobbled and therefore quieter. The wagon will wait there. The yard gate is bolted on the inside, so one of them will have to climb in through the window, open the kitchen door to the yard and then let his fellows in."

"They might climb the gate," Renshaw said. "I've done that a time or two when I was late home."

"Excellent point," Edgerton said. "It would be simpler for them and safer for us if they never need to enter the house. They will then shift the sacks that hide the hatch, open it and descend the ladder to the cellar. We want them to bring their boxes up to the yard and close the hatch door — then we will nab them."

"How many will there be?" Samuel said. "Renshaw, you and your sister have watched these people. Could you count them?"

Renshaw shook his head. "Too dark. They have a couple of lanterns, but it's hard to tell."

"My guess is four or five," Edgerton said. "One at least will wait with the horses. Mac, Spencer, I want you two to wait in the shadows out there, and when you hear us tackle the men in the yard, you must hold the horses and capture the man with them. Broughton, Neate, Chandry and I will secure the men inside the yard. That is where the mill will be."

"What about me?" Renshaw said, his chin lifting. "I can fight, too."

"You are the man who will raise help if all goes to pieces," Edgerton said. "You will stay in this room and if you hear any of us shout *'Constable!'*, you will race out of the front door and raise help — constables, the watch, neighbours, whoever you can get hold of quickly. You are the only one of us who would know where to go. Now then, weapons."

He laid several pistols on the table.

"Is that necessary?" Samuel said. "These men are unlikely to be armed, surely."

"In which case, a pistol aimed with a steady hand will bring them in line quicker than scuffling in the dirt. Broughton, you can shoot, I take it? You, Neate and I will take the poppers."

"I ken which end to point, too," Mac said. "Five years in the army."

"Which regiment?" Edgerton said.

"King's Own."

"The Borderer's, eh?" He slid a pistol across the table to Mac, who caught it deftly. "Try not to use it."

"Aye, sir." He hefted the pistol, then tossed it from hand to hand. "Braw piece o' tin, sir."

"I am glad you approve," Edgerton said, laughing.

"Pity ye'll want it back."

"Impudent Scot," Samuel said. "There is no doing anything with him, I regret to say, Edgerton."

"As long as he can shoot straight, he can be as impudent as he chooses, but I will have the pistol back later, if it is all the same to you, my Scotch friend," Edgerton said. "Now, gentlemen, let us consider our battle plans in more detail."

The evening passed slowly into night. Lanterns were prepared, pistols loaded, door hinges were greased. Mac and Spencer, their faces darkened with mud, disappeared to take up their post in a dark corner of the alley. Then all the lights were doused, and they began the long wait.

The watch came past at midnight, calling the hour. Several drunken revellers made their noisy way home shortly after. A cat yowled somewhere. Samuel followed Edgerton's advice, and rose from his chair several times to walk about, the better to stay awake. Even so, he was beginning to slip into a doze when a quiet *'Hsst'* from Edgerton alerted him.

Not far away, some sort of conveyance passed over cobbles. Not necessarily sinister, for anyone might be abroad at this hour quite legitimately. The sounds dropped away, but did not disappear, as if the cobbles had given way to dirt under the wheels. And then there were the unmistakable sounds of a vehicle making its way along the alley, and drawing to a halt.

They had come.

Samuel took up his position just inside the door of the consultation room with Neate and Chandry. Only Edgerton remained in the kitchen, watching the yard from the window, ready to retreat hastily if the thieves entered the house.

But they did not. Renshaw's guess was right, for one man climbed over the yard gate, then opened it to let the others through. Edgerton gestured to the others to return to the kitchen. Samuel waited just inside the door for the signal, the pistol heavy in his hand. Edgerton had his tucked into a pocket, but Samuel liked the reassuring feel of it in his hand. Even if he never fired it, he could deal a heavier blow with it than with mere fists. He had never been much of a fighter in his youth, and was quite happy to leave the derring-do to heroic types like Edgerton.

There were faint noises from the yard as the sacks were moved and the hatch door opened. Then silence.

"Only two of them," Edgerton whispered. "They are in the cellar now. Remember, we wait until they close the hatch before we move. Chandry, as soon as I give the signal, uncover the lamps."

Then they waited again, as the thieves came and went, loading boxes into the wagon, then returning to the cellar for more. There was nothing to be seen, for only Edgerton stood watchfully by the window, but Samuel was fully alert now, straining for every little sound, and found he could visualise the scene in the yard quite well. The thieves worked without talking, but there were shuffling noises, a thump, a low grunt and then a heavier thud as the hatch door was closed.

And then the wait was over. Edgerton threw open the kitchen door, two lamps shone out and he and his friends boiled out into the yard, Samuel in their wake.

"Stand!" Edgerton yelled. "Stand or I shoot!"

Several things happened at once. Shouts from the alley suggested that Spencer and Mac had also made their move and were meeting with some resistance. One of the two thieves made a bolt for the gate and freedom, pursued by Neate, who dropped his lantern in the process. The other pulled out a pistol and took aim at Chandry's lantern.

A loud *crack* echoed around the yard, followed almost at once by a second shot, a scream and a whinny of alarm from the horses in the alley. The gunman dropped his weapon and bolted, but Edgerton was quicker and brought him down with a flying leap. Samuel saw a chance to be useful, and raced across to help pin the man to the ground.

Then the last lantern went out, and the yard was plunged into inky blackness.

For a moment there was near silence, the only sound the heavy breathing of several men, and Mac's low soothing murmur to the horses.

"This one is secure, Captain," called out Spencer from the alley.

"And this one," Neate said from close by.

"Excellent," Edgerton said, breathing heavily. "Broughton, I have this fellow tight. Would you be so good as to find some light? The lantern we did not use is on the kitchen table. Try not to trip over Chandry."

Chandry? But there was no time to puzzle over that. Samuel jumped up and began to inch his way carefully to where he guessed the house to be. Before he could take more than two steps, light blazed out from the kitchen door, the lantern held high in Renshaw's hand. From behind him, a small figure darted into the yard with a cry.

"Mikey! Oh, Mikey!" Charlie dashed out to where Chandry's prone body sprawled motionless, face down in the dirt, and even from the far side of the yard, Samuel could see the spreading pool of blood. He had not been of great use in the fight, but an injured man was very much a matter he could deal with. He crossed the yard in three long strides and fell to his knees beside the fallen man.

"Renshaw, light over here! Charlie, hold the lantern for me, while Matt helps Captain Edgerton. A little higher. Good, good."

Kneeling beside Chandry, he rolled him onto his back, and the pain must have brought him round briefly for he screamed once, and then lapsed into unconsciousness again.

"Oh please God, don't let him die!" Charlie cried, the lantern wobbling dangerously in her hands.

"He will not die if I can prevent it," Samuel said grimly, hastily unwrapping his neckcloth and attempting to staunch the blood. There were noises and scuffling sounds elsewhere, but he ignored them, all his attention focused on his patient.

Edgerton knelt beside him. "What do you need?"

"Cloths, water and more light," Samuel said tersely.

Edgerton tore off his own neckcloth, then disappeared momentarily before returning with two more. Taking the lantern, he said, "Charlie, cloths, water, more light — *at once!*"

She disappeared. Samuel swabbed blood as Edgerton held the lamp, swabbed, wiped, found the place on Chandry's neck whence all the blood emanated, pressed his fingers firmly on the spot, waited. More light appeared. A bowl of water, towels, smaller cloths. Keeping his fingers on the place, with his other hand Samuel dipped a cloth in the water — by some miracle, it was warm — wiped away blood. Then again, and yet again, until much of the blood was gone and Chandry's neck was almost clear of it.

"Charlie, I need needle and thread — nothing too delicate."

She disappeared again, asking no questions, which was good, for Samuel had no answers. Chandry's life hung in the balance, and he could not as yet say which way it would tilt.

There were more lanterns now, and a ring of silent faces around him, watchful, anxious. Where had they all come from? It hardly mattered. Charlie returned with the needle, already threaded with a stout black cotton. Samuel began to sew. Stitch by careful stitch, never removing his fingers from Chandry's neck, he closed the opening in the vein in his neck. And when eventually the last stitch was in place, he said, "Scissors." Silently Charlie handed them to him, he snipped the thread, and removed his fingers. The vein held.

He sat back on his heels, and gazed around at perhaps a dozen faces staring down at him, puzzled. Who were they? Where had they all come from?

"Will he do?" Edgerton said.

"He will do, for now," Samuel said. Charlie burst into noisy sobs. "He is not out of the woods yet," he said more gently, "but with careful nursing, he should be as good as new before too long."

"Thank you, thank you, thank you!" she cried, too distraught to formulate any more complicated thought.

"For doing what I have been trained to do?" Samuel said in surprise.

Edgerton laughed. "If ever you find yourself in need of a job, Broughton, the army could make good use of you. That is a cool head in a crisis you have there. May we move him inside now?"

Samuel nodded, straightened his aching back, rose to his feet. How long had he been kneeling there in the dirt, fighting to save a man's life? It seemed like no time, but his muscles were complaining. He stepped back and several willing hands moved forwards with blankets to wrap round Chandry and then to lift him gingerly from the ground and carry him inside. Again Samuel looked around in surprise at the multitude of onlookers, many of them half-dressed, some still in nightgown and cap. Several carried makeshift weapons, from stout sticks to a musket and a blunderbuss.

One of the watchers nodded to him. "Neat piece o'work, master." Samuel recognised him as the linen draper from next door, with his two sons.

"Thank you. I suppose the shots woke you?"

"Aye. Came round to help, but we weren't needed, thank the Lord. Be all right, will he?"

"I hope so."

"Pleasant fella, and I wish him no harm, but I've had to lock my daughters up for their own good, and I'll be plenty glad when he goes back to Cornwall or wherever he's from, I can tell you."

Samuel had Chandry carried into the consultation room, where he set about lighting as many candles as he could find. Charlie brought more water and a pile of clean cloths, then Samuel set about cleaning and bandaging the wound. Neate and Renshaw held Chandry upright for this operation, but Chandry began to come round and started to thrash about.

"Charlie, hold his hands, will you?" Samuel said. "Talk to him."

"Mikey?" she said, kneeling beside the chair Chandry occupied. "Mikey, it's all right. Keep still."

"Charlie? What... happened?"

"You were shot, but Dr Broughton saved you. You'll be right as rain in no time."

"Oh." And then he passed out again.

When Samuel was finished, Neate and Renshaw carried him through to the small bedroom off the kitchen, with an anxious Charlie fluttering alongside. As Samuel was tidying up, Edgerton came into the consultation room, holding a bottle aloft.

"Medicine for the physician. Do you have glasses? Ah, I see them." He poured two glasses, and settled himself in Samuel's chair. "I have left the men to clear the battlefield while the officers recuperate in barracks."

"It was not much of a battle," Samuel said, amused, pulling out another chair and taking a sip of brandy. "No more than a skirmish, I should have said, but you are the expert, Captain."

Edgerton laughed. "I have seen a lot worse, it is true, but, skirmish or no, we did what we set out to do, and may plume ourselves on a successful mission. But tell me of Chandry — how soon shall I be able to remove him from here?"

"Not for a few days, at least."

"Damnation! There will be no way to prevent him from breaking Charlie's heart. Or is it too late already for that?"

"I fear so. The linen draper's daughters were preserved from that fate only by lock and key, it seems. He does have an extraordinary power over women."

"And very useful it is, too, in certain circumstances," Edgerton said. "Ah well, if he is to be caught, he could do worse than Charlie Renshaw. She is a clever little thing."

Samuel sipped his brandy thoughtfully. "It did not seem to me that Chandry stepped out of line at all, or gave the girl any reason to raise her hopes. He always behaved impeccably towards her when I was here, treating her very much as an elder brother might, without a hint of flirtation."

"So he assured me," Edgerton said. "He feared that Charlie was becoming attached to him, and we hoped that tonight might see an end to the business and no harm done. But if he must stay here to recuperate, inevitably the nursing will fall to Charlie. In such romantic circumstances, whatever attachment has already sprung up will be quite fixed."

"But that does not mean that he must marry her," Samuel said sharply. "He has done nothing at all wrong, so why should he be forced into matrimony?"

"Oh, he is ripe for it," Edgerton said easily. "He has reached that stage in his life where the pleasure in romantic freedom begins to pall, and a calm domestic sphere begins to seem very appealing. I have seen it in many of the men I served with in India, and it happened to me, too. A man grows restless, feeling there is something missing in his life and along comes a young lady who looks upon him favourably and there he is — hooked and netted. There is nothing so alluring as a pretty young woman visibly pining for one, as I can personally testify, and it is useless to resist, quite useless."

He grinned roguishly, but Samuel was not fooled. Although Edgerton affected indifference, the open adoration in his eyes when he gazed at his wife was plain for all the world to see.

"Even so, no one should be pushed to marry against his will," Samuel said.

"He will undoubtedly be willing, by the time she has nursed him back to health," Edgerton said. "Do you think all marriage must be between two people equally deep in love? For my own part, I concede that there ought to be *some* affection in the case, but it matters not where it lies. If the wife be fonder, then the man may allow himself to be led into felicity by her tenderness, and if he is the one in love, then he may gently school her in the delights of matrimonial harmony. So long as one enters the married state open to the idea of love, a very little will do the business. Or do you feel that a marriage founded on rationality is a better prospect for happiness?"

This was cutting too close to the bone for Samuel's liking. He had no wish at all to talk about either of his marriages, the one past or the one yet to come, and especially not with a man as observant as Edgerton. Even now, he felt that the man was watching him, weighing him up and seeing all the secrets of his heart.

Perhaps Edgerton sensed his reluctance, for he went on easily, "For myself, I could never have married a woman who was not head over heels in love with me." He laughed, shaking his head. "Lord, that would be dull! I need a woman with fire in her, and not all Luce's fifteen thousand pounds would have got me to the altar if she had not shown me the passionate side of her character."

Such sentiments stood opposed to all that Samuel had believed for years, and yet was it not very much the same idea that Susannah held? *'We all need affection in our lives, and that is not weakness but part of what makes us human.'* So she had said, and now Edgerton was saying the same thing — that he had married his wife *because* of her passionate nature, not despite it. And that was such a novel concept to him that he could not make head or tail of it.

"You do not think," he said slowly, "that a passionate nature in a woman could... lead her astray?"

"Does it do so in men?" Edgerton said. "When a man strays from his wife's arms, is it because he is too passionate to be constrained or is it a weakness in his character?"

"Weakness of character, of course," Samuel said at once. "But women—"

"Are no different from men, Dr Broughton. Before I married, I was befriended by any number of married women, and some of them liked to flirt and some of them liked to go beyond that. And some were passionate and some were cold as ice. It is a question of virtue, not passion. A woman of good moral character would never be tempted to wander, any more than an honourable man would, and the degree of passion infusing their veins is irrelevant. But within a marriage —" He sighed, a little smile playing about his lips. "Ah, that is another matter altogether."

Samuel was fascinated by this glimpse of a different kind of marriage, but there was no time to consider the question just then, for Neate put his head round the door. "We have scraped the blood off our three villains after our little *contre temps*, and we have a bit of a problem."

"Blood?" Samuel said.

"What sort of a problem?" Edgerton said.

"Come and see."

Neate opened the door wider, and Samuel followed Edgerton through it into the kitchen. There, sitting at the kitchen table, their hands bound and their faces bruised, were three men he recognised.

Silas, the Manor footman. Timothy Rycroft from Maeswood Hall. Henry Winslade from the Manor.

"Oh, wonderful," Edgerton said resignedly.

25: Confessions

"So you were stealing your father's wine, Winslade?" Edgerton said. "A fine example of filial duty."

"Merely redistributing my own wine," Winslade said sulkily. "Or it will be, in time. No law against that, is there?"

"We shall see if your father agrees," Edgerton said crisply. "He is the magistrate, after all. And then there is the little matter of Lucas Renshaw..."

"Wait a minute, Captain," Samuel said. "I need to examine those bruises first. This fellow has a fine black eye brewing."

"No more than he deserves," Neate muttered.

"They can talk while you work your magic," Edgerton said. As Samuel turned for the consultation room to fetch the necessary equipment, the captain added, "Better bring the bottle through, too. I have a feeling we are going to need considerably more brandy. Now then, Winslade, let us have the story, and the truth, mind. I want no Canterbury tales, or I shall simply haul you off to the constables and have you charged."

"With what?" Winslade said. "We have done nothing wrong."

"Attempted murder of Michael Chandry."

"An accident!" Silas said quickly. "Heat of the moment… pitch dark… could have happened to anyone. Besides, he's not much damaged, is he? He will survive, seemingly."

"Only through Dr Broughton's skills," Edgerton said. "There is plenty more besides that. Affray. Breach of the peace. The theft of a quantity of wine."

"It is mine!" Winslade yelled, as Samuel lit more candles and sat down to examine Silas's black eye.

"If it is yours, then you will have all the appropriate papers to prove your ownership," Edgerton said smoothly. "Date of purchase, amount paid, name and direction of the vendor, certificates of duty paid and so forth."

"Duty?" Winslade said, nervously.

"Duty," Edgerton said firmly, pouring brandy into kitchen mugs and passing them around the table. "If all of these transactions are above board, you will have no difficulty proving it to the magistrate."

Even under the flickering light of lamps and candles, Winslade could be seen to pale.

Silas shifted restlessly. "Don't say anything, Master Henry."

"No, the game is up," Rycroft said softly. "Truly, Henry, we had best come clean. Your father will forgive you, I am sure, for you were only raising a little extra blunt to maintain your position in society. He will understand."

"It's all very well for you two," Silas shot back. "You're gentry, so everyone will smile and say what a lark! *You* won't be turned off without a reference."

"I will write you a reference, if it comes to that," Winslade said, tiredly. "Look, Edgerton, there was no need for all this heavy-handed business, as if we were common thieves. Setting about us with guns and fists and who knows what. You are acting entirely beyond the bounds of what is proper. I have a good mind to lay a complaint against you myself."

"By all means," Edgerton said genially. "Let us have it all out in court, if you wish, and you can explain exactly how so much of your father's wine ended up here, ready to be sold on to any number of inns and houses in the next county, and just why all your transactions are conducted under cover of darkness. I am sure your father will be most interested to hear it when he holds his next magistrate's session."

"There is no question of *us* laying a complaint," Rycroft said sharply. "Be sensible, Henry. We have been caught, fair and square, and the time has come to own up to it and take whatever penalty your father imposes."

"I suppose we must confess," Winslade said, grimacing. "It is annoying, but I am not afraid of my father."

"Or you could just *shut your mouth!*" Silas said. "All this talk of owning up and confessing — are you crazy? Shut down the game if you like, but to be sitting round the table drinking brandy together as if you were all friends is plain stupid!"

"I daresay you cannot understand it, Silas, but there is a code of honour amongst gentlemen," Rycroft said with dignity. "Once found out, one owns up to one's mistakes."

"I know honour when I see it," Silas snarled. "Honour is sticking by those that are loyal to you, and not squealing when you're caught. *That* is the proper code of honour."

"He has a point," Winslade said uneasily, his glance shifting from Silas to Rycroft and back again.

"For heaven's sake, Henry, stiffen your spine!" Rycroft said. "Face up to it like a man. You have been educated, you have been given sound principles, yet you dither about and wring your hands like an old spinster. You are worse than Miss Gage. Edgerton, even if my two partners in crime have not the sense they were born with, I shall tell you whatever you want to know."

"Traitor!" hissed Silas.

"Indeed you are, Tim," Winslade said. "If you do this, I shall—"

"Enough!" Edgerton said, sharply enough that they were momentarily silenced. "Neate, will you be so good as to gag these two, if you please? It is the middle of the night, we are all tired, and I grow weary of their maunderings."

A short scuffle ensued, which Neate won handily, reducing Silas to impotent grunts. He turned to Winslade, another cloth in his hand, but Winslade glared at him.

"If you *dare* lay one finger on me, I shall have you charged with assault. You are nothing but a valet, after all, and should show a little respect to your betters."

Edgerton and Neate roared with laughter, and Neate had him gagged in a matter of seconds. Winslade's eyes bulged with rage, but he subsided into silence.

"Now, Mr Rycroft, you may commence your tale," Edgerton said, as pleasantly as if this were a pleasant social occasion. "And be sure to include the precise details of what became of Lucas Renshaw."

"I trust also you will account for the traces of an older bruise on your face," Samuel said. "That would have occurred about two weeks ago, around the time that an intruder here bumped into Mr Chandry."

"That was Chandry, was it?" Rycroft said. "I have said I will tell you, but it seems you know a good part of it already. Very well. Let me start at the beginning. Henry and I were always short of the readies, he because his father was short himself and I because my stepfather was a miserly so-and-so who thought it amusing to raise Jeff and me as gentlemen and then not give us the money to live up to that position. It was abominable, and so we both had to live on our wits. We tried cards but neither of us was good enough to profit by it, not honestly, at least, and we drew the line at becoming sharps."

"How noble of you," Edgerton said.

Rycroft took that on the chin. "We do have *some* standards," he said with a hint of a smile. "We were drowning our sorrows at the Manor one day, as was our wont, when the bottle ran out, and Henry decided it would be quicker to fetch a fresh one from the cellar himself, rather than wait for Binns to do it. We both went, and found Silas down there, industriously bottling a whole pipe of claret. He helpfully offered to put a few dozen to one side for Henry's own use, not recorded in the cellar book, so that his father would not know how much he was consuming. That seemed like a good idea to me, but there were limits to such a scheme. If the squire was expecting six hundred bottles from a particular barrel, and only four or five hundred were recorded he would want to know why. However, if the bottles were *smaller*, he could have his six hundred, and there might be a couple of hundred extra, to be sold off at a tidy profit."

"So that was how it was done," Edgerton said, with a satisfied smile. "I would never have guessed it."

Rycroft smiled again. "A very simple strategy. I would have tried the same scheme at Maeswood Hall, except that Rushbrook is entirely incorruptible, and my stepfather kept a close watch, too. It could only be done at the Manor, where Binns was too old for cellar work and left it to Silas. He knew Renshaw, who lived here alone at that time, with a large, empty cellar, and Dr Beasley, who was physician here then, never set foot in it. Henry ventured into Staffordshire to find customers, Silas, Renshaw and I helped to deliver the goods, and within a twelvemonth we had a viable business and pockets jingling with coins, and no one any the worse off by it."

"Except the squire," Edgerton said.

"True but Henry would inherit the Manor, including the cellar and its contents, in due course, so we regarded it as merely an advanced claim on his inheritance," Rycroft said with a shrug. He paused to take a sip of brandy, no easy task with his hands still bound. "He felt free to decide what he would do with that inheritance, and if he chose to sell some of it a little in advance... well, he will have to convince his father of that argument, but at the time, with money in our pockets at last, we felt it was reasonable."

Edgerton nodded, but made no comment, merely passing the brandy bottle around again. Samuel had long since completed his examination of the three men, and his eyes were heavy with lack of sleep. What hour was it now? It must be three or four of the morning, but the curtains were drawn tight so there was no way to see whether the dawn was yet creeping over the town. He suppressed a yawn, and tried to concentrate.

"Everything went on swimmingly until January, when Lord Saxby died," Rycroft went on. "I had never thought much about what would become of my brother and me in such an eventuality, because his son would inherit and Miles was a generous, open-hearted boy who had a fondness for his half-brothers. And besides, Lord Saxby was the sort of hearty, energetic man for whom death seemed far off. But die he did, and his heir with him, and we found ourselves waiting for the arrival of a complete stranger, a man on whom we had not the shred of a claim. Sooner or later the new Lord Saxby would arrive, and we would be turfed out of our home and left to fend for ourselves. It was necessary for me to find myself a source of income, and one sufficient to permit me to maintain my place in society. I had always taken little part in the wine enterprise, but now I began to take a larger part. Henry permitted me to develop my own list of customers, in Cheshire, primarily, so we would not trip over each other, Silas increased the amount of wine we produced and we began to expand. We even started selling other commodities, like candles, oil and tea, to increase our profits. And then—"

He took another sip of brandy with his bound hands, and Edgerton silently topped up his mug. Somewhere in the street a door banged. It would not be long before the town began to come to life.

"Then we discovered that Renshaw had been feathering his own nest," Rycroft said sombrely. "As I was searching out new customers, I started to encounter those who already bought wine on a similar arrangement, and it did not take much effort to discover that it was Renshaw. We were careful with the cellar book at the Manor, in case the squire ever took it into his head to examine it, but we were less careful here, so it took us a while to notice that Renshaw was on the take. He would pinch a bottle here, or two there, and hide them away somewhere, then he would hire a small cart and take off for somewhere beyond our usual circuit, selling bottles door to door for cash. We confronted him, and he denied it at first but—"

He heaved a breath, exhaled, then gulped another mouthful of brandy. "It was just an *accident*, I swear," he said. "Things got heated, and there was a quarrel, it is true, but nobody touched him. The poor fellow just toppled out of the wagon and hit his head. He was beyond mortal aid before we reached him, and that is the Gospel truth, as God is my witness!"

"Where was this?" Edgerton said, his voice neutral.

"About three miles or so east of here. We were just starting a delivery run, and Renshaw was very full of himself, happy as a grig, and we all knew why — he had been lining his pockets at our expense. Silas had had enough of it and confronted him, and they fell into an argument as the wagon was moving along, with Silas driving and Renshaw beside him on the box. Renshaw stood up and started yelling and maybe the horses took fright at all the noise, for they lurched forward and Renshaw fell out, and hit his head on a mile stone. Henry and I were riding behind, and by the time we got to him, he was stone dead."

"Convenient," Neate said.

"It is the truth, I swear!" Rycroft said. "We had no idea what to do, but Silas said—" He stopped, as Silas glared at him, unable to defend himself because of the gag. "Look, I do not blame Silas, for we all agreed to it. Perhaps it was wrong of us, but if we had brought him back here, there would have been the devil to pay and a huge dust-up and everything shot to pieces, and truly his death was an accident. We felt — we *all* felt — that we should not pay for his stupidity in standing up in a moving vehicle."

"And what did you do with the body?" Edgerton asked conversationally.

"Left it where it lay," Rycroft said tersely. "We were sure someone would find it eventually and assume he had been attacked by footpads or simply fallen from a vehicle — as he did."

"So much for owning up to one's mistakes," Neate said.

"I have said it was wrong, but nothing we did could bring back Renshaw, only make things incomparably worse for ourselves," Rycroft said. "I am not proud of it, but there is a difference between owning up when caught out and voluntarily leaving oneself open to trouble. We never did find Renshaw's money, by the way, although we searched his room thoroughly."

"Not thoroughly enough," Edgerton said. "It was under a loose floorboard, and is now safely in the hands of the young Renshaws, who have more need of it than you."

"Strictly speaking, it should be returned to the squire, from whom it was stolen," Samuel said.

The others all turned to him with slightly puzzled faces, as if they had forgotten he was there.

"He makes a good point," Neate said, with a slight lift of one shoulder.

"It is an interesting question," Edgerton said, draining the last of the brandy into his glass. Neate silently disappeared to find another bottle. "Here we have the dilemma in a nutshell — if one takes the high moral ground of owning up to one's mistakes and makes a clean breast of it to the squire... well, he has his missing wine and money returned to him, but there will be any amount of unpleasant consequences. His son and heir revealed to be a common thief, for one. A neighbour's son, ditto. A dead body to be accounted for. And a personal point, quite trivial, perhaps, but worth mentioning — he might feel that Neate, Chandry and I, not to mention Dr Broughton, have stepped beyond the bounds of neighbourly goodwill in pursuing this matter quite so enthusiastically."

"Are you suggesting that these miscreants should get off scot-free, Captain?" Samuel said.

"Not exactly, only that the punishment should be proportionate to the crime. At this precise moment, the squire is sublimely unaware of the business. He has noticed no deficiency in his cellar, nor, I presume, commented on the frequent absences of his heir."

"As long as the wine kept flowing, he never cared about it," Rycroft said. "Is that not so, Henry?" The gagged Henry nodded vigorously. "Susannah was the one who noticed the orders increasing, and grumbled about it."

"She also recognised the bottles when she saw them here," Samuel said. "She it was who made the connection to the Manor, but she suspected Binns."

"Ha! Binns!" Rycroft said. "No, he knew nothing about it. Well, I do not blame Susannah. We always knew that the bottles would be recognised sooner or later, but we could not order plain ones without arousing suspicion. Was that how you got involved, Edgerton?"

"No, Dr Broughton asked us if we could discover what had happened to Lucas Renshaw, and then the young Renshaws discovered the wine hidden in the cellar. That was what set us off."

Samuel barely heard him. Blame Susannah? How dared he even think of such a thing! Why, she was no more responsible for the fix in which Rycroft and Winslade now found themselves than the hapless Binns, or the squire. It was ludicrous.

His anger took him by surprise. He was almost as defensive as if she were his wife already, and not someone he barely knew and could hardly afford to marry at all now. He was assailed by a sudden longing for that event which caught him off guard. It was disappointing that she was now in mourning, and their wedding must perforce be delayed, but he was not in such a hurry as to make the wait a penance, surely? Or was he?

His mind conjured her face without any hesitation — those lovely grey eyes framed in dark hair, and that sweet smile! And then there were her kisses... If only they were married already! If only he could go home and find her waiting there for him with a welcoming smile. She would sit beside him, snuggling against him as he wrapped an arm around her waist and she would *listen* to him. Now that he thought about it, he realised that no one had ever really listened to him before, not in that honest, open way she had, not judging, just allowing him to speak. Corinna had been too cynical, Strickland too critical and his friends too detached to be confidants, but Susannah was different. Ah, Susannah... Susannah...

He jerked back to alertness, rubbing his tired eyes, as Neate returned with another bottle, saying brightly, "No idea what it is. Nothing is labelled in your cellar, Broughton."

When it had been opened, discovered to be an excellent claret and tasted appreciatively, Edgerton went on, "As I was saying, the squire knows nothing about it. If the wine is quietly returned he will be none the wiser, and if you two gentlemen will undertake upon your honour to attempt nothing of the kind again, I believe the matter may be laid to rest. Neate, will you remove the gags so that Winslade and Silas may speak for themselves?"

"For myself, I am happy to give such an undertaking," Rycroft said.

"And I," Winslade said rather breathlessly, as soon as he was able. "It was something of a lark at first, but I shall be glad to become respectable again."

"That is agreed, then," Edgerton said.

"You seem to be leaving rather a large number of loose threads, Captain," Samuel said. "For one thing, Miss Winslade knows about the stolen wine and is entitled to an explanation. There is also the bag of money that Renshaw left here. You cannot restore *that* to the squire without explanation. And then there is Renshaw's body."

"I have not forgotten any of these points," Edgerton said. "I agree that Miss Winslade must be told, if only to prevent anything of the sort occurring again. I believe we may depend upon Winslade to confess all to his sister. As for Renshaw's body, I shall look for it tomorrow — later today, I mean, but I am sure we shall find it gone. Some farmer will have picked it up, and taken it off for a pauper's burial at the nearest church."

"What about me?" Silas said. "You haven't said anything about me not doing anything of the kind, but I'm happy to swear to it, too, if you want."

"Well, now, that is something of a problem," Edgerton said. "You have demonstrated quite clearly that you operate to a different code of honour from that of your betters, which makes me wary of leaving you in the same position of trust as before. Who is to say that you might not continue the little scheme, but on your own account?

And I should hesitate to send you off with a glowing reference to be footman or even butler in another household, with the skills you have lately acquired."

"You're not going to haul me up before the beak, are you?" he said in alarm. "That's not fair, when *they* get off with everything, just because they're gentry. That's not right at all!"

"No, indeed, but you must see our problem," Edgerton said gently. "We cannot simply let you loose to do as you will, but a change of career might be just the thing. You are young, fit, sharp enough to make your way in the world — what do you say to the army?"

"The *army?* To march off to France to be shot at by Boney? No thanks!"

"But think of the fun, Silas," Rycroft said, his thin face suddenly alight with enthusiasm. "To be doing something useful, something *important* for the country, keeping everyone safe. I should love to feel I was not just a useless drain on the family."

"Why not sign up, then?" Samuel said.

"No money to buy my colours," he said ruefully. "I have been saving, but I have no more than a quarter of the amount I should need."

"How much do you need?" Winslade said.

"Another nine hundred pounds or so, for a decent regiment," Rycroft said ruefully. "I shall never make it now."

Edgerton sipped his wine, then said, "Are you serious? Because Renshaw had accumulated four hundred, and if Winslade can chip in a few more—"

"You would do that?" Rycroft said, his voice low and trembling. "You would lend me the money? Then Silas could be my batman."

There was a long silence, as glances were exchanged. No one objected to the scheme.

"Well, that seems to be settled," Edgerton said, with an edge of surprise in his voice. "And now perhaps we can all get some sleep."

26: Lack Of Sleep

Susannah listened in growing indignation to Henry's explanation. It made perfect sense, of course — the increased orders for wine and other household commodities, the frequent disappearances when he was supposedly staying with friends and returned home with pockets jingling with coins, the closeness to Timothy Rycroft. And Silas... yes, it all made sense. But really!

"Whatever were you thinking, Henry?" she said crossly.

"I was thinking that it was a simple way to supplement my income and not bother Papa for the wherewithal. He has worries enough of his own over money."

"Even so..." She sighed, defeated. Henry had always had a wild streak in him, and no amount of remonstrance would change him.

"You will not tell Papa, will you, Sue?" Henry said anxiously. "There is no need for him to know, surely? Edgerton thinks it best not to tell him, what with him being a magistrate. It would put him in an intolerable position, you must see that. And all the wine will come back here, so there is no harm done, not really."

"And Timothy is truly to go into the army?" she said, astonished.

"Yes, there will be enough money for a decent regiment. He will take Silas with him as his batman, but Robert will move up to his place and Pugh's eldest is ready to train up, so there will be no inconvenience. Everything will be just as it was, but Papa must not know."

"I do not like secrecy, Henry, I make no bones about it," she said. "I will not tell Papa about it, for there is nothing worse than a tattle-tale. It is for you to confess or not, and that must be left to your own conscience to determine. But I will not lie for you. If Papa ever asks any awkward questions about this, I shall refer him directly to you, and so I warn you."

He smiled in relief. "Thank you, sis! That is all I ask, and I promise I will be on my best behaviour from now on."

"Do not make promises you may not be able to keep," she said, but without heat. "I hope you will stay at home for a while now, brother, for I think it is good for Papa to have another man in the house. I do not suppose you can deter him from this match he has set his heart on, but perhaps you can keep an eye on him. Is he making a complete fool of himself? She is very young, after all."

"You mean is he wasting his time with Alicia Rudd? No, I believe not. Her father has approved the match, after all, and she is tolerably encouraging, it seems to me, from what I have seen of her. I do not go with him every time he calls upon her, of course, but he likes me with him sometimes to make his attentions seem less direct."

"But he is so much older than she is!"

"Older is also wiser, more sophisticated and more mannerly," Henry said. "And you have to admit that he looks very well for his age, fitter and more stylish than many a younger man. Certainly more stylish than his son and heir! She is dazzled by his charm, I think. Papa can be very charming, you know."

She laughed, knowing it well. "Charming and easy-going, but this girl's father may not be. I would not wish her to be browbeaten into accepting Papa, if she is not inclined for it. A pretty girl with a good dowry could have her pick, I wager, and there will be plenty of younger men drawn to her."

"Lord, Sue, you sound as if you do not want Papa to be happy! You know he is miserable without a wife, and if this girl marries him, he will shower her with affection, as you know well. She would do better here as the squire's wife, mistress of a fine establishment, than with some spotty younger son squeezed in with her in-laws. Be reasonable. You are just cross because she will put your nose out of joint. You like being mistress of Cloverstone Manor a little too well, if you ask me."

"It is unseemly to be courting when Mama is barely in her grave," she snapped, but she knew that was not the reason for her disquiet. Papa had never lasted more than a few months between wives, and the world would not censure a widower who quickly sought a new mother for his many young children. A widow must remain decorously aloof from society for many months, but a man was allowed to get on with his life.

No, Henry was right — a new wife would displace Susannah, and give her no reason to object to living with the Beasleys when she and Samuel were married. She was honest enough to admit the truth in her own heart, even as she wondered just why it would be such a wrench to leave the Manor. She wanted to marry Samuel more than anything in the world, yet the prospect of leaving her home of twenty-six years made her feel like a deep-rooted plant being dragged from the earth forcibly. The pain was very real.

~~~~~

Samuel felt as if he were in a perpetual fog. Lack of sleep affected him that way every time. He longed for his own bed and the bliss of many hours of refreshing sleep, but he could not leave Chandry unattended. He had passed the rest of Friday night half-dozing on the horribly uncomfortable leather sofa in the consultation room, then got through Saturday as best he could, checking on Chandry, dealing with a scattering of kitchen-door patients who realised he was still around, and trying to snatch the odd half hour of sleep in between. On Saturday night he watched Chandry so that Charlie could sleep, which left him even more exhausted on Sunday. He dragged himself to the local church, where Mac kept him awake by poking him vigorously in the ribs at five minute intervals. Then there was another disturbed night, for even though Matt Renshaw was watching Chandry, he woke Samuel anxiously every time Chandry grunted in his sleep.

Mac seemed impervious to the disruption, losing not an ounce of his good humour no matter how little sleep he got. Samuel kept him busy with a trip to Whitfield Villa to collect a change of clothes and his shaving equipment, and letters to Susannah and the Beasleys. The story that had been agreed was that a patient with a severe wound needed constant attendance for a few days. Susannah responded with an understanding note that hoped Charlie was feeding him well, but there was no response from the Beasleys. The reason for this became apparent on Monday morning, when a carriage drew up outside the house, and Dr and Miss Beasley descended.

There was no avoiding the inevitable, so, after warning Chandry in hurried whispers, Samuel led the Beasleys to the little sleeping area off the kitchen, where Chandry sat propped up with pillows on a low pallet, with Charlie reading to him.

"Chandry! Good gracious!" Beasley exclaimed. "Why, whatever happened to you? Broughton, you did not mention that it was Mr Chandry who needed your attention."

"I did not want to worry anyone," Samuel said. "Fortunately, he is well on the mend now, as you can see."

"But his neck is bound! What has happened here?"

"I was set upon by footpads on Friday night," Chandry said, with convincing glibness. "They pulled a knife on me, and I would have bled to death if Dr Broughton hadn't been here."

Miss Beasley frowned, as if puzzling over the obvious flaws, but Dr Beasley accepted the story at face value, the physician in him far too interested in Chandry's injuries to ask awkward questions, and the moment passed off smoothly.

After they had gone, Samuel retreated to his consultation room where he tortured himself by examining his accounts and trying for the fortieth time to foresee a month when he might be earning more than he spent.

His next visitor was Edgerton, who settled himself on the leather sofa that Samuel had come to despise, and accepted a glass of something from one of the random bottles brought up from the cellar — Canary, they agreed after some tentative sips, and not a very good one.

"Your cellar is like one of those children's games where one puts a hand into a bag and pulls out an object. It might be a silver sixpence or a marble or a sugar mouse, or it might be a dead rat. Or perhaps the dead rat game was just my family, who knows. But still, the similarity is there. That claret the other night was exquisite, but this is... less wonderful."

"Renshaw was illiterate, unfortunately, so when he pinched bottles for his own cellar, he had no idea what he was taking. Have you had any luck tracing his remains?"

A shadow crossed Edgerton's face. "No, and it worries me. I have checked the records at all three of the parish churches in the region and there is no record of a pauper's burial at any of them. It is hard to believe that anyone stumbling across the body would convey it further afield than that. Neate and I have thoroughly searched around the mile stone where the man fell, but he is definitely not there, so we are at a standstill, sadly. It would have been pleasing to draw a line under at least one of our investigations, for I am no further forward with Mrs Winslade's death, and there is another matter awaiting our attention, also. Nothing can be brought to a conclusion! It is most frustrating. However, it is of yet another matter that I wish to speak to you."

There was something in his expression that made Samuel sure that this was bad news, but he merely said, "Go on."

"Willerton-Forbes returned from London on Saturday." He paused, but Samuel said nothing. "He has... *concerns.*" Still Samuel was silent, so he went on gently, "You do not ask what these concerns might be, Dr Broughton, so I will tell you. The first concern is your wife's death. You were tried for her murder and subsequently acquitted, but that leaves many questions open. Was she murdered at all? If she was, who murdered her and why? And if she was not, why were you accused of the crime? And there are elements of the case that worry him greatly, as indeed they worry your friends. The most troubling aspect of all is that you have consistently refused to answer any questions relating to the fatal evening."

"I cannot," Samuel growled. He was having trouble breathing... one breath... another... be calm, be calm.

"So you have said," Edgerton said evenly, "and naturally that is your decision to make. However, your refusal to speak fuels the speculation that is still rampant in certain circles. Your friends are loyal, Broughton, and say not one word against you, but even they wish you would break your silence. The one sure way to bring all Strickland's malice against you to an end is to discover precisely how your wife died. Why does Strickland hate you so much, by the way?"

The question was casually spoken, but Samuel knew Edgerton well enough to be aware that he was watching his response very carefully. Yet he could say nothing as he struggled to breathe, his pulse racing.

Edgerton went on smoothly, "That too causes speculation, as you may imagine. Should you ever wish to speak of it, you would find us the ideal people to investigate. We are very discreet and also very, very thorough. But that is for you to decide, and we will not press you. There is another matter, however, which has given rise to some anxiety in Willerton-Forbes, and I must tell you that he is not a man much given to anxiety. His legal mind divides the world neatly into problems which may be fixed in law and problems which may not. If they may be fixed, he sets out to fix them, and if they may not... well, he loses no sleep over them. But he has discovered a problem which is indeed causing him to lose sleep, and it concerns your daughter."

"Cressy? He has concerned himself with Cressy? He had no business to do so!"

"It was not intentional," Edgerton said hastily, raising his hands placatingly. "His interest was in Strickland, and so he went into Hertfordshire and asked about, and what he heard there caused him to have grave misgivings."

Samuel's heart turned over in fear. "She is not ill? Hurt?"

"No, no, nothing of the sort. She is well cared for, and well loved, but— Broughton, I do not know whether you are aware, but your daughter is known in Hertfordshire by a different name."

"What name?"

"She is called Corinna Strickland."

No... no... breathe... breathe. Corinna was her middle name, but Strickland? He had claimed her as his own?

Edgerton went on slowly, "Everyone knows that she was once Cressida Broughton, but Strickland insists on the new name, and he spends all his time there with her. He has given up his London practice entirely and now spends all his time in the country with his granddaughter." A long pause. "She is very like her mother, I understand?"

Samuel nodded. He could manage that much.

"Pettigrew feels that... this is worrying... not a natural state of affairs. It is almost as if Strickland is trying to relive his own daughter's life in his granddaughter. He feels that you should remove Cressy from his care as soon as possible, and will do everything in his power to help you achieve that. As will we all. Broughton? Are you... quite well?"

He was not, of course. How could he be well when Cressy was in *his* care? He had assumed that it was Strickland's mother who had charge of her but this—! It was worse than he had ever imagined.

"I will leave you to consider all I have said," Edgerton said gently. "Be assured that we are ready to assist you in any way we can, at any time, Dr Broughton."

When he had gone, Samuel laid his head down on the desk and gave way to utter despair. What in God's name was he to do? Cressy, his sweet, beloved Cressy, was being consumed by Strickland, changed into something more to his liking, some grotesque parody of her mother. Yet what could he do? How could he fight Strickland? He had sworn an oath... a binding oath... Breathe... breathe...

"Samuel?"

His head shot up. There she was, his Susannah, her face filled with concern.

"Oh, my dear!" she said softly. "Whatever has happened? What is it?"

Mutely, for he could find no words, he held out his arms and she was there beside him, holding him, holding him tight, murmuring into his hair. And he wept like a babe in the comfort of her embrace, while she murmured, "Hush... shhh, now... there, my love... hush now..." into his ear.

Somehow, the words came and he poured it all out in a confused jumble. He hardly knew what he said, but she listened quietly, and once or twice asked a question, and nodded and held him tight, and, odd as it seemed, he felt better. Somehow nothing was quite so bad when Susannah was there with one hand warm on the back of his waistcoat, and the other tangled in his hair.

Eventually, exhausted, he looked her in the eye. "You must think I have run mad."

"No, merely stretched beyond endurance," she said. "What you really need is a walk by the river, followed by a hearty dinner and a good night's sleep, for you look as if you have not slept for a week. Then you will know what you should do."

"What do you think I should do?" he said.

"After the walk, the dinner and the sleep? I think you should talk to Mr Willerton-Forbes. And then I think you should go and rescue your daughter from this dangerous madman."

"You truly think him dangerous?"

"Clearly Mr Willerton-Forbes does, or he would not speak in such terms."

He liked that about her. There was no prevarication, no sidestepping round the issue. He had asked and she had answered, as she always did, openly and honestly.

"May I kiss you?" he said tentatively.

"Of course," she said, clearly surprised.

"I did not wish to presume."

She smiled then, that smile of such sweetness that her whole face was alight. "I am entirely yours, Samuel. You may kiss me whenever you wish."

So he kissed her, a gentle kiss of gratitude. He had no words for what he felt at that moment, but he knew beyond all doubt that Susannah was an angel sent from Heaven to rescue him from desolation.

When, eventually, he lifted his lips from her sweet mouth, he rested his forehead against hers. "Tomorrow I shall talk to Willerton-Forbes, but... I should like you to be with me, if you would be so good."

"Of course, my love," was all she said, but her smile filled him with joy.

27: Mr Willerton-Forbes Tells All

To avoid awkward questions, Susannah waited until her father had left for Shrewsbury before ordering the carriage, so it was almost noon before she arrived in Great Maeswood and turned into the drive of the Dower House. Mrs Edgerton met her at the door and ushered her inside.

"We are so glad you felt able to come, despite your mourning," Mrs Edgerton said, as she assisted Susannah out of her bonnet in the front parlour. "Pettigrew is so agitated — I have never seen him so upset, and as for Dr Broughton, I do not think he would have come here at all without your good offices to persuade him. He is here already, looking like a man at his own execution, poor fellow. I do hope he can set all this behind him, for clearly it distresses him so. Was he so very much in love with his wife? I suppose he must have been."

Susannah did not feel she could break Samuel's confidence by explaining that he had never loved his wife. Or so he said. A niggle of doubt crept in. Perhaps he had only said so for Susannah's sake. He was a very private man who would not want to talk about his feelings, in fact sometimes it seemed as if he would deny that he had any. *Love had nothing to do with it, not on her side and certainly not on mine.* Was that true? Perhaps today she would find out.

Taking a deep breath, she followed Mrs Edgerton across the hall to the study where the gentlemen waited, seated around a small table laden with glasses, decanters and dishes of biscuits and sweetmeats. The gentlemen all rose as she entered, and Captain Edgerton held a chair for her. Mrs Edgerton poured her a glass of wine, pushed a dish of something towards her and then graciously departed. Susannah was alone with Samuel, Captain Edgerton, Mr Willerton-Forbes and Mr Neate.

Samuel looked like death warmed up, as Susannah's old nurse had been wont to say, and his hands were shaking, but he gave her a tremulous little smile. Any smile from him was something of a triumph, so she smiled back as warmly as she could, and was pleased to see his expression lighten somewhat.

Mr Willerton-Forbes cleared his throat, took a sip of his wine, and then cleared his throat again. He was nervous, too, she realised. That was worrying, for she had never seen the lawyer in the least ruffled before.

"Miss Winslade, Dr Broughton, thank you both for coming today," he began. "Dr Broughton, you need not say anything at all, but I should like you to know all that I have discovered in London of your wife's death, and then I will explain my thoughts on the matter. Is this acceptable to you?"

Samuel nodded, briefly. His breath was laboured, and his skin had a pasty sheen, as if he were sweating. In any other man, such signs would suggest a guilty conscience, but Susannah knew otherwise. He might be suffering from deep-seated distress, but not guilt, of that she was sure.

"I began with the newspaper reports of the trial," Mr Willerton-Forbes went on, "which were quite extensive. I do not imagine you read them yourself, but the gentlemen of the press, if they deserve such an epithet, know that their more prurient readers enjoy every detail of a murder trial, especially one involving the great and the good of this country. I will not tire you with any of that. I spoke also to Sir Edward Browning, the barrister who defended you, with the coroner and magistrate who were involved, and with your friends named on the list that you graciously supplied to me. This has enabled me to piece together a picture of you and your wife, of your marriage and of the fatal night when Mrs Broughton met her end. Do have a little more Madeira, Dr Broughton. You are very pale. Or a brandy, perhaps?"

Samuel shook his head, but took a small sip of wine with trembling hands. It made Susannah's heart ache to be unable to hold him, soothe away his fears, bring him some little comfort in his distress. All she could do was to stretch out her hand to hold his. He lifted his head to look at her, and there was that momentary smile again — just a flash and then it was gone. But it was something! She could not do much, but whatever aid was in her power he should have.

Clearing his throat again, Mr Willerton-Forbes continued his story. "That evening, the third day of June, Mrs Broughton had guests for dinner, six long-standing friends of hers. You were not expected to dine with them, and that was quite usual. You and your wife maintained quite independent circles of friends. Just before seven o'clock, therefore, you looked in on the guests, wished them a pleasant evening and departed for White's, where you dined alone.

Stranger at the Villa: Strangers Book 3

At approximately nine o'clock, you left White's. At approximately the same time, Mrs Broughton's friends were leaving for the opera, but Mrs Broughton was not to accompany them. She had accepted invitations to a number of different events that evening. Accordingly, she went upstairs to change her gown for something more formal. Her maid had left her and had returned downstairs when she remembered a forgotten item, and went back upstairs, where she overheard a violent argument taking place in Mrs Broughton's bedroom. Two raised voices were heard, that of a man and a woman. That was a little after nine. The argument was quickly over, and at about ten o'clock, it seems they both left the house."

Mr Willerton-Forbes took another, longer sip of Madeira, and refilled his glass. "This is where things become a little tenuous, because after the dinner guests had departed, the front door was locked and bolted for the night. This was a normal state of affairs, and anyone from the household entering or leaving the house after that would use a small side door that led directly to a narrow passageway between houses. Both you and Mrs Broughton had a key, as did the housekeeper and footman. The housekeeper's room was directly above the door, and she could hear it open and close. She could not see who was entering or leaving, but she noted the time because she suspected the footman of dalliance, and was gathering evidence.

"The housekeeper heard the door about ten o'clock, and it was presumed that Mrs Broughton and the man who had been with her both left the house at that point. From shortly after ten until twelve, you were at a small club off Mayfair, Dr Broughton, playing chess with a physician friend, a regular arrangement. You left at about twelve, and the housekeeper heard the door a few minutes after twelve, as you presumably returned to the house. That was usual for you, since you rarely stayed out past midnight. Mrs Broughton, meanwhile, was attending some of her various entertainments that evening. Her precise movements cannot be determined, since she dispensed with her own carriage after the first event, but she was seen by several people. The housekeeper notes that she returned at about two o'clock, which was perfectly normal for her. She undressed herself, which again was usual. And nothing further was known until about eight in the morning when her maid found her mistress dead in her bed, and her screams alerted the household."

He paused, looking across the table at Samuel. "Is there anything you wish to say at this point, Dr Broughton?"

Samuel shook his head. His hands were shaking again.

Mr Willerton-Forbes nodded, as if he had expected such an answer. He went on, "You were summoned, and Mrs Broughton's father, Sir James Strickland, and then the coroner. A quantity of laudanum was found in Mrs Broughton's room, and an empty glass containing traces of laudanum, so it was presumed that she had taken some when she returned home. Her maid said that she occasionally did so when she had the head ache. At first it was assumed that there had been a tragic miscalculation and that your wife had inadvertently taken too large a dose, but when Sir James heard about the quarrel, he immediately began to suspect something more sinister. And that was when you were arrested on a charge of murder, Dr Broughton."

The whole room was silent, as if waiting. Susannah felt as if a great weight were pressing on her chest, for Mr Willerton-Forbes was not relating all this for his own amusement. He was leading up to something terrible, she knew it, but she could not guess what, only that she felt a profound dread.

"We need not dwell on the trial," Mr Willerton-Forbes said. "Sir Edward Browning defended you ably, and showed the jury that there was no evidence that Mrs Broughton had been murdered at all, it was mere supposition, and even if it had been the case, anyone could have come in through the side door, for the lock was easily picked or the key could have been copied at any time. And there was no motive. The only suggestion of such was the quarrel, but then a glass containing brandy was found on Mrs Broughton's bedside table. Since she never drank spirits herself, it must have belonged to her male visitor, and a man who stops to drink brandy is hardly likely to turn to murder. That brandy glass was a significant factor in the trial. A great many friends came forward to testify to your good character, and your devotion to your wife. No one had ever witnessed you raise your voice to her, or appear anything other than entirely contented, in seven years of marriage. No one could suggest a single reason why you should want to kill her." He sipped his wine thoughtfully. "You have fiercely loyal friends, Dr Broughton."

Susannah shivered, although the room was warm. Was he suggesting something subversive in having friends who spoke up for Samuel? That perhaps they were concealing something? She was beginning to understand how little she knew of this — indeed, of Samuel's life altogether. There was something to be said for a longer courtship, and a period of getting to know one another better.

"I spoke at length to Sir Edward Browning, your barrister, and he was most helpful. He told me of a circumstance which was not mentioned in the trial, namely that Mrs Broughton was with child, and would have been confined not long after Michaelmas."

Samuel's head shot up. "Michaelmas? Then it *was* mine!"

"You doubted it, Dr Broughton?" Mr Willerton-Forbes said, with an edge of excitement in his voice.

"Of course!" he said, a little frown of puzzlement on his forehead. "She said it was mine, but then she always had lovers."

"Did she?" Mr Willerton-Forbes said softly.

Again Samuel looked puzzled. "Yes. There was no secret about it. She told me about them. There were always lovers, even before we married."

"Ah. How interesting. And she would have been... oh, eighteen or so at that time?"

"Not quite eighteen."

"You see, Dr Broughton, this is where matters become murky again," Mr Willerton-Forbes said. "There was a man in Mrs Broughton's room that evening, that much is known, but his identity is not. Sir Edward considered the possibility of a lover, naturally, for that would be by far the quickest way to scotch the case against you, and the separate lives you led would also suggest it, but he could find not one shred of evidence for it."

"Nevertheless, she did have lovers," Samuel said. "Very occasionally our paths crossed at some affair or other, and she always had a man on her arm, always."

"She had cicisbeos, certainly, and some of them very highly placed — the military, the diplomatic world, the nobility and even higher than that. For that reason, her delicate condition was not mentioned at the trial, in case there should be unseemly speculation on the matter. But lovers? Sir Edward could not find one person who even wondered about it. But if there were no lover, then the only person who could have been in your wife's bedroom that evening was you, Dr Broughton."

Samuel opened his mouth as if to speak, then clamped it shut again.

"What a pity," Mr Willerton-Forbes said softly. "For a moment there I thought you were about to deny it. But you never have. In fact, you have spoken not a single word about that night, even when you were accused of murder. Sir Edward wished to have your version of events to impart to the jury, naturally, for what could be more convincing than the words of an unquestioned gentleman proclaiming his innocence in ringing terms. But you would not speak of it, there was the quarrel and the lack of any other suspect, and so he was forced to conclude that you had, in fact, murdered your wife."

"He did not!" Susannah cried. "He could not possibly have murdered Corinna for he knew she was with child. He would never, *ever* have harmed a child. If he did not speak in his own defence, he must have had a good reason."

"Your logic is impeccable, Miss Winslade. Yes, indeed, a good reason, but what? When a gentleman remains silent in such circumstances, it is usually because he is protecting someone."

"So you are saying that *Samuel* had a lover?" Susannah said.

"That is one possibility," he said calmly. "He could also be protecting his wife, or his child. Impossible to say. But his silence has been very damaging. Even the barrister who defended him believed him guilty, and his friends are uneasy about it. They have defended him, of course, but in their hearts they wonder about it. Dr Broughton is a very reserved man, they told me, very private, very restrained. Perhaps, if pushed beyond endurance, his self-control would snap and—"

"*I did not kill my wife!*"

Mr Willerton-Forbes let out a long sigh, and leaned back in his chair, resting his laced fingers on his rounded stomach. "Then who did? Or was it an accident?"

"I do not *know!*" Samuel said in frustration. "I wish I did, but I do not. You cannot know how that question haunts me."

"Can you perhaps tell us about it and—"

"No!" His breathing was ragged again, and he buried his face in his hands.

For a moment there was silence in the room, and the three men watched him sympathetically. Susannah was sympathetic, too, but she knew he would never be able to set the past behind him unless he spoke about it.

"Samuel..." she began tentatively. His head lifted again, and she dared to reach out to him, to take hold of his hand in both of hers. It was cold, and without thought she rubbed it gently with her thumbs. "Samuel, do you truly wish to find out what happened that night?" He gave a little nod, but his eyes were wide with... what? Not fear, but perhaps sorrow. "Then the only way is to talk about it. You are not on trial now, and nothing you say will ever leave this room, but you have here three people who spend their lives investigating such cases. Is it not worth a try? If Corinna *was* murdered, do you not want to bring her murderer to justice?"

"No."

"What? Why ever not?"

He said nothing, and it was Captain Edgerton who answered. "Because he wishes to protect that person, that is why."

"Why would he protect a murderer?" Susannah cried. "That makes no sense!"

"Ah, but it does," the captain said. "Bear in mind that there is a period of the evening when Broughton's movements are unaccounted for, from the time he left White's until the time he arrived to play chess with his friend. Suppose he spent that time in the company of a lady — a lady who is deep in love with him and would be delighted to be rid of the inconvenient Mrs Broughton."

"Michael, Michael," Mr Willerton-Forbes said sorrowfully, as Mr Neate rocked with laughter. "You allow your imagination to carry you too far."

"He has forgotten the quarrel, too," Mr Neate said. "Who was that, if this was all about a lady?"

"An assassin, paid for by the love-sick lady," Captain Edgerton said.

"No, no, no," Mr Neate said. "Too fanciful by half. I think the quarrel *was* with Dr Broughton, but they made it up. Then Mrs Broughton accidentally took too much laudanum and now Dr Broughton is consumed by guilt, and that is why he cannot speak of it."

"Gentlemen, please!" Mr Willerton-Forbes said sharply. "You are *both* too fanciful. Engage reason, if you please. No one could enter Mrs Broughton's bedchamber who was not a member of the household, or else held a key to the side door used in the evenings. The only male servant, the footman, was at a nearby tavern, so Dr Broughton is seemingly the only person who could have quarrelled with Mrs Broughton that evening. But there is one other person who may have had a key, who would have been admitted without question by Mrs Broughton, namely the same person who leased the house in the first place."

"Sir James Strickland?" Susannah said. "But... why? Why would he visit his daughter at night?"

"Now that I cannot answer," Mr Willerton-Forbes said. "Strickland, however, interests me greatly. He was most helpful to Dr Broughton at the time of his marriage, in a number of ways. He seemed very supportive and then... he accused him of murder, in a case which even the coroner thought was more than likely an accidental excess of laudanum. He took everything from Dr Broughton, emptying his house of all its contents, and effectively preventing him from pursuing his profession. He even took his child. And now, when Dr Broughton is beginning to rebuild his career, he drives all the way to Shropshire for the sole purpose of damaging his reputation. Why would he do such a thing? That was the question that drove me to London, initially, and then to Hertfordshire and there I saw—"

"Cressy!" Samuel cried. "You saw my daughter."

"Sadly, no. Doubtless the intrepid Captain Edgerton would have climbed walls and so forth to gain admittance, but I am more a man of words, rather than actions. I talk to people, Dr Broughton, including the local parson, and an acquaintance who lives nearby, who introduced me to some of Strickland's friends, informally, you understand. A dinner guest is able to hear a great deal of local gossip that would not be afforded a stranger. What I was about to say was that I saw much in that gossip to disquiet me. Your father-in-law was very fond of his daughter — your wife. Everyone agreed on that point. They were very close. In fact, she was far closer to her father than her mother, and once she outgrew the nursery, she spent most of her time with her father in London. He was very careful to keep suitors well away from her, and yet somehow, by some means, she found herself with child, whereupon she was hastily married off."

He fell silent, gazing at Samuel, as if expecting him to speak, but he said nothing. There was a tenseness about him, though, as if he were waiting for a blow to fall.

"Dr Broughton," Mr Willerton-Forbes said gently. "Cressy was not your blood. Have you never wondered who fathered her?"

"No." His voice was so low as to be almost inaudible.

"And perhaps that was why Strickland came to you to marry his daughter, since he knew you would ask no questions. But I think you know the answer anyway, do you not?"

"No." A mere whisper.

"But you suspect. As those who know the family did. As I did, when I heard all."

The shock of understanding hit Susannah like a hammer blow. She gasped, hands to mouth.

"Yes," Mr Willerton-Forbes said sadly. "I am very much afraid it is so. Sir James Strickland is Cressy's grandfather, but he is also her father."

28: Hertfordshire

Oddly, Samuel was not shocked. As soon as Willerton-Forbes spoke the words, he knew the truth of them. So many small pieces of evidence over the years suddenly came into sharp focus. The way Strickland had looked at Corinna, the way he *touched* her... a hand on her arm, her shoulder... a flick of one finger against her cheek. When they met, he always kissed her on both cheeks, one arm around her waist. And he was always visiting. When Samuel had seen his last patient each day, he generally went up to the drawing room to see Corinna and more often than not he found Strickland there, lounging in a favourite chair with a glass of brandy at his elbow, holding forth on some subject or other. Whenever he went into Hertfordshire, he expected her to go with him. Not Samuel. He was rarely invited. But Corinna... he never liked to be apart from her.

"Yes," he said slowly. "Yes. It could be."

"But that is so horrible!" Susannah cried. "For a father to do that to his own daughter! It is *evil!*"

"It is," Samuel said. "I think... I think I have always known it, in some way, that he was *too* close, *too* affectionate for a father, but I never saw the full truth of it until this moment. Oh dear God! He has

Cressy!" The burning fear that swamped him was primal in its urgency. "I must rescue her!"

"Yes, and soon," Mr Willerton-Forbes said. "However, the matter is no longer urgent. I persuaded my father, who knows Strickland slightly and lives not far away, to invite him for a visit. He should be at my father's house now, and he and Mother will keep him occupied until you can get to Hertfordshire and take her out of Strickland's reach."

"But how can it be done? He is her guardian now."

"Not in law, Dr Broughton. You are her father, after all. Sir James has no rights over Cressy, and in fact has not attempted to claim any. I took the precaution of checking the Court of Chancery records, and he has not applied for guardianship, nor would it ever be granted, while the child has a living father. So you need only walk up to the door and take Cressy away with you."

"That is all?"

"Precisely so. Since you will have us with you and the law on your side, even Sir James Strickland cannot prevent it. But do you agree with me, Dr Broughton? That it might have been Sir James who quarrelled with your wife that night?"

"Brandy... he drank brandy," he said distractedly.

"Ah, interesting."

"It is possible, but... all my ideas of that night are overturned now and I do not know what to think."

Susannah was still holding his hand, and now she gave it a gentle squeeze. "Is it not time, Samuel? Time to speak of it?"

She was right of course, but could he do it? Instinctively, his heart thumped with painful pressure, and his breathing was shallow. He *could* not, he had sworn— But that was all swept away, for there was a higher imperative now. For Cressy's sake, he must and would speak!

Briefly, he nodded. Then he took a deep breath... and then another, as he marshalled his thoughts.

"That day... seemed perfectly normal, except that Corinna came down to breakfast. She never did so before, but that day she did, and when we were alone she told me that she was with child. She asked me if I were pleased — well, of course I was! I had long wished for another child, but had almost given up hope. I did not care if it were mine or not. That had never mattered with Cressy, and it would not matter with the new child, either. But she told me it was mine. I was... surprised. I was not often invited to her bed, and— Oh, forgive me, Susannah!"

"It is quite all right," she said, smiling her lovely smile. "I am not some green girl straight out of the schoolroom, to swoon away at the mere mention of marital relations."

That made him laugh suddenly. "You are a most unusual woman, do you know that? Anyway, it had been some months, and so I was surprised. But then she laughed and said, *'Or perhaps it was one of my many lovers, who knows. Perhaps my very special lover.'* That was how she always talked, and I never thought anything of it. I just assumed that she meant it. But the rest of the day was as usual, nothing untoward. I left the house that evening at seven, as you have said, and dined at White's, leaving at nine, but not to return to the house. I cannot tell you— No, I must, I think, but I can provide no one to verify my whereabouts, for I do not know her name. Yes, I was with a lady, but not for any underhand motive, I give you my word. I was never unfaithful to my wife."

He was addressing Susannah, fully aware that he was pleading, but for some reason it was desperately important that she believe him.

"Then I accept your word on the matter," she said placidly.

Her trust took his breath away. Could he ever be worthy of such generosity of spirit? What a wife she would be, and that time could not come soon enough for him.

Collecting his scattered thoughts with difficulty, he went on, "She was a patient, a woman who had called upon my professional services previously and wished to talk to me again. She held a high position, however, and wished to exercise the utmost discretion. I never knew her name or rank, and only ever met her in discreet lodgings in obscure streets, a different one every time. That night I talked to her, or rather she talked to me and I listened, for an hour or so, but then she had to attend some function. She was going out of town the next day, so she asked me if I would return at midnight. I left, I played chess, as you know, and returned at midnight, and she arrived there a few minutes later. I left shortly before two o'clock."

"So you were the one who returned at two," Captain Edgerton said excitedly. "So who returned at midnight?"

"Corinna, I assume," Samuel said, "for she was home when I returned. Her bedroom door was ajar, and so I went in... I went in..."

It was difficult to breathe again, each gasp dredged up from deep inside, harsh and laboured.

"Take your time," Susannah said, and her sympathy gave him a burst of energy.

"She was asleep... curled up in bed. My candle did not disturb her, so I left her to sleep, may God forgive me! How many times have I relived that moment? Could I have saved her, if I had known? Or was she even dead at that point and I, for all my much-vaunted expertise, failed to understand it? Was I even worthy to call myself a physician?"

"You would have known," Susannah said quietly. "The dead are... different. You would have known."

"I agree," Edgerton said, unexpectedly sombre. "I have seen more of the dead than I ever wanted to, and Miss Winslade is right — there is a distinct difference. Once the life force has fled, everything changes."

Samuel nodded. "You are right, of course. But now you see why I could not speak, for I knew nothing. I do not know, to this day, how Corinna died, whether by accident or intent, by her own hand or another's, and if the latter, by whom. If I told the truth, there would be a great search for my distinguished patient and for Corinna's lover, if indeed she had one. There would be an ocean of rumour and half-truth and speculation, damaging to far more than just myself, and I had sworn to Strickland that I would never say or do anything to damage him or his family. Better by far that everyone should think I murdered my wife. I wanted to tell everything... to clear my name... to stand up in court and proclaim my innocence loud and clear, as any honest man would, but I was honour-bound to secrecy — to my patient, to Corinna's lover, and most particularly to Strickland. "

"You were prepared to hang to protect Strickland's reputation?" Mr Willerton-Forbes said gently.

"What did I have to live for? As soon as Strickland accused me of murder, I was finished, my reputation destroyed. A man cannot live without his reputation, his *honour*. I was done for, and all I could do was to ensure I took no one else down with me. I was astonished when I was acquitted. I had no idea what to do with myself, but one of my friends had acquaintances in Edinburgh and put me on the mail coach with a letter of introduction. Even then, I could not understand why I was still alive. I used to go and sit by the river — it is more than a river, wide and slow-moving and remote. Uncaring. For hours, sometimes, I would sit staring out at the far shore, until a mouthy Scotsman found me, and nagged me back to the world, and gave me hope."

"Mac," Susannah said, smiling. "Your groom."

"Yes. He just attached himself to me, somehow, and now I cannot shake him off. But he saved my sanity that time, and I believe that you — all of you — have saved it this time. I truly thought it was the end, when Strickland came here. I had recovered my reputation once, but I could not do it a second time."

"In Shropshire, we do not desert our friends," Susannah said. "Londoners may be fickle, but we are loyal."

Samuel's throat was so tight that he could not speak, and it was Neate who said cheerfully, "We Londoners may be fickle, but we are also very stupid, or at least I am, for I confess I cannot work out what happened to Mrs Broughton in the slightest. We have a man who arrived at nine and quarrelled with her, then they presumably both left at ten. She returned at midnight, Dr Broughton returned at two in the morning when she was sleeping peacefully, and there is no scope in this neat arrangement for a murderer. Nor are we any further forward in determining whether Mrs Winslade was murdered, and we have not managed to find Lucas Renshaw's body, even though we know precisely where, when and how he died. In short, we are utter failures, and should hang up our investigative hats immediately."

"And Dilys Hughes — never forget Dilys Hughes," Edgerton said despairingly. "One day I shall find out what happened to her, I am determined on that."

"We have had *some* successes," Willerton-Forbes said mildly. "We have resolved the mystery of the wine in Dr Broughton's cellar, for one thing, and I hope we will make progress soon on another project."

"We have plenty of time yet for that," Edgerton said.

Susannah laughed. "You are very secretive, gentlemen, but I believe I may guess at that project in particular."

Willerton-Forbes looked surprised, but Edgerton laughed. "Do tell us your guess, Miss Winslade."

"Very well," she said, a smile lighting up her face. Samuel melted a little inside as he looked at her. How lovely she was when she smiled, her eyes alive with amusement! She went on, "I have heard that you were in Overbury recently asking questions about Mr Truman, who was born and raised there, and since I happen to know that Cass's trustees wish to be sure that her future husband is not a fortune hunter, it is not hard to guess what you are about."

The men exchanged glances. "You are very astute, Miss Winslade," Willerton-Forbes said. "However, we would appreciate it if you would not mention this to anyone, not even Miss Saxby."

"No, indeed. But you have many months before the wedding, and there are more urgent matters to be dealt with. Samuel, you must go at once to Cressy and bring her to Shropshire. We will take good care of her here, you may be sure."

~~~~~

Samuel was terrified. His head told him that he had every right to go to Hertfordshire to claim Cressy, but his heart... oh, his heart! Would she even know him, after two years? Even if she did, would she want to leave? She had been uprooted from her familiar life in London and taken to live with her grandmother — and her grandfather, for he had all but given up his London practice after Corinna had died and stayed in the country. She had even been given a new name, for she was Corinna Strickland now, not Cressida Broughton. What had they told her about her father? Had they told her anything? She must surely have thought that he had abandoned her.

If Willerton-Forbes and Edgerton had not been with him, he was sure he would have turned tail and gone home again. As it was, he sat passively in the carriage with Willerton-Forbes, saying nothing, for the lawyer was engrossed in the many pages of Corinna's marriage settlement, a kind of dry-as-dust document that appealed to his lawyerly instincts.

Three days of travelling... three days of Edgerton's cheerful bonhomie, and Willerton-Forbes' recitals of the law. Three days of dread... but it could not be avoided without shame, and so, late in the third day, they turned off the leaf-shaded lane into the grounds of Purnell House, Strickland's residence.

Willerton-Forbes had assured them that his father would keep Strickland out of the way, but there was a carriage drawn up at the front door as they arrived, with luggage being unloaded.

"That is my father's carriage," Willerton-Forbes said, pulling a face. "It looks as if we will have to deal with Strickland after all. But it is of no consequence. We have the law on our side, Dr Broughton, never forget that."

The carriage decanted Samuel and Willerton-Forbes, Edgerton dismounted and they walked up the steps to the front door, standing wide open. Samuel hesitated, but Willerton-Forbes marched straight into the hall.

"Courage, my friend," Edgerton said, and with a quirk of one eyebrow, he followed the lawyer. Samuel had no choice but to scuttle after them.

The hall swirled with servants and boxes and packages. The butler materialised out of the maelstrom, an imposing giant of a man with a misshapen nose.

"May I help you?" he said.

"Do you remember me, Castleman?" Samuel said softly.

There was a flash of shocked recognition, then years of training snapped into place. "I am afraid—"

"Please tell Sir James that I wish to speak to him. My companions are Mr Willerton-Forbes and Captain Edgerton."

"Sir James is not receiving."

"Oh, I think he will receive us," Edgerton said, with a wide smile, shifting slightly so that the sword at his side was in clear view.

"Make an appointment, gentlemen. This way out, if you please."

He gestured towards the door, but Samuel was not about to be deterred by an uppity manservant. He was about to respond when an inner door opened, and Sir James Strickland and another man emerged together. They stopped, and stared at the three men standing in the middle of the hall. Sir James glowered at them, but the other man smiled gently. Samuel guessed from a slight family resemblance that he must be the Earl of Morpeth, Willerton-Forbes' father.

"Why, Pettigrew, what a pleasant surprise! Sir James, this is my youngest son, Pettigrew, a lawyer as I was before my elevation. And this is Captain Edgerton, formerly of the East India Company Army. And this is—?"

He tipped his head towards Samuel. Willerton-Forbes said smoothly, "Dr Samuel Broughton, Father. Sir James's son-in-law."

"He is no relation of *mine*," Strickland said. "What the devil do you want, Broughton?"

Samuel had no trouble with butlers, but he quailed before Strickland's intense dislike. He took a deep breath, then another. He remembered the law, and Susannah's sweet face. He remembered that he was in the right. Most of all, he remembered that Strickland had done unspeakable things to his own daughter.

He lifted his chin. "I want my daughter back. I want Cressy."

"Well, you cannot have her. Castleman, remove these persons from my property."

"Certainly, Sir James." Castleman stepped forward, looming menacingly large over the group.

"I would not try that, if I were you," Edgerton said softly, one hand reaching into his pocket.

Willerton-Forbes laid a hand on his friend's arm. "Michael, Michael... you cannot shoot a butler. It is dreadfully bad form. It is also bad form to discuss family matters in front of the servants. Sir James, shall we repair to somewhere more private?"

Strickland eyed them thoughtfully, clearly weighing up the likelihood of Edgerton actually shooting someone against his clear desire to throw them all out on their ear. Discretion won, and he led them silently into the drawing room, where Lady Strickland sat, her back ramrod straight, as always. To Samuel's surprise, she expressed pleasure at his visit.

"How lovely! You have come to see Cressy, of course. She will be so pleased to see you."

"Corinna," Sir James growled.

"Oh... oh, yes. Corinna. Yes, indeed. It seemed to be for the best, Dr Broughton. I am sure you understand. But I do forget, sometimes," she added in an undertone, half to herself.

To Samuel's relief, Willerton-Forbes took over, explaining succinctly that Samuel was still Cressy's legal guardian, and now that he was settled and shortly to marry again, he wished to have his daughter under his own roof once more.

"Marry again! How wonderful!" Lady Strickland twittered. "I wish you joy. Is she anyone we know?"

"Nonsense," Strickland said, ignoring his wife. "This is Corinna's home now. You cannot take her away."

"She is my daughter," Samuel said.

"She is *not!*" Sir James's eyes bulged. "You cannot have her, do you hear? She is a Strickland and this is her home now. You know perfectly well that she is none of your blood, Broughton. You have no claim on her at all. She is mine — *mine!*"

"Sir James," Willerton-Forbes said, in his gentle but implacable voice, a sharp contrast to Strickland's loud bluster, "the law says otherwise, and you cannot defy the law. The scandal that would ensue in any attempt to do so would be most distressing for everyone. Dr Broughton is grateful to you and to Lady Strickland for caring for his daughter while he was away in Scotland and unable to provide her with a home, but that is now at an end. He wishes to take her with him today. Where is Cressy?"

"You cannot have her! She is my own precious girl!" His voice rose to a dangerous crescendo, and he took two steps towards Samuel, fists clenched.

Edgerton and Neate were there before him, pistols in hands, standing protectively in front of Samuel.

From behind them came Willerton-Forbes' even tones. "Yes, you may shoot Sir James if you need to. Self-defence is acceptable in law."

For several long seconds, no one moved or spoke.

Then Lady Strickland said quietly, "She is riding in the paddock."

Sir James deflated in an instant. With a growl of anger, he turned and walked across to the window. Edgerton and Neate lowered their pistols.

"I will have her things packed up," Lady Strickland said.

"Thank you," Samuel said, crossing the room to take the hand she held out to him. "I am so sorry to descend on you without warning but—"

"I understand," she said, but he wondered if she did. Had she any idea what her husband had done?

Samuel dimly remembered the way through the house to the stable door, only going wrong once, and thence to the paddock. And there she was, but goodness, how she had grown! She sat side-saddle on her little pony as if she had been riding all her life, clad in a neat habit and stylish bonnet, cantering in a big circle round the paddock, with a groom running alongside. A few logs had been laid out as simple jumps, and over she went, without the slightest hesitation.

As she came round the loop again she saw the little group standing watching her, slowed and then came to a halt, staring at them. She said something to the groom but he shook his head. Urging her pony forwards at a walk, she neared the open gate where they stood. Oh, her sweet face, those rounded, rosy cheeks, the fair curls peeping out from her bonnet... His Cressy, a little older, a little more of a lady now, but still his beloved daughter.

She stopped again, and then... "Papa? Papa!"

The horse sped up to a trot, then a canter. Nearer and nearer she came, her face alight with joy. She drew the pony to an abrupt halt directly in front of Samuel, cast aside the reins, swung her leg off the pommel and practically threw herself into his waiting arms.

Tears trickled down his face and he cared not one whit, for he had Cressy again and the world was a glorious place.

"Papa? Have you come to take me home?"

"Yes, sweetheart, I have."

29: Coming Home

Samuel gently set Cressy on the ground again. Much as he wanted nothing more than to hug her tight, the most urgent necessity was to remove her from Strickland as soon as possible. He introduced her to Willerton-Forbes and Edgerton, and the Earl of Morpeth, who had followed them out of the house. Like all children she was fascinated by Edgerton's sword, and he was obliged to demonstrate its use, in his usual flamboyant style, while she clapped her hands in glee.

"Wilkie has a sword, too," she said, pointing at the groom. "Two swords, and he can throw them up and catch them. Show them, Wilkie."

He was a small man, as grooms often are, but then Captain Edgerton was not overlarge, either, so the sword did not seem excessively long in Wilkie's hands. He took the sword and carefully judged the heft of it, then passed it from hand to hand. Then without warning he threw it straight up in the air, and as it fell, tumbling end over end, he deftly caught hold of the handle again.

Cressy clapped excitedly.

"Very clever," Edgerton said. "Which regiment were you with?"

"Astley's," the man said grinning, so that a row of gleaming teeth with a few gaps shone from his dark-complexioned face. "You pick up any number of tricks in the circus."

"He can walk along the fence rail," Cressy said happily, and this skill, too, had to be demonstrated before she could be coaxed back into the house, where they found two boxes sitting in the hall, together with a nervous-looking maid, cloaked ready for travel.

"Beth!" Samuel said. "So you are still here. I thought all our servants had been scattered to the four winds."

"Jes' me left, sir, to see to Miss Corinna."

"Cressy," he said gently. "Her name is Cressy. I am very pleased that you will be coming with us, Beth."

Their farewells were brief. Cressy curtsied demurely to Lady Strickland, who waved her off with a cheerful smile. The giant butler seemed to be blinking back tears, and the housekeeper and several maids wept openly. Sir James did not come to the hall to see them off, but as Samuel helped Cressy into the carriage, he caught a glimpse of his thunderous countenance peering out of the library window.

They all found rooms for the night in Hertford, the Earl of Morpeth included, taking a large private parlour where Cressy clung to Samuel's arm as if she would never let him go. Since that was exactly what he intended, he made no move to detach her, and so they sat, the two of them, as the servants came and went, the conversation ranged back and forth and dinner appeared, was demolished and vanished. Cressy ate little and Samuel nothing at all. He could barely believe, even now, that his precious daughter was safe with him again.

When she fell asleep on his shoulder, he carried her up to her room and left her with Beth. As he re-entered the parlour, Edgerton was shuffling a pack of cards.

"Will you play, Broughton?"

"Thank you, but no. I shall sit here in a glow of brandy-soaked relief that we succeeded in extracting her from that strange household with so little difficulty."

"What was so strange about it?" Neate said. "To my eye, all these rich houses and their occupants are eccentric in one way or another, and that one seemed no worse than usual."

"Lady Strickland seemed almost glad to get rid of Cressy," Samuel said thoughtfully. "Then the butler is a former prize fighter, and one of the grooms is a circus acrobat. Yes, I would call it very strange. Edgerton? Are you quite well?"

The captain had frozen, an expression of utter shock on his face. *"Wilkie!"* he groaned. "Wilkinson! An acrobat! A man agile enough to climb to an upper window and strong enough to put a pillow over Mrs Winslade's face. And it is possible — it is *entirely* possible — that he did exactly the same two years ago and murdered Corinna Broughton."

~~~~~

'Hertford, 6th August. My dear Susannah, Cressy is in my care again and we expect to reach Great Maeswood on Tuesday. I should like you to be at Whitfield Villa when we arrive, if you can possibly manage it. I cannot wait to introduce Cressy to her new Mama. Yours in haste, Samuel.'

~~~~~

Stranger at the Villa: Strangers Book 3

The letter from Samuel had not reached Susannah until Monday afternoon, throwing her into an unaccustomed spin. So soon! She was to meet her soon-to-be daughter in just a few hours, and the instant she walked out of church as Samuel's wife, she would be a mother, too. She was used to children, for she had eight young brothers and sisters, but then she had known them since birth and her affection for them and theirs for her was long established. Poor Cressy had been uprooted not once but twice in her young life, first when her mother had died and now when she was returning to her father's care. How would she cope, poor child? At least Samuel was known to her, even if Susannah and the Beasleys were not.

The Beasleys! Were they even aware of Cressy's impending arrival? She summoned the carriage and drove at once to Whitfield Villa.

"Oh, Susannah! I am so thankful to see you, I cannot tell you!" Miss Beasley cried, racing down the steps to grab her arm before she had got halfway out of the carriage. "Tomorrow! They will be here tomorrow, and I have not the least idea what to do or what the child will need. A nursery maid! How shall I find a nursery maid at such short notice? And clothes, gowns — what will she eat? I am so distracted I do not know which way to turn, I declare."

Susannah laughed, her own trepidation lost in these easily answered mundane questions. "Miss Beasley, this is unlike you, to be so put out by a domestic matter. You are so imperturbable as a rule."

"But a child! I know nothing about managing a child."

"Then it is fortunate that I do. To start with, she will bring all her clothes and other belongings with her, and she may bring a maid, too. If she does not, you may borrow Jenny while you look about for someone. As for food, why she will eat plain nursery fare. You can leave all that to Mrs Shinn."

"Oh yes, yes, of course." She laughed, her panicked voice already returning to its usual gentle tone. "Thank you, Susannah, you are such a help. We have a room for the nursery and a room for her to sleep in, but of course we have nothing suitable for a child of eight — no toys or books, no slates or dolls. I suppose she might bring things of that nature with her, too, do you think?"

"She might indeed, but I shall have Alice and the twins look out some things for her."

"Oh, that is a kindness," Miss Beasley said. "You will be such a help, for of course you are quite used to children, having so many little brothers and sisters. I do not know when there was last a child in this house, for Aunt Margery had none, and Roland has never married. Will you come and see the nursery?" Susannah had got into the hall by now, and was handing her bonnet and gloves to Thomas, when Miss Beasley came to a complete halt and grabbed her arm again, her cheeks pink with pleasure. "A child! Here in this house! Just think! Is it not wonderful? Thank you Thomas, that will be all. Come, now, will you inspect our proposed nursery and cast your experienced eye over it?" As they climbed the stairs, she laughed, and said, "You must think me terribly foolish to flap about in this irrational way, but I did think we would have time to prepare, you see. Even when Dr Broughton went away, I did not quite expect that he would bring the child back with him directly. It is wonderful, of course, but rather a surprise, and I do not know what she will like. I do so want her to be *happy* here."

"All children need is food, space to run around and love, in plentiful amounts of each," Susannah said. "The rest — book learning and moral guidance and how to eat soup silently and what shape of bonnet suits them best — well, there is all the time in the world for that later. But for now, Cressy has her father, and she will have you and Dr Beasley, and before too long she will have me, too, and no books or dolls can substitute for those. She will be happy."

In the nursery, the housekeeper and a maid were busily raising a great cloud of dust by shaking the rugs out of the window. Susannah coughed, and found a handkerchief to cover her mouth and nose.

"Perhaps you can get Lil Irvine to come up from the Smithy to help out," she said. "The Boar's Head might lend you one or two of their maids, too."

"Yes, of course, I should have thought of that. How wonderfully practical you are. Come and see the bedroom we think might do. It is sometimes used for a guest, so it is not quite so neglected."

It was a good sized room, but filled with dark, heavy and overpoweringly grown up furniture. Susannah thought of her young sisters' rooms, with their pretty wallpaper and brightly painted woodwork, and wondered what an eight-year-old child would make of this gloomy room.

"Of course, we will have it refurbished," Miss Beasley said, as if reading her mind. "Cressy may choose her own wallpaper and colours and rugs. Perhaps she will like to go to Shrewsbury to look at furnishings."

"You are too good, ma'am," Susannah said.

Miss Beasley's face clouded for a moment, but then she seemed to come to a resolution. "Miss Winslade, pray forgive me if I am speaking out of turn, but it would be most helpful to us if we could know whether you and Dr Broughton will settle here or perhaps elsewhere." She plumped down on the edge of the bed, smoothing the counterpane with one hand. "If we are prepared, you see, we would take care not to get too attached to Cressy and… and…"

And there it was, the question that she and Samuel had been putting off for far too long, a question that she was not sure she wanted to face. Perhaps she would never be ready to face it. But she knew the answer — her clearest reason for staying at the Manor was now gone, for her stepmother was dead and her father would soon install a new wife in her place, one who would have no need of Susannah. Besides, Papa had barred Samuel from the house, and when she married, she would be barred, too. There could be no home for her at the Manor. Her sense of loss was almost overwhelming, but she could not be unmoved by Miss Beasley's situation.

Susannah sat down and put her arm around her. "There now, do not cry, dear Miss Beasley." She offered her a handkerchief, and Miss Beasley blew her nose in a business-like manner. When she began to apologise for her weakness, Susannah interrupted her. "No, no, you have every right to ask, and we were quite remiss in not making our intentions clear long since. Samuel and I will make our home here at Whitfield Villa."

Such difficult words to say! Such a distressing road to take, to leave the only home she had ever known, where every tree, every view from every window, every quirk of that eccentric old house was as familiar to her as her own hand. However would she cope with a new home, a new husband, a new daughter all at once? It was terrifying.

But Miss Beasley went pink with pleasure, and murmured her gratitude in her usual quiet way, and Susannah smiled and hoped that her doubts did not show.

~~~~~

Susannah took her three oldest sisters, Alice, Mary and Jane, with her, together with Jenny, the senior nursery maid, in case she was needed. Miss Norton, the governess, insisted on joining them. "Just in case Miss Broughton brings a governess with her, madam," she said. "She will like to have another of her profession to welcome her." Susannah suspected that the driving factor was curiosity rather than professional courtesy, but she agreed to it. At least the girls would be better behaved under Miss Norton's watchful eye than in Susannah's more lenient care.

The girls had filled two boxes with books, toys, pictures for the walls and colourful rugs, and spent the day happily arranging their treasure in the nursery and bedroom. Miss Beasley followed them from room to room, a beatific smile on her face.

The carriage arrived even sooner than it was looked for, and the entire household gathered on the steps. They had agreed that only Susannah, Dr and Miss Beasley would do so, but the Manor party edged out from the hall in excitement, and the servants peeked out of the door, agog to see the new arrival.

Samuel was smiling, that was Susannah's first delighted thought, as he stepped down from the carriage. He looked towards the crowd on the steps and he *smiled*, just as she remembered from that long-ago visit to London. The dark gloom had left him at last.

He turned to the carriage, reached out a hand… and there she was, solemn-faced, clutching a doll to her chest. She was taller than Susannah had expected — a long, slender child, taller even than

Alice, two years her senior. And her hair! It was much paler than Samuel's, falling in spun-gold curls to her waist, which Susannah, with her drab brown hair which never held a curl, could only envy.

"She is so pretty!" Alice muttered under her breath. It was an assessment no one could argue against.

Cressy held tight to Samuel's hand as he led her up to the house, and the pride in his voice as he said, "This is my daughter, Cressy," almost brought Susannah to tears.

There were introductions, including Cressy's maid, who was whisked off in triumph by the servants to be pressed for every drop of information about Miss Cressy. Then there was a tour of the house, with Alice and the twins showing the newcomer all the good things they had brought, while she nodded, solemn-faced, and clung to Samuel. Then there was a walk around the gardens, the pigsty and the chicken run, and still she held tight to her father. The three Manor girls then turned to a game of battledore and shuttlecock, with Miss Beasley and Miss Norton joining in just as enthusiastically.

"Shall we sit down?" Samuel said to Susannah, pointing to a bench in the shade of a gnarled old apple tree.

They sat, Samuel in the middle, and talked about nothing very much — the journey, the inns, the state of the roads, the weather, all the subjects that people turn to when they want to say more but feel hampered. But after a while, Cressy let go of Samuel, sitting forward slightly as she became engrossed in the game on the lawn. And eventually, she turned to Samuel and placed her doll on his lap.

"Will you look after Maisie for me?"

"Of course I will."

"You will not go away?"

"Absolutely not."

She skipped off to join the game. With a sigh, Susannah wrapped her arm around Samuel's and twined her fingers with his. "You look so happy to have her back."

"Happy… yes, of course, but a little dazed, too. I thought it would be more difficult, but Willerton-Forbes waved the law under Strickland's nose and Edgerton waved a pistol, and he gave in. Or at least, he made no further fuss."

"I am so glad. But where are your faithful henchmen? Have they gone directly to the Dower House?"

He laughed. "Nothing so tame! Willerton-Forbes has gone haring off to London on some mission of his own, and Edgerton and Neate have stayed in Hertfordshire to try to compile evidence that one of Strickland's grooms, a man called Wilkie, is also Wilkinson, who stayed at Astley Cloverstone for a while about the time your stepmother died."

"No!"

"Indeed. Wilkie used to work at Astley's as some sort of acrobat, seemingly, so he could easily have climbed up to her window. He might even have killed Corinna, since there was a tree in the courtyard below her window just right for climbing. I should not like to attempt it myself, but Wilkie is small and light."

Before this interesting news could be developed further, the housekeeper ran out from the house. "Miss Beasley! Miss Beasley! There is a carriage coming up the drive, with a coat of arms on the side!"

Dr and Miss Beasley disappeared in haste, but Miss Beasley returned a few minutes later, smiling. "It is a Lady Jennett, Dr Broughton. I recognise her! She is one of the lonely ladies in your drawings. She says she has come all the way from London to see you and will not be denied."

Samuel laughed. "Lady Jennett? Good heavens! Of course she may see me, but she must come out here to do it, for I have promised my daughter I will not stir."

Miss Beasley raised her eyebrows. "You would put the needs of a child above those of a noblewoman?" she said in gentle surprise.

"Unquestionably, at least for today. In a few more days perhaps Cressy will allow me to disappear from her sight for short periods, but not yet, seemingly. She is watching me even now."

Miss Beasley disappeared into the house again, and emerged with two ladies in tow. It was not hard to identify the older woman in richly decorated attire as Lady Jennett. The other was much younger, dressed in a plainer but much more elegant ensemble. Susannah and Samuel rose to greet them.

"There you are, Dr Broughton!" Lady Jennett boomed, her voice ringing around the garden. "What a dance you have led me, vanishing off the face of the earth for two entire years."

"I was in Scotland, Lady Jennett."

"Precisely. A wild, uncivilised place. And now I find you hiding in— Lucy, dear, what county is this?"

"Shropshire," her companion said, trying not to laugh.

"Practically in Wales! You could hardly have got further away from society."

"Oh, I could. Ireland? America?" he said.

For an instant, she was aghast, then burst into raucous laughter. "What a card you are, Broughton! But I have found you at last, and now you must return to London at once."

"I am very sorry to disappoint you, but I have no intention of doing so," Samuel said. "This is my home now."

His words gave Susannah a momentary pang, until she wondered whether perhaps he meant Shropshire rather than Whitfield Villa. Then she reproved herself for the thought. The Villa would be *her* home soon, and she must get used to that.

Lady Jennett frowned at him, then, seating herself on the bench, she patted the space beside her. "Well, since you will not even come into the house, we must needs talk out here. Lucy, dear — oh, this is Mrs Leonard Audley, Broughton — Lucy, do go away for a while."

Miss Beasley had rushed off to arrange refreshments, so it was left to Susannah to accompany Mrs Audley away from the bench, although Lady Jennett's voice could be heard as a low, distant rumble wherever they went.

"So very sorry to inflict ourselves on you in this ramshackle way, but she positively insisted," Mrs Audley said in an undertone, her eyes brimming with amusement. "You must be Miss Winslade — Dr Broughton's betrothed? She saw the notice in the paper, you see, so she set off from London determined to find him, but she will not stay at an inn like normal people. Oh no! She can only stay with friends or relations — sometimes very distant relations, it must be said. Leo is a second cousin to her husband... or is it third and possibly removed? I am not sure. So complicated, these things. So it has taken her weeks to plan her journey and track down all these distant relations and write to them, and then she says that she cannot stay for under three days, for that would be dreadfully rude." She giggled. "She is quite a character, is she not? But I am very glad she brought me here, for I have long wanted to see Great Maeswood. I have a friend living here, David Exton, do you know him? He has a little cottage somewhere hereabouts. Green Lawns, it is called, although I should never dare to call upon him, for he is quite a recluse and would not thank me for it. I daresay he would not even receive me. Oh, chickens! How lovely! I used to have chickens once, and they were such sweet little creatures. I gave them all names, you see, but now I have two poultry maids and when I ask what names they have given the chickens, they look at me as if I am quite insane. What a lovely house this is," she said suddenly, spinning round so that she could see the full western side of the house. "Large enough that there is always a corner where one might hide away from unwanted visitors, but not so large that one becomes lost trying to find one's own dining room. Or one of them, anyway. We have three, and I am always arriving at the wrong one, and Leo has to send the footmen scurrying about to find me."

Susannah could not help laughing. "You are speaking of Stoneleigh Hall, I collect. I was invited there once, for your wedding celebration, but I daresay you do not remember me."

"I beg your pardon — I do not, but then *everyone* was invited for our wedding celebration, and I was in such a daze, I had no idea who was whom. Apart from the bishop... I remember him, for he was as fat as a butterball, and his wife as thin as a rail. There was a duke there, too, but I cannot tell you which one. Leo just called him *'Duke'* so I did the same, but I never knew his full title. It was the most tremendous fun, though, and everyone knew who *I* was, so I never had to remember names. I just smiled and nodded and tried not to drink too much champagne. At least I was not late for the ball, for Leo sat outside my dressing room and took me down himself, for he said if it were left to me I might never make it to the ballroom. I should be sure to end up in the library or the billiard room. Now, the Bath house is not near so bad, for even I cannot get lost there, but Stoneleigh—! I feel like a doll in my own house, sometimes. Whereas this house is the perfect size. I have grown accustomed to Stoneleigh, and I love my kitchen garden, but if I could choose a house for my own pleasure, it would be something like this one."

"But you could live anywhere!" Susannah cried.

"Oh yes, and Leo said once that he would live in a cottage and keep chickens if that was what I wanted, but I could hardly expect him to do so. I do not mind Stoneleigh, not really, because we are together. I am happy there because Leo is there, and I should not be happy in *any* house that had no Leo in it."

And with those words, the last shreds of Susannah's doubts crumbled to dust. Surely they were the truest and wisest words ever spoken. She would live at Whitfield Villa and be happy, because Samuel would be with her. She had come home.

30: *Calling The Banns*

It took Samuel more than an hour to hear the recital of Lady Jennett's concerns about her health, and even then she was only persuaded to leave by the reassurance that he was not about to go haring off to Ireland or America or other outlandish parts of the world.

"You will be here when I call tomorrow?" she said sternly.

"Tomorrow I shall be at my Market Clunbury consultation room. 12 Chester Road."

"Market Clunbury? Where is that? Never mind, Lucy will know it. Lucy? *Lucy!* Over here, dear. Where is Market— Market what was it? Oh yes, Clunbury. Is it easy to reach from Stoneleigh? I have no desire to spend hours being tossed about in the carriage."

"It is the town we passed through on the way here, Lady Jennett."

"Ah. Well, that is not so bad, but if you are determined to settle so far from the metropolis, Broughton, I shall just have to settle here myself. Lucy, you must look about for a house for me. I shall not want anything grand, no more than ten or a dozen rooms, and some grounds — a lake. I must have a lake or two, and some woods, with decent shooting, for when my brother visits. I am sure you can find me something near to this Clunbury place, and this village. What is it called again?"

"Great Maeswood, Lady Jennett," Samuel said, trying not to notice Susannah's eyes brimming with merriment.

"I shall see you tomorrow, Broughton. Come along, Lucy."

The garden became a more tranquil place once Lady Jennett and Lucy Audley had left. Susannah sat on the bench, and smiled invitingly at Samuel. Willingly he took his place beside her. He was still holding Maisie, he discovered. The children had retreated to the shade of a Norway Spruce on the far side of the garden, where lemonade and gingerbread men had been brought out to them, and Miss Beasley and Miss Norton were sitting side by side on the grass, murmuring together.

"Miss Beasley is happy," Susannah said. "This is what the house needed, I think — children. It always seemed a very gloomy sort of place to me before, but I have never seen it like this, with the garden full of life. I shall like living here, I think."

That was a surprise. "It is settled, then?" he said cautiously.

She turned her lovely eyes towards him. "Oh yes. It was foolish of me to hesitate, but I felt needed at the Manor, you see, and I could not think what I would find to do here, when Miss Beasley is mistress of the house. But Mama is gone and Papa will soon replace her, so I should be very much in the way there."

"Not to mention that your father has banned me from the house."

She laughed. "He will come round, you will see. He is never cross for long. But I shall not change my mind. Marriage is a new beginning, so there should be a new home, too."

His heart was so full he hardly knew what to say. She was so open, so guileless, so... so *wonderful*, that he wanted to kiss her there and then, and let propriety go hang. "I wish—"

A little smile curled her mouth. "What do you wish?"

"That we could be married soon — very soon. How long must we wait, do you think?"

"I had thought a few months, but Cressy makes a difference. We were betrothed before Mama died, after all, and have already passed the month that Papa insisted upon. Shall we walk across to the parsonage to see if Mr Truman is at home?"

And so they did, accompanied by Cressy and Maisie, and found Mr Truman at home and very happy to agree to call the banns and officiate at their wedding.

Samuel was in something of a daze that evening. It was a happy daze, to be sure, but still he could hardly believe his good fortune. When Cressy went to bed, he left her door ajar so that he could go and peep at her, just to reassure himself that her return was not just a dream. Several times during the night, he found himself padding up the stairs to the nursery floor, creeping into her room and gazing down at her sleeping form, dimly perceived by the low night light. And then, smiling, he would return to his own room, contented. For two long, desolate years he had felt as if his heart had been torn from his body and ripped apart, and now at last he was heart-whole again.

Or was he? There was another cause for happiness in his return to Great Maeswood, in Susannah's smiling face. He had arrived exhausted and anxious, but seeing her standing on the top step, smiling warmly, had brought him a jolt of pure joy. To go away and come back to such a smile — even now, the thought of it made him want to laugh out loud. His Susannah, his lovely Susannah, waiting to greet him with a smile of welcome, just as a wife should. As Corinna *never* had. But then Corinna had never been his, as Susannah was. She had never gazed at him, eyes softened with affection. She had never kissed him that way, as if she truly wanted him. But Susannah did want him, enough to put herself forward when he had glibly mentioned marriage. And he wanted her. But was that love? What was love, anyway?

~~~~~

There was a parcel waiting for Samuel on his return from Hertfordshire, left by the smith's son, his task of framing Mrs Cokely's portrait completed. Samuel took it to Bramble Cottage, accompanied as he was quickly becoming accustomed by Cressy and Maisie. Miss Cokely admitted them with a delighted smile, not at all downhearted despite her mourning. Her black gown was plain but neatly fashioned, for she had undoubtedly stitched it herself. While she sighed over the sketch of her mother, and praised it far more than Samuel felt was at all justified, Cressy walked wide-eyed in wonder around the little parlour, gently touching the hats and bonnets and bows and soft feathers.

"They are pretty, are they not?" Samuel said, and she nodded happily. "But not so many as last time I was here," he went on. "Are you not making your bonnets any more, Miss Cokely?"

"Oh yes, but I have sold a great many lately, Dr Broughton, and all thanks to Mrs Gage. She went off to Shrewsbury in one of my bonnets, and visited every milliner's shop in the town, examining all their wares and what do you think she said? She told them that they were well enough, she supposed, but not as fine as Miss Cokely's of Great Maeswood. And so several of the milliners came here, and bought a great many hats and I have orders for more and can barely sew fast enough to keep up with it all. Was that not kind of her?"

"Indeed it was," he said. Poor Miss Cokely, who had barely managed before with her mother's annuity and must now support herself solely from her bonnets. "I wonder..." he said thoughtfully. "You must miss your mother dreadfully, and nothing will ever entirely replace her, but I wonder if you have thought of letting her room to a lodger? It would be company for you of an evening, and perhaps you might find one with nimble fingers to help you out."

"Oh... a lodger? A lady lodger, who would pay for her board? Oh, but I would not at all know how to go about finding such a person, Dr Broughton, and how would one know if she were respectable or would make off with Mama's silver spoons in the night?"

"One would ask for references, naturally, and a month's rent in advance."

"References... in advance... I could post a notice in the *Clarion* or the *Chronicle*. But I should not want anyone just turning up on the doorstep."

"You can have the applications sent to the newspaper office — or to my consultation room in Market Clunbury, if you prefer. Then I can bring them to you."

How kind you are," she said, smiling widely. "How very kind. A lodger... company of an evening. Oh, that would be most agreeable."

~~~~~

Susannah was now thrown into a flutter of excitement. She was not a person who easily became agitated, but there had been so many abrupt switches in her life lately. From long considering herself unmarriageable, she had almost overnight found herself betrothed, and then in mourning. But her marriage was to be delayed no longer. This was really happening to her! In a very short time she would be Mrs Samuel Broughton, wife of an impoverished country physician, stepmother to a child of eight and leaving the gloriously rambling Manor for a much smaller property. Her life would be incomparably different. But better, she was sure of that, for she would have the man she loved.

He did not love her, but he felt *something* for her, she was in no doubt about that. When he had said wistfully that he wished they could marry soon, there had been a light in his eyes that could not be misinterpreted. She had never been a beauty, but he *wanted* her, she could see it in his face, and the sight of it had made her quiver inside with joy.

The day after the visit to Mr Truman, Jeffrey came to see her. This was not the confident, rather bullish Jeffrey she was used to, but a miserable wreck of a man.

"You are calling the banns," he said abruptly, without any effort at a polite greeting. "Truman was full of it at the Gages' card party last night. Is it true?"

"It is."

She was in her sewing room, working on a cambric round gown, and he simply collapsed onto the worn sofa with a heavy sigh. "You are really going through with it, then?"

She said nothing, and he hung his head, looking so dejected that she could only pity him.

"Oh, Sue—!" He looked up at her with such pain in his eyes that she laid down her sewing and crossed the room to sit beside him.

"Jeffrey," she said gently, "I wish you could be happy for me. I am marrying the man I love, after all."

"I am... I am happy for you. I wish you joy, Sue, truly I do, with all my heart, but... I just cannot imagine how I can go on without any hope at all. I mean... you have refused to marry me a dozen times, but while you remained unwed, there was always this little corner of hope in my mind, that one day you would see me differently and... and now there is no hope. Not a shred. You will marry him and I shall be alone for the rest of my life."

"Jeffrey, you do not want to hear this, I know, but you *will* find someone to love, I am sure of it — someone who loves you the way I love Dr Broughton. Somewhere in the world is the perfect wife for you, and it may be that now that you have stopped hoping for me, you will be receptive to finding another love."

"I shall never love anyone but you, Sue. How shall I go on? Everything is so pointless."

"Life is never pointless. You can still make something of yourself. What happened to those grand schemes to remake the Grove gardens and make your fortune as a landscaper?"

"What does it matter now?"

"Jeffrey Rycroft, I do not want to hear such talk! You cannot make me your wife, but you can still make me *proud* of you! You can still work hard and be successful and earn enough to take back Melverley."

He straightened his back a little. "Yes! I shall make you proud of me, Sue! I shall be so successful that you will tell all your children that you could have married Rycroft, the world famous landscaper, and they will wonder why you were so foolish as to turn me down."

She laughed. "That is more like yourself. Go out there and conquer the world, Jeffrey!"

Not half an hour after he had left, Binns arrived, breathless from the stairs. "Whatever is the matter?" she cried, thoroughly alarmed, for he never came all the way up to the sewing room.

"The Master," he gasped. "Home... brandy..."

"At this hour? Oh dear."

She flew down the stairs, and along corridors to her father's book room, to find him pacing up and down, brandy glass in one hand, decanter in the other, grumbling in an angry monologue.

"Too good for her, that's what it is... foolish chit of a girl... damned cheek... little minx..."

"Papa? Are you unwell?"

"Unwell? Ha! Perfectly well, never better. Fit as a fiddle."

"Then... what has happened?"

"She would not have me, that is what has happened."

"Oh," she said, understanding. "The banker's daughter."

"Said I was too old, if you please! Am I not in my prime? Never lost my figure and always well turned out — better than Henry! Ha! She thanked me very prettily, was much obliged... honoured and so forth, and then said I was too old for her, if you please, but if Mr *Henry* Winslade was minded to marry, she would be very happy to receive him. Henry! Who always looks as if he has been dragged through a hedge backwards! Stupid girl!"

"Oh, Papa, I am so sorry. Were you... very fond of her?"

"Fond? Oh... not in love with the girl, or aught of that nature. Love comes later, you know, for a man."

"Does it?"

"But what I am to do now I cannot imagine." He plumped down in his chair beside the fire, and topped up his brandy glass. "I am not a man who can live without a woman, daughter, and it is best if— Well, never mind. That money that came from the business in Market Clunbury — you are putting it to good use, I hope."

"Yes, Papa. It is paying for a splendid trousseau, but there will be plenty left if—"

"No, no. It is yours. I do not want such ill-gotten gains. Ah, you look surprised, but the business that Lord Saxby willed to me — it is a den of iniquity, daughter. I shall never go there again."

"A gaming den, Papa?"

"That and... other things. Saxby led me astray there, but that is done with. I have learnt my lesson, but I need a *wife*, daughter. A wife will keep me right, and keep the house right, too, once you are gone. Susannah, you must forgive me for speaking intemperately to Dr Broughton. I was distressed about Lilian... not in my right mind. I had a letter today from a Lady... oh, something or other, travelled all the way from London to consult him, and wishes to assure me that he is perfectly sound."

"She wrote to you, having never been introduced to you?"

"It was done through the Audleys of Stoneleigh Park. We know *them*, and this Lady... whatever..."

"Jennett."

"...is staying with them. Mr Audley's secretary came by in the carriage — *one* of his carriages, at any event — to deliver such letters to all his acquaintances. I wonder... would it be disrespectful to Lilian's memory to invite Lady Jennett to dinner? I should not like to be backward in any attention." And then he grinned, entirely himself again. "Besides, it would put Lady Saxby's nose out of joint, eh, if we invite her ladyship first. And I should so like to hear all the London *on dits*." And then he added the words that made Susannah's heart sing. "We can invite your young man, too, if you like."

It was as strange an evening as Susannah could remember. It was, strictly speaking, too soon after Mama's death to be entertaining, but seeing her father full of life in the company, she could not begrudge him the pleasure. She had the delight of Samuel beside her, although he could not stay long after the tea things arrived, for he knew that Cressy would be fretting for him. But Lady Jennett dominated the conversation, and had soon wheedled the sad story of his rejected suit out of Papa.

"But my dear Squire Winslade," she boomed, as they sat, replete, around the dinner table, "what you need is a pretty young widow! These schoolroom girls never answer, for they know nothing about managing a house properly and keeping the servants up to the mark, and they still harbour romantic notions and that never does. Ten to one if you had married her, she would have fallen passionately in love with the curate and caused you no end of embarrassment. No, a widow is the very thing, and I know just the place to find one — Bath! The whole town is positively heaving with widows, all looking for a second husband, and a fine looking man like you will have no trouble at all. Find yourself a woman who will appreciate a man in his prime, Squire. If I were not so comfortably situated as I am, I should marry you myself, I declare! Bath is the very place for you. I can give you letters of introduction, or Mr Audley may do so, for he has a house in the Royal Crescent, you know. He knows everyone there, I wager. Well, Squire, I do not know when I have had such a fine dinner outside London. One never expects much in the provinces, but that was really very tolerable. You must dine with me as soon as I am settled in my new abode."

"Oh... you are... staying in Shropshire?" the squire said tentatively, looking dazed by the onslaught of Lady Jennett in full spate.

"Indeed I am, since I cannot persuade Dr Broughton to return to civilisation. I have never been entirely well since he left London. I tried first one physician, then another, but none of them answered. Now that I have tracked him down again, I do not plan to let him escape me again. I enquired of an attorney in Market... Market..."

"Clunbury," the squire murmured.

"Precisely, and there is a house that might suit me perfectly — the Grange. Do you know it?"

"Know it? I could fire an arrow from the roof and have a fair chance of hitting it," the squire said. "The estate used to be Manor land, before this house was built. We shall be neighbours, Lady Jennett."

"How splendid!" she said. "You shall be the first to dine with me — if you are not a-wooing in Bath! Ha ha ha!"

"Delightful," the squire said, and it was a credit to his breeding that he sounded almost sincere.

~~~~~

Samuel was visited by Captain Edgerton and Mr Willerton-Forbes, both looking rather smug. They met in Samuel's study, where Willerton-Forbes placed a large purse bulging with coins on the desk.

"Yours," he said, with a pleased smile. "A modest advance on your next quarter-day payment."

Samuel lifted it, felt the weight of it. "Payment?"

"Interest on Mrs Broughton's dowry, Dr Broughton, which is now wholly yours."

"Is it?"

Willerton-Forbes sighed with theatrical zest. "Tsk, tsk, Dr Broughton. Did you not read the settlement papers?"

"Corinna's dowry was for her use, and after her for Cressy, I thought."

"True enough, but *you* have full control of it. Your wife received her allowance because *you* had authorised the bank to transfer those funds to her. Sir James made one attempt to withdraw from the account, but the bank manager set him straight on *that* score. Thirty thousand pounds your wife brought to the marriage, and since nothing has been withdrawn from it since her death, the capital has increased a little. Thirty-three thousand or thereabouts. It is entirely yours to use how you please. You could settle some money on Miss Winslade, for instance."

"But it is Cressy's money," he protested.

"No, Dr Broughton, it is yours. That is how the law works. Unless a wife's portion is tied up in legal knots and trusts tighter than a miser's purse, it belongs to her husband in its entirety. Now you can use it to protect your family — all your family — for the future. I should be very happy to advise on a settlement, if you wish it. I do so enjoy a marriage settlement. But enough of my doings, for Michael has interesting news."

"Wilkinson is gone," Edgerton said. "Fled in the night, leaving behind in his room a number of valuable items that have now been returned to their rightful owners. No doubt his pockets were filled with pilfered coins and small items. Sir James admitted that he first encountered the fellow when he caught him in his bedchamber with a fistful of fobs and cravat pins. His skills as an acrobat enable him to scale any wall and enter an open window to steal. Sir James thought that giving him honest work might induce him to give up his thievery, but his gratitude seems to have inspired him to even worse villainy. It is almost certain that he murdered Mrs Winslade to aid Sir James's campaign against you."

"Good heavens! He thought my reputation would be damaged by a wealthy patient dying unexpectedly, is that it?"

"So it would seem, but he miscalculated, I believe. No one was surprised that a woman already suffering from consumption should die. It was your wife's death that excited the gossips."

"Did he murder Mrs Cokely, too?"

Edgerton laughed. "It is a coincidence, is it not, and I do so dislike coincidences. However, despite my best endeavours, I can find no connection between Wilkie and Mrs Cokely, so I believe we must set her death down to natural causes. On the other hand, it is very possible that he also murdered your wife."

"There was a tree in the courtyard that an agile man might climb," Samuel said thoughtfully. "It is flimsy evidence, though. Not enough to hang him, even if you can find him."

"Oh, we will find him, and if we can connect him to *both* murders, I believe we could make a convincing case against him."

Samuel nodded thoughtfully. "And Sir James knew nothing of this? Of the murders, that is?"

"He says not, and we cannot prove that he did," Edgerton said with a rueful grimace. "He wishes to come and see you — to explain himself, he says. I suppose an apology would be asking too much. Will you see him?"

"Does he know what we suspect of him — that he is Cressy's father as well as her grandfather?"

"It was not a subject we could raise with him, naturally."

Samuel nodded. "But I can. Very well. I will see him."

31: Playing Games

Sir James Strickland arrived on a grey, drizzly day almost as dark as Samuel's mood. He knew it had to be done, for so much had been left unsaid in that brief confrontation in Hertfordshire, but he had no appetite for it, all the same.

Strickland was different, there was no doubt. He seemed shrunken and sagging, somehow, like an air balloon that was beginning to deflate.

"Is she well?" were his first words. "It must be unsettling for her."

"Cressy is very well."

"Might I see her?"

"I think it best if you do not see her again."

"What, never? But I am her grandfather! She needs to know her family, Broughton."

"I am her family now. What is it you want of me, Strickland? My forgiveness? As a Christian, I give it. As a *father*, you must know that I can never permit you near my daughter, not after what you did to her mother. It is unthinkable."

He spoke with confidence, but he could not be sure, even now, that his suspicion was right. Strickland audibly drew breath, shock writ large on his features, and Samuel waited for him to deny it. Surely he would deny it!

But he did not, his gaze dropped, and he twisted his hands together. "She made me do it," he said, his tone whining. "She was always such a flirtatious child. Little girls are, it comes naturally to them, and Corinna was a dreadful tease. No man could help being drawn into her orbit — except you, seemingly," he added savagely. "You were immune to her wiles, that was why I chose you to marry her. I knew you would never take her away from me. She was mine, always mine, my precious girl, my darling Corinna..." Horrifyingly, he began to weep, noisy sobs that made Samuel writhe with embarrassment. This was his mentor, the man he had looked up to for years, crying like a baby over the daughter he had ill-treated in the most abominable way.

"Did you tell Wilkinson to kill her?" Samuel said.

"No! I was angry with her, yes, because after all the trouble I had taken with her, she had betrayed me. She swore that she would never let you into her bed, that she would never love anyone but me, but that day she told me—"

He stopped, weeping too much for speech, but Samuel could complete the thought. "She told you she was with child, and that it was mine."

"*Yes!* How could she?" He pulled out a handkerchief and wiped his face. "You were nobody, the son of a provincial saw-bones, so thrilled to be in London, to learn under my tutelage, so grateful, or so I believed. But you never knew your place, did you? I gave you *everything*, I *made* you, and how did you repay me? First you took all my patients, and then you took my precious girl from me, you... you *traitor!* She wrote to me, that day, a long, meandering letter, babbling about love and what a wonderful father you were and how she wanted a *real* family, as if I were not real enough for her. I went straight round there to have it out with her, but she would not listen. We argued... we had never argued before, not once, but we argued that night. I followed her out of the house, I pleaded with her, but she would not see sense. I said—"

This time Samuel could not guess his meaning, so he waited.

"I said I wished she were dead, and Wilkinson... he was driving my carriage that night and I suppose he overheard. He must have gone back in the middle of the night, climbed up to her room and killed my darling girl. Oh, my lovely Corinna! And I thought it was you, Broughton. I *wanted* it to be you."

"You hated me... because she chose me," he said wonderingly. "She turned away from you, and chose me."

"She said she *loved* you," he spat, anger suffusing his face now. "What did her paltry feelings for you compare to what *I* felt? We shared the deepest love that—"

Samuel jumped to his feet. "You disgust me! Leave at once, if you please."

With an effort, Strickland rose to his feet too. He was growing old, Samuel realised. He had always seen him as a vital, energetic man, a towering giant of a man, full of wisdom, of sophistication, of *honour*. Now he was merely a shrivelled old man.

"Ah, you think you are so powerful now, Broughton. But you are still nobody. Look at you, a provincial saw-bones just like your father. You will never amount to anything, you know. You will never be a great man."

"I do not aspire to greatness," Samuel said quietly. "Only to move through the world with honour and compassion."

But Strickland only snarled at him.

~~~~~

Susannah watched the carriage rattle up the rutted drive and sweep round in front of the Cloverstone Manor. Almost before Robert had opened the door, Cressy was tumbling out, to be encircled by Alice, Mary and Jane in a cloud of excited chatter. With only the briefest wave of acknowledgement, the four raced off around the side of the house, some game in mind already.

Samuel stepped down from the carriage, holding Maisie. "I suppose it is a good sign that she is too excited to remember her doll," he said. "Is it normal, all this running about? She was used to be a very quiet child."

"It is normal, and very healthy," Susannah said, laughing. "After all, she is getting plenty of sunshine and exercise, and is that not your own prescription? Ah, Beth, they went that way. You had better take Maisie."

The maid bobbed a curtsy, and set off after the children, clutching Maisie firmly under one arm.

"Shall we walk?" Samuel said, offering Susannah his arm and pointing in the opposite direction.

"Are we not going to watch the children?"

"No, they have Beth, Miss Norton, Miss Matheson and Nurse Pett to dance attendance on them. Mac, when you have put the carriage away, go and find Beth and tell her that Miss Winslade and I have gone for a stroll by the river."

"Aye, sir," the Scotsman said with a knowing grin, and flicked the reins to set the horses moving.

"What a delightful notion," Susannah said as they walked away from the house. "I like to have you all to myself, and I have little opportunity these days, now that you are so much in demand."

"Thanks to Lady Jennett," he said. "She used to tell me that I was the only physician who understood her constitution, but I never suspected she would follow me all the way to Shropshire."

"But not to Edinburgh."

He laughed. "No, that was a step too far. Foreign soil, you see. No self-respecting English lady would venture across the border."

Susannah chuckled. "Perhaps I am not sufficiently self-respecting, but I should love to see Scotland."

"Then we shall go one day. When I am rich," he said grandly, making her smile. "But I have any number of new patients now from amongst the gentry. Only yesterday, for instance, I was called to wait upon the Honourable Hannah Amsworth of Little Sutton Hall, just the far side of Market Clunbury. There was nothing greatly amiss with her that a little sunshine and exercise would not cure, but we had an enjoyable conversation. And then, just as I was leaving, she asked if I would mind looking in at the lodge cottage, for there was a man there whose condition was concerning her. Two of her grooms were out exercising the horses early one morning, and found this man quite unconscious at the side of the road. They arranged for him to be conveyed to the lodge, and the local surgeon was summoned, who said there was a head injury, which he treated, and the fellow would either recover or not, as God pleased."

"A man found at the side of the road?" she said, puzzled.

"Precisely. Well, it pleased God to allow him to live, and he recovered... somewhat, being able to rise from his bed and walk about and eat and drink and to make himself useful in simple tasks. What he did not recover was his wits, for he has no memory of... anything at all. Not his name, nor anything that might connect him to family or employment or habitation."

She stopped. "Oh! When did this happen? When was he found?"

"Ten weeks ago," he said triumphantly.

"Then... is it... can it be—?"

"Lucas Renshaw? That is my suspicion. He is younger than I had expected — for some reason I had supposed him to be of middle years — but there is a certain family resemblance to the Renshaw brood. Charlie and Matt are on their way there now to verify it." He sighed. "Michael Chandry is driving them, for there seems to be no detaching him from Charlie's side now."

Susannah chuckled. "Ah, but will he stay by her side long enough to get to the altar, do you think?"

"Possibly, in time, but Charlie has a remarkably cool head for a girl of seventeen. She has told him that she will not marry until she is of age, so if he wants her, he will have to wait four years for her. I suspect he will do it, too. He seems very contented. Ah, here we are."

They had reached the spot she had guessed was his objective, the sheltered little clearing beside the river where they had first talked of marriage and later had sealed the deal, and then the dreadful day when Strickland had come.

"May I remove my coat for you to sit on?" Samuel said, gesturing to the fallen tree where she had sat before.

"You may remove your coat, if you wish, for it is a hot day, but I shall sit on the grass. It is very dry, and my black gown will show no stains, fortunately."

He hesitated momentarily, but then removed his coat and sat beside her, crossing his legs neatly. She removed her bonnet and gloves with a sigh. "That is better. So hot, today! But this shade is refreshing."

"Do you think Cressy is wondering where I am?" he said, then sighed. "Probably not. She does not need me now that she has friends."

"She will always need you, but in a different way. A father is the solid bedrock upon which a child may build, but he does not need to be there every minute of the day."

"But we were so close in London. I spent a great deal of time with her, reading to her, teaching her."

"You are an adult. She needs to be with children, too. She needs to play like a child, Samuel."

"What does that mean? To play like a child?"

"Who played with you when you were a boy? Your nurse? Your mama? Your papa?" There was a long silence. "Did anyone play with you?"

"I played cricket at school," he said doubtfully.

She laughed. "Lie down."

"What?"

"Lie down and close your eyes. We are going to play a game."

"A game?" He was puzzled, but obediently he lay down and closed his eyes.

Susannah stretched out alongside him, smiling as she admired his long lashes, the contours of his chin, the lock of hair that always fell across his brow. "Now tell me what you hear."

"Apart from your voice? The river. That constant but ever-changing burble."

"Very good. What else?"

"Something humming — a bee or insect of some sort. Oh, a cricket! There it is again. A cow lowing far away. A rustle in the trees — a slight breeze is stirring the dry leaves. Oh — what was that? Something went into the water with a plop. Was it a kingfisher?"

"No, I think not. Just a frog, I suspect. Now tell me what you can smell."

"Smell? Mmm... your perfume, mostly. Lavender, perhaps. And something else... a floral scent, mingled with grassy, earthy smells."

"Clover." She pulled a stem of meadow cat's-tail from the grass. "Now tell me what you feel." Softly she feathered it across his cheek.

He laughed, and tried to blow it away at first. "What is that?"

"What does it feel like?"

"Ticklish," he said, still smiling. "May I look?"

"No. Now what do you feel?" Dropping the cat's-tail, she leaned nearer and touched the lightest of kisses on his forehead, his temple, his cheek.

His eyes flew open. "I feel that you are tormenting me. Kiss me properly."

"Not yet."

"What is this? What are you trying to do to me?"

She smiled down at him. "I think when you were a little boy, nobody showed you how to play, how to do nothing very much. Children have to learn how to be children before they can be adults. Cressy has my young sisters to show her the way, but you had no one. I daresay you always had your head down in your books, doing serious, important things, but one of the greatest joys in life is to lie in the grass like this, simply allowing the world around you to seep into your bones. You are a very serious man, Samuel, and I want to show you that it is possible, and even enjoyable, to be frivolous occasionally, to be silly and spontaneous and light-hearted."

"Why?" he murmured, but his lips curved up in a smile.

"Because I remember you when you were not so serious. I remember when you smiled all the time, even when you were only being polite to a tedious fourteen-year-old girl from the provinces."

"I am from the provinces myself," he said, "and although I do not remember you, I cannot believe you were ever tedious." Abruptly he rolled over, pushing her onto her back, his face above hers. She gave a squeak of surprise, and he laughed. "My turn to be spontaneous. Close your eyes."

Thrilled with this unexpected response, she did so, and he began to pat little butterfly kisses all over her face. "Am I tormenting you?" he whispered.

She gave a gurgle of laughter, reaching up to pull him closer, and he fell into the kiss with an enthusiasm that took her breath away. For a long, long time the world faded to nothing, and a hundred kingfishers might have danced on their heads for all they knew of it. When, eventually, he drew back a little and she dared to open her eyes, he was smiling down at her with such warmth that she could almost imagine him to be in love with her.

"That was delightful," he said.

"You are not angry with me for my enthusiasm?"

"Not in the slightest," he said softly. "I was terrified to encourage your ardour at first in case you turned into another Corinna, with a multitude of lovers, but it is clear to me now how wrong I was about that. Poor Corinna! She deserved my pity, not my censure. I knew she was a deeply unhappy person, but I never fully understood why. If she had told me all that her father had visited upon her, I could perhaps have helped her. We could have been close... At the least, I would have understood her a little better. But she always kept me at a distance. Not like you! You are so honest and open and straightforward and will never deceive or betray me. Or exclude me. You have made it very clear that you want our lives to be entwined. And I find I like that idea — I like it very much. So upon reflection, it seems to me that enthusiasm in a wife is a desirable quality, Susannah dear."

"I love you so much," she said softly.

His smile widened even more. "What *is* love? What does it *feel* like? For I feel something... I cannot put a name to it, I just know that the world feels *right* when you are here, that *I* feel right, and that I want to be with you and protect you and make you happy. Is that love?"

"We can call it love, if you like," she said. "Because it sounds very much like it, to me."

"Oh." He sounded pleased. "Then... I love you, Susannah Winslade. I love you a little bit more with every day that passes, and I cannot wait to make you my wife and begin our life together, a life that will be silly and spontaneous and frivolous and not serious at all."

She burst out laughing. "That sounds perfect. Oh! Did you see that? A kingfisher... just above the water. Beautiful. Did you see?"

"No." He was still smiling down at her, his eyes alight with love. "I was watching something even more beautiful — your face."

"That settles it," she said severely. "You must be very badly in love if you think I am beautiful."

"But you are," he said simply. "You are not merely a beautiful outer shell, you are beautiful all the way through. The very core of your being is wondrous and shining and splendid. You brought light and love to my darkness, and I am honoured and very privileged to share your life. My darling Susannah, I am going to cherish you for ever."

Her heart was so full that she could not speak a word, but she made no protest at all when he bent his head to kiss her again, a kiss of the greatest tenderness and joy and promise for the future.

THE END

The next book in the series is *Stranger at the Manor*, wherein the squire's impoverished cousin arrives, and discovers that mousy Phyllida Beasley hides a shocking secret. You can read a sneak preview after the acknowledgements, or find out more at my website http://marykingswood.co.uk/.

Thanks for reading!

If you have enjoyed reading this book, please consider writing a short review on Amazon. You can find out the latest news on all my books and sign up for the mailing list at my website http://marykingswood.co.uk/.

Family trees and maps: Hi-res versions of these are available at my website http://marykingswood.co.uk/.

A note on historical accuracy: I have endeavoured to stay true to the spirit of Regency times, and have avoided taking too many liberties or imposing modern sensibilities on my characters. The book is not one of historical record, but I've tried to make it reasonably accurate. However, I'm not perfect! If you spot a historical error, I'd very much appreciate knowing about it so that I can correct it and learn from it. Thank you!

The great houses: Most of the houses I describe in the books are creations of my imagination, or 'generic' styles of a particular era, but sometimes I base them on real houses. In this series, Maeswood Hall, home of the Saxby family, is based on Stourhead House in Wiltshire, designed by Colen Campbell. Lower Maeswood Grove, where the Gage family lives, is loosely based on the Queen's House,

Stranger at the Villa: Strangers Book 3

Greenwich, designed by Inigo Jones. The Squire's home, Cloverstone Manor, is based on Hatfield House, another Inigo Jones project.

Isn't that what's-his-name? Regular readers will know that characters from previous books occasionally pop up. Lawyer Mr Willerton-Forbes, his flamboyant sidekick Captain Edgerton and the discreet Mr Neate have been helping my characters solve murders and other puzzles ever since *Lord Augustus*. Michael Chandry, first seen helping after the shipwreck in *The Clerk* and more recently in *The Duke,* is now a crime-solving partner to Captain Edgerton and his pals. Mrs Leonard Audley, the former Lucy Winterton, appeared in *The Chaperon*, *The Seamstress* and *Woodside.*

About the Strangers series: There's a famous saying attributed to John Gardner that authors like to quote: that there are only two plots - a stranger arrives in town, or a person goes on a journey. Most of my books have been based on the latter, in its loosest sense (sometimes a journey of discovery, rather than a literal journey, but a major change, of death or misfortune or even good fortune which propels the main character in a new direction). So I wondered what the other side of the coin would look like - a stranger arriving in town. And there was my series title - Strangers.

Book 0: Stranger at the Parsonage: a new parson arrives at the village of Great Maeswood, and tragedy strikes the baron's family. *(a novella, free to mailing list subscribers).*

Book 1: Stranger at the Dower House: a widow moves into the long disused Dower House and makes a horrible discovery in the wine cellar.

Book 2: Stranger at the Grove: an estranged brother is forced to return to his home and face up to his past.

Stranger at the Villa: Strangers Book 3

Book 3: Stranger at the Villa: a new physician arrives in the village, but is he all he seems?

Book 4: Stranger at the Manor: a destitute man comes looking for help from his cousin, and uncovers some mysteries.

Book 5: Stranger at the Cottage: an out-of-work governess tries to start a school in the village.

Book 6: Stranger at the Hall: the newly discovered heir to the barony arrives to claim his inheritance.

Any questions about the series? You are welcome to email me at mary@marykingswood.co.uk - I'd love to hear from you!

About the author

I write traditional Regency romances under the pen name Mary Kingswood, and epic fantasy as Pauline M Ross. I live in the beautiful Highlands of Scotland with my husband. I like chocolate, whisky, my Kindle, massed pipe bands, long leisurely lunches, chocolate, going places in my campervan, eating pizza in Italy, summer nights that never get dark, wood fires in winter, chocolate, the view from the study window looking out over the Moray Firth and the Black Isle to the mountains beyond. And chocolate. I dislike driving on motorways, cooking, shopping, hospitals.

Acknowledgements

Thanks go to:

John Gardner, whose alleged saying about strangers and plots inspired these books.

Allison Lane, whose course on English Architecture inspired me.

Shayne Rutherford of Darkmoon Graphics for the cover design.

My beta readers: Charles Crouter, Barbara Daniels Dena, Amy DeWitt, Melissa Forsythe, Pat Oen, Rosemary Paton, Quilting Danielle, Melanie Savage and the readers of Rachel Daven Skinner of Romance Refined.

Last, but definitely not least, my first reader: Amy Ross.

Sneak preview: Stranger At The Manor: Chapter 1: The Banker

AUGUST

Peter Winslade descended gingerly from the coach, brushing the worst of the dust from his coat, and stood in the yard of the Cross Keys Inn at Astley Cloverstone. The swaying of the coach had made him rather nauseous, but it was still a jolly adventure to ride on top, watching the fields and woods and villages go by. There had been something of a breeze up there, too, which he would not have obtained from an interior seat. Nevertheless, it was pleasant to stop moving at last, to see his boxes being unstrapped, to know that this time the coach would leave without him. He had arrived.

The ostler's eyes slid past him as he led the spent horses away to the stables, and he moved on. Then he saw the name on Peter's box as it was handed down and stopped, turning to look more closely.

"Mr Winslade? Lord, sir, ain't seen you this many a year."

"It cannot be Tommy, can it? Gracious me, you were only this high when I last saw you. How are you? And your sister — Mary, is it?"

"We're fine, sir, and thank 'ee kindly fer askin'. Hoy, Billy! See to these horses, will 'ee? Well now, sir, 'tis right kind o' you to come, even though you've missed the funeral."

"Funeral?" Peter said in alarm.

"Aye, Mrs Winslade was took... oh, almost a month past, now, poor lady."

"Dear me. I had no idea."

"She were very sick. Carriage ain't here yet, Mr Winslade."

"Oh, they are not expecting me at the Manor, so they will not send the carriage."

"Well, give me ten minutes to see the coach away and they horses properly settled, and I'll run you up in the cart wi' your boxes."

"Thank you, but I shall walk, I think. It is such a warm day, a stroll beside the river will be most refreshing."

He shook more dust off his hat, replaced it and then set off at a brisk pace, his cane tapping rhythmically. The stage coach overtook him just before the bridge, clattering off in a cloud of dust towards Great Maeswood and on towards Shrewsbury. Peter coughed, brushed the new film of dust from his coat and turned onto the river path.

Three days ago, he had left behind the smoking chimneys and foul air of Leeds, so hot he could scarcely breathe. Three days of lurching about on the roofs of slow-moving cross-country stage coaches, of waiting hours in noisy, sweltering inns for the next cheap coach to arrive, of snatching a few hours sleep on a bench. Quite an adventure!

Now he was back in sleepy rural Shropshire, the trees rustling above his head providing him with blessed shade. By his side, the Wooller River burbled gently over the pebbles, although without much energy at this time of year. Three coots paddled industriously upstream and disappeared into the reeds.

When he came to the wooden bridge, where there was a patch of shingle edging the water, Peter bent down to scoop water into his hands, drinking thirstily and then splashing his face. It helped a little to refresh him as he left the water behind and began the long, slow climb to the house, emerging in a short time at the bottom of the deer park. The heat was fierce as he strolled through the meadow, swinging his cane jauntily. He was almost at his destination.

Cloverstone Manor was a fine old building in the Jacobean style, with mullioned windows and elaborate chimneys outside, the interior a maze of dark-panelled rooms, and all of it expensive to maintain. Peter would never say so to his cousin, but he was secretly very glad there had never been any possibility of it coming to him.

He rang the front door bell and waited. And waited. Twice more he rang, and eventually the door creaked open a notch, and a very elderly butler peered out. Heavens, was that Binns? How frail he had grown.

"Yes?" Binns said.

"Is the squire at home?"

"I will enquire, sir. What name shall I give?"

"Tell him his cousin Peter is here to see him."

Binns started. "Mr Peter? Is it you? Come in, sir. Come in at once." He opened the door wide and ushered Peter into the hall. "Are the grooms dealing with your horse, sir? Or your carriage?"

"No horse or carriage, Binns. It is Binns, is it not? I walked up from the village, and my boxes will follow."

"I will ask Mrs Cobbett to prepare a room for you, sir." He nodded to a footman standing the shadows. "Robert, pray inform the master that his cousin, Mr Peter, is awaiting him in the book room. This way, sir, if you please."

Peter followed the butler at the excruciatingly slow pace that seemed to be all the fellow could manage. After what felt like half an hour of long galleries, stairs, then more meandering galleries, he was shown into a room that might once have been a cosy, masculine apartment, but was now a scene of devastation. Every surface was covered with newspapers, opened letters and scraps of paper, with abandoned glasses and decanters half buried in the debris. Peter shuddered. Three pointers dozing on a sofa looked up with interest as he entered the room, only to lay their heads down again almost at once. After pointing out a decanter and what might once have been a clean glass, the butler withdrew.

On the mantle, a clock ticked mournfully, measuring out the seconds. One of the dogs rose, turned round, settled again. Out in the garden, a gardener was industriously clipping something. Snip... snip... snip...

The door was thrown open, and there was John, looking not a day older and just as stylishly dressed. A warm smile lit his face, and Peter could only hope the smile would stay in place, for all his hopes depended on it now.

"Peter! My dear fellow! What a wonderful surprise! Whatever brings you to our little backwater, eh?"

Too soon to answer that. "I was so very sorry to hear about Mrs Winslade," Peter said. "I knew nothing of it until I heard at the Cross Keys just now. How you must feel it, Cousin!"

"Oh... yes, poor Lilian. Of course, she was very ill. Consumption, you see. She barely left her room these last two or three years."

"Consumption is an evil thing," Peter said. "At least her suffering is at an end, so you have that comfort."

"Yes... yes, of course. A great comfort. Peter, I am so very glad to see you, but I am this minute leaving for Bath. Henry and I are going to... recover our spirits a little, you know how it is. A change of scenery and air, new faces... it will do us a world of good."

That was a setback. His disappointment must have shown in his face, for John went on at once, "But that need not affect your plans. Stay here if you wish, and see all your old friends. Susannah is here, for a few weeks anyway, until she marries."

"I had supposed she must have married long since," Peter said, distracted by this news. How out of touch he was! But he had been so frantic these last few weeks that he had ignored his mail.

"No, no, quite an old maid, we all thought, but along came a new physician over at Great Maeswood, and there we are. So you are very welcome to stay here. Or come to Bath, if you wish."

Peter laughed. "No, no, a repairing lease in the country will suit me very well."

"Repairing lease? Not in the basket, surely, Peter? I thought the bank was doing well."

"So it was." He sighed, tried to find some light-hearted way to speak of it and failed. "The bank is gone, Cousin. Failed. Smashed. I am done for. Once the house is sold, it will cover all the debts, I hope, but there will be nothing left. I am come to throw myself on your mercy and beg for your charity — a roof over my head while I regroup and look about me for some employment. A temporary home, that is all. I will not inflict myself on you for a day longer than necessary."

"In God's name, Peter, never talk about *charity* to me. You are *family*, so of course you may stay. Make this your home for as long as you wish — for ever, if you like. I shall be glad of the company, to tell the truth, because Henry is too restless by half to sit and talk to his father, and Susannah will soon be taking *her* conversation away from me. But your father's house — it must be sold? There is no alternative? I thought you were too wily a man to lose your money. Not like me, eh? I frittered most of mine away, but you were always the prudent one of the family. Have a drink. You must need it. Brandy? Where is the tray? Oh, never mind, this glass will do."

He half filled an empty glass and pushed it into Peter's hand, although it was the last thing he needed. He had not eaten since last night, and he was too light-headed with hunger for spirits. He took a polite sip, and hoped John would not press him further. Topping up a half-full glass for himself, John pushed the dogs off the sofa and waved Peter to a seat.

"Now, tell me all about it."

He was a good listener, Peter had to give him that. Considering that he was practically out of the door on his way to Bath, he made no effort to rush the story, not interrupting at all, and Peter found himself spilling out the whole, foolish tale. How he and his partner, Kenneth Linch, had built their banking business by means of small loans secured by land to local farmers and mill owners. How Linch had become friendly with Lord Silberry, a personable man with a fine estate, who wanted to borrow a larger amount, but unsecured. He could not underwrite it with the estate since it was entailed, but he would repay it from his tenants' rents and agreed to a high interest rate. Peter had not wanted to do it, for it went against all their principles, but Linch had persuaded him, and for a year or two, all was well. Silberry paid the interest due, and although the ship he had been long expecting from India, which would pay off the principal, was delayed, he could still meet the interest payments. But then the harvest was bad, and rents were poor and he could not pay in full, and the next two quarters he paid nothing at all. Gradually funds at the bank began to dwindle and then…

"You know how it is," Peter said. "It only takes one person to get wind of a problem and everyone was at our door wanting their money at once, and no bank can survive that."

"And this Lord Silberry gets off scot-free, I suppose?" John said. "That is not right, not right at all."

"The fault was ours for accepting the loan," Peter said, gently. "We took a gamble, and lost. It was very wrong of us."

The door burst open and a handsome young man rushed in. Henry, Peter presumed. The son and heir. Carelessly dressed, and with the slightly arrogant swagger so common to men of that age. He was four and twenty, and Peter was only fourteen years older, but he felt like a grandfather by comparison.

"Father, the carriage is at the door."

"Yes, yes, but make your bow to Cousin Peter, who is to make a stay at the Manor for a while. I hope he will still be here when we return from Bath."

Henry bowed and said all that was proper. His manners were good, anyway. Then his father chased him away to supervise the loading of the luggage.

"I am sorry to leave you so abruptly, but all the arrangements are made — changes of horses, overnight stays, and so on."

"Of course you must go. Cousin, I cannot begin to express my gratitude for—"

"Tush to all that. Family, remember? You would do the same for me in a heartbeat. Not another word about gratitude."

"It goes against the grain, but it shall be as you wish. But how may I make myself useful while you are gone? Is there anything you wish me to do to repay your hospitality?"

"Stay here until I return, that is all I ask. I shall be back in a month or so, in time for Susannah's wedding and the Michaelmas ball."

"You will not hold a ball, so soon after Lilian's death?" Peter said, shocked.

"Oh… well, not perhaps quite as we usually do, but there must be some celebration for the wedding, you know. One must acknowledge the occasion, although how I am to pay for it… Peter, you are good with money. Do you think you could get my accounts into some semblance of order?"

Peter laughed and shook his head in bemusement. "Cousin, I am the man whose bank crashed, remember? And you want me to deal with your accounts?"

"Well, someone needs to, and it is beyond my ability." He waved a hand vaguely to encompass the piles of paper heaped everywhere. "Will you? Have a look at them, anyway. Look, the keys to everything are here. See if there is anything in this house worth selling, just to get my head above water again. I do so hate having to watch the pennies. If you find anything, you can keep a tenth of whatever it makes. No, no, I insist. You must be properly rewarded. But if you think it will be too difficult—"

"No, I should enjoy it, and I will certainly look for anything that may be sold. May I talk to your banker and attorney? I shall need letters of authority from you."

"Very well. See if you can find ink and a working pen in this shambles, will you?"

It took ten minutes to locate them, and a matter of seconds for John to dash off a letter *'To whom it may concern, My cousin Mr Peter Winslade is acting as my agent. John Winslade'* on the back of a tailor's bill.

And then he was gone, and Peter was alone. The dogs rose as one and reclaimed their places on the sofa.

~~~~~

Peter had a home, he had work to keep him busy and he had a full belly, too, for the housekeeper, Mrs Cobbett, splendid woman that she was, had caused a tray of cold meat, bread and cheese to be placed in his room, with a jug of ale to wash it down. Thus fortified, washed and changed into clean clothes already arrived from the inn and bestowed neatly in presses and drawers, he had two hours to pass before dinner. Time for a walk.

Great Maeswood was no more than two miles away as the crow flies, and a pleasant walk it was too, for a man with sturdy legs and an energetic nature, back across the deer park, across the river and along a leafy lane between fields already cleared of their crops.

No one was about in the village, for it was the hour when the working people were at their dinner, so he walked down the road and through the lych gate without meeting a soul.

St Ann's church was like a thousand other churches in small, rural parishes — modestly sized, unadorned, undistinguished. A few marble plaques on the wall testified to the piety of a succession of Saxbys and Gages and Ramsbottoms and Platts. A wooden board recorded in gold paint the names of the parsons, from John Wilmott in 1484 to the recent names of Sherrington, Cokely, Lancaster and Truman, the latter's paint shiny and new.

Peter found a pew near the pulpit and knelt down to express his gratitude to God for his good fortune in his cousin, whose charity had undoubtedly saved him from the work house. He had not got very far when he heard a door open and close, and someone entered the church from the vestry, humming softly. A woman, he thought. He tried to continue his prayers, but the humming was of just that level that is almost but not quite inaudible, and impossible to ignore. Smiling, for whatever she was doing she was happy about it, he rose from his knees and sat on the seat. Closing his eyes, he listened to the tune, trying to work out what it was.

Quick steps came down the aisle, closer and closer, and a face peeped over the pew wall. "Oh, I do beg your pardon," she said, in a softly melodious voice. "I heard a noise and thought it was one of the Preece boys hiding from his mother again. I was just about to box your ears."

A woman of about his own age, drably dressed, with a little froth of a lace cap but no wedding ring on the hand resting on the pew wall. A middle-aged spinster, then.

"I have not had my ears boxed these twenty years or more," he said, laughing. "What were you humming? I could not quite make it out."

"*Hark! The Herald Angels Sing*", she said. "I do so love the Christmas songs, and that one seems to go so well with my polishing."

"What are you polishing?"

"The brass and silver."

"May I help?"

Her eyebrows shot up. "Are you serious?"

"Perfectly. I enjoy polishing and I also enjoy the Christmas songs, so I cannot imagine a more perfect occupation."

She found him another cloth and they polished and hummed and then sang all the Christmas songs they could think of, until he turned to her and said, "What next?" and she said, with surprise in her tone, "Everything is done, and in half the usual time. Thank you very much, stranger, although... I feel I should know you. Have we ever been introduced?"

"Probably, a long time ago. I have not been here for more than ten years. I am Squire Winslade's cousin, Peter Winslade."

"Oh, the *banker!* I know you now. I am Miss Beasley. Phyllida Beasley."

"Ah, Dr Beasley's sister. I remember. How delightful to meet you again, Miss Beasley, and under such charming circumstances. Alas, you are out of date, however. My bank is no more." A hesitation, but it could not be kept secret. "It failed."

"Oh no! How dreadful! Whatever went wrong?"

She was so sympathetic and interested and horrified and angry on his behalf, that he told her not just the bare bones of it, but the very worst of it, too. "Ten employees at the bank are now out of work, not to mention my own servants — six of them, and my partner was in worse case. He has a wife and five children who are now scattered amongst three or four relations, and a dozen servants let go, and I do not know when they will find work again. One never minds for oneself, you see, but one's dependents find themselves cast into darkness through no fault of their own. Mrs Linch and the children — blameless. The servants — quite blameless. Yet there they are, wondering how on earth they will manage this coming winter."

"But you have lost more than they have," she said, leaning forward eagerly. They were sitting in the Saxby family pew, plush with rugs and cushions and hangings against a stray draught, where lay the final brass they had polished. "A servant with good references will always find employment again, but you have lost your business, your income, the house you inherited from your father... everything!"

"Not everything," he said, with a smile. "I have my health and strength. I have my mind, such as it is. I was very fortunate to have a house to sell to discharge all my debts, otherwise I should have ended in a debtors' prison or the work house. I should certainly have been bankrupt. And I am very blessed indeed to have a good, kind cousin who offers me a home for as long as I want it, and something to do, to keep me busy — I am to put his accounts in order, if you please. I came directly here to thank God for my good fortune."

"You call it good fortune to be expected to set Squire Winslade's accounts in order?" she said, her face alight with merriment. "Most people would regard it as a penance."

"It is a new adventure, Miss Beasley."

"You have an odd definition of adventure, Mr Winslade."

"Ah, but you see, all of life is an adventure, Miss Beasley. Life itself is the adventure."

"Is it so?" she breathed, smiling at him with clear, dark eyes, and he felt something shift inside him. Some dark, hidden spot that had been frozen for half a lifetime had started to melt.

END OF SAMPLE CHAPTER *of Stranger at the Manor; for more information or to buy, go to my website at http://marykingswood.co.uk/*